RUSSIAN SALAD

RUSSIAN SALAD

Julia Watson

BANTAM BOOKS

TORONTO • NEW YORK • LONDON • SYDNEY • AUCKLAND

RUSSIAN SALAD

*All of the characters in this book are fictitious,
and any resemblance to actual persons, living or dead,
is purely coincidental.*

A BANTAM BOOK : 0 552 40645 0

First publication in Great Britain

PRINTING HISTORY
Bantam Books edition published 1993

Copyright © Julia Watson 1993

The right of Julia Watson to be identified as author of this
work has been asserted in accordance with sections 77 and 78
of the Copyright Designs and Patents Act 1988.

Conditions of sale
1. This book is sold subject to the condition that it shall not,
by way of trade or otherwise, be lent, re-sold, hired out or
otherwise circulated in any form of binding or cover other than that
in which it is published and without a similar condition including
this condition being imposed on the subsequent purchaser.
2. This book is sold subject to the Standard Conditions of Sale
of Net Books and may not be re-sold in the UK below the net
price fixed by the publishers for the book.

Set in 11/13pt Plantin by
County Typesetters, Margate, Kent

Bantam Books are published by Transworld Publishers Ltd,
61–63 Uxbridge Road, Ealing, London W5 5SA,
in Australia by Transworld Publishers (Australia) Pty Ltd,
15–25 Helles Avenue, Moorebank, NSW 2170
and in New Zealand by Transworld Publishers (NZ) Ltd,
3 William Pickering Drive, Albany, Auckland.

This book proof printed by
Antony Rowe Ltd, Chippenham, Wiltshire

For all the Ws from 8 to 80

Chapter One

The first time Alice Mason passed through customs at Sheremetyevo Airport, she was seven months pregnant. George had gone ahead with their two large suitcases, while Alice stood at the side of the table holding Harriet tightly by the hand. The customs officer, a young man with scrubbed cheeks, threw open the first case. Inside, pressed neatly together edge to edge, lay boxes and boxes of condoms. The officer studied the suitcase for a moment, then plucked a packet out and turned it over carefully in his hands. Drawing his gaze briefly across Alice's inflated stomach, he looked up at George and said, 'So yours don't work either.'

George had been delighted by the incident. It seemed a splendid two-way introduction: of the Russians as a nation of humourists and George as a man to be reckoned with. Alice observed that he did not, on retelling the story at those first dinner parties among Moscow's foreign community, reveal that the condoms had been intended for Russian friends and contacts made during earlier reconnaissance trips. There was no harm, as chief and sole correspondent of the *Sentinel*'s first Moscow bureau, George felt, in provoking a little pleasant speculation about the extent of one's abilities.

Now, three months later, Alice thought there could be little doubt remaining as to George's abilities, or indeed those of every member of Moscow's foreign press corps.

Whatever else Mr Gorbachev was provoking, and it appeared at this point that the Soviet people and foreign powers alike felt considerably provoked by the man, he was generating enormous amounts of work for those covering his new reign. George left the flat at half past eight each morning and generally did not return before nine at night. Once the children were in bed, Alice waited in the sitting-room, watching television: not an entirely satisfactory occupation since, while the set produced pictures of the most vivid colouring, there was no sound. Some problem with compatibility, George explained vaguely. Jonathan, the British diplomat whose flat was across the corridor, said they should have ordered a telly from Helsinki, not imported one from the Tottenham Court Road. What could those people with their discount technology possibly know about Soviet systems?

But George, with a Soviet set in his office (which Jonathan assured him would some day blow up in his face – all Soviet tellies did eventually), saw no need to invest in another. Particularly when the *Sentinel* was unlikely to foot the bill. So Alice put records on the stereo and turned to ballet programmes. Or borrowed videos of old Hollywood films from the American television company next to George's office and tried lip-reading. It didn't bother her much. It was one of those things that quickly became par for the course here.

In Moscow, she reflected, she had picked up more about irrational behaviour patterns than at any time since Biology and Reproduction loosely introduced her class to sex. Now, for instance, she was hovering in the kitchen, waiting to dart to the front door at the first suggestion of movement outside. It was imperative to prevent the anticipated chime of the bell from waking Daisy, while not quite imperative enough to challenge the pronouncement of the computer salesman's wife downstairs that 'in this compound, we do not leave our doors wide open'. Harriet had stuffed the last of their soft Western lavatory paper down the loo and blocked it. When Galina arrived that morning to clean the flat, she had taken one look at the swill on the tiled floor of the tiny bathroom, thrown her coat back on, demanded a half bottle of vodka from George's supplies, and fled.

To anyone but a Soviet resident, this would have appeared an irrational response. But Alice, now the old hand, had at once understood her scheme. Volodya and his sidekick, Ivan, were janitors of the foreigners' compound, assigned as handymen to execute household repairs, their services included in the rent. Except, as Alice had learned, they would not remove themselves from the warmth of their basement boiler-room unless someone swung a bottle of vodka before their eyes. Galina was tougher than most of the other maids in the block: she would whip the bottle just out of reach and dangle it like a carrot as she led them out of their lair towards the lift. Other maids produced one bottle to persuade them into the lift and another if they finished the job. With the clamp-down on alcohol that had earned Gorbachev the nickname 'Lemonade Joe', vodka had become scarce, with toothpaste and eau de cologne the favoured substitutes. Alice had quickly come to appreciate the janitors' desperation for bottles of any size, and Galina's frugality with them.

Back in London Alice had been alarmed to learn they would have a maid. 'Ah, Moscow, dear boy! Last outpost of the decent white servant!' a Foreign Office crony of George's had crooned when he had learned of George's assignment. It had seemed to Alice somewhat in conflict with the notion of a socialist people's state. But as George had pointed out, Galina would be working for two employers – the Masons and the KGB. The latter would expect regular reports on the domestic activities of the former.

Both the flat and Galina had been assigned to the Masons by UPDK, the Diplomatic Corps Service Bureau that made sure the only apartments available to foreigners were in fenced-off non-Soviet compounds guarded by sentries, and that their only employees were carefully vetted Soviets who had earned these plum assignments through merit, connections or bribery. The apartment was luxurious by Soviet standards, actually two flats on the fifteenth floor broken through where the kitchen met the dining-room. George, in Moscow when the demolition had taken place, had witnessed the procedure with some alarm before the janitors had hustled him away. Two women in baggy army fatigues had shuffled in while he was taking measurements and, without any reference to building plans, had set about bashing at the wall with road picks. He had a horrible feeling he would have to stretch beyond his conviction that the fifteenth-floor flat floated unconnected to the corp, much as archaeologists need faith to see an entire being in a motley collection of bones.

The small dining area was the mirror image of the kitchen, as the narrow room behind it was a repetition of the room in which Harriet slept, and the master bedroom at one end of the flat echoed the sitting-room right at the other. Each of the rooms looked on to a balcony that ran the length of the two flats, with access from all but Harriet's and Daisy's bedrooms. If you leaned far enough out and round the balcony at the sitting-room end, you could just make out the spires of St Basil's in Red Square.

Directly below the balcony the view was less exotic. Most of the open wasteland that surrounded the foreign compound and each of the similar apartment blocks in the area was in a state of static development, rubbled banks of snow-covered earth, sections of man-sized concrete piping, builders' debris and broken machinery littering the landscape.

Galina had sailed into the Masons' lives at breakfast on their second day. She followed proudly behind a sumptuous bosom that appeared to be uplifted only by the regal carriage of her shoulders. Alice, still in her pink towelling dressing-gown, was nonplussed. The woman obviously had her own key.

'Galina, madam,' she announced. She stood in the doorway to the dining-room and bowed slightly from the waist. George was hunched over his tiny shortwave radio, which he had wedged behind the hot pipes that ran up the corner of the room. This apparently gave him a clearer reception of the BBC World Service, which he was at that moment trying to hear. He flapped an arm behind him at Galina and shouted, 'Hush!'

George had given Alice a phonetic list of the Russian words for 'clean', 'iron', 'cook', and 'wash', and had advised her to point to everything else. He had not, however, prepared her for the social aspect of the relationship. She gestured at Harriet, who was placidly chewing toast while scrutinizing this new arrival, and said, 'Harriet. She's' – Alice held up her fingers in a spread – 'four.' She could hear herself speaking more loudly than she had intended. Then she pointed at her own swollen stomach through the dressing-gown. 'Baby.'

Galina leaned over the breakfast table and formally shook hands with Harriet. Alice thought this a promising sign. Harriet did not take to being swept into the bosoms of strangers and objected strongly to kisses from mouths as scarlet as Galina's.

Alice studied her employee furtively, an inane grin exhausting her cheeks. Early fifties, she guessed. With the navy blue tailored suit, red stiletto court shoes, matching handbag, black hair drawn into a tight French pleat and dramatically made-up face, the woman looked more like the manageress of a small ladies' clothing shop in a genteel English market town than a maid.

But Alice need not have been alarmed. After some astute sizing up of her own, Galina quickly abandoned her Sunday best and worked in ankle socks, beaten down slippers and an overall with a small hole over the heart which, as the days went by, expanded until at last a large well-covered breast poked through. For public viewing, she was a game dresser and enjoyed fashion, particularly if it was witty. Joke earrings in amusing shapes pleased her and she appeared to have a large collection of sloganned t-shirts about whose provenance she was always vague. Alice soon learned that direct questions to Soviets about where they had acquired something always provoked a hazy reply. George's favourite t-shirt, produced with a mischievous moue at the beginning of their second month was a shocking pink affair which read across the front 'The essence of journalism is . . .' and on the back '. . . the free lunch!' Galina had a particular fondness for exercise clothing, often appearing only in footless tights and a baggy sweatshirt that hinted at a figure as great in centimetre sizing as her age.

Her pride in her body, large though it was, contrived to make her appealingly sexy. She flirted outrageously with Volodya and Ivan and any other Soviet male who chanced to come to the front door. By the end of their first fortnight together, Alice had concluded (not without some envy) that Galina was well contented with herself, and it was this that accounted greatly for her appeal.

She had already drawn a group of other maids to the flat to pay court. The fact that she was not prepared to dress the part of *babushka* to which her age assigned her was what appeared to fascinate them. They would pop in to deliver or exchange small packages wrapped in brown paper, and pluck, a little shocked, at Galina's leg warmers as she sat on a dining-room chair, legs akimbo, soapy hands planted on bare knees, chuckling at them in amusement. At moments like these, Alice felt she was an intruder in someone else's flat. But after the early days of wariness Alice felt that they had developed the foundations of a workable relationship, and that spending the day together in the cramped apartment might not be so intolerable. Besides, Alice had no territorial feelings about housework.

Now, she took hold of the thick plastic bag of beetroot Galina had brought with her that morning, and shook them on to the chest freezer that served as the main worktop in the tiny kitchen. They rolled out, wizened, caked with earth and not very large, like the testicles of some tropical animal. Still, there were enough for bortsch for eight, so long as George kept his guests to that number. Surely he would – he knew they couldn't comfortably seat any more. But George's dinner parties had a tendency to grow.

Galina had been delighted to hear that the Masons would be entertaining. Her previous employers, German diplomats who filled her conversation, had called upon her – for extra pay, she emphasized – to serve at their parties. She announced with considerable pride that she owned a splendid pair of Western black court shoes (very high heeled), a black dress and frilly white apron. Alice was alarmed. The dining-room was so small there was barely room for guests, let alone Galina swooping about on tottering stilettos with dishes of food. Besides, the kitchen was exposed to the dining-room and Galina could not be relied upon not to settle congenially down on her stool, plate on the chest freezer, to gnaw a chicken bone in full view of the guests.

Alice once tried her out at a luncheon party. Galina had repeatedly glided into the dining-room, bosom thrust well to the fore, dropping little remarks into the conversation. She was keenly anxious that everyone should enjoy themselves and Alice could almost sense her longing to help pop forks into mouths. The Masons never again held a luncheon party at the flat.

The doorbell chimed. Alice dropped the peeled beetroot into the pot and ran through the dining-room to the door. It wasn't the janitors. It was Babs, wife of Jonathan Simpson, the British Embassy first secretary who lived across the corridor.

She looked at Alice and shrieked, hands at her mouth. 'My God, you've cut yourself!'

Alice glanced down. Her fingers were stained a rich ruby. 'Beetroot. I'm making bortsch.'

'Bortsch! Gosh, how jolly enterprising. I'd better not bother you, then.' She hovered hopefully.

'You're not bothering me. Come in, won't you? You can watch me chop.'

Babs shifted uncomfortably. She butted the toe of her sneaker at the doorframe. Babs was a devotee of American college-girl dress. Alice had never seen her during the day in anything other than track suits. They didn't do a great deal for Babs' soothingly wide posterior but they did contribute to her shower-fresh air of junior games mistress.

'Actually, I was hoping you could pop over to us.' Babs rubbed the side of her short nose and looked at Alice expectantly. 'There's something I'd quite like your view on.'

How tiresome, thought Alice. 'Just let me wash my hands. I'll be right over.'

As she crossed the corridor slippers whispered across the scuffed floor tiles, and Alice sensed rather than saw the fluttering of some dark material disappearing swiftly through the door at the far end of the hall. It clicked softly shut. Alice's young Japanese neighbour. Sometimes Alice caught sight of her as a ripple of floating kimono in whte-socked feet. Once she had startled her at the food chute and the poor girl had blushed deeply then, repeatedly bobbing her smooth dark head between touching palms, backed silently into the flat; her fortress against the threat of the barbaric on both sides of the compound fence.

Chapter Two

The Simpsons lived in controlled chaos. When Alice rang the bell, there was a scuffling sound behind the door and a voice at handle height shrieked, 'It's my turn!' Then followed a loud wail and a thud against the thin hardwood panel before the door was opening. A child of six stood there in a patterned viyella nightie, curls floating about her face. Behind her, a small pyjamaed infant stared up at Alice through tear-filled eyes, gobbling frantically at a long and grubby rag.

'Hello, Emily. Hello, Becka. Aren't you at school?'

Babs appeared clasping two tumblers of pink liquid. 'Hey, back into bed, you two! At once! They've got the 'flu. Wouldn't you know it? Hazel's day off, too.' She handed the tumblers to Alice. 'You bring those, and I'll get them settled again. Look, I tell you what.' She propelled the children into the sitting-room. 'Hop on the sofa, and if you're very good and don't fight while I talk to Alice, you can watch a video of Playschool. OK?'

The two children shrieked, and the smaller one flapped the rag at her elder sister.

'Put that down, Becka! There are enough germs around here as it is.'

The Simpsons' flat was bigger than the Masons', four instead of two flats knocked into one. Though the sitting-room was large, it was choked with Foreign Office teak and swathes of faded chintz. Alice knew from experience that the sunken sofa was only comfortable to look at, while its matching armchairs, with the spreading dimensions of middle-aged country matrons, trapped the sitter in their depths, making it impossible to rise without assistance. There were few books. Instead, out-of-date fashion and home magazines, lacquered covers dulled and cracked from repeated turning, were piled on the bamboo and glass coffee table. Except for an orderly set of Victorian hunting etchings above the sofa, the walls were bare. Nowhere was there any indication they were in Moscow: none of the usual souvenirs – the Palekh boxes, the garishly coloured pottery figures, the wooden eggs, the stacking matrioshka dolls of other diplomatic households.

Only the photographs ranged along the windowsill added any personal note. In one of a matching pair in tooled silver frames was a picture of Babs and Jonathan, Babs white-suited, in absurdly high court shoes, hair held back in a velvet band, cradling an infant swaddled in a christening blanket. In the other was the Simpson family, tanned and shiny with the red-tipped noses and vermillion eyes of flash photography, hunched over ice cream sundaes. Lined up behind were pictures of the Simpsons at country weddings, at tea on summer lawns, picnicking in rowing boats, on windy hillsides, at gymkhanas, and a recent group in front of the Kremlin. Babs' fair hair now layered to feather about her soft face.

Babs pressed the play button on the video and the children fell silent, faces turned expectantly towards the television screen. She straightened and gazed anxiously at Alice. 'Will you come and look at something? I want to know what you think I should make of it.'

She led the way, almost tiptoeing, down the corridor to a small room beyond the children's bedroom. Furtively she turned the door handle. With the door ajar, she stared defiantly back at Alice.

'I know this is dreadful. I know perfectly well I shouldn't be doing this. But I need your advice.'

Intrigued, Alice stepped into the room. It was small, with barely enough space for more than the bed. Under the window was a chest of drawers with a pot of straggling Busy Lizzie plants that had outgrown their strength. By the door was an almost empty bookcase with a row of Russian dolls queuing along the top shelf, and several paperbacks lined up below. The room appeared to Alice as unremarkable as the rest of the flat.

Babs pointed. 'It's that.'

Pinned to the wall above the bed was a collage of photographs, letters and mementoes. Alice peered closely at them. She recognized Hazel the nanny, pale-haired and thin, the flesh on her stretched and single-toned like pastry rolled out beyond the limits of its elasticity. The girl stood slightly cupped in on herself, hip bones thrust forward, shoulders drawn round, protecting the centre core of her body. An angular man with greying hair stood alongside her, an arm possessively across her shoulders, while to the side hovered a woman with badly permed hair, a defensive expression and three smaller children lined up in front of her.

'Her family, is it?'

'Not that, Alice.' Babs sounded irritated. 'There. Above the Leaning Tower of Pisa.'

Alice's eye travelled across holiday postcards, Moscow bus tickets, and Bolshoi theatre programmes to a small hand-written note: 'God protect Emily and Rebecca from the weakness of their parents and lead Mr and Mrs Simpson away from the path of the Devil,' she read.

'Ah.' Alice was nonplussed. The capital D for devil was perhaps unusually dramatic, but otherwise it seemed to her a rather touching supplication. Yet Babs, standing there expectantly plucking at the hem of her sweatshirt, obviously had not been affected in similar fashion. Alice strove for an appeasing response. 'It is a bit solemn, I suppose. Quite earnest, really. In a young girl, I mean.'

She faded. What exactly was she supposed to say? So far her relationship with Babs had not progressed to the level of intimacy that would have guided Alice in guessing what Babs hoped for from her.

Babs burst with indignation. 'It's downright interfering!' she exclaimed. 'What right has she got to judge us? I think Jonty and I should be allowed to choose our own paths. Don't you? Anyway, what's all that stuff about the devil? You'd think we were Satanists, or something.'

'It could be a perfectly simple prayer, Babs. I mean, they've made the language quite modern these days, haven't they? It's quite touching in a way that she has the interest of the entire family at heart and not just the children's.' She paused. 'Isn't it?'

Clearly it was not. Alice searched again for the right approach. 'Is she an especially devout girl, do you know?' She tried not to make it sound like a disease.

'She goes to Bible study group one night a week with some American nannies.' Babs sounded deflated. 'To be honest, till this came up I'd always thought it was a euphemism for the Dive Bar at the Canadian Embassy. And she does attend church when the vicar from Helsinki comes on his rounds. Would you say that qualified as devout?'

Alice reflected. 'It's a bit tricky, isn't it, complaining about a girl being religious? On the whole I would have thought it argued in her favour.' She looked enquiringly at Babs.

Babs reddened. 'I know.' She sunk down on Hazel's bed and slowly expelled a long breath. 'I'm being absurd. That's what you're saying, isn't it?' She toyed with her fingers in her lap. 'It's so hard keeping things in perspective when you've been cooped up here any length of time.' She glanced accusingly at Alice. 'You haven't been here long enough. Except for my half day computer classes when I can escape to my oasis at the Anglo-American School – and that's only twice a week, for heaven's sake – I'm stuck most of the day in the flat. The only other distractions are embassy coffee mornings, which I dread; cooking for the Dive Bar when it's my turn which is worse; or learning how to batik or speak conversational Chinese or something equally futile with the ladies of the International Women's Group. And on top of all that we're bugged, we're reported on, we're followed and I can't even have a pee without wondering who is listening in upstairs.'

'So that makes you constipated, too?' Alice smiled encouragingly. She wasn't sure how to handle Babs in this vein.

Babs smiled ruefully. 'I'm sorry. I suppose you're thinking I'm over-reacting. But it does get on top of me sometimes. D'you know?' She looked Alice over. 'Perhaps you don't yet. But you will.' She sighed. 'You're probably right. I'm much better off with a Bible thumper than a girl who hangs around the Marines. I had one of those last time.'

'I never said that.'

'No, but it's true.' She hauled herself up, twitching smooth the quilt. 'Come on, let's get out of here before we're caught. I'll put the kettle on.'

Alice, following her out of the room, lingered with her hand on the lightswitch. She turned aside, curious, to the bookcase. The shelf below Hazel's collection of painted Russian woodwork held no more than a handful of paperbacks, titles that might have been found in any young girl's collection. Alice glanced at them: a couple of historical romances, a detective novel, a spy thriller,

Russian in 20 Minutes a Day, the Bible and a book called *Utterly Female*.

Intrigued, Alice pulled it out of the shelf and turned to the back cover. The blurb was designed in day-glo pink to sting the eyeballs.

> Over 100,000 copies sold! More than 32 weeks on the US bestseller lists! With intimate sensitivity and understanding, author Suzie Sapmann has written the book that cures all marital problems.
>
> When marriage hits a glitch and the going gets rough, *Utterly Female* will tell you, step-by-step, how to rekindle that fire in your man.
>
> Suzie knows. She's been there.
>
> So if you, like Suzie, discover you are no longer Number One in your man's life, reach for this bestselling guide to sexual and spiritual harmony and let Suzie show you how to hit star-billing once more in the long-running marriage show!

Alice was startled. Titillating literature for the pure in heart! Without considering what she was doing, she slid the book into her shift and left the room.

Uncomfortably aware of the peculiar new outline to her ribcage, she put her head round the door of the kitchen. 'Babs, I should be on my way to pick up Hattie. Could I take a raincheck on coffee?' Babs turned, surprised. 'But listen.' With one arm guarding her waist, Alice inclined more of her body carefully into the room.' Why don't we all go tobogganing this weekend? If the girls are better.'

Babs put the kettle down. 'I'm sorry you've got to run. But thanks for coming round.'

She sounded hurt, and looked so forlorn that Alice stepped quickly across the kitchen and threw her arm carefully across Babs' shoulders.

'Hey, cheer up! I'd give my back teeth for a nanny like Hazel! She's a treasure. Whatever plans she has for your future.' Alice peered into Babs' face. 'See if you can't have a rest, why don't you? While Emily and Becka are still glued to the telly. I bet you're tired out with two sick children.'

'Yes,' Babs said emptily. 'I probably am.' She let Alice out and gently shut the door.

From the autumn bonfire smell of *papirossi* cigarettes seeping into the corridor, Alice could tell Galina had successfully coralled the janitors. Above her head the neon light flickered and popped, flaring across the turquoise gloss of the rough cement walls like an electrical storm across a summer sky. One of the Yemeni women from the sprawling family crammed into the flat along the hallway was bent over the open rubbish shute, pouring cooking debris into it from a plastic sack. She saw Alice and hastily pulled the cloth of her headdress into place over her nose. A tumble of potato peel and tea leaves spewed slowly to the filthy tiled floor as she stooped to her task.

Goddammit, thought Alice, it's no wonder we have cockroaches. But still she smiled fixedly at the woman until she had let herself back into her flat. United we stand.

Galina was planted, legs wide, fists on hips, blocking the hall at the doorway to the tiny lavatory. Daisy, heavily swaddled in blankets, was slipped through one arm like a large marrow. Her button eyes blinked at Alice and her mouth worked like a goldfish gulping at the side of the aquarium.

Galina turned triumphantly to Alice and gave her an exaggerated wink. Volodya and Ivan were both pressed inside the lavatory, doing, as far as Alice could gauge, absolutely no more than she and Galina had already attempted themselves. Volodya had stuck a spanner into the rim of his knitted ski hat, presumably to indicate that he was a man at work. But otherwise, the only tool the two men shared was one of George's precious wire shirt hangers, which they had twisted grotesquely out of shape. Ivan leaned against the British Tourist Board photographs of placid thatched cottages with which Alice, in an attempt at a little local counter-propaganda, had papered the lavatory. He was flicking the ash from his *papirossi* on to Volodya's ski hat. Volodya looked up at Alice as she squeezed by, wiping his hands on his faded blue cotton dungarees.

'Big shits in the West, eh?' he declared with satisfaction, in Russian.

Galina cuffed him across the shoulder and gave a kick to his thigh that provoked a genuine yelp of pain.

Alice held her arms open to receive the gulping Daisy and indicated her breast. '*Moloko*. Daisy, milk?'

Galina flapped an arm at her. '*Nyet, nyet*. Daisy *horosho. Paka!*'

Later, Alice understood. That was fine by her. There was something very soothing about abdicating responsibility for Daisy's feeding times. She bore Hazel's book to her bedroom and placed it carefully in her bedside drawer. Then she returned to the hall where she slid into her snowboots. Grabbing her coat off the stand, she declared, 'Hattie. *Payedu*. I go.'

'*Shapka!*' Galina scolded, picking Alice's fur hat off the hall shelf. She placed it firmly on Alice's head and patted her approvingly on the arm. '*Za* Hattie. Madam go.'

Volodya glanced up curiously as she opened the front door. Alice looked back at the three of them at ease in her flat. She knew what Babs had meant. If there was anyone who didn't belong there, it was her.

Chapter Three

Outside in the compound the cold hit Alice like a slap, making her eyes water and her nose run. She sniffed the air and at once her nostrils blocked, ice forming on the hairs inside. The *dezhornaya*s, the women concierges who did a better job at running the compound than the male janitors, were out in the parking lot with their wide metal shovels. With grating sweeps they pushed the morning's snowfall on to the rising banks of snow that each day diminished further the already inadequate parking space. One of the woman had climbed up into the garbage container and was standing astride the rubbish shaking out any printed Western plastic bags she could find. Food scraps, crushed tin cans and putrid nappies tumbled out on to the reeking mass before she cast her emptied treasure fluttering to the ground.

There were few cars at this time of day, most of them the smaller second cars of the wives. It was another anomaly Alice had had to accommodate: the graduation from their cherished, much battered Citroën 2-CV to two-car family status. Before Daisy's birth, Alice had determinedly used the metro and bus system. Determinedly, because the state of apartheid created by Soviet officialdom to cordon off the foreign community reached beyond the fenced-in compounds and hard-currency-only stores to influence the attitude of the Soviet populace. They had learned, with sound historical justification, to fear foreigners on their soil and that fear translated into obstruction, abuse and criticism. On the metro, fierce *babushka*s in too-short coats, stout boots and fur-rimmed felt hats had had no qualms about piercing Alice's extended stomach with stubby fingers and berating her for appearing in her condition in a public place in wintertime. In fact, Alice had noticed with surprise that she was indeed the only pregnant woman she had seen out.

On one occasion, queuing at a bus stop after a walk in Gorki Park in a press of cold, tired Muscovites burdened with net bags, she and Harriet had been rounded on in English by a man who accused them of occupying space in the crowded bus when, as foreigners, they could well afford to travel by taxi.

At last, with a baby and its support system soon to be added to her retinue, she had capitulated. A second car was only practical. George had made a trip to Helsinki while Alice was in London for Daisy's birth, bringing back the little Fiat that Alice now loved with a ridiculous passion.

It was her home from home, her small refuge at times of incipient claustrophobia in the flat. She ran her eyes along the number plates of all the Unos that sat among the other compact models the community tended towards for their second cars. The foreigners were allocated specifically coded licence plates, distinctly coloured, numbered and initialled. In this fashion, militiamen the length and breadth of the Soviet Union could establish, at the lift of a telephone or walkie-talkie, precisely whose car had just passed by. Alice was rather amused by the scheme, relishing the suggestion of celebrity that came with knowing that her number would be fed by militiamen into some central computer the instant she left her own compound or arrived at another.

George was less amused. The front tyres of his Saab had once been slashed while the car was parked outside the

Press Centre, he assumed in retaliation for a piece he had written criticizing the Soviet presence in Afghanistan. And within a week of importing it into the country, the Saab had been stripped of all its metal insignia. These emblems, George was told, were coveted collectors' items among Russians whose only hope – if they could ever aspire to own a car at all – was for a Soviet Volga, Zhiguli, or Zaparozhets. Even more prized were windscreen wipers, which all drivers, Soviet and foreign alike, removed whenever their cars were parked in public places. As George discovered with the slashing of his tyres, spare parts of any sort did not exist on the open market. He had been forced to telex Helsinki for new ones.

The lock to Alice's car had iced up again. She reached into her pocket for the lighter she carried for the purpose and ran a flame over her key. It eased in like a blunt knife through thick lard. She sat back to let the engine run long enough to release the frozen gear shift. She checked her watch – midday – and turned on the radio. A voice with a mid-Atlantic accent was saying '. . . in the 42/41 metre bands.' Then followed the discordant clangs from the Kremlin bells that rang in the news. Good. What had happened in the limited zone Radio Moscow defined as the world?

'This is the Moscow World Service. The news, read by Maria Dudena. First the news headlines. The General Secretary of the Communist Party has extended congratulations to the leader of the Yugoslav Communist Party on the occasion of the fortieth anniversary of its founding. Cosmonaut Alexandr Yeliseyev has been appointed rector of the Bauman High School of Engineering, the nation's oldest techincal institute. Foreign Minister Andrei Gromyko went walk-about in Moscow this week to find out how the socio-living conditions of the people are being satisfied.'

Alice switched over to tape. She slipped a Dire Starits cassette into the deck and the car filled with noise. She checked that the windows were wound up tight, the gear stick loose, then eased out of the car park. As she coasted slowly past the sentry's box shouting 'Money for nothin' and chicks for free' in visible puffs of breath into the freezing air, she saw him pick up his telephone and dial.

Serpuhovsky Val is a treelined boulevard that lies between the Donskoi and the Danilov monasteries in the south of Moscow. Trams run in single file up one side towards the city centre and southwards down the other to the wide and soulless intersection of Tulskaya Street with the Warsaw Chausee. Just beyond, in a southern swoop of the Moskva river, stretch extensive marshalling yards. It is a grim area of featureless concrete buildings, with not even the propaganda placards of the Masons' early days in Moscow to add colour any longer to their cement façades.

Alice turned right into the traffic flow. Snow lay neatly piped like toothpaste along the branches of the barren boulevard trees. Beneath them on benches middle-aged women with tea-cosy silhouettes squeezed together like pigeons, clutching their shopping bags possessively to their chests and inclining their heads together in gossip. Down the snow-compacted paths of the central garden loped a cross-country skier in royal blue track suit and red knitted cap. It was the only colour in a landscape of greys and white.

At the T-junction by the cinema, a woman as old as the Soviet Union bent over the points where the tramrails converged, plucking at the ice with a metal pick. Her feet were encased in felt *valenki* boots, yet otherwise she was clothed only in pullovers, a thin scarf tight on her head. While Alice waited for the traffic to clear, a tram rattled up behind the woman and flashed its lights. She took no notice, chipping doggedly at the ice. The young female driver gave a turn of her metal screw-bell and the old woman shambled off the rails with a contemptuous backwards jerk of her arm at the tram.

The snow was thick and yielding under the car wheels, as dense as sodden sand above a retreating tide. It was thicker still on the windscreen where it dropped like globs of whipped cream from a beater. As Alice nosed the car into the traffic round Dobrininskaya metro, she was distracted by the sight of a queue down the side of the pink circular building. Briefly she considered stopping to investigate. Galina had said there were oranges on the streets. Then a gap widened immediately in front and she eased the car forwards.

The Koltso ring road was built under Stalin's orders, a wide circular highway that hacks a formidable route across the convoluted and narrow streets of old central Moscow. Acres of ancient buildings, stuccoed palaces, merchants' houses and gold onion-domed churches were demolished to accommodate its ten lanes. Driving on it without mishap requires nerves of steel, panache and a profound lack of reverence for the highway code. Cars, lorries, tourist coaches and open trucks loaded with tumbling cabbages, logs and bricks slalom from lane to lane, weaving in and out of fleeting gaps like country dancers, so intent upon accomplishing the next manoeuvre before the formation changes that there is seldom time to flash the indicator. If, indeed, the indicator works. Moscow cars run as much on their drivers' adrenalin as they do on choking Soviet petrol.

Alice turned off the Koltso at Kalinin Prospekt and headed towards the block on Kutuzovsky where the British Embassy playgroup was housed. She parked under the eye of the sentry down the side street outside the Commercial Section, glancing briefly at its photographic window display of scenes from British life. There were glossy pictures, two foot square, of the Prince of Wales and the Princess in her sumptuous wedding gown; photographs of the royal couple emerging from the clinic with their first baby; of swans on the lake in St James's Park and industrial plants in flowered meadows, and several pictures of the Queen Mother. As always, a group of Russians clustered about this curious display. Even Alice found it difficult to fathom the message that lay behind the choice of illustrations.

Inside the tiny playgroup foyer a huddle of mothers pressed against the glass doors, staring through at the auditorium beyond. Alice stood on tiptoe and caught sight of Harriet in the line-up of singing toddlers. She had raised the hem of her dress high across her chest and appeared only mechanically engaged in giving the song her vocal support while staring blankly towards the long frosted window. Then class was dismissed and the wife of the British Consul strode briskly towards the door to admit the impatient mothers. With a rustle of quilted coats and slithering of furs, each mother or nanny pushed to be first to scoop from the oncoming rush her own small child into a doting embrace.

As Alice strapped Hattie into the car, she turned briefly to look over her shoulder at the building above the playgroup. Kutuzovsky 7/14, familiarly known as 'Kutz', the first and largest of Moscow's foreign compounds, stretched blank and forbidding for several hundred metres along Kutozovsky Prospekt. Somewhere inside, George was busy with his writing. Alice wondered what time he would be home. She had forgotten to get a new video and there was no ballet scheduled for television that night.

Chapter Four

George, on the fifth floor of Korpus 6, was well behind in his work. He had come in that morning, eager to start on a story about Gorbachev's recent promise of a new latitude for the Soviet press, to find Harold slumped over the telex machine, an empty bottle of vodka beside him on the floor. George slung the bottle into the brimming wastepaper basket, and looked over Harold's shoulder.

SOVIET TROOPS WILL WITHDRAW FROM AFGHANISTAN QUOTE ONCE FOREIGN INTERVENTION IN AFGHANIS-TAN HAS CEASED AND WE HAVE GUARANTEES THAT IT WILL NOT BE RESUMED UNQUOTE, DEPUTY FOREIGN MINISTER MIKHAIL KAPITSA SD IN MOSCOW YDAY PARA

TAKE IN REUTERS

George sighed. The news story was no longer 'yday', but the day before that. Harold must have been drinking since yesterday evening. George wondered where Nadya could have been, though by now her indifference to her husband's habitual drunkenness no longer startled him.

He went into the outer office and dialled her home number. 'Nadya? It's George. I'm in the office. So's

Harold. Could you come down and help me with him?'

George waited at the window that looked out over the compound car park. He watched as incoming Volvos and Saabs and Mercedes cruised up and down the lines for the parking slots of departing cars. Soviet office drivers stood about in clusters by running engines, stamping their feet and blowing on their hands.

The front door clicked and George turned. Nadya stood in the doorway looking grim, her arms folded over her perky bosom.

'Where is he?'

George jerked his head towards the telex. 'I'll give you a hand.'

Nadya was a small, compact woman, with the soft feathered-fowl plumpness that pleased the Russians. But she was a thoroughly capable and remorseless woman. She hooked her hands into Harold's armpits and dragged him off his seat, toppling the chair to the floor. George picked up Harold's legs, and they carried him out of the office to the lift. Nadya had held it on their floor by propping its wire gate open, and George could hear shouts of complaint from below. They pushed Harold through the two half doors and swung the gate to behind them. Nadya punched the button and the cupboard-like lift rose slowly upward.

'Why didn't you come for him, Nadya?' said George.

Nadya shrugged. 'He falls so drunkenly asleep he does not care where he is, why should I?'

They heaved Harold's comatose form into the flat, through the sitting-room, and dumped him on to his bed.

'Will you be coming down?' George spoke tentatively. Nadya would sometimes explode unexpectedly, waving her arms and shouting at him in Russian. George hated that.

'Of course. I come now.'

George sighed. It was enough contending with Moscow, a new job, London, the Soviet system, Soviet bureaucracy, and God knows what else, without having to depend on a drunk for office space and his mercurial Soviet wife for secretarial skills. The *Sentinel* was respected as a newspaper that cherished the memory of the 60s, minority groups, offbeat causes, sexual equality, and home-knitted jumpers on its journalists. As a principled paper, it conveniently believed that big budgets corrupted correspondents and relied heavily instead on their initiative. This paid off. With every newspaperman's pride in his work at stake, *Sentinel* journalists exercised the utmost ingenuity in organizing support systems for themselves that cost the paper remarkably little in operational budgets.

On his second reconnaissance trip to Moscow, laden with blank cassettes, disposable razors and cartons of Marlboro in the naive hope of bribing UPDK's rental department into giving him an office (he had not then appeciated that the price was more likely to be a new video system), George had been introduced to a temporarily sober Harold Armitage. Harold, he quickly learned, was about to lose his telex machine because he had omitted to pay its running costs for several months. Only later did George discover on what Harold had been spending his telex budget. George had offered to pay Harold's back bills and half the office rent if Harold would let him share them both. The deal was done, with Nadya thrown in as translator, secretary, and office manager, to be paid, under the desk, in hard currency.

Harold was the longest surviving member of the Moscow press corps. He had come to Moscow in the late 1950s as the correspondent for a popular British daily. A Russian scholar, he had a nose for Soviet affairs that regularly put him on the front page of his paper. But he had fallen in love with Nadya, a dancer in the corps de ballet of the Bolshoi, and had opted to stay beyond the period allotted to his posting. His newspaper had been quietly relieved. There was no-one among its staff expressing any enthusiasm over the prospect of covering Brezhnev's Soviet Union.

Then Harold had become what his fellow foreign correspondents called 'Sovietized'. Which meant he had stayed on too long for his own good: too long to find a familiar niche back home, too long to keep in mind that despite his appreciation of the Soviet Union and its customs, he was nevertheless a foreigner. He began to drink. He stopped making much effort to be part of the Western community that would have stood by him, and was rarely seen outside his attendance at press briefings. He was permitted to marry Nadya because the Soviet authorities gambled that by this time Harold had probably left a return to the West too late for a comfortable 'rehabilitation', so it was unlikely that Nadya would be leaving. And her legitimate placement in the middle of a foreign compound, many Westerners pointed out, was strikingly handy. Nadya, whatever her relationship with the KGB, realized that even if Harold would never be her ticket to the West, at least he could provide access to Moscow's foreign currency stores and to goods ordered from Western catalogues in his name. It was better than nothing.

'There is a press conference at ten,' Nadya remarked, as though assessing the weather.

George checked his watch. 'My God, Nadya, that's in fifteen minutes! Where's Sasha?'

She turned casually towards the window, and pointed. 'Down there. Don't worry, the car's ready.'

'Jesus wept,' George muttered. Grabbing his coat and *shapka*, he ran for the door. There was no sign of the lift. 'Christ!'

He swerved at the stairs, barrelling down them two at a time. 'Sasha!' he yelled as he emerged on to the parking lot. 'Press Centre. Now! Fast!'

Sasha touched the rim of his *shapka* and slid behind the wheel of the Saab. He had the car on the move, screeching

33

and slithering out of its space, as George threw himself into the passenger seat. This was the kind of driving he liked best.

Once on the Koltso, Sasha headed the car into the Zil lane. He and George exchanged grins. The centre section of Moscow's main roads was kept clear for the Politburo in their Zils, and the Chaikas of lesser officials. But foreigners generally found that it they drove with enough speed and ostentation round Moscow there were few militiamen with the confidence to challenge them. One of George's most gratifying Moscow moments had been his formal accept-ance by cheering correspondents into the K Club, member-ship of which entiled driving past the Kremlin at 100 kph.

Sasha switched on the headlights full beam and pushed the speedometer towards seventy. George felt the exhilar-ation of a schoolboy on a prank. They rushed through amber lights and past the glass boxes of traffic cops raised on platforms above the road. Then Sasha swung the Saab across four lanes of oncoming traffic and shot into the Press Centre forecourt.

George almost toppled out and pushed past a clutch of Japanese hovering by the glass doors into the press building. He showed his pass to the militiaman on duty and shouldered his way towards the coat counter. The place was filling fast with correspondents impatient to secure a good seat. Still, the cloakroom attendant determinedly main-tained her slow and steady pace, slopping back and forth in flattened slippers from counter to coat rail.

George felt a tap on his shoulder.

'Salutations, George.'

He turned and smiled at the gaunt and bearded man behind him. Svenson was a one-man news service for Scandinavia's radio stations. 'Today Sweden, tomorrow the world!' he liked to say, his voice rolling and swooping like an adolescent boy's.

'Here, let me help with some of that.' George bent towards a cumbersome tape machine.

'I am very lucky to get in,' Svenson puffed as they lugged his equipment up a flight of glistening marble steps which would not have been out of place in a luxury bathroom.

'Oh yes? How's that?'

'My press card is still up for renewal, so I have to hang around the entrance like a prostitute and tout for someone yenerous enough to bring me in as a guest.'

'That's too bad. How long have they had it?'

'Three weeks now. Unfortunately it ran out right after I broadcast a piece about Sakharov being confined to Gorki. When I went to my minder to see what was the delay in getting it back, he had the transcript on his desk.' He gave a laugh. 'You know what the Foreign Ministry told to me: That Dr Sakharov had not been exiled to Gorki at all, yust lives there as one would in a large industrial city such as for example Detroit! Anyway, they still have my press card and no-one answers my questions about when I can expect a new one.'

They entered the conference room, where foreign television news crews were setting up their cameras. Sound men ran back and forth trailing microphones to the dais. George looked about. Slumped back in their tangerine seats in the centre of the auditorium, he spotted two members of the British press corps.

He eased himself in beside them. 'Greetings, comrades.'

Charlie Prowse was reading from his notebook, pulling gently at his dark Zapata moustache. Under his black corduroy suit he wore a vibrant Hawaiian shirt swirling in exotic fruit. The head of Winston Fitch was sunk deep into the folds of his tweed jacket.

George nudged Charlie Prowse. 'That's a pretty appalling shirt, Charlie. What's up with Winston?'

Charlie cast a brief glance over his neighbour. 'London

called,' he said, and turned back to his notebook. George leaned across him and touched Winston's sleeve.

'What have they done this time, Fitch? Cancelled the luncheon vouchers?'

Winston Fitch kept his chin buried in the rough cloth and snorted. 'The truth is funnier. Foreign editor asked me to give Philby a bell. See if I couldn't stand up some wind that the Home Secretary is the Fourth Man.' He frowned. 'Or is it Fifth? I can't keep track.' He turned to George with exasperation. 'They haven't a bloody clue, have they? How am I expected to find Philby's phone number when there isn't even a bloody telephone directory, for God's sake?' He threw his hands despairingly into the air. 'I ask you. What kind of superpower is it anyway that doesn't even run to a lousy phone book?'

'Upper Volta with rockets,' Charlie Prowse obediently murmured from his notebook.

George jogged him.' Burkina Faso these days, Charlie.' Were those bananas on Charlie's shirt or what?

'And do they truly imagine Philby's name would be in it if there was a bloody phone book?' Winston's pale hair flopped over one eye. He stared at them bleakly through it. 'All right. Say I did have his number. Then what. Can they seriously believe he'd confirm the story?'

'Would make a superb page one, though,' mused George. '"KGB Colonel admits British Home Secretary top Soviet spy!"'

'"Top Dog Top Rat" if it were my paper,' observed Charlie, flapping his yellow tie. He turned his head and his dark curls dragged along his collar. 'I don't know why you take it so hard, Fitch. My own esteemed editor wanted a profile last week on the Soviet media's top gossip columnist. With photograph. Do we love it, or do we love it?'

Winston appeared not to have heard. He gave a short bitter laugh. 'Why don't they fly out here, see what it's really like? We're no further away than Athens, after all. Two days is all it would take. Then perhaps they might be a bit more realistic before they roll back from the pub with fatuous suggestions for their Man in Moscow.'

Charlie patted Winston on the knee. 'Haven't you noticed that when foreign travel is called for, it's always to places with a decent meal at the end of the journey?' He turned to George. 'You know, they should never send bachelors out here. Unkind. You need a nice Soviet girlfriend, Fitch. All cuddles and kasha. Soon make you feel better. Life is too short to take one's paper seriously.'

'In Moscow,' retorted Winston, 'life is a damn sight too long.'

The briefing produced no surprises. Peace was its main theme.

'God! Not world friendship again,' sighed Charlie and slid lower into his chair.

George doodled. While US and Soviet negotiatiors would be meeting shortly for the next round of Geneva talks, a Congress of Intellectuals For A Peaceful Future was being held in Warsaw, followed the next week by a Together For Peace conference of international non-government organizations, with a Bike For Peace rally planned for Leningrad in the summer.

George yawned and toyed with his pencil. He couldn't make anything witty come out of the peace movement acronyms. There was more interest in the elegant cut of an obviously new and Western-made suit that the Foreign Ministry spokesman was wearing. The Horse, some press corps wags called him. It wasn't a bad nickname. Not only did most official policy statements issue from his mouth, but his initials were an irresistible 'G.G.'

Questions followed on the Star Wars issue, on Strategic Defensive Initiatives, and on the Greenham Common women, giving the Pravda correspondent a chance to comment that they were victims of Western hypocrisy over human rights.

'At least we didn't get the usual stuff about the norm of international law being flouted in Nicaragua,' Charlie observed as they rose.

'Charlie,' begged Winston. 'Please. Leave off the jokes about flouting poor Norm, will you for once?'

'Are we still seeing you and Lisa for dinner on Friday?' George asked Charlie as they reached for their coats.

'*Absolutna*. Must meet your better half properly. We've only touched hands at the Embassy Christmas cocktail so far. I'm looking forward to closer acquaintance.' He raised his eyebrows and leered at George.

Outside the snow was falling sluggishly out of a leaden sky. It would have been pleasant to drop everything and go home. But even if he booked a telephone call to the *Sentinel*'s copy desk to dictate his day's stories from the flat, there were Sasha and Nadya looking to him for some kind of order to shape their day. One of the side effects of state control, George had found, was the inability of the Soviets to take any form of initiative. With considerable skill everyone in every sector of society made sure the buck would never stop with them. George knew that without him there to direct them neither Sasha nor Nadya would do anything with their working day. Yet presumably, he mused, as Sasha once more flung the Saab into the Zil land, he and Nadya must have caught some of the current of excitement, working, as they did, with the press corps? There were, after all, exhilarating times. Surely they must be affected?

Certainly George was convinced that they were covering what he felt in his bones would become the most compelling story in the world. It had been some years since he had felt so stimulated by his work. He returned reluctantly to the flat at night and rose in the mornings eager to leave it. In one sense, he almost couldn't do enough work. While he and most of the Moscow press corps were reporting that Gorbachev was a man to be watched, the outside world was still viewing the acitivities of the new regime with wariness and scepticism, a fact reflected in the amount of space newspapers were giving to day-to-day Soviet developments. These were absurdly modest, George felt, when balanced against the enormous changes taking place. George itched to fill the foreign pages, the feature pages, the editorial pages, with news and comment. But as his editor patiently repeated, there were other parts of the world to be covered as well.

So it was with extreme frustration that he read the message on the telex machine.

ATTN HAROLD ARMITAGE

NEED FULL COVERAGE OF MOSCOW STORY ON DAILY BASIS STOP ARE U WILLING/ABLE UNDER DIFFERENT BY-LINE TO STRING FOR THIS PAPER QUERY WILL PAY TOPS FOR NEWS AND FEATURES, TELEPHONE NUMBERS FOR EXCLUSIVES STOP INTERESTED QUERY

REPLY SOONEST

CHEERS

BOB MATHISSON DAILY POST

Damned Harold was barely in a fit state to file for his own paper, thought Georg, let alone take on a second. Blast the man! What a terrific opportunity!

George's irritation was aggravated by the knowledge that no-one was likely to ask him to write psuedonomously for them. It wasn't that he was too new to Moscow. It was more that the image of the *Sentinel* suggested none of its dedicated reporters would dream of tapping a typewriter for any other, less pure in heart, organ. Yet there was he, frustrated with excitement by the urge to spread the Gorbachev gospel as wide as it would go!

He tore the telex from the machine and put it on Harold's desk.

'Nadya?' he called across the office. 'CAn you come in? There's work to be done.'

By four o'clock night had come. Meagre streetlamps dotted the compound like distant stars. In Serpuhovsky Val, Alice was wiping the debris of ingredients for sugar biscuits from the top of the chest freezer. Daisy was tucked up alongside in her carrycot, her small face puffy, forehead wrinkled in the concentration of sleep, tiny fists clenched against her chest.

'Go and wash your hands, Hattie. It's almost supper time.'

'Not hungry.' Harriet was lying speadeagled across the kitchen floor.

'You're in the way, sweetheart. I shall trip over you.'

Harriet rose and clambered on to the chair by the freezer. 'Don't want any yucky supper.'

'How do you know it's yucky when you haven't had any yet?' Alice was terse. 'How do you know it isn't hamburger and chips, or fish and chips, or pizza, or something?'

''Cause it never is, 'cept when we go to Granny's.'

'What a deprived life. Besides, I often make you hamburgers and chips. And tonight it's delicious stew, so stop moaning.'

'Yucky stew again!' Harriet kicked the freezer. 'Why can't we have pizza?'

'Because, light of my life, dear heart, this is Moscow and they don't bloody sell it.' Alice drew a steadying breath. 'Now be a good girl, please, and go and wash your hands.'

Galina appeared in the dining-room, shrugging into her

coat. She was clutching a plastic bag clinking with George's empty bottles.

'*Da zavtra*, madam.'

'Till tomorrow, Galina,' echoed Alice.

Galina bustled towards Harriet through the gap into the kitchen and planted a noisy scarlet kiss on Harriet's forehead.

'*Paka*, Hattie.'

Harriet threw herself at her. 'Don't go, Baba!' she wailed. 'I don't want you to go!'

'For heaven't sake, Hattie.' Alice was irritated. 'Just go and wash your hands. Baba will be back tomorrow.'

'Come,' Galina volunteered. She led Harriet into the bathroom, pointing to the lavatory as they passed it. 'Much paper, Hattie, *nyet*,' she cautioned. 'OK? *Horosho?*'

'*Horosho*,' Harriet grumpily agreed.

But bathed and sweet smelling, warm in a winceyette nightie, Harriet became a soft and pliant creature, nestling into Alice's lap for her bedtime story. Her hair clung damply to her shiny face and Alice felt her eyes prick with compassion for this small and vulnerable person. She tucked the child in bed and switched off the light.

In her own room Daisy lay quiet in sleep. Alice touched her breasts, tense and sore with milk, and debated waking the baby for a feed. She shrugged and turned from the cot. Daisy would wake soon enough. She went instead into the sitting-room and opened the balcony door, tiptoeing carefully into the snow. The cold was exhilarating, a reminder of childhood holidays and the first plunge into the stinging waves of the Atlantic. Alice felt the skin of her body contract like a sea anemone at the touch of a finger. At this height the night was still and Alice felt detached from the world. Sounds of the city rose up to her, muted, as though from a very great distance. Along the boulevard below rattled late evening trams, loose wheels stumbling over irregular points with the noise of coins shaken in a tin box. She could hear the crank of gears and the grumbling of ancient engines as lorries took the turn at the end of the street. Now and then the heavy, regular throbbing of the night-caught city was punctuated by the brief toot of a driver's horn.

Directly opposite, twenty metres or so beyond the compound fence, rose a replica of the foreigners' apartment block. In the treacle-thick darkness Alice watched as figures flicked in mellow light across windows not yet curtained. There seemed so many people busying about in the small flats. An interior from the Dutch school, she mused, as faces touched with the sheen of heat came briefly together above the amber glow of a Soviet table lamp then moved out of sight behind the walls.

She flicked the snow from the balcony balustrade and leaned delicately over on fingertips to look down into the compound below. By the gleam of the light inside the box she could dimly make out the movement of the militiaman at his observation window. As she watched, a yellow taxi swung through the compound fence and slowed in front of him. The militiaman stepped out, peered into the back of the cab, and saluted. The taxi drove into the broad rectangle of light cast on to the snow through the large lobby pane. Alice saw first a turban, then its wearer emerge gingerly from the passenger seat and hurry across the ice. The taxi reversed away, a small green light now burning at its windscreen.

George returned at half past nine. He looked drawn, his eyes red. Alice had made curried beetroot and cabbage with coconut cream and spices from her supplies. It was not a happy concoction. Devising imaginative recipes from prosaic local ingredients Alice looked upon as creative therapy. She could summon up pretty close to twenty ways with beetroot. But this particular number would have to be deleted. By the time she had tidied supper away and laid the table for breakfast, George was in bed asleep, a paperback tumbled on his chest. Alice gently removed it from his hand and pulled the sheet up under his chin.

She lay beside him for some time, listening to the central heating bubble and swill inside the water pipes. Outside, in the corner of the snowy balcony, pigeons gently rolled their throats, gurgling comfortingly.

Then, carefully drawing back the bedclothes so as not to disturb George, she swung her feet on to the floor and into her slippers. She reached into her bedside table, and tiptoed down the passage to the lavatory. Here she switched on the light, thrashing with a slipper at the cockroaches activated by the sudden glare, pulled down the lid, sat upon it, and opened Hazel's copy of *Utterly Female*.

Chapter Five

The Friday dinner party was not an overwhelming success. Whether the food or the mix of guests was at fault, Alice couldn't quite decide. No-one, except George, made any remark about the bortsch, which she had thought deliciously rich and soothing. Nor had they taken particularly enthusiastic helpings of the pelmeni she had treated like ravioli, bathing the little Russian dumplings in a chunky tomato sauce. With tomatoes costing twenty pounds sterling a kilo they might at least have said something. If it were a manifestation of bias against Soviet cuisine, then Alice thought it unsympathetic and snobbish.

Alice prided herself on her cooking. When George had returned to London after an early reconnaisance trip with a spartan list of groceries available in Moscow, Alice had gone out with an empty suitcase to a Chinese supermarket behind Leicester Square. She had filled the case to capacity with Asian, Indian and Chinese foodstuffs, determined to transform Soviet basics into ethnic exotica and generate a little culinary excitement at her dinner parties. She would not be prevented from cutting a social swathe in Moscow circles simply through a local lack of ingredients. Some enterprise was necessary.

Her spices had come into play within a month of arrival. George had telephoned one afternoon, squeaky with excitement, to ask her if he could invite a couple of Soviet contacts to dinner. They were terrific acquisitions, he confided short of breath: one a candidate member of the Politburo, the other high up in the Foreign Ministry. Both had served at some time in Jakarta and George had boasted to them of Alice's skills with sate and a wok. Would she conjure them up an Indonesian fest? Fine, said Alice, just fix the date. He had, replied George. How about tonight?

Alice was outraged. Did George not remember where they were? This was hardly the place to ring up at five hours' notice and order up Indonesian specialities as though she was some kind of take-away outlet! How was she expected to get chicken at this hour?

But of course, at a pinch she knew she could. And wasn't this just the type of challenge she expected herself to rise to? She left Harriet with Galina, squeezed her by then camel-humped stomach into the back of a passing cab flagged down with a packet of Marlboro, and clattered off to the foreign currency grocery 'Beriozka' in the Mezhdunarodnaya Hotel.

That much, at least, she had known. Unfortunately, what she did not learn until she had set the opur ayam in the oven to keep warm, switched the grill on high to barbecue the sate, and turned up a front burner for the wok, was that the wiring of the flat could only carry eight kilowatts of energy. The oven fused. The flat plunged into darkness.

Fortunately, George's guests were already seated at the candlelit table and unaware of any loss of power. What to do? She would have to jump the fuses. Fearful of what tampering with electricity might do to her unborn baby, Alice sunk her feet into her red wellington boots and, easing her swollen stomach behind the head of the man from the ministry, squelched out of the flat into the hallway. On tiptoe at the central fuse box she pushed back the short circuit button. Then with her eyes squeezed shut, both fingers crossed and her breath held still, she mumbled a brief prayer and flung the switch.

Back into the flat she stomped, trilling breezily with laughter as she squeezed once more behind the man from the ministry and into the kitchen. George, she noted, was looking singularly abstracted, but his 'acquisitions' appeared to find nothing remarkable in Alice's behaviour.

The lights were on again throughout the flat. the oven, however, was not. Alice swore. Now what? She grabbed the wok in one hand, the grill pan of skewered chicken in the other and, bearing them high above the ministry man's balding head, pressed once more behind him. George by now was looking deeply unhappy, while his contacts had begun to shuffle in their seats and toy thoughtfully with their glasses of vodka. Alice smiled warmly at them all and marched anew out of the front door.

She turned to the flat next door where the representative for Alitalia airlines lived and briskly rang the bell. The door opened a crack and the eye of Mrs Alitalia peered through. She took in Alice and her wok and opened the door wide. She looked harassed. A lock of her usually impeccable hair had fallen across an eye, her make-up was shiny with sweat and she was wringing her hands out in a heavily tomato-stained apron. This did not appear the optimum moment to ask a favour.

'My oven?' Alice ventured. 'Kaput. My husband? Important guests. Molto important. May I borrow some space?' She shook her wok at her neighbour and looked hopeful. 'On your stove?'

The Italian woman gave an unexpected snort of laughter and pulled Alice into her flat.

'Me,' she announced with grim satisfaction, 'I make spaghetti bolognese *per tutto l'Aeroflot!*'

At this Friday's less fraught dinner, Alice had found it

difficult to deal with a group of guests who all knew each other far better than they knew Alice and George. There were intimacies and gossip in which they could not entirely share. Who was Abel, who had apparently been asked (could it really be true?) by his American television company to interview Stalin for a personal assessment of Gorbachev?

George was more in tune. At least he knew the men. He bent between them in a peculiar handwoven shirt from Guatemala, pouring Beriozka Chianti. Alice wondered if he had dressed with Charlie in mind, for Charlie was wearing a turquoise shirt that seemed to be covered with open pink umbrellas. Or were they breasts? Charlie's wife, Lisa, had been friendly, though. No sooner had Alice placed the dish of pelmeni upon the table than Lisa, staring intently at them, had insisted that Alice immediately write down the sources for some of Moscow's more Western-style food-stuffs. She knew, she said, where you could buy frozen game birds – unplucked and ungutted, of course, but so far as she knew no-one had yet been poisoned, ha ha. As the pelmeni were passed round Lisa became quite relentless with her listing. There was a Polish frozen food shop for blackcurrants – strawberries too ('Are you getting all this, Alice?') and chopped french beans. There was even a restaurant ('You're not writing this down, Alice.' 'I am, I am.') at whose back door a lobster from Havana might be obtained for a small 'sweetener' and many roubles.

Lisa was what Alice's formal and formidable grandfather would have described crushingly as 'a curious little person'. He would have been mistaken. She was indeed very short, her lack of stature emphasized by a long black shirt worn over a pair of baggy black pants that flapped about her ankles. When she had struggled out of her snowboots, she had slipped on a pair of black suede wedge-soled sandals that elevated her an inch above Alice's shoulder. She wore her dark hair cropped to a brush and no make-up at all. The whole presentation contrived to give her the alternative London look of a footsoldier in a Maoist army corps stationed in Covent Garden. Alice was surprised to learn that she had been a highly respected programs analyst in a multinational computer firm before they came to Moscow. Now, she announced with a certain grimness, she was a student of Russian literature and a specialist in shopping for luxury goods.

Once the pelmeni were served, the conversation turned to what people had eaten recently at other dinner parties. Avocado pears! chimed Angela, the wife of the British banker, Geoffrey Rimstead. Oh, God! Avocados! groaned the others. Roast lamb with peas! put in Charlie. Cheesecake 'with real tinned mandarins on top!' enthused the girl from the British Council. Alice thought it all sounded like the menu for one of her old publishing house's staff Christmas parties.

But the avocado pears inspired the raconteur in Charlie. They had a neighbour in Kutz, he said, who went off on a shopping spree to Helsinki. 'She asked around if anyone wanted anything brought back. Who didn't? Same thing, of course: avocado pears!'

'Why?' asked Alice, puzzled.

'What else!' exclaimed Angela.

'So she's sitting in the train on the way home, and it stops at the border for a check. And the customs officials, wouldn't you just know it, barge right into her compartment. And tell her, surprise, surprise, to open her suitcase. There, inside, what do they see but wall-to-wall—'

'Avocados!'

'So, of course, out comes the requisitions form. Bye-bye avocados.'

There were groans of sympathy round the table. Charlie held up his hand. 'Ah, but wait! They don't know what this weird-looking stuff actually is, do they. So one of the customs boys picks an avocado up, sniffs it, rattles it, and says, "What do you do with them?" And Joan, knowing just where her hoard will be going, looks up at him without batting an eyelid, and says, "You boil them very slowly for four hours!"'

Charlie Prowse had seemed to Alice a slightly juvenile individual, attractive in a dark, tousled rock musician kind of way. His glossy hair curled well over his collar and he sported a Mexican moustache. Clearly his main pleasure was to shock. According to him, Gorbachev was a second Stalin, one senior diplomat a roaring drunk, another entangled with his (male) Soviet secretary, and Serpuhovsky Val one of the raunchiest compounds in town. Here visiting trade delegations were invited by certain unattached businessmen to have the full sum of their appetites satisfied by sumptuous imported feasts spread out above the table and by versatile Soviet wenches strategically positioned below it.

At one point, discussing the difficulty of buying light bulbs that worked, Charlie had looked up at the ceiling, cupped his hand round his mouth and, raising his voice, intoned, 'Boris? Alice needs light bulbs. Ones that won't burst. Is it too much to ask of the great motherland?'

'Charlie!' Alice had scolded, embarrassed. But the rest of the table had laughed. Surely the fact that their flats and offices and cars were bugged was one of those things you simply didn't mention.

Alice did not, of course, wish them to think she was naive on this subject. The Masons had abandoned with the birth of Daisy their opinion that surveillance of foreigners was a fiction relished by Westerners brought up on a Cold War diet of spy thrillers. George's mother had telephoned him from England around six in the morning Moscow time, with the news that he had a new daughter. George had at once summoned his fellow correspondents to join him in a celebratory champagne toast. As each recognizably licence-plated car drove into the compound, the militiamen had leapt from his sentry box crying, 'It's a girl! It's a girl!' George, in his telephone calls out, had not specified.

'If we're going to have uninvited guests in our living quarters,' Charlie told Alice once he had broken off his conversation with the ceiling, 'I think we should be allowed to talk to them, don't you?'

It was two o'clock by the time George and Alice had finished clearing up. They had discovered early on that it was unwise to leave unwashed pots and pans to soak overnight in the sink. When they came to them in the morning, they would be overrun with cockroaches waving their antennae like glossy chestnut coloured prawns as they picked their way delicately across the caked-up plates. George would sluice them with scalding water from the tap and then have to pluck their squirming bodies from the plughole once the sink was empty. Galina had done something with an egg yolk and borax mix to put paid to them, but the cockroaches seemed blessed with immortality. They even survived Harriet stomping on them in her snowboots.

'At least tomorrow is Saturday,' said George, wiping his hands on the sodden tea cloth. 'Day of rest, children permitting.'

'I thought we might go sledging with the Simpsons after lunch. At Kolomenskoye. We haven't been there yet. What do you say?'

'I say it's time for bed.'

Alice sighed. George, she guessed, was already paving the way for opting out of a family outing in favour of a kip on the sofa.

Chapter Six

Twice in the night Daisy woke Alice for a feed. Alice sat with her in the darkness of the baby's room, sniffing the top of her fuzzed hair as she sucked. Then Harriet shook Alice awake at seven, hungry for breakfast. George slept on, out of contact.

Harriet climbed from the chair on to the top of the freezer, and sat there banging her heels, waiting for her porridge.

'You'll have to get off, Hattie,' said Alice. 'I need a milk.'

She reached down into the cold for a carton of frozen milk. Soviet milk being unreliable in availability and freshness, Sasha drove once a week to collect imported English milk from the Commissariat of the British Embassy, a grocery shop set up in one of the rooms of the old stable block behind the main building. Alice had once peered in silent fury round the open Commissariat door at the shelves of cornflakes, marmalade, lavatory paper, tins of fruit and vegetables, packets of pasta and pulses, chest freezers with heaven knows what treasure stored in their depths. Only British diplomats and British Council students holed up in grim language institutions on the outskirts of Moscow were allowed access to this Aladdin's cave.

'Because,' the wife of a British diplomat carefully explained, 'Moscow is not designated a hardship post.'

For a moment, Alice had been speechless. 'How can it

possibly not be a hardship post!' she had exploded, incensed.

'Because' – the woman was patient – 'we have a diplomatic bag and a Commissariat.'

'Except that *we* are not allowed to use them!'

In fact, Alice did not hanker after Commissariat goods. Not only was Harriet's diet better without the addition of Smarties, Angel Delight and fish fingers, but Alice had once noticed on a package of chocolate digestives that tumbled out of Babs' shopping bag a 'Best before' date that had expired eighteen months previously. It was the principle of the thing.

'What do you think about going tobagganing?' Alice asked Harriet.

'Too cold.'

'Shall we see if Emily and Becka want to come?'

Harriet yelped and slid off the freezer.

'We have to get dressed first,' said Alice. 'Tights on under your trousers, please.'

George was still cocooned in the duvet. Alice, peering over him, thought he looked as exhausted asleep as he did awake, and left him.

She and Harriet stepped hand in hand out of the flat and across to the Simpsons' front door. Alice wrinkled her nose. There was a sweet sickly smell of putrefying vegetation. Round the food chute were lumps of fat, small chicken bones, and vegetable peelings. Over the debris scrambled the moving mass of cockroaches.

When Harriet, held aloft, rang the Simpsons' bell, the door was opened not by Babs but, to Alice's discomfort, by Hazel. Could the girl posssibly have some special instinct that would reveal Alice's 'borrowing' of her book?

'Hello, Hattie. Good morning, Mrs Mason,' Hazel said brightly, her Yorkshire accent lengthening her vowels. 'Babs isn't dressed yet. Do you want to come in?'

Alice liked Hazel, found her reliable and ordinary. Sometimes, on her evenings off, she babysat for Alice, one of the few childminders who did not eat the Masons out of house and home while they were absent.

'Just say to Babs we thought we might go sledging this afternoon. Why don't you tell her to bash on our door when she's ready if she wants to come too?'

'You said we were going now, Mummy!' Harriet wailed.

'I did no such thing, Hattie. We'll go after lunch, OK? Or not at all,' she added, as Harriet began to sob.

'It's better in the afternoon,' encouraged Hazel. 'Then, when you get home, you have hot cocoa and toast.'

Alice rolled her eyes. Smiling, Hazel closed the door.

George was in the bath, steeped in steaming hot water with a book and a glass of beer, his normally curly hair plastered damply over his skull. Alice and Harriet squeezed in and Harriet leaned over to plant a kiss on George's trickling brow. Alice felt a prick of irritation and envy.

'Did Daisy wake?'

George turned towards her, dragging his eyes from his book. Water rolled in a slow wave and slopped over the side of the bath.

'Who?'

'Daisy,' Alice said tersely. 'Your daughter.'

'Quiet as a mouse.'

Alice went into the baby's room. Daisy lay purple and sticky with rage, bawling lustily. Her fists were clenched and her legs kicked at the air. Alice rushed to the cot, plucked Daisy from it, wrenched up her jersey and connected Daisy to a nipple. At once there was silence.

'I'm a garage,' Alice muttered to herself. 'That's what I am. A bloody garage.'

But the image was not entirely correct. Recently she had only been servicing the baby. George increasingly had been too tired to take advantage of the restorative powers of

Alice's body. He was working far too hard, in her view. Even when he got home there was usually telephone calls from the *Sentinel* wanting copy changes or copy adds. The fact that London was three hours behind Moscow time stretched George's working day. Being patted on the rump before he turned from her in bed and fell at once asleep was frankly not enough. She was going to have to take matters in hand.

Holding Daisy firmly to her, she rose, and tiptoed back to her bedroom. Harriet was still ensconced in the bathroom with George. Alice groped about in her bedside drawer and pulled out *Utterly Female*. Transferring Daisy to the other breast, she sat down to read. So far all she had done was flick through, stopping only when random trigger words had caught her eye. It hadn't been a rewarding method. Obviously she was going to have to grit her teeth and start at the beginning.

According to the author, marriage was like bread. 'If it gets a little stale, you have to warm it in the oven.'

Alice turned the book over to look at the back cover. What kind of author was it who would turn out cereal-packet psychology like this? There was a photograph of Suzie Sapmann in a frilled denim shirt and imposing earrings. She had the kind of fixed tumble of blond curls favoured by manufacturers of long-limbed plastic dolls and women who respond hotly to the sound of steel-string guitars. Her bosom must have been eased into its container cups with a serving spoon. Alice couldn't imagine she would have much problem with her bread. Or butter. Alice was wrong.

With the very real concern she felt, Suzie explained, for sincerely promoting a trusting relationship with her readers, she wanted to share with them the pure truth. She would lay it all on the line, tell it like it was. Like it had been for her.

'After ten treasured happy years my marriage had gotten stuck in the proverbial rut,' read Alice, agog. 'The warning flag went up. I knew in my heart we were swimming in dangerous waters. My husband and I loved each other, truly cared for one another. But the freshness was gone, that spark that makes a relationship grow and glisten. I had to face facts: my man was plain bored with me. And sooner or later that would spell T-R-O-U-B-L-E. In desperation, I turned to God.'

Gracious! thought Alice. Was He more her type?

'I prayed to Him for guidance,' Suzie rolled on. 'He answered me that the path to true joy started right back with me. And when I lay down in the loneliness of the night, my husband asleep beside me unaware of my torment, I knew He had sown the seeds of a plan to put the sparkle back into our marriage.'

This had to be the most unadulterated tripe ever published, Alice thought. Riveted, she read on.

'Follow my step-by-step guide, and you too will find fulfillment in your relationship with your man and, through him, with God who – after all – is the Maker of all men.'

Ha! exclaimed Alice. The meat at last. Daisy uncoupled with a plop and stared at her through raisin eyes. Alice looked down upon this miraculous creature, clasping the tiny warm head between her hands. 'What you have to look forward to, eh, little one?'

Moving her absentmindedly back to the other nipple, Alice flipped on several pages until suddenly the print became studded with asteriks.

'Follow Through The Fantasy!' shouted the chapter heading, and underneath: 'Doing It His Way!

'*He likes see-through negligees? Wear them!

'*He likes transparent undies? Flaunt them!

'*He likes candlelit dinners? Arrange them!

55

'*He likes snacks in bed? Make them!

'*He likes scented baths? Fill them to the brim!

'Relax! Enjoy! Let your imagination run free! Nobody's watching but him!'

Alice wondered how the author would have expressed herself without the use of exclamation marks. She found this ranting made her tired and turned further on. She came to another chapter headed 'Undressing, and How To Do It!' and stopped.

'Who undressed you first? No, foxy lady. Before him. That's right! Mother. And what was her style? Throw it all off, fold it up neat and into a nightshirt quick as lightning so baby is lying in bed sweet as an angel waiting for her daddy to come kiss her good night.

'And I'll bet that's how you're still doing it. So now's the time to add a little spice to the routine with my Four Bedroom Tips!'

Alice soldiered on.

'Number 1 – Don't undress. Strip!

'Number 2 – Strip with style! Sensuous is S-L-O-W!

'Number 3 – Those pantihose must go! From here on in, it's silk stockings and garter belts!

'Number 4 – Undress from the top down, not the legs up! Those stockings come off last!'

God seemed to have been left out at this juncture. Cheap smut hiding behind holy coat-tails. Alice was surprised. Hazel may well be a devoted Christian, but Suzie Sapmann's book, in Alice's view, was no more than a thin excuse for a bit of basic titillation.

She placed Daisy on the changing mat and reached out for a clean bodysuit. The baby lay, legs executing a strong backwards frog kick, watching Alice closely as she moved about. Alice gently squeezed her plump flesh, pressing it tenderly where it lay in creases around the wrists and knees. So much to grow into, she thought.

'Alice!' George shouted out in the corridor. 'Have you seen my broomball stick?'

'It's probably still in the car.'

'Are you sure?'

'No,' she replied complacently.

George burst into the nursery. He bulged under several layers of track suit, polo shirts, and scarves. By contrast, on his feet he wore nothing but a simple pair of gymshoes.

'Are you coming or not? It's really time we went. The game starts at ten.'

Alice snapped the poppers on Daisy's clothing. 'Where is it?'

'British ice this week. Against the Finns, God help us.'

'Why not? Yes, we'll come. Hattie can play on the swings. Get her into her snowsuit, will you?'

As they drove out of the compound, a grey Volga pulled away from the pavement behind them. George angled the driving mirror. 'Me and my shadow,' he trilled, 'driving down the a–ve–nue!'

'Are you sure?' asked Alice, turning round to peer out of the back. 'I never seem to notice them.'

'That,' replied George, 'is because you never look.'

Chapter Seven

The golden domes of the Kremlin gleamed in the thin morning sunshine on the opposite bank of the Moskva as they approached the British Embassy.

The palace of a pre-Revolution sugar baron, the British Embassy dominates the river view from the Kremlin palace. There is a story that on Christmas Eve, 1952, Stalin, befuddled by vodka, peered out of his office windows and saw the American Embassy's Stars and Stripes flying above Prospekt Marx to the north and the Union Jack fluttering on the south side of the river. Panic stricken, he became convinced that the Kremln was under attack. Despite the peaceful dawn, both embassies were encouraged to move to more distant quarters. The British stayed put, flag defiantly flying.

Today it hung limp in the centre of the snow-humped lawn. The Soviet guards on either side of the ornate gates cast an eye over the Saab's 001 number plate and stepped aside, saluting. As George drove round the side of the yellow and white stucco building, the grey Volga cruised slowly past the embassy and on down the embankment.

He pulled in at the stable block beyond the tennis court and parked outside the doctor's surgery. Already the teams and their supporters were gathered in the play area, strapping baseball guards to their shins with gaffer tape, easing on their helmets and taking swipes in the air with their sticks. Two low hockey goals had been set up on the iced-over tennis court and some of the players were skidding between them in their plimsolls, testing the polish of the surface.

Broomball is played with short household switches whose twigs have been tightly bound to curve like scimitars. It was a game at which the Finns in Moscow excelled because they took it extremely seriously, while the Pits, George's team, a motley collection of British and American journalists and businessmen, appeared to go out of their way as a matter of principle not to win. Year after year, and the end-of-season dinner-dance the league threw at the Frency Embassy (a dinner so good that for some it was the prime motive for joining the game), the Pits, with whoops of triumph, took the booby prize for most goals lost to any opposition.

Breath and cigarette smoke fanned on the cold air. Players' wives tucked cans of lager into the snow and banked up thermoses of coffee on the picnic table. Harriet struggled through the snow towards the swing. Daisy had been left in her carrycot in the car.

'I'll give you six pushes, Hattie,' said Alice, 'then I'm going to watch the game.'

It was played in fifteen-minute shifts, with no rules that Alice could identify but plenty of noise. She drew close to the tennis court fence. Lisa Prowse was already there, in an ankle-length black quilted coat.

A shuffle of players padded towards the ice. George trod tentatively on to the court. Suddenly the game seemed to have begun. While George stood there, getting his bearings ('He'd better not stand still too long,' said Lisa, 'his soles will stick to the ice'), a mighty Finn broke free from a huddle in the far corner of the court, propelling in front of him a child's rubber ball. Behind him came the pack of bodies, ululating frantically. A player skidded up on plimsolls from the side and cannoned into George. They both fell hard on the ice. Alice straightened anxiously. There was the thump of sticks as the players hooked away the ball and swarmed off down the other end of the court.

'Go, George! Go, George!' Alice and Lisa cried in unison.

George looked back over his shoulder at them, waved his stick, and collapsed back on to the ice, a marionette with loosened strings.

'Go, George! Go, George!' repeated Alice and Lisa, giggling hard.

'Piss off!' retorted George, crawling along the ice. At last his feet found purchase. He rose and slithered off towards centre court, where the game appeared to have stalled as both sides struggled to crook away the ball.

'They could get seriously injured playing this game,' Alice remarked uneasily.

'Not only could they,' replied Lisa calmly, 'they do. The doctor's forever tending bruised limbs, blackened eyes – concussion, even. And never a season goes by without someone shipped out to Helsinki with a broken something. Probably why they play it.'

Alice clamped her gloves over her mouth. George was back down on the ice. He hauled himself up on his stick and was at once thrown back to the floor by a scrum of bodies reversing into him at speed. Alice grasped the tennis court fence. They thrashed their sticks at the ball that rolled between their slithering feet, unheeding of George behind them on the ground. Alice closed her eyes. George hooked his stick through the flailing limbs about him, and caught a Finn around the ankle. The man tumbled to the ice beside him. Using his opponent's helmet for purchase, George clambered up and was at once surrounded by players shunting him along with them down towards the far goal. Somewhere among the feet was the ball.

'Hit the bugger, George! For Bog's sake, hit it!' screamed the Pits supporters from the sidelines.

'Bog?' said Alice tensely. 'Bog who?' She wished the game were over.

Lisa snorted. 'Russian for God.'

George thrust about, trying to find enough space among the padded bodies to make a sweep with his stick. His feet were freezing and no longer under his control. Suddenly the scrum broke wide and George was left standing alone, bewildered, while the players trotted off the court.

'Come on, George! Come and grab a beer!' cried Charlie Prowse. The teams crowded about one another, clapping each other on the back. 'Played like a trooper, mate,' someone said to George. 'Good lad!' said somebody else. 'Developing nicely there.'

George was exhausted, aching, cold and confused. He couldn't tell who any of these people were nor which side they were on. All he knew was that he was grateful that his part in the game was over and that he wanted to lie down somewhere warm and comforting.

Alice approached. 'Are you all right?' she asked, peering anxiously into his face. 'Can we go? Hattie's freezing, and so am I.'

George heard Alice's reassuring voice from somewhere very cold and very far away. She tucked her arm through his. 'You look a bit dazed, my sweet. I'd better drive.'

Back at the flat, George clambered once more into the hot bath it seemed to Alice he had only just left. He groaned and sighed and loudly lamented his bygone days of youth and fitness.

'For heaven's sake, George,' said Alice irritably. 'Just have your bath and shut up.'

It was clear that George would not be undertaking any further physical activity that day. Alice would have to go sledging with Harriet on her own. At least, she conceded, it meant she could leave Daisy behind in his care.

She dished up the remains of the pelmeni for lunch.

Harriet spat out the doughy casings and poked about with her fork for the meaty stuffing. George chopped them up into tiny cubes then flattened them into the pale of his plate with the back of his knife. Alice was a wonderful woman. It wouldn't do to upset her over her cooking. Alice compressed her lips and said nothing.

In the Simpsons' flat the family were eating perfectly formed orange-crumbed fish fingers and brilliantly green peas. There were bottles of HP Sauce and Heinz tomato ketchup on the table. Harriet looked longingly at Rebecca and Emily's plates.

'Sorry,' said Alice, not the least bit repentant. 'We're interrupting.'

'Pull up a pew,' said Jonathan. He was in a loose Guernsey fishing sweater, unshaven, the red stubble on his cheeks in alarming contrast with the wiry blond waves of his hair. 'Where's the scribe?'

Alice sat and drew Harriet on to her knee. 'George has smothered himself in wintergreen and is canvassing for sympathy. I wasn't up to it, so I came over instead.'

'Ketchup, Becka,' Emily intoned.

'You already got some.'

'Pass me the ketchup this minute,' muttered Emily through clenched teeth, 'or I'll saw your head off.'

Rebecca began to wail. Babs leaned forward and snatched the ketchup off the table. She looked significantly at Emily and held the bottle behind her back. Emily sighed. 'May I have the ketchup, please, Mummy?' she said sweetly.

Harriet observed this interchange closely. She turned her head into Alice's chest. 'Why can't we have fish fingers, Mummy?'

'George pulled a muscle?' Jonathan spoke with his mouth full.

'All of them, I think. He's been playing broomball. Don't ask me why. He hates games.'

'This juice is sour,' Emily announced. 'Can I have some milk, Mummy?'

Babs groaned and took the glass into the kitchen. She returned with it full – to the brim, Alice noted with interest. Their own supply would not stretch that generously. 'There,' said Babs. 'What do you say?'

'Thank you, Mummy.'

Rebecca sped her glass into the middle of the table. 'I want milk too!' she cried.

'Copy cat, copy cat, eat a rat,' Emily chanted.

'Do be quiet, Emily, for heaven's sake. You're being perfectly obnoxious.' Babs rose once more to her feet. Alice considered that by now she would have gone on strike. 'Hattie, would you like some milk? Does anyone else want anything? Speak now or for ever go without. I'm not bobbing up and down again.'

Jonathan prodded a fish finger and held it aloft on his fork, oblivious of the family. 'It's the camaraderie thing,' he mused, taking a large bite. 'All boys together.'

Emily knocked over her glass of milk.

'For goodness sake, Emily!' Babs exclaimed. 'Can't you be more careful!'

Alice was rising from her seat, but Jonathan put out a hand to restrain her. 'Emily will fetch the cloth. Won't you, Emily.' The child sighed loudly and pushed back her chair.

'Wait till the snow melts,' Jonathan continued. 'Then they all join the Hash House Harriers instead and run around Gorki Park in false noses and Superman costumes.'

'I want to do a wee,' wailed Rebecca.

Alice looked at Jonathan blankly. 'Whatever for?'

'Fun, of course. Especially here. You know, a touch of the old "up yours, tovarich", while keeping fit and filling your weekend. Good clean entertainment. No harm in it, really. Keeps the foreigners happy and the Sovs confused. Isn't that what it's all about when you come down to it?' He swept a slice of bread round his plate, then pushed it aside. 'Good grub, Babs.'

Husbandly praise dispensed, he rose. 'Right. What's on the menu for this afternoon? Tobagganing, is that it?'

Rebecca, Emily and Harriet all began shouting at once. Jonathan held up his hand. 'Quiet!' he bellowed. 'Now we shall all repair to our posts, dress appropriately, and meet in the car park in – synchronize watches – fifteen minutes. OK, team?'

'OK,' agreed Alice. 'But I don't think George will be coming.'

The Simpsons owned a Volvo estate with red diplomatic number plates and a smashed in front headlight where Babs had made contact with a Soviet drunk who had toppled out into the road in front of her. Fortunately his companions had been sober enough to remember that drunkenness was no longer acceptable. They had restrained the man in his attempt to break up more of the Volvo with his shoe and hauled him cursing away. As Jonathan pointed out to her at considerable length, Babs could have got herself into serious trouble and didn't she know to be always vigilant for such obstacles and how did she think they were going to get the bloody headlight mended anyway? But in fact he had negotiated with the embassy's Soviet garage mechanic and several bottles of whisky to have it repaired just as soon as the British Minister's car was back on the road.

'I want to sit next to Hattie,' Emily announced, reaching for Harriet's hand.

'I want to sit next to Hattie,' wailed Rebecca.

'You can both sit next to Hattie,' soothed Babs. 'She will sit between you.'

Out at Kolomenskoye Alice's spirits lifted. The old country estate of the czars stands high above a southward bend in the Moskva. The Volvo passed through vast studded fortress gates set in whitewashed walls several feet thick that glared against the snow. Alice sucked in the icy air. It was clean of the taste of dust and lead that hovered in the centre of the city.

The children ran ahead, dragging their sledges past a startlingly blue domed church. *Babushka*s in flowered shawls hovered on its covered staircase. The adults walked in silence along the avenue, their boots compacting the snow with the teeth-jarring squeak of polystyrene packaging. Jonathan and Babs called out every once in a while to check the children and in the lifeless trees about them sinister grey Siberian crows, heads blacked in hangman hoods, cawed emptily back. Sometimes they flew down, heavy and ungainly like an open book tossed across a room, and bounced along the ground as big as rabbits.

The path emerged through another fortified gateway and Alice gasped with pleasure. The wide river lay below them, frozen but for a narrow central channel. On the opposite bank stretched a flat expanse of snow-covered fields, and far in the distance the tall buildings and factories of Moscow's southern suburbs. Immediately ahead a white church rose from a high galleried base in the embrace of two exterior staircases. A faceted steeple soared into the air, chalk stone against chalk sky, punctuated by the black dashes of crows looping predatorially about its pinnacle.

Emily, Rebecca and Harriet plunged through the snow with their sledges to the summit of the steep hill beyond the church. A current of toboggans rushed headlong towards the river bank, random skiers weaving a reckless course around them. Alice watched them closely. This was clearly a run where it was essential to have perfected the art of the ninety-degree turn before attempting the descent. The frozen Moskva looked picturesque but unwelcoming.

Babs was careening down the slope with Rebecca, Emily

running after them, her arms spread wide. In the distance, Alice saw Jonathan perched on one of the cannons up by the church, hands deep in his pockets, bare head hunched defensively into his shoudlers. Down the slope slid tin trays and frozen scraps of cardboard packing-case that span madly round and round in their descent. Along the crest of the hill, like Indians poised for attack, stood the watchful adults. They shouted encouragement, barked orders, adjusted scarves and hats and wiped dripping noses. Now Babs was rising from the river bank, towing Rebecca on the sledge, Emily pushing from behind.

Alice and Harriet hurtled together down the slope, Harriet screaming in terror and delight. Alice's cheeks burned, her nose ran and her chest tightened with elation. Particles of ice pricked her face and the raw wind seared her skin. Suddenly, there came a heavy thud from behind and the toboggan was kicked off course. Alice and Harriet were flung on to the snow while the sledge careened off down towards the river. Harriet wailed, snow shovelled inside her jacket, and Alice looked around for their assailant. Lying spreadeagled behind them in the snow, laughing hugely and waving about her head an iced-up square of cardboard boxing, was a middle-aged *babushka*, stout legs akimbo under a short, ill-fitting coat. She raised her head from the snow and flapped her makeshift sledge at them.

'*Atlichna, da? Kak atlichna!*' she chortled. Alice smiled widely at her. Yes, it was fun. Really, it was!

Babs panted up alongside. 'Are you all right? You took an awful tumble.'

Alice laughed. 'It's a terrific slope! I wish George had come. He would have loved it.'

Babs gazed back towards Jonathan. 'More than can be said for Jonty. Perhaps we should think about packing in. The sun is beginning to go down. It will get cold fast now.'

Long stains of darkness were swilling across the sky and

the hillside was beginning to empty. The children sagged sleepy and silent against each other in the back of the car. Alice stared out into the dusk as the Volvo swept by busy pavements of people trudging with bulging bags past dimly lit shops. By the time the car drew into the compound it was quite dark and Harriet was asleep in the corner.

George, to Alice's surprise and delight, had made spaghetti for Harriet's supper, and it was sitting in a bowl above a pot of boiling water, keeping warm. He was perched on top of the freezer with Daisy in his arms, reading aloud to her from a newly arrived ten-day-old copy of the *Sentinel*. Daisy was regarding him steadily, bubbles forming and popping at the corners of her mouth.

'Guess what we did, Daddy!' cried Harriet. George slid off the freezer and squatted down on the floor, adding Harriet to his embrace. Alice looked at him fondly. Just as she was becoming tense and irritable over George's apparent lack of contribution towards domestic affairs he would do something unexpected, like make the supper or the beds. It was quite provoking, really. It meant that Alice, poised to do battle, was forever postponing confrontation. Perhaps he had developed a marital sense that warned him when an argument was in the air, and timed his random – 'token' would surely have been too sour an adjective – gestures accordingly.

She took Daisy from him and, sitting in the kitchen chair, raised her to her breast. George fed Harriet, listening earnestly to her description of her daredevil tilt downhill. Every now and then he smiled conspiratorially at Alice over Harriet's head.

He even cooked supper for them both – the same spaghetti base to which he added, at carefully timed intervals, extra chunks of chopped onion, whole cloves of garlic, and black olives Alice had found at the foreign currency food Beriozka. He stood over his pot, a book in

67

one hand, stirring with the other, a glass of red wine strategically placed within reach. When they had eaten, he sent her off to the bathroom while he cleared the dishes.

'Your turn to relax.'

But Suzie Sapmann would not have approved. The water was scalding. Alice lay back, watching her body turn puce. The heat slackened her, drawing out the tiredness and inducing a trance-like languor. Eventually she hauled herself upright, water sluicing from her, and reached over to the bathroom cabinet above the basin. From it she took a small phial of bath essence and a bottle of baby oil, shaking one and squirting the other into the steamy water. The tiny room filled with the smell of sandalwood and Alice's skin slithered with lanolin. She rubbed at it lazily and rolled in the water.

'Phew! That's a smell and a half!' said George, closing the door behind him. He knelt down beside the bath and leaned over to kiss her slowly on the mouth. 'You look like a beetroot,' he remarked fondly as he rose.

He bent over the basin, his mouth bubbling with toothpaste, and gurgled into the bowl. Then he cupped his hands under the running tap and flung water at his face. Alice lay back and watched him, the familiar, friendly shape, the curling hair, the broad shoulders, square frame, and firm bottom pressed against balding corduroy. Alice climbed out of the bath and George eased out behind her with a quick squeeze of her buttocks.

Alice wiped around the basin and mopped up the floor. Why was it George's ablutions involved flooding an area twice his size with toothpaste foam and puddles? She rubbed the steam from the mirror and peered into it. Damp had seeped in behind the backing and eaten at the mercury so that the bottom quarter was pockmarked with dull spots. It cast a confusing reflection. She rose on tiptoe and leaned in close, thrusting her tongue so far down her chin that a perfect doctor's aaah involuntarily erupted. She parted a clump of wavy brown hair on her right temple and stared with dismal satisfaction at the strands of silver as thick as fuse wire amongst the dark. So far there wasn't enough to show. Still, the fix was in. In six years she would be forty. She twisted her head from side to side. Brown eyes riveted to their double image stared implacably back. She considered the face dispassionately. Skin in good shape. No acutely disturbing lines. The light crow's feet around the eyes more due to laughter than to age – evidence of character, yes? No deep furrows, no puckering around the mouth. Neck taut. Time not yet wreaked noticeable havoc.

She smoothed her hands over her modest breasts and down across her stomach. In my prime, she thought. And bloody well stuck with it in the Soviet Union! Where were the morale-boosting department stores, cosmetics counters, nice places to lunch, office cronies? Those placebos of the youngish matron warding off approaching middle age while still heartily embroiled in her own virility?

She brushed her teeth and sprayed herself erratically with cologne. Tentatively she opened the bathroom door. Then hesitated briefly in the corridor to remind herself of what she had read that morning.

'Show off your body and let your man enjoy it'? Something along those lines, at any rate.

Alice swayed languidly into the bedroom. In the doorway she paused, sliding one arm high up the frame and tossing her hair thickly against it Miss Calendar style. George might appreciate an introductory stare at the goods on offer.

The room was softly lit by the lamp on Alice's bedside table. It cast a gentle glow across the hump in the duvet on George's side of the bed. The hump stirred and bent her knee, drawing her leg slowly up the door. Then she pushed off and undulated slowly into the room, closing the door

gently behind her. She leaned sacrificially back against it
for a moment.

'George?' Alice whispered throatily into the gloom.

But George was already asleep.

Chapter Eight

The alarm went off at a quarter to seven. It was still black outside. George stretched beneath the warmth of the duvet. He could hear the sound of cars revving up in the car park below and the scraping of snow shovels against the gravel. His face felt sore, the skin tight, and his trunk ached as he turned over. He touched himself gingerly here and there with his fingertips. Touching didn't hurt. Breathing did. He swung his legs out of bed and tottered yawning to the bathroom. Alice was already in Harriet's room, helping her with her clothes. George reached for the light, then reeled back into the corridor in disgust.

'Alice! There are cockroaches up and down my toothbrush!'

'It's hardly my fault, George.'

'Can't you get Galina to do something?'

'She says its the Yemenis down the corridor. They chuck their left-overs at the food chute. Not in it.'

'Then talk to the Yemenis. Tell them to co-operate.'

Alice appeared at the door to Harriet's room. 'The entire UN Peace Keeping Force has been attempting to talk to the Yemenis for years,' she said calmly. 'What hope do you think I have?'

'Alice,' George admonished with his toothbrush. 'You are becoming a racist.'

George dressed and took the shortwave radio into the

kitchen. Nearly time for the half-hour news. He twiddled the dial. The familiar comforting sound of the BBC World Service crackled into the kitchen. Some young man was reading his journal of a voyage by raft down the Amazon when gradually the account faded and fuzzed over into the vapours of the rain forest. George snatched up the radio and pressed it to his ear. He heard an echo of voices through muffled heaviness, as if emerging from a dose of anaesthetic. Grabbing the chair, he clambered up and stuck the radio on top of the refrigerator. The intrepid diarist struggled from the rustling undergrowth.

Alice led Harriet into the room. 'Whatever are you doing up there?'

George was now huddled on top of the fridge, cramped beneath the ceiling.

'Quiet!' George shouted, concentrating on the thin squeak issuing from the airwaves. Still, at least he now had contact.

He listened hard until the end of the bulletin, then snapped off the radio. 'Not a word about the Party Congress,' he said irritably. 'Gorbachev's first, the most important for a whole generation, and the West is taking not a blind bit of notice! When are we going to sit up and pay serious attention to this man?'

'Do you want your breakfast up there, George?'

He clambered down and morosely scraped butter over a thin slice of black bread. The musty, malty salty taste revived him. Russian bread typified the Soviet nation, he thought with satisfaction: heavy, dense, but at bottom a sound commodity that could be put aside for considerable time yet still emerge ready for use as a reliable base for noble augmentation. He studied his slice with interest.

'Did you know they use this stuff to brew a kind of non-alcoholic beer?'

'Doesn't surprise me in the least,' said Alice. 'You nearly

ready, Hattie? Time you went.' She bent down and wound Harriet's scarf around her neck. 'You look a bit peaky, sweetheart. Are you feeling all right?'

Harriet considered. 'My throat's scratchy.'

'Oh, sweetheart, no! You're going to Veronica's after playschool. Shall I tell her mummy you can't come?'

Harriet at once looked as cheerful as Alice had anticipated. She hopped up and down on one leg, chanting, 'Bronca, Bronca! Yippee, I love Bronca!'

'Tell the school, will you, George, that Lisa Prowse is taking Hattie home today?'

As George kissed Alice goodbye, Jonathan emerged from his front door. Babs stood behind him in a lavender quilted dressing-gown, her hair mussed around a shiny unmade face.

'Becka!' she bawled over her shoulder. 'Harriet's daddy is waiting! Come here this minute!'

She bent to kiss Emily and propelled her gently by the bottom towards Jonathan. Rebecca clumped up behind her dragging a satchel along the floor.

At the far end of the hallway another door opened and a Japanese man whose hair had the sleek sheen of a long-playing record came marching up the corridor, carrying a large attaché case. As he drew near the group he brought his heels together, bowed abruptly, and turned smartly off towards the lift. Babs laid her hands on the heads of her children.

''Bye, darlings. Be good.' She and Jonathan pursed lips at each other across the width of the corridor. With a wave at Alice, Babs gathered up her dressing-gown and retreated behind her door.

'Shall I carry that?' George offered, leaning down for Rebecca's satchel. She swung it out of his reach with a grunt.

'Now, miss!' Jonathan brandished a warning finger. 'I'll

have no rudeness from you! Emily, run and call the lift.'

'But I want to call the lift,' cried Rebecca. 'It's my turn!' She tore off towards it.

'It's not. It's my turn,' said Emily, rushing after her.

'Daddy!' Rebecca wailed as he approached. 'The man pressed the button!'

'Rebecca!' Jonathan spread his arms helplessly and smiled weakly at the grinning Japanese. 'Children! Aren't they frightful?'

The Japanese once more brought his heels together and bowed at them. They all turned in a line to wait, staring at the slab of veneer while behind it the lift dragged heavily upwards. Rebecca gave the door a kick.

'Becka!' Jonathan pulled her sharply back and Rebecca's face crumpled while she considered the usefulness of tears.

The lift door slid open. The children hurried in, pushing past the Japanese who slipped unobtrusively into a corner behind them all.

'Daddy, Becka's squashing me!' complained Emily.

'Do stop making such a performance,' said Jonathan irritably.

George studied him out of the corner of his eye. Quite the city gent, in beige twill coat and black briefcase. He twitched his own beat up sheepskin jacket about him and settled his *shapka* more comfortably on his head.

'Don't make any concessions to the cold, then, Jonty?'

'Hardy Brit,' replied Jonathan, a little smugly.

Foolhardy, more like, thought George. 'Catch your death without a hat.' He stared at Jonathan's highly polished black brogues. 'Don't your feet freeze?'

Jonathan looked down, surprised. 'God, no. Never leave the embassy, once I'm in. Becka, do stand up, there's a good girl.'

'But Emily pushed me!'

The lift juddered to a halt. There was nothing to indicate

74

on which floor they had stopped. A woman sculpted in rippling black leather pressed in. She broke her staccato barrage of Spanish at a girl in taut yellow jeans and shocking pink skiing jacket to murmur a Russian greeting to the occupants of the lift. George could barely move. He wondered how Harriet was managing down at knee level. Once more the lift halted. This time the door drew back upon a man with a djellabah hanging below his thin winter coat, clutching a curly-haired boy in each hand.

'Ha!' exclaimed the Japanese with a suddenness that startled them all into twisting round to stare at him.

The Arab gazed at the crush inside the lift. Jonathan applied a regretful expression and the door squealed shut.

'There'd better not be any more stops,' said Emily in a threatening tone.

Rebecca had worked her way to the front of the lift. As it opened at ground level she tumbled out and skidded into the hall. A sweet cloying smell of joss-sticks hung stale in the hothouse air. One of the *dezhournayas* with a metal bucket was busy slopping a mop along the slush-slicked floor.

'Becka! Do you always have to push? *Scusi*,' Jonathan apologized to the Spanish woman. She gave him a distant smile and patted Harriet pointedly on the head. Harriet smirked.

'I've had to learn how to say sorry in every language since Becka was born,' said Jonathan tersely. He bent down and tapped her on the nose. 'Behave, you.' He urged her towards George and turned away with a brief wave, leading Emily towards the front entrance. 'Enjoy school, Becka. See you tonight.'

George followed him. Outside, the compound was as active as a railway terminus forecourt. Cars were being noisily revved up, exhaust waffling into the icy air. Soviet drivers swayed from foot to foot on the frozen asphalt, waiting with hands on handles to open doors for their assigned employers. Children scrambled into soothingly warmed Mercedes, Volvos and Saabs. Women in tailored coats, fur coats, quilted coats, in saris, pantaloons, burnouses and blue jeans, drew their feet neatly in behind them and slammed their doors. Up and down between the rows, stooped between buckets of steaming water, went the Soviet *dezhournaya*s in work fatigues, slapping dripping sponges against the muddied metal of the foreigners' cars. Round the road into the compound came the maids in ones and twos, some with arms linked and heads bent conspiratorially together, bodies rolling between bulging string bags.

George crossed the car park with Rebecca and Harriet, saluted in Russian, the one languge common to each, by the medley of foreigners progressing towards their own machines. The water the *dezhournaya*s had used to wash his Saab had frozen over its bonnet in thick runnels of ice, curled like bacon rind. He strapped the two children into the back seat and slid behind the wheel, waiting for the engine to warm up. Come the day when Rebecca and Harriet were old enough to join Emily at the Anglo-American School he would be able to leave the compound earlier, if he chose. He grinned to himself. The pre-Moscow George Mason had not been known for keenness in arriving early at his desk.

The new American Embassy compound was a curious complex that disoriented him every time he saw it. Above the wall of red brick that separated them from the street rose a row of townhouses that might have been scooped up from any middle class urban development around Washington DC. That was perhaps the point: home from home. The main gate was not yet open, but George knew the code for access through the sidegate. He parked and let the children out, and the sentries at either side of the entrance watched implacably as the small group approached. George nodded to them. Inside the gatehouse he punched the numbers that released the lock and pushed the two children through the door.

After their discovery that the Soviets had so successfully bugged their new consular building as to render it unusable, the Americans' sensitivity to the possibility of Soviet ears' overhearing the lock combination had resulted in a ritual that had become the stuff of uproarious anecdote. According to the stories, staff had been called in one at a time to face in silence an official seated behind a desk. Once eye contact had been established the officer held up his fingers in the numbers of the code, to be silently memorized and confirmed in their own finger formation by the recipient of the great secret.

The precautions were in vain. The first time George had arrived early to find the main gate closed, the Soviet militiaman had stepped out of his sentrybox and, with the greatest courtesy, had punched the combination for him.

Inside, the embassy building was like the sports complex of a new American suburb. Ahead was an Olympic length swimming pool, a beauty parlour, and a PX store, open to all American nationals, whose shelves accommodated the same range of goods to be found in any modest supermarket back home. George led the children past the open door of the basketball court and upstairs to the room given to the nursery school. He helped Rebecca out of her snowsuit and boots and tied the laces of her indoor shoes. Harriet sat on the bench alongside, swinging her legs. Without a word, Rebecca marched away from them and through the door to the school.

George took Harriet's hand. 'Your turn. Playgroup ahoy.'

By the time George drove into Kutz, the clock on the car read nine fifteen. Harold was standing at the telex machine, reading from the long train of printed paper that covered the floor behind it.

'I see you've done a piece on the suggestion that the Soviets might float the rouble,' he observed without looking up.

George struggled out of his coat. 'Bogomolov was trumpeting the possibility, yes. You don't think it's likely?'

Harold shrugged. 'I wouldn't say it was unlikely. As an idea, you understand. Gorby's clique seem to be able to go about proposing all manner of schemes. Very refreshing too, of course. But until they actually stick a to-be-done-by date on any of them I don't think they'll carry much weight in the West. Still,' he said, turning at last to George, '*po zhivyom uvidim*, as they say. Let's wait and see.'

He moved towards his desk, propelling himself carefully by the furniture. 'I'm told you had to assist me to my truckle bed. I hope the exercise didn't cause any undue strain – physically or otherwise.'

George looked up from his mail, reddening slightly. 'No, no, absolutely not.' He busied himself with the papers on his desk. 'Did you spot the telex from the *Post*? Sounds like a nice bit of easy bread, doesn't it?'

Harold cleared his throat. 'Not my cuppa really, dear chap. I've enough on my plate as it is.'

George looked up. Harold was standing at the office window, staring down into the compound, one hand spread through his thinning hair. He was a tall man, imposing, with a natural elegance, always impeccably dressed so long as it was in his own room that he awoke in the morning. Today he wore a wide striped blue and white starched shirt tucked into charcoal grey flannel trousers under a pair of scarlet braces. At his double cuffs flecked a brief gleam of pearl. He revolved round and faced George, letting his gold-rimmed half-moon spectacles fall to the tip of his nose. He peered over them at George.

'You take it.'

'What?' George was startled. He couldn't think for a moment what Harold was referring to.

'You take the string,' said Harold. 'Why not? It's pseudonymous. Make yourself a few extra pennies.'

'You make yourself a few extra pennies, Harold' George said crossly. 'You're the one they asked for. Besides, it's no skin off your nose. Just a re-write of what you're doing already. Seems to me it's just what you need: something to get your teeth into.'

'And away from the neck of the vodka bottle?'

'You said it, Harold. Not me.'

'I have a more fulfilling relationship with vodka than I could ever hope for from the *Post*. I relinquish the position to you, dear boy, to do with as you please.' He made a wide sweep with his arm and bowed slightly to George.

'God, Harold, you can piss a man off sometimes!' George sat down brusquely at his desk and pulled a copy of *Sovietskaya Kultura* towards him. The silence dragged. Eventually George flapped the pages of the paper and announced, 'Ivan Frolov, Chairman of the Scientific Council on Philosophical and Social Problems of Science and Technology, says there is need for the activization of the human factor.' He looked over the top of the newspaper at Harold. 'Interpretation, your honour, veteran Moscow observer, if you please.'

Harold accepted the truce. 'It means get the Soviet workers working, as if you didn't know.'

'By the way, where's Nadya?'

'Does your question necessarily follow? Actually, she's on the long haul towards the dentist. I thought you wouldn't mind.'

'I'm not sure I understand you.'

Harold sighed. 'She needs two back teeth filling. Has needed for some time. But of late they have become hideously painful. Fortunately one of her old dancing pals came round last night with a couple of tickets to the Bolshoi next week.' Harold sat down at his desk and began searching through his drawers. He seemed to feel the explanation was adequate.

'Harold, I am still in the dark.'

He looked up, surprised. 'It means she can get the length of wool the dentist wants in exchange for the work on her teeth.' He saw George's expression and leaned forward patiently. 'The contact with the cloth wanted some Polish sausage. And the friend with the Polish sausage wanted some tickets to the Bolshoi. Last night Nadya provided. This morning she is at the dentist.'

'Ah. Soviet health care in operation.'

'You have it exactly.'

George rose. 'So I'll have to make the tea.'

'Good man. A touch weaker this time, if you please.' Harold inserted a piece of paper into his typewriter. 'Have you been out and about in this fair city of late?' he called into the kitchen.

'Not for a couple of days.' George put his head round the door. 'Have I missed something?'

'It's worth a stroll through the stores along Kalinin Prospekt. Down Gorki Street, too, Nadya tells me. They are apparently stuffed – no, I should correct myself. There are 'some samples' of French scent and silken stockings to be garnered by the astute shopper. Finnish raincoats too, I gather.' He pushed back the typewriter carriage and posed his slender hands upon the keys. 'If we are to have five thousand delegates to the Party Congress at large in the capital we must convince them the Soviet Union can provide, must we not? One wouldn't want them to depart with the notion that the Three Sisters were striving for the wrong paradise.'

'Could be a nice colour piece,' mused George. 'Perhaps I

should take a quick look.' Behind him came the hiss of boiling water and he turned back into the kitchen.

He emerged shortly with two glasses of tea steaming in their metal holders. 'I say, why don't we both of us take a stroll, and finish up with lunch at the Praga?'

'Lunch is not a meal I partake of with relish. Still,' Harold considered, 'I dare say I could toy with some vodka and a dish of caviare while you tuck in.'

George checked his watch. 'I'll have to knock off a congress curtain raiser first. Shall we aim to leave in an hour?'

'Perfect. It wouldn't do to arrive much before two anyway. One is required by law, remember, to remain sober until then.' Harold began tapping delicately at his typewriter with two long fingers.

George sat down at the telex machine and gazed vacantly outside. Sasha had arrived and was buffing the Saab's windscreen with his coatsleeve. George fed the tape puncher and went through the routine that set his brain in motion: shuffling about on his chair, scratching his chest, clearing his throat, sniffing noisily and, at last, typing.

ATTN FOREIGN
EX MASON MOSCOW

CONGRESS OPENER

WITH HIS FIRST CONGRESS AS PARTY LEADER COMMA MIKHAIL GORBACHEV IS EXPECTED TO PRESENT A COMMON SOCIALIST RESISTANCE TO THE DEVELOP-MENT OF THE STAR WARS PROGRAMME STOP PARA THE DARFT PROGRAMME OF THE 27TH PARTY CON-GRESS OF THE COMMUNIST PARTY THAT WILL BE FORMALLY ENDORSED IN MOSCOW THIS WEEK PLEDGES TO WORK WITH ALL SOCIALIST PARTIES

WORLD WIDE TO PREVENT NUCLEAR WAR STOP PARA IN HIS SPEECH EXPECTED TO LAST NEARLY FIVE HOURS MIKHAIL GORBACHEV WILL PUSH FOR A NEW SEASON OF PEACE AND GOODWILL STOP PARA UNDERLYING THE PARTY LINE COMMA PRAVDA'S EDITORIAL COMMENTED YDAY COMMA OPEN QUOTES WE THE SOVIET PEOPLE ARE DOING ALL WE CAN TO SAVE OUR COMMON HOME COMMA OUR FRAGILE PLANET EARTH COMMA FOR ALL MANKIND AND FOR ALL FUTURE GENERATIONS STOP CLOSE QUOTES

Why they couldn't rent a more up-to-date telex with punctuation marks infuriated George. The offices of other foreign bureaux were equipped with the most modern telex machines that never seemed to break down. While correspondents transmitted copy smoothly out, other telex machines clacked smoothly in throughout the day, conveying world news coverage from Reuters, Agence France Presse or Deutsche Presse Agentur. They also carried the Soviet TASS New Service telexes that spewed out news, press releases and official announcements in English. Since neither Harold nor the *Sentinel* could be persuaded that such equipment would greatly relieve the burden upon George to keep his finger on every pulse that quivered, he had had to find other means of acquiring information.

He had developed the art of the informal barter. Dropping by a bureaux that did not operate on the *Sentinel*'s territory for an exchange of ideas, interpretations and decent ground coffee, George would help himself to a glance through the reams of tumbling telex print-outs. At the same time, he would pass on rumours and leads from his own contacts. Both parties seemed content with the unspoken arrangement and George was particularly grateful for the regular excuse to escape the office.

There was a thud in the hall, and the door slammed.

Sasha staggered in bearing a large cardboard crate. He dumped it down by George and plucked out a small green bottle.

'*Vot, nachalnik!*' he declared with pride. 'Look, boss! "Narzan!"' He swivelled the label round and pointed. 'Best mineral water there is. Found it up by Riszkaya Station. If you can let me have a couple of those eye make-up palettes I can fix the old bat that runs the shop to set us up with regular supplies of Polish apple juice as well.' He tapped the side of his nose and winked.

'Help yourself,' said George. 'They're in the cupboard.'

Sasha unlocked the doors and reached into what George called the slush fund. He glanced briefly over his shoulder and clamped his hand round three small make-up boxes, then locked the cupboard once more.

'*Paka, nachalnik,*' he called, disappearing quickly towards the door.

'Hoy! Hang on a minute!' George was finally brought back to the present. 'Bring the car round to the Praga at three and wait for us, will you?'

Sasha tipped his hat. 'Horosho.'

'You know,' Harold observed once Sasha had left, 'you really shouldn't let him help himself to that cupboard. One day you'll find it bare. If I were you I'd move what's in it somewhere else and keep the key with you. It isn't kind to tempt the man.'

George nodded. 'Want some water?'

'I have always held the view that water was best left for washing in.'

George uncapped the green bottle still cold from the boot of the car. He put it to his lips and let the bubbles foam against his teeth. He swilled it around his cheeks, his head to one side, considering, and swallowed.

'Yes. Well, I wouldn't want to disappoint Sasha after his foray into the northern outposts of the city, but I really think I prefer the old Borzomi to this stuff. At least it had a taste of sorts.'

'You must understand, George, that Narzan is by far the better water, despite disputable lack of character, because at the moment it is the more scarce of the two.' Harold cranked the roller of his typewriter and pulled out his copy. 'Once Borzomi becomes *defitzit*, Sasha will consider it his duty to seek out the very last bottle in town and bear it to his master.' He stood up, folding his spectacles in his shirt pocket. 'I don't know about you, but I have had enough of this mortal toil.'

'I'm through, too. Let me just run it across and we'll go.'

George punched the *Sentinel*'s telex number and held the tape as it fed into the machine.

'Another deeply worthy analysis hits the deck.' He shut down the connection and tore the file copy out of the machine, flinging it on to the pile on the windowsill. 'Take me away from all this, Harold. I'm all yours.'

Chapter Nine

They walked across Kalinin Bridge in the sunshine, Harold in a fedora with his navy cashmere coat slung over his shoulders, George trudging alongside in sheepskin car coat and silver quilted moonboots. He took surreptitious glances sideways at Harold.

'You know, you look just my idea of a Cambridge spy,' he remarked.

Harold put a leather-gloved finger to his lips. 'Dear boy! Hush, hush! Careless talk costs lives! I merely attempt to present a figure of the classic British gentleman that our socialist Soviet friends most admire.'

The pavements of Kalinin Prospekt were packed on both sides of the street. Shoppers laden with swollen string bags collided in their rush for buses and taxis with the queues that stretched from the ice cream carts. George and Harold were buffeted by well-wrapped, middle-aged women who used their stoutness as a battering ram against the crowds. Strolling at a slower pace, arms linked and cheeks rosy below fur-haloed hats, were the younger girls on breaks from shifts in nearby shops, their white overalls showing beneath their short coats. Along the gutter, sometimes in the gutter, padded the men, hands punched into the pockets of their cheap nylon parkas, eyes squinting against the smoke from their *papirossi*. Why, wondered George, were older Soviet women always so fat and older men so thin?

He and Harold turned into the Gastronom halfway down the Prospekt. Stale heat belched at them as they entered. George grabbed for Harold's sleeve to steady himeslf as his feet glided away from him in the black slush on the tiled floor. Behind the counters, women in white headscarves and overalls silently reached for the proffered sales chits and cut and chopped and weighed produce from the meagre displays before them. Harold led George past the lard and cheese counter towards the back of the shop. Here the queue had disintegrated into a shapeless mob, pushing and shoving for access to the front. George peered on tiptoe over the tops of their heads. Two men were unloading tins of Danish pressed ham from cardboard packing-cases.

Harold turned to him. 'Will you indulge?'

George shuddered. 'Can't stand the jelly.'

'Consider yourself fortunate that you can afford to be so particular,' Harold admonished. He waved a hand towards the juice counter beside them. 'Before the clamp-down on alcohol, you could buy a glass of Soviet champagne here. I think that's rather a civilized touch, don't you? Particularly when one has had to engage in the kind of battle these sterling heroines of socialism experience each time they go shopping.'

They pushed their way back on to the street. The air was searingly cold, but George could feel the sun upon his shoulders. Only the tips of his fingers, in gloves too tight, were pained by the chill.

In *Dom Knighi*, the House of Books, George came upon a Soviet cookbook, *Discourses on the Russian Kitchen*. He examined it with interest. Harold approached, an art book of the treasures of the Tretyakov Gallery tucked under his arm.

'I have a find! Have you?' He took the book from George. 'Good sir, you do indeed! I shall acquire one of these for Nadya. I don't suppose she has ever seen a Russian cookbook.' He studied it closely. 'Most of the recipes include ingredients that are actually available, by heaven. Now that is a veritable achievement. You must buy several copies, George, for your slush fund. They are gold dust, I assure you.'

He gathered up six copies and dumped them, along with his art book, in George's arms. 'I shall repair to the *kassa* to pay for our booty and you will stand by and guard it until we can take it back to the appropriate counters for packing. We can't afford to leave them here with this crowd. They will all be vanished by the time I have parted with my money.'

He sauntered off and placed himself at the end of the queue for the cashier. George looked uneasily at the six cookbooks. Surely cosmetics and tights made more seductive sweeteners.

With their parcels under their arms, Harold and George descended into the underpass that led across to the Praga restaurant on the other side of the street.

'We're a bit early, Harold,' said George. 'We shan't be able to order booze before two.'

'Fear not. Soviet memories of legal restrictions become vague at the sight of American dollar bills. They are secreted in my wallet, George, precisely to ease this kind of official obstruction.'

Harold pushed through the glass doors of the building and made his way towards the cloaks counter where he flung down his coat like a matador. Then he led the way up the stairs past smaller dining-rooms that lay beyond red-plush curtained doorways, along carpeted corridors where waiters in dinner jackets and bow ties, damask napkins still folded formally over their forearms, slumped against the walls, up to the Hall of Mirrors on the top floor. He stood imperiously at the entrance to the wide marbled room and lifted his hand.

At once a waiter in a burgundy jacket scuttled across the restaurant, skirting at speed the fountain that played in the centre. He ignored the Soviet couple who had been standing patiently in front, ushering Harold and George towards a table between columns near the window. Harold allowed his chair to be pushed in for him, then, turning back towards the man, he pressed his hand warmly between his own and murmured, 'Vodka. Five hundred grams.'

George flapped the stiff damask napkin across his knee, and picked up the menu the waiter had left behind. He riffled through its several pages. 'Everything will be off except the mushrooms, the tomato and cucumber salad, the smoked salmon, the caviare, the fried fish, the steak and the Chicken Kiev.'

'So blasé so soon?'

'Not blasé, Harold, irritated,' George said. 'No-one expects anything of any menu in any country but what the management chooses to print upon it. What I find mildly insulting to my intelligence is the listing of a series of dishes which everyone knows cannot be provided by which we must pretend are simply unavailable today.' He slammed the menu shut. 'I'm having the *gribi v'smetanye*. At least you can't fault the Russian way with mushrooms. And some caviare. How about you?'

'I shall join you in the caviare.'

Their waiter returned, placing two carafes upon the table. One was full of water, the other icy with chilled vodka. He poured two small glasses. Before George's had been filled, Harold had thrown back his head and swallowed his vodka in a single gulp. He motioned for the waiter to replenish it. George sipped, savouring the oiliness of the spirit. A bowl of caviare sunk into a metal container of chipped ice was placed gently between them, gleaming grey beads heaped against the glass.

'Wonderful stuff,' said George. He spread a slice of

compact brown bread thickly with butter and ladled caviare upon a corner. 'Now I know what tapioca was like before it went through the wash.'

'Quite,' said Harold. He dipped the teaspoon into the bowl, then brought it, heaped, directy to his lips. George watched, silently aghast, as the spoon slid between Harold's parchment yellow teeth and at once withdrew clean. Harold raised the tiny vodka glass and flung the chilly liquid at the back of his throat. Thoughtfully he pursed his lips then touched them delicately with his napkin. George reflected that a gecko would have empathized with the spectacle.

Harold coughed gently into a closed fist. 'I think I should tell you that I'm thinking of divorcing Nadya.'

George dropped his bread back on to his plate unbitten. 'Good Lord, whatever for?'

Harold poured himself a third shot of vodka. 'You might say, for her sake. Though I confess I am not a naturally altruistic man.' He stared thoughtfully away across the room. 'I sense, as I know you do, George, that there are greater changes about to take place in this vast nation than any of us can predict. There is a potent new mood in the air. A sense of hope, of a new direction forward. In that most of us agree, even if our masters back home have not yet fully grasped the fact. But what is particularly significant in this, it seems to me, is that it appears to have filtered down beyond the ranks of the *nomenklatura*, the privileged, the intelligentsia, to the Ivans and Petrovs of the street.' He paused, toying with his fork. 'If such is indeed the case, Nadya will be able to fix much better for herself than by staying with me.'

'This sounds quite extraordinary to me, Harold. In fact, I don't buy it. What does Nadya have to say?'

'I haven't talked to her.'

'You're thinking of divorcing her and you haven't talked to her! I'm appalled.'

Harold picked up his glass and tossed back the shot of vodka. He smiled wistfully at George. 'My time here has passed. Not, though my esteemed colleagues would doubtless dispute this, with regard to the length of my stay.' He raised a hand to prevent George from speaking. 'No, more with reference to the nature of the period. My niche is in a Chekhovian Russia of intrigue, double-dealing, and despair. In a Brezhnevian system where threats, extortion and bribery are the goads to action, I thrive. I know how to operate. It is my milieu. I don't relish what I sense our new General Secretary is striving for. I am a Cold War man. I'm no good with peace, goodwill and friendship. If moderation is to be the order of the day, then I shall be better off back home where at least a familiar, more practised facsimile is in place.'

'Harold, you have no more idea what is in place "back home", as you call it, than you have of live in Zimbabwe. You haven't lived there in, what, twenty years?'

Harold did not reply for a moment. He pinched his nose between finger and thumb, then said, 'There is also, I should tell you, the fact that my first wife has recently been widowed.'

George looked at him in even greater surprise. 'I didn't know you'd been married before.'

'Indeed, yes. She came out with the children when I was sent here by the *News*. She stuck it as long as she could – two winters, to be precise – then swept up the girls and withdrew home to Saffron Walden. The guilty party was Moscow.'

Harold's eyes had become hooded and his drawl pronounced. 'Anyway, I am allowing myself to hope that should I return to England, contact with her, now that she is alone, would not be unwelcome.'

'Why would you hope that? Have you been in touch recently?'

'Certainly. She has always written every year at Christmas. To keep me abreast of the girls' activities.'

'And you have established that she'll have you back?'

'Ah, no. I have never written to her.'

'Forgive me, Harold, but it really doesn't sound like much to go on. For this you are filing for divorce and leaving the place you've lived in in reasonable comfort and pleasure for the past two decades?'

Harold focused hazily upon George. 'What would you have me do, George? Drink myself into the gutter like a good Soviet husband and drag Nadya down with me? In Saffron Walden my wife would insist upon my good behaviour, and I would do my best to oblige. The English predilection for dry sherry would force a change in my drinking preferences. New leaves would be turned over. And in return, my wife—'

'Your ex-wife.'

'—would cherish me. My slippers would be placed to warm beside the fire. There would be beef and roast potatoes for lunch on Sunday. I would address the local Rotary on my life as a foreign correspondent. Nadya is a good woman. But I desire in the evening of my life to be cared for.'

'You're right about the level of your altruism, Harold.' George felt depressed. He slumped back in his chair as if a thick clammy blanket had been tossed about his shoulders. 'I can't believe your presumption that your wife would want you back! You're the past, Harold, not her future. Has it occurred to you that she may have half of Suffolk queuing for her hand now? Why should she accept you?' He signalled for the bill. 'You know what, Harold? You're a selfish, self-deluding old bugger. Totally gaga.'

Harold rose, grasping the corners of the table. 'Isn't that what they all say?'

The Saab was drawn up outside the restaurant, its

exhaust fumes pluming on the sharp air. Sasha jumped out and held the door. As they settled themselves in the back, Harold shook his finger at George. 'Next time you come here, dear boy, make sure you bring an empty jar or two. While you eat, Sasha will have them filled round the back door with caviare.'

George looked at him, an eyebrow cocked. But Harold was staring out of the window towards the star-shape pavilion of the Arbatskaya Metro station.

'The chocolate cake is worth having, too,' he added ruminatively.

By the time the car turned in at the gates of Kutz, Harold was asleep, his head thrown back into the corner, mouth slack, his breath rattling.

'I'll help him up to the apartment, *nachalnik*,' Sasha announced with a softness that surprised George. He shook Harold gently awake.

'*Gospadin* Harold,' he whispered. '*Eta* Sasha. *Vsyo normalna*.' Everything's fine.

Chapter Ten

The telex machine was stuttering as George opened the door. He stood over it, unwinding his scarf, while the message came through.

ATTN HAROLD ARMITAGE

U STILL UNANSWERED STRING REQUEST STOP NEED CONGRESS OPENER URGENTEST STOP ARE U COVERING FOR US QUERY

REPLY SOONEST

BOB MATHISSON DAILY POST

George tore the message from the machine with irritation and tossed it on to Harold's desk. He sifted through the messages on his own: Wolfe's in Helsinki needed confirmation on the typeface for his business cards; Vneshtorg Bank of the USSR's absurd ten per cent service charge for account administration to sign; Radio Liberty transcripts to read-and-return to the office of the amenable Chicago correspondent upstairs; the milk bill from the British Embassy commissariat to pay plus a written complaint that the Masons still had not settled up for their Christmas turkey; and a request to phone Alice.

The telephone rang three times in the apartment before

George heard Galina's heavy panting at the instrument.

'Allure?'

George winced. The Soviet pronunciation of the universal telephone response was so insufferably genteel. 'Hello, Galina. *Eta* George. Alice *tam, pazhaluysta?*'

He could hear her slippers on the parquet down the end of the hanging receiver.

'George?'

'Alice.'

'You were going to let me know if it would be all right to take Daisy along to dinner tonight.'

'Right. Hell, I forgot to phone you back. There's no problem. Apparently there's some bedroom near the dining-room where you'll be able to hear if she cries. I'm hoping to be back by seven so I can change.'

'I thought it was casual.'

'Informal.'

'What's the difference?'

'A clean shirt.'

'I hope we're not going to be out too late. Harriet's got a temperature. I don't really like leaving her to babysitters when she's not well.'

'Can't you dose her up with something? There's enough medication in the cupboard to cure the Third World.'

'Sometimes, George, I think you deliberately miss the point. I've given her what I can. Now Galina's busy rubbing her feet with vodka and her chest with lard.'

'What's she planning to do? Cook the poor mite?'

'Folk remedies often work just as well as modern ones.' Alice's voice was stiff. 'I read it in the *Sentinel*, I believe.'

'The Soviets haven't got any modern ones.'

Alice sighed. 'I'm not going to debate the issue now, George. I've got shopping to do. See you later. And make sure it's not late.'

She had put the phone down before George had thought

to tell her of the merchandise at large in central Moscow. But as a long established owner of a Burberry and a mountain of British supermarket make-up, doubtless Alice's shopping aspirations were for more mundane scarcities.

Nadya brought him the early evening copy of *Izvestia*. 'Congress, congress. Such excitement,' she said tightly through swollen cheeks.

'Nadya, what are we going to do about the *Post*? If Harold hasn't sent something by tonight, they'll drop the offer and find someone else to string.'

She propped her arms on his desk and leaned down over the spread of her fingertips, head bowed as she considered the question. George could smell dental antiseptic on her breath. Most Russian dentists didn't have supplies of the stuff. At last she looked up and stared directly at him.

'Actually, it would be terrible pity for Harold. Maybe when the spring comes, he will be better. As when you met him, by the way. Winter is very bad time for Harold.' She paused. 'But you know today he will not write for anybody. And perhaps not tomorrow. Or after that. So.' She shrugged, yet did not shift her gaze from George.

He chewed his pencil thoughtfully, still caught in her stare. Eventually he spoke. 'What you're saying is I should do it, aren't you? Cover for him.'

She stared implacably back. 'I did not think of it.'

George pursed his mouth and blinked. Finally he spoke. 'All right. But only to tide him over, mind. And you realize' –he shook the pencil at her – 'that if my paper ever found out, I'd be in deep doo-doo. Absolutely no-one must know. No exceptions. Understand?'

Nadya barely nodded. George studied her. Then he leaned across his desk. 'Should you by any remote chance feel like prostrating yourself with gratitude on the floor in front of me, please don't give it a second's thought. I'd be hideously embarrassed.'

A small smile touched Nadya's mouth. 'George, actually you are terrible man.'

'But you love me anyway. There you are, easy to say, wasn't it?'

At last Nadya grinned. 'So.'

George inserted a clean sheet of paper into his typewriter. 'In fact, perhaps my thanks to you are more in order. I've always wanted to have a bash at writing for the pops.'

He made a show of closing his eyes and pursing his lips in thought. He flexed his fingers above the machine, then plunged them to the keys. He dictated out loud as he typed: MOSCOW HAD ITS FIRST TASTE OF SALES MADNESS COMMA OXFORD STREET STYLE TODAY STOP THERE WERE TEARS OF HAPPINESS AS HUNDREDS OF LUXURY GOODS FROM THE WEST POURED INTO THE SOVIET CAPITAL'S TOP SHOPS STOP PARA

He halted a moment, chewing the inside of his cheek. WOMEN FAINTED IN THE CRUSH AS SOVIET MOBS FOUGHT OVER MERCHANDISE SELDOM SEEN BEHIND THE IRON CURTAIN COMMA INFORMED SOURCES SAY STOP PARA

'God! I just love these one line paragraphs!'

'It is terrible, George. You are very clever.'

He grinned up at her. STYLE HUNTERS GRABBED FASHION MACS, EXOTIC PERFUME, NAUGHTY NIGHTIES AND GLAMOUR COSMETICS SUDDENLY ON SALE ON THE EVE OF THE PARTY CONGRESS THAT HAS DRAWN THOUSANDS OF DELEGATES FROM ACROSS THE USSR TO MOSCOW STOP

'You appreciate that this is a prime example of the free press in action. Here, Nadya,' he slapped the page, 'is the Western proletariat's prose style of choice! I only wish I could work in an "I stood and watched helpless as" intro, but that would be pushing it.'

Nadya patted his shoulder. 'Actually you are not too terribly unhappy to cover for Harold, I think.'

George put his finger to his lips. 'Speak not of it, woman. This is not happening.'

He stared at the copy. 'And what are we going to call ourselves when this is done? George Armitage? Harold Mason?' He pursed his lips. 'Hmmm. A little too closely connected. Boring besides. What we need is something credible yet with a certain punch.' He stroked the skin below his nostrils thoughtfully with his forefinger. Then suddenly he banged his forehead with the flat of his hand.

'Eureka! What a man! I have the very thing! God, I'm hot! How about Myra Drewsbarr?'

Nadya looked unimpressed. 'I think it sounds very strange. And why a woman, actually?'

'Nadya, you're such a sexist. Number one, having a woman has got the right feel to it. Pop papers like a bit of totty around their by-lines. And two, it's the joke. The pun!'

'The pun?'

'Of course it is! Don't you get it? Myra Drewsbarr.' George enunciated slowly. '*Mir i druzhba*. Peace and friendship! Go on, tell me you love it!'

'I think this is not a subject for mockery.'

'Nadya, you are bowed down by the weight of your Russian soul. It's pure genius.'

She did not comment. 'When you have finished your typing, I will punch it througgh.'

'Good lass. And get hold of Sasha, will you? There's all these letters to deliver.'

Nadya was scornful. 'You cannot imagine he will be back until too late?'

'Why, where's he skived off to? I thought I left him taking care of Harold.'

Nadya paused and turned in her passage through the door. 'By this moment probably Sasha is one of your unconfirmed Soviet citizens fainting over the perfume counter.'

'The skunk! He never asked me if he could go shopping! I'll kill him!'

'Actually, probably he knew you would say no. But if he does not go home tonight without some trophy, Natalya will kill more efficiently than you could.'

Alice, too, was out shopping. Not, as George had correctly surmised, for raincoats, nor for lipstick and stockings. He had, however, been way off course in assuming she was in search of more mundane acquisitions. 'Mondaine' would have been a more apposite word. While she wouldn't go so far as to say that the tripe Suizie Sapmann had written with regard to perking up one's marraige had triggered any serious response, there seemed no harm in building up an arsenal of seductive equipment should the time arrive when it became necessary to go on the offensive. With equal amounts of resolve and hopelessness, she was walking the backstreets behind the Bolshoi Theatre in search of lascivious underwear.

She knew there was not the slightest chance that she would find what she wanted in a department store. The Universalni Magazini – from General Store No. 1, whose initials produced the acronym GUM, downwards – only stocked a limited range of styles deemed by the state designers to be appropriate for the people. Lascivious was never an adjective in their brief. What she counted on was that the Bolshoi, sited in what could loosely be described as the theatre district of Moscow, might have attracted to its neighbourhood *Atelye* bespoke tailors who either worked on stage wardrobes or created theatrical confections privately for members of the profession.

Were she Russian there was no doubt she would be able to get hold of what she wanted. Someone in her circle would either have secreted away or know where she could acquire almost anything out of the ordinary. It was the common-place that was hard to find, the toothpaste, the tights, the tampons. But if sables, antiques, diamonds or Dior were your desire, or caviare, Kalashnikovs and icons, someone always had a source. At a price. Nothing was legal but everything was possible, George maintained.

Away from the compound and out of the car she felt liberated. A fresh fall of snow in the gardens down the centre of the boulevard was still unmarked, the sky clear and the sun dazzlingly bright. It was easy to imagine the fun-decked merchants' daughters of the past stepping gingerly across the wide pavements into waiting troikas and skimming away with a jangle of bells along bare-treed boulevards silent with snow. Here at its heart the ancient city had not changed. Palaces and old merchants' lodges in sugared-almond pastels, with thick stucco walls and tiny windows, glowed pink, pistachio, peach and blue against the white. Alice dawdled down the narrow side streets where modest brown-painted wooden houses, fretwork window frames pricked out in white, squatted between the undistinguished blocks of postwar apartments.

On the boulevard ring Alice hesitated, intrigued, at one of the archways between the row of Chekhovian dwellings. From the busy main street, she suddenly found herself in a courtyard where two men sat on wooden boxes round a bucket of burning pitch. They were warming their hands at the flames while one drew steadily from a bottle. His companion waited, watching carefully. A young woman stood silently observing the pair, rocking a pram to and fro under the cover of a naked bush that grew out of the stone wall of the house at her back. Alice was an intruder from another century.

She reached the corner where the Moscow headquarters of the MVD police looked down Petrovka Ulitsa, and turned right, then left. She was heading up Pushechnaya to a small *Atelye* just before the Alitalia ticket office. She hoped fervently she would not bump into their next-door neighbour.

In the windows on either side of the door were fans of machine-embroidered handkerchiefs spread before a stretch of net curtain that hid the rest of the *Atelye* from view. Alice hesitated briefly, drew a deep breath, then pushed the door and stepped down into the shop.

It was empty, lit with the sterile pink-toned glare of fluorescent lighting. Counters ran down both sides of the room and behind each rose the glass-fronted drawers of a haberdasher's cabinet. At the back hung a blue sateen curtain, through which now emerged a corpulent elderly woman in a grey wool dress. Alice wondered by what desperate stretch of the imagination she could have supposed, first, that she would be able to find suggestive underwear in this shop and, second, that she would have the courage to ask for it.

The woman spoke. '*Dobry den*.'

Alice smiled weakly in response to the salutation and took a step forward towards the counter.

'*Dobry den. Ya hatchu*' – she wanted what? – '*ena . . .*' Alice's vocabulary failed her. Reddening, her heart jerking about uncomfortably behind her ribs, she made a sweep with both hands down her torso.

The woman nodded and gestured for Alice to open her coat. With a quick glance she appraised Alice's figure.

'*Tochaya*,' she observed. Thin. She turned behind her and opened a drawer. Alice let her coat fall together and leaned tentatively against the counter, her hands clasped tightly behind her back. So far it had all gone rather smoothly. It was true that words often impeded communication.

The woman was flicking dismissively through neatly stacked wads of shiny pink stuff. At length she pulled out a flesh-coloured rectangle of material and placed it on the counter. She ran her forefingers swiftly over it and looped them under two embedded straps then swung the article into the air with a flourish. She flapped it once briskly and it soared into shape. Alice was confronted with two sharply pointed cones of shiny satin, overstitched in concentric circles from tip to base in thick purple thread. She stared at it in awe. It seemed to stare back. It was the largest, most formidable, most impenetrable piece of underwear Alice had ever encountered. It stretched down far below its mighty cups, wired and boned, to encase the waist. This was more than a brassiere. This fortress for the fuller figure qualified for talks at the next summit.

Alice shook her head regretfully. She held up her finger for the saleswoman's attention, then she very carefully described against her body the shape she was looking for. As her palms reached her hips, she gave a provocative wiggle, thrust out her pelvis and looked encouragingly at the woman. Come on, you old gorgon, thought Alice. I know you're not that dim. You're just putting me through this, aren't you?

The woman frowned as her eyes carefully followed Alice's fingertips round from her hip bone down to her crotch then up again as Alice cupped her breasts and lifted them higher. She raised her eyes to Alice and stared at her without comment. Just as Alice had decided she had better turn smartly about and flee, the saleswoman spoke.

'Dollari?'

Alice shuffled about in her bag and flourished her American money. The saleswoman nodded. She took hold of Alice's wrist and led her through the sateen curtain to the room at the back of the shop. Alice trotted meekly at her heels, not entirely convinced she and the saleswoman were working towards the same goal. It was stuffy, three seamstresses in scarves and aprons rumbling at treadle sewing machines in a windowless space the size of a one-car garage. From hooks and wires along the wall and ceiling hung rows of brassieres and boned stays, swinging above the heads of the machinists like pink carcasses.

The saleswoman summoned Alice to a halt. She picked her way carefully over the drifts of cloth that lay under each machine and stepped to the corner where, covered by a black shawl, stood a dressmaker's mannequin. Alice stared apprehensively as she took hold of one corner of the shawl and, with a magician's tug, whipped it off.

Alice was speechless. Underneath was a basque that defied immediate description. In Russian the same word root is used for 'beautiful' as for 'red'. While Red Square is in some sense beautiful, Alice was not sure if the same word could be applied to the basque. But it was most certainly red. The kind of deep, committed hue of holly berries, traffic lights and ketchup.

Tentatively she drew nearer while the machinists, wreathed in smiles, ceased their labours to watch. Down the middle of the basque ran two wide parallel lines of ruffled red nylon lace. Along the top of the sweetheart bodice marched a row of red satin pleats like castle crenellations. And in ever widening bands around each cup were appliquéd circle upon circle of sparkling rhinestones. In red.

'*Krasivaya, da?*' said the saleswoman proudly.

'*Krasnaya, da,*' allowed Alice.

The machinists clapped with delight. The elderly saleswoman turned to the basque, releasing some closure concealed between two rows of lace. It fell heavily in a heap around the base of the pedestal and the saleswoman bent to retrieve it.

'*Paprobytye,*' she urged, holding the garment out to Alice.

'*Paprobytye,*' echoed the machinists, giggling.

The last thing Alice wanted to do was try it on, and certainly not in front of such an attentive audience. Still, she threw her coat over a chair and began to unzip her skirt.

The women stared with interest as she stood revealed in her Western underwear. She reached and took the basque. The machinist closest to her also stretched forward and tentatively stroked Alice's buttocks.

The basque had been made for a figure at least twice as voluptuous as Alice's. When she held it by its straps, Alice could swirl around inside it without the material touching her skin at all. She sighed at the shop women with disappointment.

'*Nichevo!*' The saleslady bustled towards her.

Of course it mattered. It was blatantly the wrong size. But the woman had grabbed a little tin as she passed by the machinists and now set about pinning and tucking the basque to shape around Alice. Finally she signalled to Alice to step out of it into her own clothes, and flung the garment at the nearest worker.

She guided Alice by the elbow back into the front shop and pushed her down into a chair. She smiled at her, nodding reassuringly, and sat down herself in another chair behind the counter, arms folded across her vast bosom. Through the curtain, Alice could hear the machines chattering busily once again.

She waited. The saleswoman waited. Every now and then they turned their faces from the direction of the street and exchanged the vaguest of smiles.

The light from outside was beginning to show dark through the glass front door when the sateen curtain was tossed aside and a machinist stepped into the room flourishing the basque. It had lost several inches. She looked enquiringly at Alice, but Alice emphatically did not want to try in on a further time.

'*Spasiba. Bolshoi spasiba,*' she thanked her. The machinist bobbed her head, smiling, and disappeared into the back.

'*Skolka stoyit?*' asked Alice.

The saleswoman drew a pad of paper towards her and on it carefully wrote 'US$50'.

Alice was aghast. Fifty dollars might well have been what she would have expected to pay for the piece in the West. But at black market rates, which is where her dollars would go, that fifty dollars translated into around three hundred roubles! What an idiot she had been not to negotiate a price before any work had been undertaken.

'*Ochen mnoga,*' she said flatly. Too much.

The saleswoman took a deep breath, growing in height as Alice shrivelled before her contemptuous regard. Alice couldn't argue. She hadn't the vocabulary. She hadn't the nerve. Without a word, she placed her handbag on the counter and drew from it, one by one, three ten dollar bills and laid them in front of her. Then she firmly closed the clasp and stared defiantly at the saleslady.

Without moving her eyes from Alice, the woman reached a hand across the counter and swept the money into her fist. Then she pushed the basque as it was, unwrapepd, at Alice. At once Alice snatched it off the counter and rushed out of the shop.

Night had fallen on Pushechnaya. The narrow pavement was busy with people newly released from work. Alice checked her watch. A quarter to six. She would have to rush if she was to have any time at all to bathe before going out. And Galina would have to be paid extra for staying on. Why on earth had she not thought to ask the cost of the corset before it had been altered! With dollars to offer she could easily have negotiated herself a bargain.

Only when she was safely cocooned in the dear, familiar Fiat did it occur to her to wonder for whom the basque had originally been intended. And would the machinists be sharing in the dollars to replace it for its rightful customer? Or would the saleswoman keep them to herself?

Angry with her feebleness, Alice fed her Dire Straits

cassette into the machine. She turned the volume up as high as she could tolerate, filling the tiny space with a turmoil of electric guitars and rumbling drums. She started the engine. Then, with a defiant look for any passers-by who might challenge her anti-social behaviour, she wound down her window to the bottom, letting the freezing night in and the cacophonous thundering of decadent Western rock music out.

Chapter Eleven

Whenever he was at the wheel, George made a particular point of driving with music blaring through the windows of the Saab. However, his choice was generally less provacative than Alice's, his preference being the surfing sounds of '60s beach party pop long scorned by fanatic Soviet collectors of black market Western rock.

Tonight as he swerved into the Serpuhovsky Val compound the Ronettes chimed loudly from the car, George supplying bass harmony at the top of his voice. When he turned off the ignition the silence that followed came as a shock. He climbed out of the car, stepping delicately behind an Indian woman whose sari trailed below her coat along the snow. Under her arms she carried several loaves of bread which looked to George in danger of falling. He hovered closely, at the ready. He felt grey.

Given the choice, he would have preferred to spend this particular evening slumped in front of his video of the Best of the Tests. There was something wonderfully soothing about watching a cricket match in the middle of a Moscow winter. The modultaed tones of commentators from parts of the country, parts of the world, where pronunciation was as thick and stretched as honey dripping from a spoon, the measured ponderings and thoughtful analyses – ah! such comforting contrast to the five foot snow drifts, the drabness beyond them, the intractability of so many of the minor officials he had to deal with during his day.

Still, it could not be denied that an invitation to dine with the Egyptian Ambassador was not to be sniffed at. Quite a coup, really, journalists not generally being the company of choice for diplomats.

He checked for letters at the metal mailboxes banked along the glossy blue-painted concrete walls of the lobby. There were several back copies of the *Sentinel* stuffed into the mouth of the Masons' box and a tumble of envelopes on the floor beneath. He gathered them up as the sound of grating metal announced the arrival of the lift.

Someone had taped a business card to the veneer wall: Faisal Youssef, Cultural Counsellor, 4th Floor. The Iraquis – or was it the Sudanese? – were having a party. And since the morning there was a new graffito in Arab script. 'Bring a bottle', perhaps.

The lift shuddered slowly up to the fifteenth floor and the door squealed back on his Alitalia neighbours glowing in evening dress. George felt even more stale. The woman smiled warmly at him, gathering up her billowing chiffon skirts as she stepped over the gap of the lift shaft.

'*Molto bella*,' offered George.

Mr Alitalia pressed a gloved hand over the white silk scarf that hung down his open coat and inclined his head. The lift door grated remorselessly back along its runner and he made an exaggerated show of wincing and clenching his teeth and rolling his eyes against the sound. Everyone smiled gamely. Why was it, George pondered, that people who had to compensate for a lack of common language communicated as though one had no brains either? They could have spoken in Russian.

When George stepped into the flat, he found Svetlana in the sitting-room with Harriet swathed in blankets curled upon her knee. Svetlana was reading to her from a large picture book. George bent to kiss the top of his daughter's head. She barely acknowledged him, her eyes heavily hooded and face drawn with sickness.

'Ah, my baby. Not well, are you?' He ruffled her hair. 'How's the world with you, Sveta? Any news?'

Svetlana shrugged and the thick dark hair that hung like a shawl over her shoulders undulated gently. '*Nichevo*. Nothing.' She smiled peacefully. 'I still wait to hear.'

'Ho well. Glad to see it isn't getting you down. Visibly, anyway.'

George found talking to Svetlana as uncomfortable as conversation must be with someone terminally ill. What was there to say?

Svetlana had married a foreigner, thus joining the ranks of Soviet refusniks, those who, applying for an exit visa at the authorised six-monthly intervals to the Soviet visa office, were systematically turned down. Svetlana's additional failing was that she was Jewish, a classification set accusingly down in her passport against the entry for 'Race'.

She bobbed her head, and her hair shifted again. She was holding Harriet's cheek cupped in a long-fingered hand and she stroked it gently with her thumb. 'What is the point? I can do nothing. In any case, no answer is better than a refusal. So. I can still hope.'

Nathan was a young American she had met when he was a student at the Pushkin Language Institute. They had been married now for four years, and during that time had seen each other for a total of two weeks. A marriage ceremony could not, ultimately, be prevented. But with malicious skill, the relationship could be wrecked. Nathan had regularly applied for visas to visit her in the Soviet Union, and each time had been turned down. There was no visa category for foreign spouses.

For her part, by marrying a foreigner, Svetlana had lost all chance of developing a decent career of her own. She had been training as a draftswoman at a truck factory. The week of her marriage she had been dismissed without explanation. The day, a fortnight later, that her husband's student visa had expired, two black Volgas had driven up to the block where Svetlana shared a tiny apartment with her mother to escort him to the airport.

Now Svetlana worked sometimes as a chambermaid, sometimes in a kiosk that sold combs, shoelaces and political badges, and sometimes in a flower shop tying red carnations into bundles in winter and red tulips into bundles in spring. At night she babysat for families of the foreign press. Nathan had confronted their dilemma with all the ingenuity of a Westerner who believes that bureaucracies are for challenging. He had written to his congressman, to the President of the United States, and to the individual members of Moscow's press corps. As a refusnik and a 'divided spouse', Svetlana had achieved a certain fame. Western journalists covering the issue usually leaned heavily on her case for material. After all, she was prepared to babysit, she was willing to be quoted, she was a useful interpreter of Soviet life, she could be interviewed while the wife was putting the finishing touches to her make-up; and she kept the press corps up to date with Soviet jokes.

'I have a new one, George. You will like, I think.' She twinkled at him. 'What is the meaning of 'glasnost'?'

George shook his head.

'A shortage of barbed wire!'

Alice appeared bearing Daisy asleep in her Moses basket. She put her carefully down on the floor.

'George, are you ready? I thought you were going to change.'

Harriet lolled her head heavily against Svetlana's shoulder.

'Mummy, I don't want you to go out,' she murmured sadly. 'I don't feel well.'

Alice was pierced by remorse. She squatted down by Svetlana and took Harriet's head between her hands. Her cheeks burned against the coolness of her palms. 'Sweetheart, I know. But we have to go out, I'm afraid. We shan't be long. Besides, you'll be asleep very soon, you'll see.'

Harriet stared miserably at her. 'But why can Daisy go with you and not me?'

'I have to feed Daisy, Hattie. It isn't a treat for her, little one. She won't have any idea where she is, she's too small to understand.'

But Harriet was sunk into her sorrow. With a sigh, Alice rose.

'We're at the Egyptian Ambassador's, Svetlana. I've left the number by the phone. George, are you coming?' she called down the corridor.

Harriet began to weep, tears seeping steadily from her eyes. She sobbed with deep gulps of despair.

'Go, Alice,' Svetlana urged. 'She will be all right. Do not worry.'

Distraught, Alice grabbed her coat and the Moses basket and stumbled out of the flat. She stood by the lift, Harriet's grief reaching to her through the door.

'Hello, there you are,' said George, shrugging into his coat. 'I didn't realise you were waiting out here.'

'I can't bear it when Hattie cries like that.'

'I shouldn't worry. The moment we've gone she'll settle down.'

'We have gone and I can still hear her.'

'Listen, there's not a lot we can do about it. Svetlana will look after her fine.'

We needn't have gone out is what we could have done about it, thought Alice. In silence she stepped into the lift. And in silence they drove to the Ambassador's residence, Alice racked with resentment and guilt. At least George seemed to appreciate that this was not an appropriate time for a blast of the Ronettes.

There were several cars dawdling ahead of them as they turned into the Ambassador's street, shiny chauffeur-driven limousines, ejecting passengers who were partially obscured from Alice by puffs of exhaust that swelled between them on the freezing air. Nevertheless, Alice leaned forward abruptly, peering through the windscreen.

'George, I thought you said it was informal.'

'So it is,' he replied complacently.

'It doesn't look like it to me!' Alice felt panic begin to seep into her. 'They've all got mink on!'

'They won't be wearing it inside.'

'Didn't you see that last woman's shoes? They sparkled as she got out of the car. Don't tell me sparkly shoes are informal. You must have read the invitation wrong.'

George reached into his breast pocket as the engine idled, and passed a thick rectangular card to Alice. 'Check for yourself.'

The car ahead moved slowly away and George coasted by the Egyptian residence, looking for a parking space. Alice leaned forward and examined the invitation by the pale dashboard light.

'You're right. Maybe I didn't see the shoes properly. Lucky lot. With a chauffeur driving they don't have to trudge into a party in their snow boots like us.'

George squeezed her knee. 'You look absolutely fine, my sweet. A sight for sore eyes. Now don't worry. You'll be perfectly dressed.'

But as Alice passed from the hall across the wide Persian carpet into the main reception room, Daisy's Moses basket hanging from her hand, she could see that 'informal' as expressed at North London parties was a far cry from the Egyptian interpretation of the word.

George and Alice stood rooted in the doorway silently

III

absorbing the glorious tableau before them. Women sparkling and exotic flashed like jungle birds about the vast
room, seductive streaks of colour against the stuffed ivory
sofas that lined the walls. Statues filled alcoves between
smooth stone columns, old mosaics hung framed along the
walls. Collections of antique jewelled coffers covered
the low marble tables set between the arm chairs. Every-
where were carefully casual assemblies of precious and
beautiful things, the toys of the very rich.

Almost at once a tall, steel-haired man detached himself
from the crowd and approached, hands extended. He wore
a dark cashmere jacket over grey flannel trousers and a
white shirt of heavy silk opened at the neck. His fingers
were smooth and as he leaned to raise Alice's hand to his
lips she smelt the scent of vanilla and glimpsed the links of a
heavy gold chain rolling on his neck.

'George.' He gave it the French pronunciation. 'You did
not tell me you had a so charming wife.'

'Kamal! Really good, hummm' – George rumbled nervously into his fist – 'good of you to invite us. This is Alice.
But of course, who else? Hi!' He broke off in a spasm of
coughing. George's growing discomfort as he took in the
casual elegance of their host, his beguiling house and
guests, had dried up his throat.

'It is a delight to meet the wife of such an accomplished
journalist. Welcome to our modest home, Alice. And this'
– the Ambassador glanced briefly into the Moses basket –
'is the family? I will bring Fatma to show you where you
can – uh – park it.'

He slipped back among the guests, a discreet dot of
charcoal against the swirl of colour.

'Couldn't we could go home and change? I feel so
dowdy.'

'It is rather dressy,' George acknowledged. 'I wonder
what they do for formal?'

The Ambassador re-emerged in front of them, pulling by her hand a woman whose face went back several centuries to the frontispiece in Alice's school history book. Seated in profile with one foot in front of the other, a chimney crown on her head and golden asp at her throat, this woman might have been any Egyptian queen. Her nose followed without indent from her brow between heavily lidded and darkly pencilled almond eyes that were set closely into its flat bridge. The corners of a full and prominent mouth stretched almost to the point above which jutted her cheekbones.

With such an extraordinarily timeless face, her grape silk palazzo pants suit with a patern of rhinestones over each roundly padded shoulder seemed an anachronism. She should have been in a simple shift, a subtle draping of some rich cloth. Alice's memory of sartorial details in *From Ur to Rome* were hazy.

She also recognised that any criticism was a defence against her sense of inadequacy at having dressed 'safe' in a black velvet skirt and plain silk blouse. She wasn't even in stilettos, damn it.

'You are Alice?'

The hieroglyph's voice was as thick as clotted cream, her rs puttering off the tip of her tongue. She held out a jewelled hand. 'I am Fatma. Please, follow me with the baby.' She peered politely into the basket. 'Ah, it is a beautiful baby. But of course. A beautiful mother.' She smiled slowly at Alice and gestured for her to follow.

She led the way down a corridor spread with overlays of oriental rugs. Upon the walls hung vast tapestries in faded blues and ochres. She halted before a pair of French doors paned in opaque glass and pushed them open. In the centre of the room beyond, under a canopy of sea-coloured silk, was an enormous circular bed. Alice stumbled slightly as her foot left the hard parquet of the hall and sunk deep into pale pile carpet. Corpulent armchairs and ottomans squatted in each corner of the room and on the walls old silvered mirrors framed in blown Venetian glass caught and repeated the tiny sparks of rainbow light that flashed from the largest chandelier that Alice had ever seen in a bedroom. It fell from the centre of the high ceiling, tier upon crystal tier like the beard of a classical god. Fatma turned a knob by the door and the light grew dim. She gestured at the bed.

'Put the basket there, yes? This room is right across from the dining room so you will hear. But if the baby cries before, the maids will come to tell us. The kitchens are close by. Come'

She reached for Alice's hand and drew her back towards the salon. Alice went relunctantly. She would have preferred to linger a while to make sure that Daisy remained asleep. At least, that is how she explained it to herself.

'I remember how it is to have small children at parties,' Fatma murmured. 'But now my two little ones are not so little.'

'That is hard to believe,' said Alice, as polite as Fatma had been. 'Are they here in Moscow?'

'No, no!' Fatma's laugh rippled softly. 'Omar, he is at Harvard. Abdul, he is only fifteen, so he is still at school. In Switzerland. Abdul comes here for holidays when we are not in Cairo. And Omar, he comes when he is tired of his American girlfriends.' She dosed Alice with another of her slow smiles. Alice wondered why she had never been able to achieve those melded strokes of copper, silver and grape on her own eyelids without looking as though George had abused her.

The crowd in the drawing-room had now expanded to airport strike density. Alice guessed there must be at least eighty people gathered for this 'informal dinner'. George was nowhere to be seen.

'Your husband has found someone to talk to, I think,'

said Fatma. A waiter hovered nearby with a salver of drinks. Alice plucked out a glass of berry red. Could this possibly be Campari soda? The benefits of a diplomatic social life. She sipped and smiled with private pleasure over the rim of the glass at Fatma, who had not taken a drink.

'Kamal thinks highly of him,' Fatma continued. 'He respects his judgement. So now we subscribe also to the *Sentinel*.' She reached out and touched the shoulder of a man standing in their path. He turned to face them, making a small bow. 'Tonio, may I present Alice Mason? Alice is the wife of George Mason, of the *Sentinel*.'

'Of course. Enchanted to meet you, signora. Antonio Carlini.' His velvet burgundy smoking jacket glowed in the amber light of a large Chinese lamp close by. He brushed her hand against dry lips. 'Italy.'

Italy? Alice supposed this must be the form for establishing one was an ambassador. She wasn't immediately sure how she should correctly address him. A quick course in protocol would have to be taken before their next diplomatic invitation.

'You are new in Moscow, I think?' The Ambassador raised one perfectly described eyebrow. His red jacket made a flattering foil for his pure white hair, Alice reflected. And I bet he would agree.

'Is it so easy to tell?' she said.

'Only because I have not had the great pleasure of meeting you before.'

Italians were bliss, thought Alice. Somehow they could always get away with the kind of corny lines which uttered by an Anglo-Saxon would simply make you feel tired.

'When you come to Kamal's next party, as now you probably will, and the one after that, and the one after that, you will find all the same people that you meet here tonight. Here' – the Ambassador swept a hand about the room – 'is *le tout Moscou*. So that if you see a face you do not recognize, it is because it belongs to a new arrival or to someone passing through.' He smiled self-deprecatingly. 'We all become greedy for fresh company. Not, of course, any company. No, no.' He pushed the offensive suggestion away with both hands. 'But now you have been granted the imprimatur of Kamal and we have faith in his judgement. So, *gentilissima signora*, you may consider yourself launched upon the *créme de la créme* of Moscow society!'

Alice caught an amused twitch of irony at the corner of his mouth as he inclined his head towards her.

Suddenly there came without warning the sound of gunshot from the street, a detonation of cracking and popping that built in intensity. Alice went cold. Revolt? Revolution? Surely not. What, then, was this dreadful chilling sound?

Next the lights went off. The room at once fell silent. Alice sucked in her breath in fright. What on earth was happening? Where was George? They had to get out. How would she find her way back to Daisy in the dark?

Then the heavy curtains at the long windows were thrown back and tight skin of night outside split across with a shimmering cascade of tiny pink and emerald stars that opened out like flowers and let fall to earth a sparkling stream of coloured sequins.

'Soveit Army Day,' remarked a voice at Alice's side.

'They have fireworks?' Alice was incredulous.

'Sure they do. On most public holidays as well.'

'I didn't know it was a public holiday. Weren't people still working?'

'Betcha bottom dollar. This is the worker state. But they get the fireworks. At nine o'clock for five minutes winter time. Ten o'clock for five minutes summer time. Lenin loves ya, baby! Whizz bang kapow! You know,' the voice leaned in confidentially, 'if you were out in the streets right now or up in an apartment you'd catch them all around you.

They're fired simultaneously from several points around the city. Quite an impressive piece of timing. Gives our military people the squits.'

The drawing-room lights came back on and there was a gentle spattering of applause. Alice half turned. The Ambassador had been quietly sucked back into the crowd. In his place was a short barrel-chested man with a grin on his face, rocking gently back and forth on his heels and staring optimistically at Alice through an enormous pair of circular glasses.

'Let me see your hand,' he said. 'The left one. Sheesh, wouldn't you just know it? Married. Don't they ever send any single women to this town?'

'I'm sorry to disappoint you. Is there a shortage?'

The little man nodded vigorously. 'There is when you're under strict orders to swan it.'

'Swan it?' Alice was puzzled.

'Sleep White And Nato. Uncle Sam insists.' He held out his hand. 'Josh Klaczynski, attaché at the US Embassy. We all seem to have Polish monickers at the embassy these days. Hey, maybe it's policy. So who is the lucky guy?' He nodded at her hand.

'George Mason, of the *Sentinel*.'

'Why, the heck! Georgie-boy? You're George's wife! Is that right?'

'I think you can safely award yourself a few points there.'

'Ho! That English sense of humour. It always gets me!'

'And I bet you love my accent, too.'

Josh Klaczynski bared his orderly teeth at her. 'You're a doll.'

She smiled at him more warmly. 'No. That wasn't polite. I shouldn't tease. Tell me how you know George. I'm not sure what an attaché does.'

Josh rubbed the side of his nose. 'Well, we're a little unspecific on that, Alice.'

'You only know who you can sleep with.'

'Boy, but you're sharp. You know that? I like broads that don't come on to a guy. So tell me, Alice, how are you enjoying this fair city of theirs?'

'I find it rather beautiful, don't you?'

'I guess I don't have that much time to go exploring. But they tell me there are indeed some very lovely spots.'

Alice was taken aback. 'So what do you do then, when you're not working? You don't stay cooped up in the office, surely?'

He shrugged. 'I play a little squash over at the Indian Embassy, summertime a little tennis at the Malaysians. End of the week I drink at the Aussies, the Canadians sometimes. Then there's the ballgame weeknights at our Embassy, filmshows. Some weekends I get to to out to the American dacha.' He touched her forearm. 'Hey! You know what I like to do down there, Alice? Cook ribs. Texas-style, with my very own Joshua B. Klaczynski special barbecue sauce. Uhm hmm! Rest of the time, with the pool and all, I guess I don't have too much reason to leave the compound.'

'But how do you get any feel for what this country's like?' objected Alice.

He studied her. 'And what would I need that for?'

Alice felt frustrated. 'Well, I don't know. For your attachéing. Reports and stuff.'

'You know, Alice' – his tone became patient – 'we have one of our guys gives us all the background we need. He has a very special job. We send him out to the bars and public toilets – excuse me, restrooms. To pick up jokes. Heck, you can really get a feel for what's going on in people's head with jokes. Real opinions and stuff. The briefs we write, on the basis of information we receive, we assess, we analyse, we discuss, I believe our superior officers back on the Hill find more than satisfactory. I do not believe it is necessary,

Alice, to roam the streets to understand this place. In actual fact, I believe you can obtain a very distorting picture if what you rely on is what you pick up from the average Joeski. There is no-one more ill-informed and boring than your man in the street. And that holds good the world over.'

Alice found this pompous recitation exceptionally dismaying. She was about to ask how the man who hung around public urinals managed to avoid being propositioned or prosecuted when Fatma appeared between them, her arms softly circling their waists.

'Please. Dinner is ready.' She impelled them gently forward.

Alice and Josh moved towards the press forming by gold and white rococo doors that had been thrown back to reveal the dining-room. A map of the tables was pinned to a green baize blackboard. Alice picked out George placed at a table between a woman with a French name and one who sounded Polish. Or American, perhaps, if Josh Klaczynski was anything to go by. Still, he did have the Italian Ambassador opposite and the Mexican one beyond. Almeira's name was legend in Moscow. He was famed for impromptu meals at midnight after his wife and the embassy cooks had gone to bed. He would take over the kitchen and, pushing back his sleeves, set about making tortillas, spinning them like plates in the air. His chili, with ingredients that came in on the Pan Am flight once a week, was reputed to draw beads of sweat beneath the eyes. His frijoles were known as the El Dorado Short Range Warhead for the amount of garlic exuded by the body after even the smallest taste. Guests were expected to sing for their supper, following the Ambassador in the Mexican Hat Dance, which he supervised from the kitchen table top, stamping his tiny feet among his cooking debris.

Alice knew nothing of her own table neighbours. She

turned to Josh for illumination but he was already weaving his way across the dining-room. Alice made her way to her seat. Grasping its spindly gold uprights for reassurance, she leaned towards the typewritten card by the plate to her left. *His Excellency the Ambassador of Cape Verde*, she read. Cape Verde. Where was that? To her right, *Mario Molina*. Startled, she read it again more closely. As she straightened she sensed him come up behind her.

'*Gentilissima signora*,' he said, inclining his head. '*Che bella sorpressa!*' The Masons' Alitalia neighbour.

'Good heavens, si! Che coincidenza!' tried Alice. Her father had brought her up to the view that in order to speak Italian one simply added an o or an a to the English word. 'Primo Serpuhovsky Val, secondo here.' The system was less than flexible. Unless they could establish some mutual language, the meal was going to be a considerable struggle.

'*Da vero*,' agreed Mr Alitalia. '*La Sua sedia?*'

He gestured at her chair. As he pushed it in behind her, someone slid on to the seat on her left. To her discomfort she observed out of the corner of her eye that it was a distinctly attractive young man, tanned, with tight curly brown hair. He smelt faintly of lemon. Sex appeal within reach always flustered Alice. He turned to her, hand outstretched.

'Madame. Jose Gomez. Cape Verde.'

Alice blushed and brought her hand, a little sticky, to his. She took her lead from the fact that he had not called her Señora. Besides, her Spanish was even worse than her Italian.

'Alice Mason. *La femme du correspondent du* Sentinel.'

'*Le* Sentinel? Ah, bon? *Je le connais très bien. Il a bien pris notre part durant les années de notre lutte contre la régime du dictateur. C'est un bon journal libéral.*'

Good grief, thought Alice. A freedom fighter! I'm sitting next to an ex-terrorist! She reflected that if she were forced to become established as Mrs Sentinel as opposed to Mrs Mason, she would do well to apply for some sort of recognition as ancillary staff. Dinners with two languages, several ambassadors, assorted foreign businessmen and a possible future as a political hostage drained one's energy pretty fast. It was all a far cry from the bring-a-bottle pasta parties of the *Sentinel*'s more usual London associates.

Jose Gomez fixed his dog-damp eyes on Alice. '*Je félicite Monsieur Mason de sa jolie femme.*'

Alice felt even more flustered and smiled weakly.

The Egyptian Ambassador rose to his feet and tapped the side of his champagne flute with his fork. The room fell silent.

'Excellencies, mesdames, messieurs, tovarishi, ladies and gentlemen. Welcome to Fatma's and my home. It is good to have you all here once again, and a special welcome to our new friends who join us for the first time.' His smile roamed slowly round the room. 'There is no need to fear,' he said gently. 'I am not becoming so fond of public speaking that I desire to make a speech before the meal as well as after it. I rise simply to tell you that tonight we are informal. We dine *au buffet*. So that now you have seated yourselves and become comfortable, I must inform you that you are required to rise and help yourselves to food. Please be sure to eat well. I do not like warmed up left-overs for breakfast. Also we shall be dancing later and for this you will need plenty of energy. Bon appetit.'

While he had been speaking four Egyptian waiters in starched white jackets had filed behind a long cloth-covered table at the end of the room. They stood to attention in front of the kind of spread Alice had only previously seen in still lives by old Dutch masters. Nestling upon vast silver platters in the centre of the table were two whole roast sheep. On either side, stretching to the edges of the crisp damask cloth, rose glistening mounds of rice studded with nuts and dried fruits, dishes of stuffed vine leaves, sagging boats of grilled aubergines, red peppers and tomatoes plumped with ground meat and pine nuts. There were sauce boats of steaming juices, tureens of tahini and chickpea mixtures, boards of unleavened bread, and great wooden bowls of lettuce.

Alice had not seen lettuce in the market for weeks. She longed for the stuff. She frequently day-dreamed of the wet cracking of the first bite of a leaf between her back teeth. The saliva rose in her cheeks. In the fridge in Serpuhovsky Val at this moment were a bag of beetroot, half a mildew-spotted cabbage, a thin bunch of parsley roots for which she had paid one rouble, an American Express-bought chicken, and some terrifying left-over decomposing on a plate. Here, within inches of her reach, was heaven. Alice could feel her chest tighten and cheeks flush with anticipation as she took the gold-rimmed plate from one of the waiters stationed behind the table.

His eyes dropped briefly to her blouse. Alice instinctively looked down. A cold chill shrieked through her body. Her chest had not tightened at the prospect of the meal ahead. Her breasts were taut with milk, and they had begun to leak. At both points, a large damp flower was blossoming across her silk shirt.

In horror Alice dropped her plate on to the table and, with both hands cupped over her breasts, retreated backwards towards the dining-room doors.

In the corridor outside she reversed sharply into Fatma emerging from the bedroom rolling freshly glossed lips together.

'Alice. Is everything all right?'

'Oh, Fatma! I'm so embarrassed. I'm going to have to go home. I should have fed the baby earlier. The milk. It's ruined my blouse. I can't possibly stay. I'm so sorry. I can't believe how awful this is!' Alice's voice hiccupped. 'Could you find George for me? We'll have to go. Oh, it's just dreadful! I do apologize.' Alice wanted desperately to cry.

Fatma patted her arm. 'Please. Do not upset yourself. I understand, of course. It is no problem. These things can happen. Go and feed the baby. I will bring George.'

Alice ran into the bedroom, unbuttoning her shirt as she went, throat tight and nose prickling with tears she certainly did not intend to shed in this house. George would kill her. She shook Daisy awake and stuck her roughly on to her nipple. The other one sprayed fiercely in sympathetic pumping.

George came in, wiping his mouth on a napkin. He was looking irritated. 'What's up, Alice? Fatma said you had a problem.'

'Oh, George. We'll have to go. I'm so sorry. I should have fed Daisy earlier. But she was asleep and I didn't realize I needed to.'

'So you're feeding her now. Good for you. Why do we have to go?'

'Because I leaked all over my blouse. Oh, George. Look at it! I can't go back in there like this!'

'Can't you borrow something of Fatma's?'

'Of course I can't. I don't know her well enough. Besides, she's an ambassador's wife. Anyway, she didn't offer, so I certainly can't ask.'

'Christ, Alice, didn't you feel the milk coming? It's not as if you're a novice at this sort of thing, is it?'

'I'm sorry, George. I thought it was the food.'

'The food is superb. Best meal I've had since we've been here. Shit. I'm sorry, I should be more sympathetic, shouldn't I? The Italian Ambo was giving me a terrific line on the Euro-Communist view of Gorby.' George toyed with his napkin. 'I suppose we'll just have to make our apologies, then, and go home. Is that it?'

Alice nodded miserably.

'Shit.'

George stalked out of the room and Alice moved Daisy to the other side. He returned wordlessly with their coats and held Alice's out for her. The patches on her shirt had met in the middle. Silently Alice packed Daisy back into the Moses basket. The noise of the party came at them as they quietly shut the bedroom door behind them.

As they tiptoed past the dining-room Alice saw that both sheep had been carved down to their carcasses, the mounds of rice flattened, and the bowls of lettuce were quite empty.

Chapter Twelve

'Madam,' Galina announced with some satisfaction, 'the washing machine is kaput. She stood in the doorway to the dining-room where Alice was writing to her mother, clutching a sagging bundle of wet bedclothes. Alice sighed. Whenever there was a disaster to report, Galina signalled it by a return to the formal address.

'What's the matter with it?'

Galina held out the dripping linen. 'The spin cycle isn't working.'

Alice laid down her pen. 'What can we do about it?'

'It's the door that's at fault. There's a connection between the handle and the machine when the door's shut that sets the cycle. Some piece in there isn't making contact.'

Alice stared at her, impressed. This was serious analysis. 'Do you know anyone who can come and mend it?'

Galina waved an arm dismissively. 'Madam, in Siberia Galina worked at an electrical engineering plant. I know machinery. I will do it.'

Alice gazed at her. What a very diverting nugget of information. This woman was making regular reports on the state of play between George and Alice and who they were having to dinner, yet Alice knew almost nothing about her.

'We can still use the machine to wash. But I shall mend

the spin cycle. And madam will be very pleased with me.'

Galina fixed Alice with a look that Alice understood at once. A mended machine for something from the slush fund. Alice nodded slightly and Galina caught the movement. Satisfied, she gathered up the wet sheets to her damp bosom and retreated to the washing machine. Alice turned back to her letter.

'A letter from me hasn't gone astray, Mama,' she had written. 'You've answered all the questions I asked in yours. So I must have numbered one of them wrong. I always forget to jot down where I am in my counting and it gets hard to keep track. But I must say, Mama, I'm not really sure we have to go through this rigmarole. I know our letters take weeks to arrive, but they do get here, even if their envelopes have a curiously pleated look around their seals.

'The children are fine. Hattie made a plaster imprint of her hand at playgroup the other day. It's touchingly small. Daisy is sleeping well through the night, I'm relieved to say. Only two feeds now, thank goodness. I really need all the sleep I can get. We never seem to stop going out. Too much, I sometimes think. But it is a welcome palliative to the drudgery of the day, specially for poor old George, who doesn't seem to stop working from dawn to well past dusk. And it does mean we are eating decently! Hattie isn't, though. She's heartily sick of stew and mash followed by little wizened apples! We'd all give our right arms for a green vegetable other than cabbage. Even potatoes are so soft and scarred these days that by the time you've cut out the frostbitten bits and the green bits and the spade slashes, they're about the size of a plum.'

Alice looked up from her page and stared out of the window at the blank stone sky. So, given that was the current produce situation, what was she going to make for supper? Cooking had become an activity of intense boredom. She had protested to George that it was difficult to make ends meet on their budget. Had he realized that cauliflower was twenty roubles a kilo? That was twenty pounds sterling for two heads no bigger than a doll's!

George had conveyed her objections to the *Sentinel*'s foreign editor and received back the message 'So don't eat cauliflower', the wit of which had passed her by. Had the man truly not understood that that was all there was? Oh, God! for the fresh crunch of a fruit or a vegetable that snapped not sagged between the teeth: French beans! Iceberg lettuce! Celery! Most unexpected, most unmentionable and perverse desire of all – an avocado pear! Ah! just to slide one's teeth through its waxen nuttiness and mash its unctuous flesh against the tongue! Alice shivered. How absurd that an almost flavourless fruit should become the symbol for Moscow's foreigners of deprivation, decadence, luxury and unfulfilled yearning.

Mind you, she considered grimly, the odds were more in favour of her experiencing the sensual satisfaction of a bite of avocado than the sexual satisfaction of a close encounter with George.

These days the poor man was regularly returning home in a state of complete exhaustion. Alice wondered whether Mrs Gorbachev was losing out on her oats, too. George certainly seemed to find reporting the polictical manoeuvres of her spouse a process that was only mentally stimulating. His Party Congress speech had put Moscow's diplomats and foreign correspondents in a spin, analyzing a proposal that farmers should sell surplus farm produce at their own prices as tantamount to an acceptance of limited private enterprise. Today tomatoes, tomorrow Toyotas.

Then the announcement that summit talks planned for later in the year betwen the Soviet Union and the United States would hinge on a nuclear test ban, or an agreement to dismantle medium-range missiles in Europe. There was no point in empty talks, Mr Gorbachev had declaimed. Good Lord, what was the country coming to? Now the liqueurs and coffee conversation of Moscow dinner parties was focused excitedly on how serious were his intentions and just how far he would go.

George and Alice were summoned ever more regularly to dine with ambassadors, ministers, councillors, and foreign correspondents from other countries. It was as heady as the pre-sex period of teenage romance. Alice had almost taken out a block booking on Svetlana's babysitting services. She and George could count on not being in bed much before two at least three times a week. This was fun, but not conducive to a good sex life, five hours before breakfast not being the optimum hour to expect a performance from a finely tuned libido.

Both she and George had downgraded their wardrobes in recognition of their newly discriminating status. Alice's 'formal' wear had become 'informal', while her previously 'informal' collection she reserved for cosy suppers with the British community. George put aside his assorted accumulation of jeans, cords and cotton twills for weekend wear and now set out to the office only in suits: corduroy for everyday use, his finer worsteds for days when he would go straight from work to diplomatic dinners.

George and Alice now drove to these separately, an arrangement which regularly resulted in their introducing themselves to each other down the diplomatic line. And frequently not noticing their mistake.

Still, on nights when they weren't out to dinner, George was either off with his Russian contacts or working so late that Alice's appetite for his attentions had been overtaken by a profound lassitude by the time he staggered home. The desperation she felt about the widening divide in their interests was becoming less and less quiet. It was several weeks since George had seen Daisy awake. Would the baby reach toddlerhood unaware there was a man in her life? There certainly wasn't much of one in Alice's, Alice reflected.

Tonight, however, she was moving to alter this state of non-affairs. It would be the third evening in a row they had had no social obligations. On the first, George had been forced to cancel a casual engagement, to watch and report on an important television broadcast. On the second, he had slept from the instant supper was over. But this morning he had agreed to be home at a reasonable hour. It was the perfect opportunity. Alice was not planning to let it slip by. Tonight was the night of the corset.

'No more news for the moment,' Alice scribbled, bored with her letter. 'Hope all in order your end. Missing you, love A.'

'Galya?' she called. 'I'm just popping out to post this letter. What do you think? Shall I take Daisy? It seems a little warmer today.'

Galina had prohibited Alice from taking Daisy out until the temperature had risen closer to zero. When she had returned with her new daughter in January, Alice had had to throw a blanket over the baby's face to make the ten-yard dash from the airport door to the car. According to George, who had been warned, Daisy's tiny vocal cords could have frozen in the minus 26 degrees temperatures. In recent days, however, Daisy had been out in Serpuhovsky Val pressed, to Galina's fierce pride, against her protective bosom in a baby sling. Whether Galina was proud of the baby or of the extraordinary Western contraption she was wearing to carry her in, Alice was not entirely certain. At any rate, it got both of them out of the flat for a while, and Alice could roam at leisure through the rooms.

It was at times like these she most missed Radio 4. Unless she ran the tape recorder or the stereo, the flat was silent. Back in England, during maternity leave from her publishing job, she had organized her day to a *Radio Times* schedule: make the beds before the morning service, hoover to Gardeners' Question Time, a quick sandwich with the World at One. The ironing would take the whole of Woman's, Hour and – if Harriet was still napping – the afternoon story as well, but if George was on shift at the weekend, she saved it for the Sunday morning omnibus edition of the Archers, when Harriet would happily lol in her cot. Always, the first thing she did on coming into the house was reach for the radio and turn it on, even before she'd got her coat off and with the front door keys dangling from her teeth. At once her world would fill with living voices, some of them as familiar as friends, whose immediacy obliterated the echoing of empty rooms.

And Radio 4 did begin the day so reassuringly. The wonderful luxury of being able to stretch a warm arm languidly out of the duvet to reach for the early morning current affairs programme at the turn of a knob. No matter how ghastly the news, the measured tones of the presenters, the banter, was so British, so chin-up and stoical that one could face international disasters and the rest of the day with reasonable cheer. Doubtless it could all be ascribed by young radicals to audience manipulation and propaganda dissemination, but at least it was done with style. God, how the English-language broadcasts on Moscow Radio preached! Listeners were treated like half-witted juveniles, thumped over the head with the facts and the required point of view to match. Protagonists in current events always had their particular supporting adjectives which acted as prompts for the proper reaction. So that opponents of Communist-backed guerrillas were always 'reactionary imperialist forces' while Soviet platoons machine-gunning their way through Afghan villages were 'the forces of peace and progress'.

The disconcerting thing was that more often than not the news was read by announcers with perfect American accents. The Russians took their language training seriously enough to acknowledge that English and American were two different tongues and to support a Moscow University department for each.

Now, with no chance this washing day that Galina would go out with Daisy, Alice sought to escape herself. She could hear Daisy gurgling through the open door of her room. The baby was lying in the cot, tugging at the coarse woollen booties Galina had lovingly knitted from Siberian yarn for her tiny feet. She turned her head towards Alice and smiled an ancient toothless grin. Alice noticed that the stash of disposable nappies squeezed under the cot was beginning to look decidedly thin. She wondered what they would do if the huge supply that she had packed on to the removal lorry and which was now distributed under every bed and on top of every wardrobe came to an end before Daisy was potty trained. Galina, staunch Communist and loyal Soviet, had none the less volunteered the opinion that there was much to be said for a system that relieved mothers of the burden of handwashing fouled muslin cloths. And offered women tampons and contraceptives besides, Alice could not resist adding.

Alice stuffed Daisy into her snowsuit and pulled a thick balaclava over her head. She eased herself into the baby sling and dropped Daisy into its pouch. Galina helped her into her loden and buttoned it around Daisy. But for the head that popped out below her chin, Alice looked pregnant once more.

The ice slicks over the surface of the compound gave slightly under her boot as Alice negotiated the compound potholes. Winter was beginning to weaken. Around the remaining cars strolled the militiaman, hands clasped behind his back, eyes pinched against the smoke of the *papirossi* dangling from the corner of his mouth. He nodded at Alice.

Linking her hands below the baby sling, Alice picked her way over the tram lines to the pavement on the far side of the boulevard. Here, for a brief moment, she paused indecisively. Instead of turning right up the boulevard towards the post office, she stepped straight ahead of her into a glass-fronted shop murky with condensation, inscribed 'Fish'.

The desire to shop – even if it was only in stores called 'Fish' – frequently propelled her into suppliers of sporting goods, semolina, matches, building equipment, or pathetically stocked chemists, simply to have something on which to feast her eyes.

The tiled floor was treacherous with thin black slush and the soles of her boots slithered dangerously. She reached out for the counter. The shop smelt of brackish sea water and a single strip light fired a harsh glow upon the ubiquitous turquoise gloss paint of the concrete-walled room. Behind the cash desk was a shelf stacked high in leaning pillars of tinned fish, evidence of one industry's plan so over-fulfilled that the state could no longer press the product on the people. What they yearned for was fresh fish. But the small brick pool behind the counter had been empty of live fish for years and was now a repository for buckets and mops.

Alice followed a woman round the display cabinets, peering with the other shoppers in silence at the half-frozen blocks of whole fish trapped in ice. They seemed the only choice, apart from trays of dry smoked fish curling defeated on their sides. Alice sighed. She had thought to make fish fingers for Harriet. She reckoned that if she processed the flesh with an egg white and shaped it into bars covered with breadcrumbs, Harriet wouldn't know they were not from the British commissariat. But this ungutted fish seeping out of melting ice looked like an invitation to instant botulism.

Further up the boulevard she went into 'Vegetable

Fruit'. Here great steel grid cages taller than Alice lined destroyer-grey glossed walls. Into each had been tumbled string bags of root vegetables knobbled with dried earth. Through the trapdoors Alice pulled nets of large but pliant carrots, shrunken beetroot, and a paper bag of potatoes. Like the silent men and women around her, she sorted carefully through these, throwing back loose into the cage the hopelessly soft, the spade-gashed and the green-tinged tubers. They weren't really what she wanted. What she had in fact been looking for was onions.

She joined the queue at the cash desk where a woman with soil-streaked overalls worked the scales with one hand and her abacus with the other, never raising her eyes to the people standing wordlessly at her side.

Alice shuffled forward and dumped her nets on the gritty counter. '*Luk?*' she asked. The cashier neither looked up not acknowledged the question. Alice assumed it meant there were no onions.

Daisy stirred against her chest and stared up at her with a frown. Her mouth began to part.

'It's all right, little one. We shan't be long.' Alice fished for kopeks in her purse with arms stretched tight around Daisy's body. A handful of coins rained on to the counter. The cashier helped herself and Alice swept the rest into her cupped hand, bending to reach them. Daisy let out a wail of protest and the old *babushka* in the queue behind Alice clicked her tongue in reproof.

Alice cut back over the boulevard, weaving around two solid women slowly pulling small children on sledges down the path. She climbed the bitten concrete side steps of the long yellow brick building called 'Bread' that stood on the corner of the compound.

Inside the cold air reeked sourly of yeast. The young girl at the check out counter had her coat over her overalls and her hands reaching for coins and flicking the abacus beads were bound in scarves. Alice moved along the outer side of the wooden barricade that marshalled the queue towards the till and pushed round it to the deep wooden shelves where bread was laid out in the shadow of a solitary light bulb. The Soviets to either side of her were methodically pressing the loaves for freshness with the back of spoons tied to the shelving with string. They hissed through their teeth and rattled their tongues.

'Gdye svezhi kleb? Where's the fresh bread?' yelled the stout one to her left at the young cashier. The girl took no notice, but a door at the back of the shelves slid open and a barrage of loaves tumbled from trays pushed through from the bakery by a pair of floury arms. At once the cashier queue dissolved as men and women pushed to throw back their loaves for fresh ones. Alice was jostled left and right by grunting, muttering people. Suddenly she felt the urge to turn and run very fast out of the shop.

It was only when she had reached the flat that she remembered she had not posted her letter. Also, that she still had no onions.

'*Gospadin* Mason telephoned,' said Galina from down on the floor in front of the washing machine. She was surrounded by very small screws and washers that Alice did not want to know about. If George had telephoned then it was best to return his call.

'Hello, George. The washing machine's bust. What's new with you?'

'I've left my keys behind. At least, I hope that's where they are. Christ, that's bad news about the washer. Can you fix it?'

'Galina's taking it to bits even as we speak.'

'My God, Alice! Stop the bloody woman!'

'George, dear heart,' said Alice patiently, glad that George had voiced her own sentiments, 'Galina spent her youth in an electrical factory.'

'Did you establish as what?'

'Let me check if your keys are in the bedroom,' said Alice.

They were, on a large plate filled with business cards, loose change, rubber bands and several felt tip pen caps.

'You're all right, George. They're here.' Alice paused. 'You know, I do think we ought to let Galina have a bash at the machine. She's very keen to crack it. But I also think you might sound Nadya out on whether she knows anyone professional who could mend it.'

George grunted down the telephone.

'Are you still going to be able to get home in good time, do you think?'

'Gorby willing. I'll do my best, I promise. *Paka*, Ali. See you later.'

Galina was now in the kitchen with Daisy beating at her apron-covered chest with the flat of her tiny hand. The baby was naked below the waist, her rubbery limbs curled into Galina's lap. Galina stared down at her enrapt, squeezing Daisy's plump buttocks and chewing absently on a crust of bread that stuck out from between her teeth at one side of her mouth. Like a cow working at grass, thought Alice. Neither of them took any notice of her.

'How's the washing machine getting on?' she asked, a little testily. Galina bent down and placed Daisy on a towel on the floor where she began to howl. She ignored her and rose, smoothing her apron about her.

'It's not working yet. But it will. Never you fear.' The crust wagged up and down as Galina spoke. She pushed a strand of hair under the scarf she had tied at the back of her neck and took from the table the nets of vegetables Alice had dumped down. She poked at them critically.

'Not the freshest, are they? You should try 'Products' on Gertsena Street. Better quality. Closer to the Kremlin.'

Daisy wailed. Alice felt like joining her. 'Galina, please

put a nappy on this child before she pees all over the floor.'

Galina had criticized her ability to shop. Worse, the obviously relaxed relationship between maid and infant all at once made Alice feel absurdly jealous.

She turned and strode into her bedroom. Decisive action was necessary. She picked up the telephone from the night table and, sinking down on to the bed with it on her knee, pondered for a moment. Whom should she call who would not take control of her sudden idea? She dialled Babs' number.

'Hello, Babs? It's Alice. Oh, sorry, Hazel. I thought you were Babs. Is she there? Yes, of course.' Alice stared out at the apartment block opposite. A woman was leaning over a balcony beating a small mat with a stick. It was snowing hard now.

'Babs? Listen, I've had a brainwave. What do you miss most about England?'

'How many hours have you got?'

'I bet window shopping and lunches with the girls would come pretty high on your list, right?'

'There's not much that doesn't. What's your great idea?'

'Well, I don't see why we can't kind of transpose some of the things we would do back home to Moscow. I mean, there *are* shops, there *are* restaurants. It's just that it doesn't seem to occur to us to take advantage of them. I don't know about you, but I was pretty pleased with what I managed to get for everyone's present this Christmas, even if – God, I feel embarrassed now! – some of it was so ghastly it could only count as kitsch.' She thought fleetingly of the embroidered violet plush teacosy from Turkmenistan.

'I sent off for all mine from Liberty's catalogue.'

'Oh. Well, what about the lunches, then? George is forever eating at the Praga and the National and the Press Club. Don't you think we could make a point of having a girls' get-together, say once a month, or something? It's just that it seems to me we don't make any kind of effort to take advantage of Moscow. And it's silly because all it does is show up what we're missing and simply gets us down. Or don't you agree?' Alice heard a note of desperation creep into her enthusiasm. 'Why don't we make a formal plan to go to a different museum each week, then have lunch somewhere?'

'In principle you're right, I suppose.' Babs sounded doubtful. 'It's just I've actually eaten out quite a bit, Alice, and I can tell you Chicken Kiev at one restaurant tastes pretty much like Chicken Kiev at all the others and none are as good as Marks and Sparks' microwave version.'

'Then choose something else!'

'There isn't anything else.'

'Honestly, Babs, this is just my point entirely. We're letting ourselves go under. And it's a disgrace. Here we all are, a bunch of women who before this posting were all computer analysts, or teachers, or doctors or publishers or something, women with pride in ourselves and our skills, and we come here, take one look around and throw in the towel. Listen, you only get out of Moscow what you put into it.'

'Frankly I resent forking out for pretty dreadful food what I'd pay for a slap-up meal in England. Besides, I can cook that badly myself.'

'You're just prevaricating. What we eat isn't the point. It's the fact that we're not making a proper effort to keep our spirits up. At least, I know I'm not. And I think it's a bit pathetic. So I want to do something about it.'

'What, now?'

'Why not? There's nothing to stop us.'

'Children.'

'That's not a good enough excuse. You've got a nanny and I've got a maid.'

'What about Hattie?'

137

'I'll deal with Hattie. Sasha can pick her up from school. Then she and Becka can play together.'

'They've seen too much of each other this week. They'll fight.'

'So let them play in your flat. Hazel can distract them.'

Babs sighed. 'All right, then. So long as you arrange it. Only, absolutely no window shopping, OK? That particular ethnic experience I am not prepared to share.'

Alice grinned. 'I'll ring you back as soon as I've booked a table.'

Next, Alice telephoned George. 'George? I'm changing my life. I've had this brilliant idea.'

'You're going back to Mother.'

'Don't be silly, George. No, I'm going to organize lunches out for all us women who feel deprived of grilled goat's cheese and gossip. But I need your help.'

'There's not a single bite of grilled goat's cheese within a thousand miles, Alice. I can't do it.'

'I was speaking metaphorically, George. What I need is Sasha to collect Hattie from school today, and you to tell me how I go about booking a table for lunch somewhere nice.'

'The first, no problem. The second, impossible.'

Alice felt her jaw tighten. 'Not you too, George. What do you mean, impossible?'

'Alice, in order to get a table in any restaurant you must first write a subservient letter and present it early in the morning to the restaurant manager. Only in the event that you have been regularly supplying him with bottles of Johnny Walker or cartons of Marlboro will he even consider your request. In our case, this gives you a choice of the Aragvi, the Praga and the National. However. It is now,' he paused, 'Almost twelve o'clock. There is no way I can rush a letter to any one of these watering holes if you require Sasha to be present at the playgroup at half past.'

'You mean we can't just go to the restaurant and ask for a table?'

'If you flashed the doorman a cigarette packet or two you'd get into the building, certainly. But then you'd have to tread the careful line between tact and insult trying to bribe the head waiter for a table. And you're a woman, which probably equals prostitute in these negotiations.'

'For heaven's sake! Are the restaurants so packed at lunchtime?'

'Not especially. But that's beside the point. It's a seller's market. He's going to get paid his monthly salary even if the place is empty. But if you want one of his tables you have to make it worth his while. See? Still, I like the idea. So why don't you let me arrange you a table somewhere for tomorrow?'

Alice sighed. 'Thanks. But I think I've got to strike while the iron is hot. Isn't there anything else we can do?'

George thought. 'I suppose if you weren't desperate to eat you could try the bar at the National.'

'It's the getting out that counts. The National will do fine. Thanks, George.'

Alice and Babs drove over the Bolshoi Kammeni Bridge in a state of giggly apprehension. Almost over the bridge, the traffic lights that controlled the road entrance to the Soviet government buildings inside the Kremlin walls turned red.

And stayed red. Not a car moved, along Prospekt Marx, down Frunze Street, or west from Volchonka Street.

'Right!' said Alice. 'Which big Politburo cheese is stopping for a pee on his way out this time?'

'Wouldn't you just know it!' Babs complained. 'Every time I use this bridge!' They sat and waited.

'You don't, by chance, know where I could get any onions, do you?'

Babs snorted. 'In March? You're joking. They'll be

defitzit. Last season's mushy, next season's not grown.'

In the mirror Alice watched the driver of the car behind get out and knock the ice from his windscreen wipers. The two men in the beige Volga on one side of them unfolded newspapers and settled comfortably in their seats. On the other side the engine of the bus sputtered and died. Alice yawned and Babs put her feet up on the map shelf. They stared silently out over the snow building on the bonnet of the Fiat. Then from the Kremlin swept three long black Zil limousines, bodywork gleaming, glass opaque, back windows obscured by genteel grey curtains. They swung up past the Paskov Palace and disappeared towards Kalinin Prospekt. At once the lights turned red and the traffic began to move again.

'Some are more equal than others', observed Babs.

Alice drove on the one way system along the wide open space between the National Hotel and the Kremlin that Stalin had had cleared to provide room for marshalling troops. Fifty Years of October Revolution Square, it was called. Nifty on an envelope. She swung the car round past the Bolshoi Theatre back to the front of the National and parked between a French diplomat's Mercedes and one of the Volvos of the *New York Times*. Checking license plates was an activity enjoyed by militiamen and foreigners alike.

Babs had warmed to the occasion, despite her initial disappointment that they would not be eating in a restaurant. She had changed out of jeans and sweatshirt into a thick tweed suit with a box pleated skirt that emphasized her wide behind. She swung ahead and pushed through the heavy door of the hotel, ignoring the uniformed doorman who looked them over as they passed him.

The foyer of the National Hotel was dimly lit and quiet. Babs and Alice climbed the wide carpeted staircase that swept upwards into the gloom. From a balcony of this building, Lenin had delivered a rousing speech to the populace when the National had briefly been the base of the provisional government. Its past was more colourful than its present, but it was none the less the hotel with the most style in Moscow.

They headed for the main bar. It was empty but for the barman playing chess at the counter with a man in a shabby brown suit and two impeccably painted Soviet women at a central table. They plucked at their fluffy sequined sweaters, eyes focused on the entrance sweeping expertly over Alice and Babs as they stared in. An old woman busied around their feet with a long birch broom, expressing her disapproval with jabbing sweeps of the twigs at their glossy high-heeled shoes.

'There's a nicer bar on the next floor,' said Babs primly.

Upstairs they found a minute room decorated like an old Islamic antechamber. The walls were tiled in patterned blue and white. White open-work ceramic shades hung down over the lights. There were half a dozen low carved tables and stools and a couple of banquettes to the back. On the small bar rested an Italian espresso machine. Alice nudged Babs and pointed at it. A stolid barman wiping out a glass watched them impassively as they stood uncertain in the doorway.

Babs led the way into the room to one of the tables.

Alice squatted down on a stool and stared about her. 'Not bad at all,' she said. 'Here we are, then. Freedom. What shall we have? As it was my idea, the first round's on me.'

'You do know it's hard currency, don't you?' Babs asked. Alice nodded. 'Then I think I'd like a red vermouth. And a plate of whatever it is he's got on the counter. It's usually caviare, or something.'

'Wonderful!' said Alice brightly. This was just the ticket, she thought. Couldn't be better. Start of a whole new approach to living in Moscow. 'Sounds good enough to me. I think I'll join you.'

Babs looked dismayed. 'You're not going to drink, are you?'

'That was the general idea, yes. We are in a bar, after all.'

'You know, as driver you really shouldn't.'

'For heaven's sake, Babs. A vermouth or two isn't going to knock me senseless!'

'I know it isn't. But it's against the law to drink and drive.'

'Good grief, you don't take it that seriously, do you?'

'As diplomats, we've got to take it seriously,' said Babs primly. 'But that isn't the point. Drinking at a private party is one thing. But we're in the bar of a hotel patronized mostly by foreigners. The place is probably bugged up to the nines. And we're being watched.'

Babs stared pointedly down at the table while jerking one shoulder towards the other side of the room. Alice turned round. The barman was staring at them expressionlessly.

'How do you know,' Babs muttered, still staring at the fretwork and speaking through clenched teeth, 'that he won't pick up the phone the moment we've gone and report that two foreign women have just been consuming alcohol? They'd stop us in the car before we even got over the bridge. We'd have to spend the rest of the day walking chalk lines at the police station and probably be banned from driving to boot. Jonty would go mad.'

'Honestly, Babs. I do think you're making a bit of a thing about this.'

'Maybe. But is it worth the risk?'

'Frankly, I don't see much point in going out if you can't get a bit potted. This is not exactly the liberating experience I had in mind.'

'Still, at least we're out of the compound,' said Babs encouragingly.

Alice took a deep breath. 'I'd better get your drink, then, and my – coffee, I suppose.' She rose and approached the bar. On it lay three plates of halved boiled eggs piped with mayonnaise and grounded on slices of white bread that curled at the edges No caviare.

'*Adno* Martini Rosso *i adin kofe, pazhaluysta.*'

The barman glanced up at the clock.

'Martini *nyet*,' he said. '*Posle dva chasa.*'

Alice felt a slow grin grow across her face. She cupped her hand over her mouth and squeezed hard to repress it. She turned round to Babs.

'Babs? No alcohol before two. It's the law. Join me in a coffee?'

Their bid for freedom left both of them tight-lipped. They drove back to the compound, the conversation dwindling to the level of incompatible strangers at a cocktail party who work desperately to keep a dialogue going for fear of having no-one to talk to at all.

Alice plunged into the sancturay of the flat with a brisk farewell. She ran through it, wrenching off her skirt and shouting 'Can't stop now, must dash' at Harriet in nurse's uniform spoonfeeding Galina. In the bedroom, she pulled George's quilted jacket over her sweater and slid her legs into trousers. She grabbed her skates and jumped breathlessly two at a time down the thirty flights of the back stairs to the car. Wheels biting at the ice like a circular saw, the Fiat sped out of the compound.

The snow had stopped and the sun gleamed down from a sky wiped clean of cloud. At Gorki Park she snatched the skates off the passenger seat and ran through the gates towards the first rink of frozen pathways. Here she threw herself down in the snow, tore off her snowboots, placed them carefully against a tree trunk and put on her skates. She twisted up her hair and stuffed it into a woollen cap of Harriet's, then tiptoed cautiously on to the ice.

It was fresh, with the sleekness of a cat's back. She pushed out, gliding gently, and felt the clear air sharp against her face. She pushed out again, repeatedly, until she was flying faster and faster over the ice with a feeling of glorious emptiness. She was alone on the rink, at one with herself in a world with a floor of pearly pink and ceiling of luminous blue.

Chapter Thirteen

George was doing the bit of his job he liked best. He was out on the scent of a story. This was exhilarating anywhere in the world, but in Moscow there was often the added frisson of absurd cloak-and-dagger tactics and very real danger.

He stood at the bus stop on Kutuzovsky Prospekt. His heartbeat was running a little faster than normal and despite the cold his shirt had begun to stick to his back by the time the bus appeared, trundling up from Kalinin Prospekt.

George climbed aboard, fed his kopeks into the ticket machine and swung down to the back of the vehicle. In his rumpled parka and the rabbit-skin *shapka* swiped out of the reach of an army colonel off the counter of the Armed Forces UniverMag store, George considered he melted into the background well. Only his sturdy leather boots marked him as a man of privilege, influence or foreign nationality among the flimsy, snub-toed, laced-up plastic footwear of the Russians. He felt keenly alert to his surroundings, exhilarated and apprehensive.

An hour ago he hadn't been so happy. A terse telephone call from the drying-out tank on Tulskaya had revealed that Harold had been picked up swaying along the gutter down the Koltso not far from the Press Centre. His papers had shown him to be a foreigner and a journalist. The drunk tank wanted rid of him at once. Would someone immediately come and collect him, *pazhaluysta*.

Harold was fortunate. The usual procedure would have been to keep him overnight in a cell with intoxicated, vomiting, morose Soviets. But these days an inebriated Westerner was a profound embarrassment. So Nadya had been driven by Sasha, fresh back from delivering Harriet to Galina, on a mercy mission to rescue her husband. It was by no means the first time Harold had been caught drunk in public. But it was the first time since Gorbachev's drive against alcoholism. George had been staring sightlessly out of the office window wondering with extreme anxiety what could be done about his colleague when the phone had rung again.

'Allure, Yorgi?' The voice was muffled and heavily accented. 'This is the man who shares your love of Rabbie Burns.'

Terrific, thought George. Who does that bloody narrow it down to? There were several thousand Burns fans in Moscow, not to speak of the members of the official Moscow Robert Burns Society. Some bloody clue. Who the hell could it be?

'Ah, hello there. Yes. Listen, could you be a little more specific, do you think? Focus in a bit?' He heard himself becoming overly British. 'I'm not absolutely with you.'

'What?'

God, this was awful. 'I'm a bit in the dark, comrade. Slight identity problem. Could I have another clue, do you think? Who you are?'

There was a silence.

'The apartment of our friend from Georgia. We met there.'

'Yes. Well you see I have several good friends from Georgia. I'm sorry, but I'm afraid I'm not really the wiser. I do need just a bit more of a fix.'

There was a grunt followed by another silence.

Then the voice said, 'You took your shirt off and wrapped it round my head and we did a Scottish dance together.'

The occasion and the individual immediately crystalized, along with the thumping headache that had followed. George's temples throbbed lightly. Oh, brother, he thought. 'Right! Comrade! Of course. Got you now. God, that was an evening! What can I do for you?'

'I think we should continue our very interesting conversation.'

'You do?'

'Absolutely.'

'If you say so, of course.'

'At the place we discussed then.'

George paused. 'We did?' All he could remember was the hangover. 'In the air, was it?' he volunteered. This referred to the ferris wheel in Gorki Park, a favourite dissident meeting place. Except was it operational at this time of year?

'No,' said the voice testily. 'Under the ground. One hour from now on the southbound platform. Is that convenient?'

'I shall be there.' George hoped he'd got the right metro station in his mind.

The telephone clicked. George put the receiver back. His incompetence had probably allowed the listeners enough time to trace the call and summon a platoon to surround the caller. Certainly enough to organize a cortege to follow George wherever he went. His heart had moved somewhere close to his tonsils and his scalp suddenly felt one size too small. Still, one had to admit, this no-names-no-pack-drill routine did give a stimulating edge to what generally turned out to be pretty fruitless furtive meetings.

He left the bus beyond the two monumental '30s apartment blocks that flanked Kutuzovsky Prospekt like gates to the city and dropped down into Kutuzovsky Metro. It was teeming with people. George slipped into the bobbing swell of fur hats and waited on the westbound platform for a train to Molodyozhnaya station, out in the Moscow suburbs.

Molodyozhnaya is far enough out from the centre of the city to be above ground, and a vicious wind swept across the rails. There were few people waiting on either platform and George ran his eye quickly over each of them before mounting the train waiting on the eastbound platform to head back into the city. The carriage was almost empty. The rubber-lipped doors shot together with a thud and a two-note siren sang out, followed by a soothing female voice crooning, 'Next station, Kunchevskaya.'

An ample *babushka* in stout boots and a short grey coat, sitting legs opened wide, stared at George with frank interest the entire journey. Natural curiosity? Or official? She rose as the train drew into Kievskaya and George followed her out on to the dimly-lit concourse of the vast interchange station. He stood, jostled by hurrying travellers, unscrambling the cyrillic on the indicators above his head, and followed the directions to the circle line.

The platform for the southbound train was packed. An illuminated digital clock above the mouth to the tunnel ticked down the seconds to the next train. George let it slide in and out without him, furtively glancing about for signs of being watched. The platform filled again with people almost without pause. Ninety seconds ticked by and another train swayed down into the station. The crowd pushed forward without waiting for the carriages to release their passengers. There was a brief argument in front of George as a massive woman with a bulging string bag in one hand and a young boy in the other was shoved aside by a pretty girl. As George was about to mount, the man beside him cleared his throat and ejected a thick green gobbet on to the platform where George was on the point of placing his foot. He pressed into the carriage as the chimes went and the doors slammed. The *babushka* he was squeezed up against half turned her head and berated him crossly out of the side of her mouth.

Despite the crush, there was a seat no-one appeared interested in. George eased towards it and sat down next to an elderly woman with a well-bundled dog on her knee. As the train sighed through the tunnel, the wide cloth-covered flanks of broad *babushka*'s swung towards George. He caught the reek of paraffin heaters on unaired winter coats and the chemical undertones of cheap scent mixed with the stale fried-onion stench of old sweat. Young men in royal blue nylon track suits striped white down the leg hung on to the metal poles by the doors, rocking back and forth in sodden replicas of Western running shoes. On their heads they sported close-fitting ski caps with foreign trade names misspelt around the upturned headbands.

George left the carriage four stations later. He waited for the train to whisper back into the tunnel, then dropped to his haunches to wipe a large brown footprint off the toe of his boot.

'*Izvenitye*,' apologized the man who, engrossed in his newspaper, had stumbled over him. He hurried off towards the escalators, folding the paper and pushing it under his arm against a brown portfolio. Across its left hand inside page the word *Keremika* had been scrawled in large red letters. George rose and followed him, his mouth dry. Recognizing the man was no guarantee that he was not a KGB plant.

The escalators were packed, in places two to a step. These were what George liked least about the Moscow metro. They soared at an angle so steep and for such a distance that often, shuffling towards them little by little, it was impossible to make out how far above they ended.

Out on the wide pavement, George paused. Traffic beat

past on the Koltso and the sour metallic smell of old and unclean engines hung in the air. Along the nearside gutter a red-painted snow-gathering truck was slowly trundling, paddling the slush with two wooden oars up a slide, to scatter down into its container. George caught sight of the man with the newspaper queuing for ice cream at a Morozhenoye kiosk. They exchanged glances and George set off across the Krimski Bridge towards Gorki Park.

Snow lay humped and undulating like the fleece on a fat sheep across the frozen waters of the Moskva river. Four snow ploughs were lumbering along the Koltso, one in each lane behind the other, in a diagonal line. They cut through the ice on the road surface and skimmed it in a wave across the curved blade of each machine, passing it on to the next and into the gutter. So why is the snow truck ahead of them? George wondered.

Gorki Park is the recreation equivalent of the pig. Not an inch of it goes to waste. There are several theatres and exhibition halls, fairground attractions, bathing ponds, skating rinks, troika courses, and a hidden grove with Grecian folly called the Not Boring Garden. Martial music was blaring tinnily from speakers attached to the monumental gates as George passed through and turned left. On either side of him swarmed packs of track-suited men – from his metro carriage perhaps – bounding into the grounds towards a rank of women in overalls standing behind ice cream carts.

George walked towards the first skating rink where paths had been flooded to create the frozen circuit. This was not a time of day for skaters, so the slight figure in quilted jacket and woolly cap arched almost parallel to the ice, hands clasped behind back, was free to move at startling speed around the rink. George watched for a moment, mesmerized by this vision of physical release, then looked over his shoulder and passed on to the second skating area beyond where the faded chairoplanes and rockets lay chained up until the summer. The amonia stench of spilled urine belched out of the open door of the lavatories by the first cafeteria. He skirted the building, moving off the path on to the snow trampled lawn, down towards where the shooting galleries would operate once May Day came.

He was heading for the Keramika Bar by the duck pond. The pond was now thick with ice, the ducks picking their way delicately along its edges. George mounted the steps to the open air bar and fished in his pocket for a 20 kopek piece. There was an empty glass at the elbow of a man leaning on the shelf that ran along the side walls. George carried it to the tap and washed it out. Then he fed his coin into the automat machine at the back of the bar and waited for the foaming beer to reach the rim. The Horse and Groom the Keramika Bar was not.

He bore the glass to the garden wall at the front of the bar and, resting against it, took a sip of the yeasty drink.

'It's pleasant when the sun comes out,' said a voice beside him.

George turned his head, stared and said nothing. He moved his gaze back across the pond. The man who had been drinking at the side of the bar wiped his mouth on the sleeve of his parka and strolled out into the park. George and the man in the brown mackintosh were alone.

George said, 'How are you, Gizo?'

The man placed his folded copy of *Pravda* on the wall on top of his plastic portfolio and smiled. 'We meet in interesting times, yes, Yorgi? What did you think of the Party Congress?'

'It seems we should look forward to many changes,' George ventured. He waited.

'Some things change. Much stays the same.' He lifted the *Pravda* and unzipped the portfolio, drawing out a thick file. He slid it into the newspaper.

'This is for you. It is copies of open letters to the Central Committee. They concern the refusal of UVIR to grant exit visas to the Sildermann family and the refusal by the authorities for two years now to permit Irina Fienstein to visit her husband in psychiatric prison. We hear he has now gone on hunger strike and is seriously ill. Also there is a detailed resume of the families' attempts over the years to seek satisfaction, plus a general history of official repression of Soviet Jews as well as statements on the position of the Central Committee towards refusniks. I have included a declaration of intent by our group. And there is a copy of a plea to Western governments to protest against Soviet violations of human rights agreements.'

These days the refusniks had the PR business down to a fine art. George lifted a corner of the file and let his eyes drop to the sheaf of papers inside. His heart sank. There were at least two dozen pages of cyrillic script closely typed on onion skin paper. Judging by the general fuzziness of the print, this must be around the seventh carbon copy. In short, illegible and incomprehensible: his Russian would not be up to it. And probably unusable to boot. George sighed, depressed. It was the cheap, slick indictment of a journalist risking his resident's permit to meet a slight, but undoubtedly courageous. acquaintance risking his freedom.

Or was Gizo more likely a plant setting George up for arrest?

'I'll see what I can do. How is Irina, by the way? I saw her last month as she was on her way back from trying to visit Yosef in prison. She seemed remarkably stoic about her failure.'

'It was not a failure. Failure would be to have given up and not gone at all. The authorities do not take much comfort from our refusal to accept their decisions as final.'

'Irina can't find it too comfortable – particularly at her

age – to travel seven hundred miles by train, bus and foot to make a point she must know they will ignore.'

'Perhaps with Western press support for her cause, they will cease to ignore her.' Gizo stared pointedly at George.

George gathered up the papers and slid them into his parka pocket. 'As I say, I'll do my best. I should tell you, though, that with Gorbachev being tentatively accepted as the Soviet Union's first good guy leader, our news media are a whole lot less amenable to pushing the dissident cause. He's the front page stuff these days, not them. Still, who knows?' George patted Gizo on the shoulder. 'We must do another of those Burns nights next time you're in town. My regards to Irina.'

He turned and walked down the bar steps and across the park, neck prickling, without looking back.

In his office he sat hunched over the papers with the anglepoise turned down to shine directly upon them. It didn't help. He could barely understand a single whole sentence. The copies were smudged and in places the carbon had been so overused that whole words had not come out. George bent closer, squinting.

Then he heard the door open and close, and looked up. Nadya was standing in the doorway, unwinding a scarf from her head.

'Is Harold OK?'

'Actually, he is in terrible condition. I have put him to bed.' She frowned and sat down in the chair in front of George's desk, flinging her legs out in front of her. 'If I had wanted a drunk for a husband I could have married a Soviet.'

'Ah, but he could not have provided you with those elegant leather boots. Nor that stylish tweed coat. Nor that six room apartment upstairs, could he?'

She smiled grimly. 'Of course you are right.' She began

folding her scarf over and over in her lap. 'Do you know Harold wants to divorce me?' She looked across at George and he reddened. 'I see you do. I will not allow him, you know. He wanted me to sign some papers. What an idiot.'

'He thinks you will be better off without him.'

'Better off?' Nadya was indignant. 'The moment the divorce comes through I will lose my *propiska* to live in Kutuzovsky. To live in Moscow! I would have to go back to Murmansk!'

'I hadn't thought of that. I see your point.' Murmansk was a god-forsaken port north of the Arctic Circle, home to the Soviet Union's fleet of nuclear submarines and a stinking fish factory, that spent three winter months without daylight. 'Perhaps he'd sort of thought you had some kind of arrangement that would let you stay in Moscow?'

Nadya stared at him. 'And what kind of "arrangement" would that be, George?'

George fiddled with a pencil and shrugged. 'I understood you had good connections, Nadya.'

'Every intelligent Soviet has connections. Only the stupid ones admit to it.' She rose indignantly. 'I'm cold. I need some tea.'

'You couldn't make me some too, could you?' George wheedled. Nadya looked at him with contempt and tossed her head. She marched out into the kitchen and George turned back to his papers with a sigh. So, was she "one of them" or wasn't she? Women the world over were an enigma. He bet himself she wouldn't bring him tea.

But he was wrong. Again, he thought glumly. She appeared with two steaming glasses and brought one round to his pile of papers. She peered down at them inquisitively.

'What is that you have?'

'Actually, Nadya, it's something I could use a bit of help on.'

This could be tricky, he thought. Specially if she was indeed 'one of them'. Still, Nadya was the secretary and secretaries did what the boss dictated even if there was a more formidable boss somewhere in the background.

'It's some stuff I need to quote from. Only I can't read it.'

'Give it to me.' She ran her eyes down the top page. By the time she had turned to the second, she was clicking her tongue and emitting short puffs of breath to indicate to George just how long-suffering Soviets were with regard to the juvenile behaviour of Western correspondents.

'Really, George,' she said scornfully. 'This is stupid rubbish. Why do you have to take any notice of it? These people are just out to make trouble for the Soviet Union. They have absolutely no loyalty. They want only to debase our country in the eyes of the West. I do not understand why you foreign correspondents want always to write about dissidents. Why can you not write about Soviets who love the motherlands? Not these people who want to see our great country destroyed?'

'Actually, Nadya, I think they only want to leave it. Besides, according to their passports, they're not even Soviets. So why aren't they free to go?' he added mischievously.

Nadya fixed him with a slit-eyed look but made no remark. Eventually she spoke, 'A bottle of scent?'

'Name your make.'

And so it was that the secretary with the connections in high places and the journalist with connections in the wrong ones sat together late into the evening working over a dissident's tract for a flacon of Nina Ricci.

Chapter Fourteen

At home in the flat, Alice, too, was reading aloud, to Harriet in the sitting-room. She was almost relaxed, but not quite, sitting with half an ear open for the sound of the front door. She had sent Galina out looking for onions and was uncertain whether she would be back that day. Galina had not been sure how long this project would take, nor how far afield she would have to go. This was the time of year between seasons, she had explained carefully to Alice.

Alice had had trouble understanding why this should affect the growth of onions. Not only were there whole regions of the Soviet Union that enjoyed a temperate climate throughout the year, but if Soviet collective farms went to the trouble of centrally heating acres of greenhouses in order to provide a constant supply of tomatoes and cucumbers at astronomical off-season prices, why couldn't they plant the humble onion too? For her part, she could not see how anyone provided the most basic kind of meal without them. They were the foundation for practically every dish – in the Soviet cooking canon to boot. In fact, she found it impossible to accept that they could have disappeared without trace from every shop in Moscow, so would Galina please go out and get some.

Alice realized that her irrational bad temper was only partly to do with onions. On her return from her thoroughly unsatisfactory break for freedom with Babs, she had discovered that the water in the entire apartment block had been turned off. They were mending a pipe, Galina explained. Everyone had been warned, she said. That was what the handwritten scrap of paper attached to the front entrance was about. Alice, of course, had not been able to decipher it, so had ignored it. Outraged, she demanded why it was that in a foreigners' compound warning notices could not be written in English. So when was the water going to be restored? By midnight, but not to worry, Galina soothed. She had filled the bath and all the pots and pans in the kitchen before the tanks had run dry. There should be plenty of water for their needs.

Alice had wanted to throw herself into the centre of the compound yard and scream, 'Call this a bloody superpower? The water is cut off. The light bulbs explode and there's not a single onion to be had in the entire capital! Third World aggressor, that's all this country is!' Instead she remembered Charlie Prowse and yelled it at the ceiling. Galina patted her soothingly and said she would take Harriet and Daisy out for some fresh air so Madam (the 'Madam' was back) could lie down. Alice agreed. Not in order to rest, but so that she could sneak down the tin of salted nuts she had bought at the foreign currency Beriozka and comfort herself with cashews.

But Harriet didn't want to go out. She lay prone in the hall, sucking furiously on her thumb, while Galina stuffed her limbs into her snowsuit, bound her up in a scarf, pushed a woolly hat over her ears, her hood over the hat, mittens on to her hands and boots on to her feet. Cocooned as she was, she needed the assistance of both women to haul her upright. At once she unplugged her mouth and began to wail.

'Hattinka mine!' crooned Galina. 'Come with Baba for a nice walk, yes? We go feed the dicky birds.'

'Waaah.'

157

'We go look at the shops.'

'Waaah.'

'We go buy an ice cream.'

Harriet's eyes immediately cleared. She sprang to the door carolling, 'I want an ice cream! I want an ice cream!'

Alice took refuge in the only private place in the flat – the lavatory. She began to wrench down her thermal tights before remembering the water was off. Too late. Her body had been alerted. She sat down with a sigh.

Then the door was pulled open. Harriet stood in the corridor, scrutinizing her mother with interest.

'Me and Baba are going to buy ice cream'. she announced.

'So I heard,' said Alice tersely, tights bunched around her ankles. 'Close the door, please, sweetheart.'

Harriet popped her thumb back into her mouth and reversed into the cramped space, dragging the door with her.

'Hattie, my angel,' said Alice reproachfully. 'There isn't enough room in here for two. Besides, what about the ice cream? Baba is waiting for you.'

On cue, Galina lurched up outside the bathroom door. 'Hattinka,' she cooed, 'come with Baba.'

'Go on,' hissed Alice. 'Just squeeze out, will you? I'll see you later.' She gave Harriet a small shove.

Harriet flung the door wide and stepped into the corridor. Galina briefly met Alice's abashed gaze before sweeping Harriet away and out of the flat.

Alice felt drained. She poured two of Galina's precious pans of water down the lavatory and went to lie on her bed exhausted by the day's lack of positive progress. There was, however, one more manoeuvre that ought to produce results. She pulled herself together and rose to bring down from the top of the cupboard the red spangled basque she had hidden between her nighties.

It was getting dark outside. She crossed to the window

and drew the curtains. By the warm glow of the bedside lamp she began to remove her clothes. Then she stood and studied herself in the long wall mirror, running her hands across the flat of her stomach and upwards, gently weighing her small breasts in her cupped hands.

She smiled grimly at her reflection. 'But we never say die, do we, Alice? The show must go on!'

She reached for the basque and wrenched the cold satin up her torso. All in place, she looked at herself more kindly. 'Not bad. You'll pass. If this doesn't knock your spouse for six, Mrs M, then nothing will!'

She took a bottle of scent from the shelf, dribbling it about till it trickled in rivulets down her skin. Then she drew on her dressing-gown, secured it tightly at the waist and slid her feet into her black patent party stilettos.

The effort finished her. She lay down on the bed, staring blankly at the ceiling, listening to the sound of piano scales coming through the wall.

She awoke with a jolt, shocked that she had dozed off, as a soft wet kiss was placed on her cheek and a small hand stroked her hair. She opened her eyes and saw Harriet in her snowsuit standing beside the bed.

'Hattie! You haven't taken your boots off! Look! You've trailed black water all over the rug!'

Harriet peered anxiously down at the floor and thrust her thumb defensively into her mouth.

Alice was filled with remorse. 'Sweetheart, I'm sorry! I didn't mean to get at you. It's just we have to think of Baba doing all that washing, don't we?' She folded Harriet into her arms. 'What a lovely way to wake me up. Did you have a nice walk?'

'No,' said Harriet miserably.

'Did you have an ice cream?'

'There wasn't any.' Harriet looked as if she were deciding whether or not to cry.

'What a shame! But don't worry, we'll try again tomorrow.' Alice swung her legs off the bed and took Harriet's hand. 'Listen, let's go and get you undressed, then I'll read you a story. Is Baba still here?'

Harriet nodded. Then she popped out her thumb. 'Mummy, are you sick?'

'No, why should I be sick?'

'You've got your dressing-gown on and you were lying down.'

'I was just having a little rest, sweetheart. Now let's go and see what Baba's up to, shall we? And get your snowsuit off before you cook.'

Galina was in the hall, draped in her shawl and scarf, peeling off her thick woollen socks.

'Galya, wait,' said Alice. 'Don't undress, will you? I'd be very grateful if you could see what you can do about finding me some onions. Any kind will do. I don't care if they've shot. I don't care if they're soft. Just get me what you can.'

Galina nodded without much enthusiasm. 'I suppose I could try round Prospekt Mira. They might have some up there. But I don't expect I shall be back today, madam.'

Alice noticed the reproving form of address and felt ashamed that she was sending Galina off on what they both knew was probably a wild goose chase. Still she adamantly did not want her in the flat.

'That's all right, Galya. Bring them in with you tomorrow. Is there any money left?'

Galina nodded again. 'I've written the purchases in the book.'

She tucked her feet back into her boots and pushed her hair under her *shapka*. 'Well then. I'll be off, won't I?' She stooped to give Harriet a hug. Alice held the front door open for her and Galina swept imperiously through, without acknowledgement.

'See you tomorrow,' said Alice, and closed the door.

She helped Harriet out of her snowclothes and they settled companionably upon the sofa. The ailing water pipes spluttered along the wall behind them. Alice began to read aloud.

Towards five o'clock she heard the key in the lock.

Panicked, Alice flung Harriet aside and threw off her dressing-gown.

'Mummy! What have you got on!'

Alice ignored her and rushed to the sitting-room door. She had to be in place before George came in. She wrenched it wide and stood framed in the doorway, one leg posed across the other, a hand posed coquettishly low on her hip.

'*Prekrasnye!*' exclaimed Galina enthusiastically. 'Gorgeous!'

Oh my God, how mortifying! How come it wasn't George? Alice stood rigid with embarrassment, unable to move.

Harriet pushed past her out into the hall. 'Baba! Baba! Look what Mummy's wearing!'

Galina ventured forward, gurgling with frank admiration, and fingered the lace around Alice's pelvis. At her touch, Alice was magically released from encroaching calcification. There was probably little difference, she supposed, between the colour of the basque and the flush swiftly blotting her entire upper body.

'It's for a party,' she stuttered. 'Fancy dress.'

Harriet jumped up and down excitedly. 'What you going to be, Mummy? What you going to be?'

'Saloon girl,' blustered Alice. 'I thought I'd be a saloon girl. With a skirt over it, of course.' She smiled weakly.

'Shame,' said Galina. She walked round Alice approvingly, tweaking her satin-plated flesh. 'I'd wear it as it is. And not to a party.' She nudged Alice in the ribs. '*Gospadin* Mason seen it?'

Alice blushed more deeply. 'Not yet.'

'Ho! I'd like to be around when he does! Lucky man!' She winked conspiratorially. 'I should be pushing off, then, shouldn't I?'

At her feet lay a bundle in newspaper. She gave it a kick. 'Spring onions. I know it's not what you want. But it's better than nothing. I got them at the *zakazov*, the pensioners' and veterans' shop round the corner. Still, I'll try for the other sort, as you asked.' She looked Alice up and down. 'Right you are, then. I'll say goodbye to you. Don't want to spoil the surprise. Best of luck.' She winked again, and let herself out of the flat.

Alice slumped back against the doorjamb. Nightmare. She should have known it wouldn't be George. He couldn't have got in without ringing the doorbell. Hadn't he telephoned that morning to tell her he had left his keys behind? What an ass she was! What a complete and utter idiot!

'Mummy?'

Alice looked down. Harriet was staring up at her, anxiously. Alice dropped down to her haunches.

'What is it, my sweet?'

'Are we going to finish the story before you go to the party?'

'Yes, of course we are.' Alice hugged her tight. 'And Mummy's not going to a party. Not tonight. Let's carry on reading now, shall we?'

Harriet nodded. Then the doorbell chimed.

At once Alice sprang to her feet. Her heart thumped frantically, pressing her breasts in and out against the tight bodice with a disturbing flutter of flesh.

'Hattie, why don't you go and get the book ready while I see who it is?'

Alice did not want the innocence of Harriet's presence curbing her performance. She had wanted George home early. But not quite this early. Still, it couldn't be helped.

162

She was ready for him, after all. The two chimes went again. Alice pulled her cleavage up. She touched her hair, and felt sweat break out around her nostrils. She took a deep breath and opened the door.

The corridor was dark. One of the strip lights seemed to be off while the other was popping with a bizzare strobe effect against the blue gloss paint. Facing her in the hallway, brandishing a teacup, was Hazel. She stood there silently, absorbing the spectacle before her. As the message from her eyes reached her brain, she suddenly turned a startling red. It seemed to be the colour of the evening. Alice cleared her throat.

'Yes?' she inquired in a curious strangulated voice as though nothing were out of the ordinary but Hazel's interruption.

Defiantly Hazel brought her eyes to Alice's. 'There's a sugar shortage. We've run out. Babs wondered if we could borrow a cup.' She pushed the empty vessel at Alice. 'If I'm not disturbing you.'

Alice took it without comment and moved towards the kitchen. I don't need to explain myself to neighbours' nannies, she thought angrily. She strode back to the front door, her head held high, and passed back the cup of sugar.

Hazel kept her gaze fixed steadily at the floor. 'Thank you, Mrs Mason,' she muttered.

'Tell Babs, any time,' said Alice. Brusquely, she shut the front door.

'Right, Hattie,' she said brightly. 'Shall we finish off this book before I'm finished off?' She picked up the dressing-gown. 'I think I should put this on, don't you?' Next time the chimes went she was going to make sure she knew who was in her audience before she launched into her Gypsy Rose Lee routine.

Alice read three more stories to Harriet, glancing repeatedly at her watch as her daughter's bedtime drew near and George still had not come home. The child was lolling with the onset of sleep. She carried her into the bathroom and washed her. Harriet's eyes closed as soon as Alice laid her in her bed. Alice kissed her softly. She turned off the light and tiptoed out of the room.

George was standing in the middle of the kitchen reading a small scrap of paper.

'George!' Alice shrieked. 'How did you get in?'

'Through the front door, of course.' His attention was fixed upon the note in his hand. 'What the hell is this about?' he demanded, swatting it sharply.

'But you left your keys behind!'

'Yes, and I asked Sasha to pick them up when he dropped Hattie off from school. Alice, listen. What does this mean?' He peered more closely at the paper. Alice sank in despair on to the kitchen chair. 'I found it pinned to the front door. It says – I kid you not – "Let not the Devil" – with a capital D – "work his evil ways and fill Mr and Mrs Mason with impurity. May the Lord protect their two innocent children from their parents' sins of the flesh"!'

George turned the paper over to examine the other side for clues.

Alice threw back her head and released a deep and anguished groan. 'My God! If that isn't just exactly what we need! The prayers and supplications of born-again Hazel!'

'The Simpsons' nanny?' George studied the words again. 'But what does she mean, "sins of the flesh"?'

'What indeed, George,' lamented Alice, sprawled legs akimbo, red basque yawning through her dressing-gown. 'What indeed.'

Chapter Fifteen

The following day Alice decided her dejected acceptance of defeat had been premature. George returned home with a bunch of red roses. To be precise, six red roses, hanging their heads regretfully inside a crisp cone of cellophane paper. Alice was seriously moved. The last time George had given her flowers she had had to produce a baby for the privilege.

'Happy Women's Day,' he announced, thrusting them at her.

'Isn't it women's day every day?' she said doubtfully.

'Not in the Soviet Union. You get one official acknowledgement for good behaviour per year, and this is it.'

'George! I'm touched. What else do I get?'

'Depends. If I'm not already too drunk I might help you with your shopping bags as you stumble in from work. If I'm a liberated kind of chap with good connections who wants to be seen doing the right thing by his missus, I might even take you out to a restaurant where we can shout at each other above the crashing of the band. You will pick at a spread of zakuski bits and pieces, and I will smoke continuously over your food and raise toasts to you often enough to—'

'—still get drunk.'

'Bang on.' George sat down on the sofa and pulled Alice down on his knee. He nuzzled at her neck and Alice shivered. 'Also,' he said from the depths of her hair, 'you get flowers.'

'They're lovely, George. Where did you find them at this time of year?'

'Ah, now there's the rub.' He lifted his head and began to massage her shoulders. 'I come home on Women's Day without flowers at my peril. It's probably grounds for divorce in the Soviet Union. So in order to acknowledge the great contribution of women to the growth of the motherland, not to speak of their dual burden in running the home and a miserable job, the men attempt to sneak the day off – while the women of course labour on – in order to scurry about in search of flowers. Poor suffering slaves to tradition, those millions of us at the bottom of the social scale have to stand in queues for hours in the snow. Foreigners, fortunately, do not feature at the bottom of any scale in this country.'

'Unless we are a student from black Africa.'

'That is uncalled for, Alice. And on Women's Day, too. I shall continue: so I delved into the slush fund and Sasha and I went to a certain flower shop on Sretenka Street where the manageress is said to have a fondess for Chanel No. 5. While the proletariat lined up at the front door for the last of the tulips, Sasha and I joined the Red Army Colonels bearing their own oblations round at the back door for roses. Roses, I have to tell you, rate twelve out of ten on the good husband scale. Tulips only seven.'

He pursed his lips at her. Alice kissed them.

'George, I'm sincerely moved. I told you.'

'You ought to be. They cost five roubles each.'

'Five roubles for one rose! That's downright robbery!'

'I know.'

'But I'm worth every kopek.'

George sucked her earlobe. 'Yup. You're all worth every last drop of scent in the slush fund.'

Alice pushed him roughly backwards into the cushions. 'Who all?'

'You and Nadya and Galina and Sasha's wife,' said George, nibbling her neck.

'Do you mean to say you've given all of us roses?'

'Of course I have. If I hadn't do you imagine I would have got anything but sulks from my staff?'

'Why couldn't they have had tulips?'

'Because if the boss gives quality out, he has a better chance of getting quality back. Small price for better work and stronger loyalty for, well, the next twenty-four hours, anyway. Nadya was tickled pink. Harold usually forgets entirely.'

'You're unscrupulous.'

George grinned with satisfaction. 'Aren't I just? Let's go to bed.'

'Is that a Women's Day treat, too?'

As George was poised on rigid arms above Alice, expelling with each considered move the warm air trapped under the duvet and introducing instead a cooler current, there came the sudden shocking retort of a distant explosion. Alice was momentarily distracted, then she remembered.

Across the thin curtains flashed streaks of red and green and white, accompanied by regular pops and bangs. George began to pick up speed. Upstairs on the seventeenth floor, the man at the tape recorders adjusted his headphones as a familiar rhythmic series of stressed wood squeaks reached his ears. From the balconies across the compound came the thin voices of children, releasing Ooohs! and Aaahs! in unison. George plunged with greater determination. He clutched Alice closer to him. Rapidly they seesawed together as the sparks of colour fell in cascades faster and faster across the sky, the children's voices crying out obediently in ritual approval. Then George and Alice gave a sudden gasp of surprise and the children on the balconies shouted 'Oorah!' one last time as the fireworks faded away and George flopped back on the pillow beside Alice. The homage to Women's Day was over. Up on the seventeenth floor, the man at the tape recorders turned the volume back to normal.

George hauled himself up on his elbow and smiled down at Alice. 'Just think. If you weren't lying here with me, you could be dancing with Raisa Gorbachev.'

'If only I'd known,' murmured Alice, sleepily.

George gently drew a lock of hair off her cheek. 'You could have danced with the woman who dances with the General Secretary of the Soviet Union. Imagine it. You might have got me a world exclusive. Consider the caption for a picture of the First Lady tripping the light fantastic with a woman!'

Alice stirred. 'You're being serious, aren't you?'

'When am I not? Except you wouldn't have been invited. You have to be an ambassador's wife for that. And, besides, with yuppies in the Kremlin, no-one was sure what form this year's Women's Day women-only dance would take.' He fell back on to his pillow with his arms behind his head and stared at the ceiling. 'But in principle – as a Central Committee wife or married to a senior foreign diplomat, you would have been invited to a hoolie in the Lenin Hills thrown by the wife of the Gen. Sec. Till now, at least, it's been a lobster tea and a spin around the floor with the cream of Soviet womenhood: ladies in polyester dresses built to look like tractors who you're never introduced to.' He turned his head towards Alice. 'So you have to be sure you know your tractors – or at least who their spouses are – if you want to fill their dance cards.' He yawned and scratched his chest. 'I'm told the hokey cokey was very popular with Mrs Brezhnev. See what you missed for a grapple with your husband?' He touched the tip of her nose with his finger.

Alice looked at him levelly. 'Getting an invitation to the dance would probably be a whole lot less challenging than pinning you down to the bed awake.'

George threw his arms wide. 'Pin me! Pin me!'

At breakfast next morning their mood of companionableness evaporated sharply. George announced he was off to Siberia.

'How long for?' cried Alice.

George shrugged. 'A week? Ten days?'

'Where's Siberia, Daddy?' Harriet asked with interest.

'Ten days!' Alice was outraged. 'You never told me. What are you going to do in Siberia for ten days?'

'It's a press trip. There's no need to shout. I didn't tell you because I didn't know.'

'Will you be coming back, Daddy?' Harriet enquired more insistently.

'What do you mean, you didn't know! You apply for these trips, don't you? How can you not know about them?'

George sighed and pushed his bowl away from him. He had not finished the precious cornflakes slipped to them from the Commissariat by the visiting British dentist who had a soft spot for Harriet. 'You apply for them, but you never know if you'll actually be given a place till the last moment.'

Harriet slid off her chair and lay on the floor under the table, clattering her heels on the parquet. 'I don't want my daddy to go! I don't want my daddy to go!'

'Hattie, do shut up. So why didn't you tell me as soon as you came home last night?'

'I didn't think about it. Come on, Alice,' George protested, 'it's my job, for heaven's sake. Why all this fuss?'

Alice prodded her empty mug with a teaspoon. She also was quite surprised by her rebellion. She drew in a steadying breath and considered the question: all right. One, because George's holding back on telling her made it appear as though he felt guilty, so there must be something to feel guilty about. And Alice couldn't stand evasiveness. Plus it would be yet another opportunity for George to get out of Moscow and see the country while Alice had to stay at home.

And it was also to do with the different ways they were free to experience the Soviet Union. That is, that Alice was not free. And George was. With official sanction, too, because it was his job. Added to which there was resentment on her part that George might be reproaching her for her inability to involve herself as deeply as he in Soviet society when what was preventing her was their two small children, the queue for cucumbers, the search for lavatory paper, the hunt for detergent, the cooking for the freezer so that if George wanted to bring his Soviet contacts home there was always an Indonesian feast ready and waiting.

Alice sighed. Too many reasons, all of them probably feeble excuses for her own inertia. 'Because I'm jealous, I suppose. Ten days away from Moscow. I'd like to see Siberia, too.'

'It's not going to be a joyride, Alice. We'll have to listen to hour after hour of figures on how many gallons of milk collective farm cattle produce and how many tons of minerals the miners bring up, and reams of patriotic songs about peace, friendship and nuclear disarmament by simpering schoolchildren in brown nylon overalls and white pompoms in their hair, whose performances are designed to soften our impassive Western hearts.'

Alice snorted. 'And in the evening, knock back gallons of vodka and pounds of caviare in darkened hotel dining-rooms in between dancing obligatory foxtrots with coy young girls from local Party headquarters who would probably soar to the top of the waiting list for a larger apartment if they could only manage to get you into bed,' she countered.

George was staring at her, his mouth open.

'According to Charlie Prowse, anyway. He's been on these trips,' she said calmly. 'He told me just what they're like. In fact,' she finished, 'he said they're what make the posting worthwhile.'

George rose without a word and took his plate into the kitchen. He pointedly did not take Alice's.

He worked late that night at the office, and Alice was in bed before he came home, her eyes closed, her breathing carefully measured to simulate sleep. The alarm went at five the next morning and George stumbled about in the dark climbing into long johns, thermal underwear, and several pairs of socks. Alice dragged the duvet over her head and refused to move.

After he had gone she was filled with remorse. What if something happened to him in Siberia? What if he was compromised, went somewhere he shouldn't, did something he shouldn't, and she never saw him again? In the darkness, the Soviet Union was a vast wilderness shrouded by a thick Iron Curtain and ruled by secret police itching to set up naive foreign journalists. George was undoubtedly going to be locked away for years in a psychiatric hospital, known only by a number.

She rose at seven, exhausted. She set out with Harriet for the playgroup, in need of reassurance. She felt a tremendous desire, if she could not see George in person, at least to make contact with his spirit, so to speak, to register with his essence that she was full of regret for letting him go without having resolved their differences. Also it was necessary to get out of the range of Volodya and Ivan, whom Galina had brought back into the offensive against the washing machine.

Galina was clearly confident that they would fathom the mechanical failure in the spin cycle without further ado. Hardly had she removed her coat and introduced the *dvornik*s, flourishing their spanners, to the machine, than she had sat down at the dining-room table, Daisy across her knee, and crumbled a slice of black bread into a cup of warm milk. Open ostentatiously in front of her was a three inch thick catalogue of foreign merchandise. She looked up to make sure that Alice, zipping Harriet into her snowsuit, had registered this tome.

Alice had no idea where Galina could have acquired the glossily papered, gloriously coloured directory of goods and clothing that were without any Soviet equivalent. On George's advice she had made a point of ignoring Galina's hints and references to maids whose generous employers paid their thirteenth month salaries and New Year bonsues in kitchen appliances and designer label blouses.

'We are not a repository for Western merchandise,' he had said. 'They can't have it both ways. If they want food processors, they should either get off their backsides and produce them or they should have thought through the likely consequences more carefully before they knocked off their czar.'

Alice departed the flat without comment. She dropped Harriet at her playgroup and drove on up to George's office in Kutz. She felt more than a little apprehensive about invading it. It was, after all, his territory. More specifically, it was Nadya's.

Alice did not know Nadya well. While the women made a great show of warmth and enthusiasm towards Harriet whenever they met, she seemed to Alice rather offhand in her regard. George dismissed her indifference as the natural defensive insecurity of a Soviet woman confronted with a sophisticated Westerner of experience and possessions beyond Nadya's reach. Alice paid little heed to George's analysis. Nadya was generally better dressed than she was herself and through Harold seemed to lack for nothing. She put Nadya's nonchalance down to the instinctive suspicion of certain females towards one another. Still, they were polite enough to each other and perhaps with George away this was a good time for Alice to work on winning Nadya a little more keenly to her side.

She was standing with her back to the door slipping papers into the filing cabinet. She wore a soft forest green twinset over a Black Watch tartan kilt and her hair was pulled back into what was clearly an Hermes scarf at the nape of her neck. She turned as Alice tapped on the door-frame, lifted her chin and thrust her shoulders back in the manner of a headmistress preparing to greet a wayward pupil.

'Good morning, Alice. How are you? You are already missing your husband?'

Alice coloured a little. 'I was taking Harriet to school. I thought I'd drop by and see how you were.'

Harold was at his typewriter, his eyes focused on the paper clamped into the roller. He peered over the top of his gold-rimmed spectacles. 'Salutations. The boy wonder is on his way to Irkutsk, I trust?'

'Yes, if the plane took off all right?'

'Come now, my dear, you're surely not one of the rubber-band-as-essential-Soviet-component-part school of preju-dice, are you? I would not have thought it appropriate in the wife of a *Sentinel* reporter. The Tupelov is, after all, an almost nut for nut copy of the highly efficient Boeing. Why else are industrial spies so strategically placed? Now do sit down and make yourself at home. We don't see enough of you. Nadya will fetch you a glass of tea. Won't you, my pigeon?' Harold smiled emptily at her and turned back to his two-fingered typing.

Above his head hung a large poster of the members of the Politburo. Several of the photographs had been crossed out and others defaced with moustaches and spectacles. Next to it was a map of the Soviet Union. Alice stared at it with dread. It was an awesomely large country. George had gone an awfully long way away.

'How many sugars?'

'What? Oh, no tea, thank you. I've just had coffee. Gallons of it. To get me going. I'll float it I have anything else.' Alice was burbling. She moved round George's desk to get a grip on herself. 'Is it all right if I sit in his chair?' She touched it hesitantly.

Nadya shrugged. 'It is not a shrine, Alice.'

Alice reddened. She sat, her hands folded neatly in her lap, and stared at the papers stacked tidily in piles. That was unlike George. At home he flung his papers, his books, his dirty laundry all over the palce. Her heart was thumping and she felt peculiarly distraught. And hot, all of a sudden. No-one had volunteered to relieve her of her coat and she felt silly that she had not simply removed it when she sat down. They probably did not want her to stay. Come now, Alice, she chided herself, pull yourself together. That was a totally irrational, self-obsessed and juvenile line of thought. More likely they were so absorbed in their work they hadn't even noticed she had it on.

She reached out to steady herself and drew the nearest sheaf of telexes towards her.

ATTN MYRA DRWESBARR

EX BOB MATHISSON

ALIEV COMMENTS ON PARTY PRIVILEGES MADE GOOD FOREIGN PAGE PIECE STOP GLAD U SIBERIA BOUND STOP LOOK FORWARD TO COPY STOP ANY CHANCE FEMALE ORIENTED STUFF QUERY WOMEN'S PAGE KEEN STOP

CHEERS

BOB

Alice suddenly felt pinioned by a bleak chill that sucked the heat right out of her and left her body trembling. The telex slipped from her fingers and fluttered back on to the desk. She wondered if her jaw would ever unlock again. She sucked in air through flared nostrils and composed herself.

'Who's Myra Drewsbarr?' she said as lightly as she could. Her breath felt curiously tight in her chest.

Nadya looked up, startled, and Harold studied Alice through his spectacles with an air of puzzlement.

'My starter for ten, is it? Well, let me see now. Fine young journo, I would say,' he offered eventually, pursing his lips. 'One of the best.'

'Who works out of this office.'

'Indubitably.'

'And has gone to Siberia.'

'Incontrovertibly.'

'With George.'

'Unavoidably.'

Alice caught Nadya smiling privately to herself. She drew herself upright and briskly straightened the papers. 'Well, I should think it will be an entertaining trip, then.'

'Do I get a fortnight for two in Svedlovsk?' said Harold, tilting back in his chair. 'Or a year's supply of tinned fish? One really should play parlour games more often.'

Alice shivered in her coat. 'You like games, do you, Harold?'

'Christmas surely isn't Christmas without a round of charades, wouldn't you say so, my dear?' He addressed himself to Nadya. 'An aspect of the holy holiday Nadya has never been able to comprehend.'

But Nadya was watching Alice. Alice smiled at her brightly. If Nadya knew she was being made a fool of, she would show Nadya she did not care.

'Nadya!' she exclaimed, clapping her hands together decisively. 'I have two altogether different domestic problems. I am sure you can help me with them.' Was she not, after all, a paid member of the Mason staff?

Nadya squinted with suspicion. 'If I am able,' she offered cautiously.

'Wonderful. The washing machine and onions.'

'The washing machine and onions!' echoed Harold with satisfaction. 'What perfect symbolism for expressing the gamut of the motherland's social disarray!'

'The most immediate problem is the washing machine.'

'I am not a mechanic.'

'No, of course not. But I am sure you must know one.'

'Of man and machines Nadya is your master,' Harold said. 'And I back to my own.' He bent once more over his typewriter.

'Actually, it is a waste of your time to try to mend it,' said Nadya dismissively. 'You will have to get a new one. What is the problem with the onions?'

Alice was taken aback. 'Isn't that a little drastic? The machine's almost new. I mean, it's not as if it isn't washing perfectly well. It's only that it won't spin.'

'There is no-one in Moscow who can mend Soviet machinery. So. It is impossible they will know what to do with a foreign machine. In any case, if I did know someone you would have to bribe them with too much vodka and wait many, many weeks for them to come. And I don't believe they will be able to fix it. You see? So. You must order straight away another one from Helsinki. I will telex for you.'

'Hang on! I don't want to be too hasty. I'm sure you're probably right. But I find it hard to believe there isn't some other solution.' Alice was shocked by the finality of Nadya's advice. 'Anyway, Galina's convinced she can sort it out. She's got the janitors on it at the moment.'

Nadya scoffed. 'When you have finally abandoned your

hopes, let me know and I will put an order through for you.'

Alice smiled engagingly at Nadya. 'That's awfully kind of you, Nadya.'

Nadya grunted. 'What is your problem with onions?'

'My problem is there aren't any. And quite honestly I don't know how anyone can cook without them!'

'Communism,' murmured Harold without looking up, 'is the electrification of the whole country, plus onions.'

'Did you try the D?'

'Did I try the which?'

'The D Gastronom. D for diplomat. Diplomats only. Has George not told you about the D Gastronom?' Now Nadya smiled a winning smile.

'I'm sure he must have done,' said Alice, returning it sweetly, 'but I've forgotten. Is George also a diplomat these days?'

Nadya turned to Harold. 'So, Harold. Alice must absolutely go to the D. I will take her. We have run out of coffee. And there is no more vodka,' she added pointedly. She turned to Alice. 'We will go straight away, yes? It is just now open. Sasha will take us. To carry the shopping.'

Nadya grasped Alice by the elbow and raised her to her feet. Why, thought Alice, did she always make her feel like a child? Nadya leaned across George's desk and withdrew from a drawer a small printed booklet. She riffled its pages at Alice. 'The coupons,' she said.

Alice was rapidly being hustled towards the door of the office with Nadya pulling a black fur coat hurriedly up around herself.

''Bye, Harold,' she called back over her shoulder. 'Nice to see you.'

Harold looked up, startled. 'What? Where are you all of to in such a rush?'

'Shopping, Harold,' Nadya soothed. 'We shall be back in

177

the shake of one lamb's tail.' She bared her teeth at Alice.

The forecourt of the D Gastronom was packed with Western cars with foreigners' licence plates. That much Alice expected. What she was surprised to see was how many of those plates were the yellow-background M and K plates of the businessman – the *marchand* – and correspondent. Nadya had explained to her in the car that Ds were issued only to embassies and their staff. Better stocked than the other two Beriozkas, the Gastronom also sold alcohol and cigarettes at duty free prices. This was the reason non-diplomats were not allowed to shop there. Alice noted that the ruling had the added benefit of enforcing a divide and rule system between the foreigners almost as provocative as that imposed between foreigners and the Soviets. Before she had even assessed the merchandise Alice was offended that those already privileged with commissariats, protected mail bags and waived import fees should have the added advantage of superior shopping. And according to Nadya, who reported it with the relish of a Westerner indulging in mildly provocative anti-Soviet behaviour, there were diplomats who apparently also took extreme offence at finding their civilian neighbours using the shop.

Notwithstanding all this fascinating information, Nadya had been vague on the question of George's source for the coupons.

Sasha turned off the engine. Nadya stepped out and held her seat forward for Alice, who had travelled in the back. Alice sat silent for a moment as the heat quickly dissipated. Her hope that spring might be on its way had been premature. In the night there had been a relentless snowstorm which still had not let up. She watched as the snow whipped across the bonnet of the car and the flakes buttoned into water drops as they touched the hot metal.

'Alice, are you coming?'

Alice gathered up her handbag and braced herself for the

cold. Nadya stepped confidently past the overalled attendant seated inside the door and Alice followed with a certain trepidation. Would she be recognized as an interloper and thrown out? The attendant glanced at her without interest. He was presumably positioned to bar the way only to intrepid or uninformed Soviets.

She stared into the chill cabinets in disbelief. Here, finally, was the produce of the Soviet empire and its satellites. Inside lay boxes of frozen octopus from Cuba, bags of chopped pineapple from Vietnam, French beans, strawberries and blackcurrants from Poland, whole fish of considerable size and unfamiliar colouring from the Baltic. On the shelf above were luridly illustrated tins of papaya juice, stewed guava, and pureed mango, their contents described incomprehensibly in loosely knitted script. There were even little packets of frozen prawns from Cambodia. These she fell upon, flinging them one after another into the shopping cart.

'Excuse me,' said Nadya. 'We have only fifty dollars in the booklet, Alice.'

'Oh,' said Alice in dismay. To have come upon this hoard of treats and then be set a limit on their purchase! She straightened up and pushed the trolley towards the meat counter.

Laid out in neat rows, trussed roasts of beef, pork tenderloins, sweetbreads and brains glistened under plastic wrap. It was a shame she didn't like sweetbreads and brains. She was reluctant to turn down anything she hadn't seen on sale before except, less appealingly, as components of the cleaved animal heads laid like tributes to Salome along the counters of the free markets. She picked up a roast. It was larger than those sometimes on sale at the regular Beriozkas; clearly diplomats cooked for greater numbers. It was also more expensive. She put it back, and moved on.

In the small vegetable and fruit section were the same cucumbers, wrapped in threes, that she no longer could think what to do with, and the cabbages, carrots and potatoes of every Soviet store. The difference was that here the quality was markedly higher, the root vegetables washed clean of soil, and firm to the touch.

What was apparent after two careful sweeps of her eyes across the display was that there were no onions. So: not even at the exclusive, excluding Diplomats' Gastronom were onions available. Alice could only conclude that, with the possible exception of stocks at the secret Kremlin shops and the warmer garden plots down near the Turkish border, there wasn't a single onion to be had anywhere in the entire Soviet Union.

But what caught her eye were bags of limes tumbled into the fruit compartment next to the dried plums and yielding yellow apples the Beriozkas also stocked. There had been no lemons in Moscow for weeks. When the visiting foreign editor of a major American newspaper had recently been given a dinner by his Moscow bureau chief, he had looked with awe at the heaped bowl in the centre of the table and enthused, 'Where did you get that caviare!' The rest of the table, Moscow residents, had exclaimed, even more impressed, 'Where did you get those lemons!' George would be delighted with the limes.

The dairy cabinet yielded even greater treats: between the cartons of sour cream, the packets of sweetened curd cheese, were cling-wrapped slabs of something called 'Rokfor'. Alice picked up a lump and examined it with interest. The lines of blue that dissected the pale cheese rang disconcertingly parallel.

'There was a trade agreement once with the Italians,' said Nadya. 'They came to teach us how to manufacture cheese.'

'The mind boggles,' said Alice.

'When they left, they left us with Rokfor.'

'That well-known Italian *formaggio*.'

'Actually, I like better this one. It absolutely does not smell.' Nadya picked out a piece of orange cheese from the section labelled 'Russian Dutch-type'.

Alice looked at it doubtfully. 'Personally, I find Dutch Dutch-type tasteless enough. Do you realize, half an hour ago I'd never have thought I could get blasé about cheese! It's amazing to find any at all. Right,' she said decisively. 'I shall go for the Russian–Italian–French type.' She tossed it merrily into the trolley. This was a most gratifying shopping spree!

There was little else worth taking from the shelves but some Finnish tomato ketchup and chocolate covered bisuits that would thrill Harriet. Nadya collected four bottles of vodka, some instant coffee and a carton of Marlboro and they pushed their cart to the check-out. At the head of the queue was a young man with his hair pulled back into a ponytail, standing by a trolley laden with cardboard crates of beer. He was patting his pockets in some agitation. The dour, grey-faced woman seated at the cash register stared implacably ahead with her hand stuck out towards him.

'So. You have lost your coupons, Chuck?' said Nadya. 'Chuck is cameraman for American Television Network,' she informed Alice. 'This is the wife of George: Alice.'

'Hi there,' said Chuck, briefly glancing up. 'I guess they're somewhere hereabouts.' He started on the inside flaps of an open leather bomber jacket. The white t-shirt underneath it read 'What's a nice guy like me doing in a place like this?' A lock of lank blond hair fell into his eyes as he stooped to unzip another pocket down by the knee of his jeans. 'Shit, here it is.' He flourished a plastic accordion wallet that unwound itself like a conjuror's card trick on to the counter.

'Coupons,' snapped the check-out woman.

Chuck licked his thumb and flicked off assorted coloured

money vouchers. 'Say, if you guys are free, Ned is throwing a farewell party tonight for Abel. He's being posted to Brussels, poor sucker.'

Alice was astonished. 'But Brussels is a wonderful place to live!'

'Not if it means moving from the headline news to a slot just before the sports.' He hoisted the beers back into the trolley. 'Oh boy. I have to get this hooch home. Catch you later, OK? Eight thirty, nine. Sad Sam. Ned's place.'

Nadya pushed the trolley to the back of the queue and Alice found herself eye to eye with Babs. Her heart gave a jolt. Then she thought, dammit, we have a right to decent food, too.

'Hello, Babs,' she said breezily. 'Not one of your work days?'

'Why, Alice! Fancy seeing you here!'

To Alice's gratification, it was Babs who blushed.

Babs hovered close and lowered her voice. 'I really should have thought, Alice. I *am* sorry. I ought to have got you some Ds. But then,' she added brightly, 'you've obviously found someone who has, haven't you?'

'So it seems. Nadya is my coupon queen,' Alice said with immense satisfaction. 'Do you know Nadya, Babs? Harold Armitage's wife. From George's office? Nadya is in charge of the Ds, aren't you, Nadya?'

Nadya extended her hand and smiled without speaking. Babs was taken aback. Surely Nadya was Russian? What business did she have with coupons? Babs turned red again.

'Well!' she chirruped. 'We must organize to shop for each other then, if we're going to be using the same places.'

'Except, of course, I'm persona non grata at the Commissariat.' Alice spoke with a fixed smile, and at once felt ashamed of herself.

'Ah. Yes. That is a problem.' Babs rocked her trolley back and forth distractedly. 'Well, I don't know. Maybe there's some way we can arrange things. Now and then. Informally, as it were.'

Alice relented. Babs looked very uncomfortable. 'Actually, Babs, don't worry. I think we're doing all right. We're not quite at death's door. Yet. Maybe in an emergency.' Ahead of her the two gold-braceleted men in Gucci shoes and tasselled checkered cloths wrapped over their heads had packed their bottles of violet liqueur and eggnog into boxes and were shouldering them towards the door. Nadya pulled the trolley forward and began unloading Alice's supplies. A truce was necessary before they left the shop. 'Why don't you pop by for coffee and a natter?'

Babs smiled, relieved. 'I'd like that. I'm usually free now I've lost my job.'

'Oh, Babs. You haven't! That's too bad. What happened?'

'The school principal sat next to Lisa Prowse at dinner the other night, and discovered Lisa's a full-blooded computer expert.'

'Lisa pinched your job? What a rotten thing to do! And pretty short-sighted, if you ask me. This community's much too small for anything so underhand.'

'It's not really her fault. The principal tactfully suggested that the better interests of the children would be served if they were instructed by someone who does actually know what they're doing.' She sighed. 'It's probably no bad thing. Life's been a bit frenzied recently. Jonty's got a trade delegation over and I've been feeding them practically every night. But yes, I will drop in when I can.

'In point of fact' – Alice fixed Babs with a decisive look – 'I've been meaning to have a word with you about Hazel.'

Babs groaned. 'Hazel?'

Alice nodded and tapped her forehead. 'Nuts.'

Nadya looked from one to the other. '*Arekh*, by the way,' she said.

'*Arekh*?' Alice was puzzled.

'Absolutely. Hazel nuts. You said. Now is not the season. Not even at the D.'

Alice and Babs exchanged glances, and broke into adolescent giggles, Alice clutching Nadya's wrist to include her in the merriment. Ah! how gratifying, how unifying were the humble misapprehensions of foreigners!

Chapter Sixteen

Sad Sam was not an unhappy American. It was the Moscow Westerners' abbreviation for the most popular, most desirable of the foreigners' compounds, at 12/14 Sadovoye Samotechnaya, on the northern arc of the Koltso.

Built by German prisoners of war, Sad Sam was a compact nine-storeyed block of comparatively few flats, each one with rooms of large and airy proportions, their high ceilings, detailed mouldings and French doors leading into the main reception rooms a muted reminder of apartments in Paris or Rome. On one side, balconies overlooked a small courtyard that in winter was flooded by the *dvornik* to form an ice rink for the children of the compound. The balconies were judged more picturesque than practical since the day a Japanese correspondent stepped out on to his and dropped with it several floors to the ground below. At the front, the windows opened on to the Koltso, except that where there were families with children they generally remain firmly closed against the grey smog of petrol fumes that belched up from the eight lanes of heavy traffic pounding relentlessly past the building. Added to the fear in every mother's mind of coping with accidents or serious illness in a city with neither a steady supply of antibiotics nor modern medical equipment was the conviction of Sad Sam mothers that their children were the unwitting victims of lead poisoning.

Nevertheless, most foreigners who did not live in the compound would give their eye teeth for a Sad Sam apartment.

Alice pulled up past the sentrybox that guarded the side street entrance. There was nowhere to park. Volvos crouched bumper to bumper with Ford Sierras, Mercedes and Saabs under smooth blankets of snow. The only gap on this half of the street was filled by a small mountain of ice chippings that had been cleared like the fat off jellied stock from the pavement and road. She was too late to expect to park this close.

Still, she might not have come at all. When she had rung Svetlana to ask her to babysit, her mother had answered the telephone at first ring, her voice tight with anxiety. Svetlana had not come home from work the night before, and she had not heard from her all day. She was at a loss as to what to do. There was nothing Alice could suggest. Did one not call the police to report people missing? Ha! scoffed Svetlana's mother. It was most likely the police who had detained her. Embarrassed at her own tactless stupidity, Alice quickly rang off.

She telephoned an American nanny based in Kutuzovsky whom Lisa Prowse said she had used once or twice.

Yes, the girl ventured tentatively, she was free that evening. Where did the Masons live? Alice gave the address and there was a long pause while the girl digested the information. Was this by any chance the apartment opposite the one where Hazel Amstrutther was nanny? That's right, responded Alice. In that case, said the girl, she was certainly not free to babysit. Not that evening, or any other. And put the phone down.

Alice was astounded. The girl had sounded quite indignant. Yet it was Alice who felt indignation now. What could she possibly have objected to? Still, there wasn't time to think about it. It was getting late and if she wanted to go to Abel's farewell party – which, with George undoubtedly dancing the tango in Irkutsk in the arms of Myra Drewsbarr, she had set her mind upon going – she had better organize a sitter fast. She dialled the number of the nanny who looked after Harriet's playgroup friend, Ben.

The girl sounded embarrassed. 'I'm sorry, Mrs Mason. I really would like to look after Hattie. But I can't.'

'You're busy. What a shame. Ah well, it can't be helped. Another time, perhaps.'

'No, Mrs Mason. Not another time. I'm sorry.'

'Oh, won't the Northiams let you sit for other people?'

'It's not that.' The girl paused, then in a rush blurted out, 'It's just that I really only want to go to families where I know I'll feel comfortable.'

Alice glanced round at their sitting-room, astonished. 'Good heavens! I don't think our flat is that bad, is it?'

'Oh, Mrs Mason!' cried the nanny. She sounded quite desperate. 'You don't understand. I must listen to what my heart tells me.'

'But of course!' agreed Alice, relieved. 'If you want to bring a boyfriend with you, that's perfectly all right. As long as I can have your word, naturally, there'll be no, well, improper behaviour. No problem.'

'No, no, Mrs Mason,' the girl insisted. 'That isn't it at all.' Her anguish was palpable. 'I can't come, Mrs Mason. I'm a practising Christian.'

'So are we,' Alice protested, now utterly bewildered. 'More or less.' But the line had already gone dead.

In the end she had prevailed upon Galina to stay on, for the promise of payment in dollars so long as she didn't tell George.

It was not until she was on the Koltso on her way to the party that she had had time to wonder why it was that the two girls had refused to babysit. As soon as she put her mind to it, she had realized with the absolute certainty that cleans the brain that Hazel and her note were responsible. The Masons had been blacklisted by a bunch of Bible-punching nannies.

She found a parking space just beyond the shrouded bakery where the foreign cars gave way to the Zhigulis and Volgas of Russian residents. The militiaman on guard outside the unfamiliar embassy lodged in the end of the row stirred himself and turned to watch her as she slithered down the street clutching at the rough stucco walls of the old houses to steady herself on the ice. At the Sad Sam entrance the sentry peered out at her through the slit in his mili-box and made a note in his book. Alice kept her face turned steadfastly to the front and passed through the tunnel that opened into the courtyard. Here she paused for a moment by the dim light of a bulb fixed to the wall above her head and checked the scrap of paper she held. 1st entrance, 6th floor, she read. As she mounted the steps to the lobby, she could hear the sounds of party echoing down the stairwell. The *dezhournaya* was sitting in her room, door wide open, eyes fixed upon the entrance, knitting. She stared at Alice as she passed by, her needles clicking steadily on.

Alice leaned with her finger on the lift button and her head tilted back to gaze upwards through the wrought iron banisters at the undersides of the stone stairs winding round to the top of the cavernous building. Who was Myra Drewsbarr? Why had Harold been so evasive with his answers? Or had it only seemed so to Alice? She chided herself that she was surely seeing spectres where none lurked. And yet there had been Nadya's ill-concealed (or deliberately displayed?) smirking to consider.

The thump of the lift startled her out of her trance. As she grasped the outer iron grill, it was flung violently back from inside and a figure shrouded in a white sheet tumbled out against her.

'Whooooaaah!' it shrieked, raising its arms at her and flapping by. 'Alice, Alice,' its voice quavered, 'your time is near!'

Alice stepped in and the box lift rumbled slowly upwards. It jolted to a halt on the sixth floor. At once the doors were wrenched apart from the outside and arms reached in to pull Alice roughly out. Alice, her hand through her coat yanking at her bra to thrust her cleavage more provocatively into the V of the shirt, was unprepared for this intrusion into her private adjustments. But the mêlée was not focused upon Alice. The confusion of people pushed past her into the lift, and with a clattering of doors disappeared back downwards. Alice was left standing alone to face the gaping entrance to Ned's apartment. She drew a breath, rolled her glossed lips together, tweaked her jeans out of the crack in her bottom, and strode into the flat.

The way was almost completely blocked by rows of boots puddling melting snow on to the parquet. Alice put her plastic bag on the floor and drew out her tan leather boots. Wrenching off her outdoor pair, she toppled slightly and her foot set down on a lump of ice. The sudden chill sent her tottering headlong into the coats. All she needed now, she reflected, was to spill drink down her shirt. She bent to tuck the legs of her jeans into her boots, congratulating herself on having had the resolve to come at all, and peered tentatively into the large room where the party seemed to be focused.

Inside the doorway Alice eased into the press of bodies leaning along the bookcases. People clutching beer cans and shovelling imported cocktail nuts shouted hoarsely above a bullying beat that had drawn a swirl of dancers to the middle of the room. Alice stared at them, impressed. She had never seen such energetic ferocity of movement except in American teen films of the 50s. The women were being yanked sharply into their partners' chests then propelled away with a forceful shove while the men stood almost immobile, knees bent, toes swivelling parallel to left and right, working the women like human yoyos. They twirled back into the haven of their partners' embrace, only to be picked up and thrown into the air, or slid down low between open legs.

At the far side of the room Alice caught sight of Nadya. She was standing with her back to Charlie Prowse, talking animatedly to a bearded individual Alice recognised as the radio man who went around telling everyone 'Today Scandinavia, tomorrow the world'. She would avoid him. What was his name? As she was searching for it, Charlie suddenly flashed his hand out behind him and pinched Nadya's bottom. Surely not. Alice must have been mistaken.

'Alice Mason. Greetings. And where is your admirable husband?'

Alice turned. The Egyptian Ambassador was standing beside her, smiling gently. He was wearing a pale grey sweatshirt with 'Harvard' emblazoned across the chest and the sleeves pushed high up his arms. Alice registered sleek dark hairs lapping round the thin gold watch on his wrist and the thickening of muscles where the sweatshirt hung loosely on his neck. Golly, was he a dish. Alice couldn't think what to say to him.

'George? He's in Siberia.' She laughed for some reason.

'Siberia? He is fortunate. I should very much like to see the tundra. I imagine it in my mind like our Egyptian desert, but covered in snow. I fear this is too simple a picture.'

Alice grinned inanely. The way he rolled his tongue round his rs was delicious.

'We shall invite you to brunch when George returns and Fatma returns and he will tell us how it is in reality. I think brunch in Moscow is a good idea, no? This I have decided will be our new form of informal entertainment. I feel we shall be able to talk more freely in a completely relaxed atmosphere.'

Alice wondered what kind of complex casual dress it would entail, 'Where is Fatma?'

He lifted his shoulders lightly and the sweatshirt looped forwards at his throat revealing the fact that despite the weather outside, it was all he had on. 'Shopping,' he said with an amused smile. 'In Paris. She tells me she needs new clothes.'

For the brunches, thought Alice.

'Lucky her.'

'It is necessary, I think, to get out of Moscow every few months, don't you agree? To recharge the batteries.' Lightly he touched Alice's shoulder. 'I will get her to call you when she comes back.' And, still smiling gently, he slid away. Alice felt her face burn and leaned back against the books, slowly expelling a very deep breath.

Hardly had it left her body than she was being pulled downwards and into a thick hedge of crisp moustache. 'Alice, *agapi mou*! Stop standing on tiptoe. I can't reach you.'

Alice threw her arms out and around in an embrace of relief and release.

'I'm not. You're just getting even shorter. How are you, Panayiotis? And why didn't we see you at the Ambo's last week?'

'Koritzakimou, it is not the place for humble press councillors to attend the private dinners of their ambassadors. I hope you both enjoyed our simple Greek hospitality?'

'Simple, my foot. Your Ambassador's residence is one of the most glorious in Moscow, and the food the same. Hard to believe we were behind the Iron Curtain. Except I've never had food that hot in Greece.'

'I am amused by the Soviet penchant for giving those

nations most active as empires – even in the far historical past – the most lavish of the old czarist palaces.' He took her elbow. 'Alice, you don't have a drink. And nor do I. Come. Ned has it stashed in the kitchen. With plates of the ubiquitous fried piroshki. I hope you ate before you came out.'

Panayiotis propelled her ahead of him along the corridor to the kitchen. Coming towards them was a figure enveloped in a black cloak, the collar of which rose well above his ears. Protruding from his neck was a plastic dagger dripping static blood.

'Kurt!' Panayiotis clapped his hands together with delight. 'Don't tell me: you're a kebab. I think it suits you.'

The man smiled wanly and eased by them without comment.

'Who's Kurt?'

'The German military attaché. A very astute individual. But he has a weakness for dressing up at any opportunity. He goes running with the Hash House Harriers in a King Kong costume. It must be very sweaty.'

In the kitchen, Ned was standing on the table tossing cans of beer from the open fridge at the arms waving up at him like pond weed.

'Hello, Pano.' The voice was gloomy. 'Alice. You here?'

Alice turned. Winston Fitch stood behind her looking slightly dishevelled and extremely hot in a tweed jacket over a Fair Isle jumper. 'You are without refreshment, Alice.' He handed her a dripping can of cold beer. 'You can get your own, Panayiotis.'

'Ah, the perfect English gentleman.'

Winston slid into the space Panayiotis left. 'George not here? I hope to God he isn't filing. I am not in the mood to have to go and check the wires myself to see what he's up to. This week has been too long as it is.'

'Of course not. No Sunday paper. Anyway, he's in

deepest Siberia. I don't expect I shall ever see him again.'

'No, I shouldn't think you will.' He patted his forehead with a folded handkerchief. 'Dear Siberia! I have fond memories of watching the same shipment of radios and tape-recorders being taken of our train in each village before we were allowed on to the platform. Then, of course, last thing before the train left, we would see it all safely packed on board again. Such sublime innocents they must think us. Every stop they had an appalling pitched battle to keep the villagers from breaking into the shops as we moved on, trying actually to buy these fabled luxuries.'

'Sounds like wonderful copy.'

'My finest,' Winston agreed gloomily. 'But the subs cut every bit of it out. Thought I'd made it up. 'Twas ever thus.' He raised his beer can at her. 'My respects. I must transport myself to where the music that calms the troubled breast doth flow before my soul sinks too deep.'

He bowed and backed away, knocking obliviously into people coming into the room as he faded out of it.

Alice waited a moment, then followed him. She thought she might try to find Nadya. And was Harold here too? Ahead she spotted Lisa Prowse looking about distractedly, an unlit cigarette in her hand, and homed in on her gratefully.

'*Privyet.*' Lisa offered the Russian greeting. She flourished the cigarette. 'You don't, do you? No, I thought not. Drat. Charlie's got my lighter and I don't know where he's gone. Hang on there a sec. I have to get this thing going. Medical emergency. Be right back.'

Alice propped herself up against the wall and considered the fact that neither Charlie nor Winston were alongside George in Siberia to keep a check on his activities.

Lisa bobbed up at Alice's shoulder, running a heavily ringed hand through her stubbled hair. She was wearing a long black tunic threaded with silver over yet more baggy

Turkish trousers. She drew deeply on her cigarette, closed her eyes with satisfaction and then let the smoke trail slowly out of her nostrils.

'Sheesh, have I had a day and a half! It never rains in this place but it pours!'

'What happened?'

Lisa sighed. 'Oh, you know how it is. In real world terms, not a lot. In Moscow terms, the sky fell in.' She tapped the ash of her cigarette into her cupped palm and winced. 'First some woman rings me up to accuse me of having stolen her job.' Alice felt her cheeks tingle. 'God knows who she was, she was almost incoherent. I mean, I didn't know anyone had had the job before me. The school principal gave me the very firm impression they wanted me to set up a computer course because the school had never had one. So what this harpy had been up to if she did have the job heaven knows!' She took another drag on her cigarette. 'Then, when I stagger home, my nanny decides to inform me she is in love! Can you beat it? Too much.'

Alice frowned. 'What's the problem with that?'

'Ha! In the usual way, nothing. Only nannies in Moscow don't seem to go the usual way, do they?' Alice silently agreed. 'This nanny hasn't fallen for a marine. She hasn't even fallen for a Soviet dissident, God help me. Ho no.' She sucked at the cigarette and then blew the smoke out firecely, funnelling it towards the cigarette's tip and making its embers glow. 'No, my nanny has taken it into her head to fall in love with me.'

Alice stared at her, her mouth slack. 'Your nanny is in love with you?'

'Yup. Poor benighted kid. Charlie, of course, is hugely understanding. He says it's because she's sex-starved. All of them are. He says they all want rogering rotten. And doubtless he'd be only to happy to oblige. God knows what I'm supposed to do. If I sack her, I'll have to fly back to the

UK to find another one. I can't do that now, not with this new job. Besides, the kids adore her.'

'And I thought I had nanny problems.'

'You? You haven't got a nanny.'

'No, but it appears George and I have been blacklisted by a group of God-fearing au pairs who've decided we're in the clutches of the devil.'

'What, you and George? You're kidding.'

Alice felt rather offended. 'Actually,' she said, needing to impress. 'It's the nanny of the woman who bawled you out on the phone. They live opposite.'

'I see. My guilt goes before me, does it? Well, I suppose if you're living with a fruitcake like that, some is bound to rub off. So tell me. How is your evil manifesting itself? George boiling the baby? Or is his head taking three hundred and sixty-degree spins?'

Alice flushed. 'It's just a silly misunderstanding. I'm sure it'll get sorted out.'

Lisa nodded sympathetically. 'The ostrich in the sand approach. It's what I'm going to try for, too.'

Alice was about to protest when someone pushed by in a scarlet cloak with a basket over one arm. Alice's beer can was jostled and a gob of liquid flew out of the opening and down her shirt.

'Hoy!' she cried, and the person revolved.

Staring into her face through a pair of lensless spectacles was the hideous visage of someone whose corrugated skin had been heavily coated in white greasepaint then dabbed violently with scarlet on either cheek. Clumps of wiry grey hair protruded from under a red-spotted scarf. The figure bobbed a deep curtsey, plucking at a wide skirt of blue and white checks, and proffered a basket of dewy beer cans. With a leering grin and grating voice it said: 'Daily Mirror on the wall, who's the smartest scribe of all? Take a drink, my dear. It won't poison you. This time.'

Alice shrieked. 'Abel! You ghoul!'

'You look better than I've seen you for a long time, Abel,' observed Lisa.

'My favourite fan,' said Abel, pursing purple-painted lips at her. 'I shall miss you too, Lisa dear.'

'When do you leave?'

'How I count the minutes! Ere these revelries are ended, to be precise. I mount my trusty, tax free personal model of the newest Mercedes, and drive into the night towards Finland and freedom!' He punched the air with a clenched fist and once more knocked Alice's beer with his basket.

Ned squeezed through the crush and reached in for Abel's arm. Mounting the coffee table that had been dragged into the centre of the room, he drew Abel up after him.

'Toverichi! Sad occasion. This is positively the last appearance together in town of my humble self, your servant Karl Marx, and my esteemed comrade, Mr Freiderich Engels. Hey Freddy, put that stupid basket down and get your butt up here. It gives me grief to tell you all that no longer young, hopelessly bald Friedrich here is on the point of abandoning our glorious socialist experiment. He has been seduced by' – knowing chortles – 'no, friends. This is a clean party. He has been seduced by the promises of the Pepsi generation. Freddy is . . . Going West.'

The crowd booed and Ned poked Abel in the chest, causing him to totter briefly back towards the edge of the table. 'I said to him, Freddy, I said. What they've got, we've got. In principle. This, as we all know, is the name of a fine town in Siberia.' There were sniggers. 'Pepsi already we have. For this you do not need to go west, young man. So tell your friends, Friedrich. Please. What have you got against Soviet Pepsi? In its cloying, rotting sweetness, in the vacant promise of its bubbles, is it not every bit as undrinkable as capitalist Pepsi?'

'Actually, Karl,' said Abel, 'I want Coke.'

Ned flung one arm round his shoulders and slammed his other hand over Abel's mouth. 'This is not a Hollywood dinner party, Freddy. Keep your addictions to yourself!'

'Karl. Dear Karl. You should understand, Communism is dead. Coke is life. I know this. It says so on American television.'

Ned held him away from him and peered into his face. 'My friend, I fear you misjudge the times we live in. Here, comrade, is life. Together you and I – with a little assistance, of course, from Vladimir Ilyich Lenin – opened the way to socialism.'

'And closed all the borders.'

'Communism, Freddy, is the electrification of the whole country.'

'And no light bulbs.'

'We have brought the people literacy.'

'And banned half the books.'

'We have established sexual equality.'

'But no birth control.'

The women in the audience whistled and clapped.

'We brought them nuclear weapons.'

'But no domestic appliances.'

'We brought them—'

Now Abel put his hand over Ned's mouth. 'Karl. My friend. All I am asking is a nice drink!'

Ned swung round to the audience, his arms spread. 'First he wants coke, now he wants a nice drink!' He turned back to Abel. 'So what's wrong with vodka?'

'I can't find any.'

Ned turned front again. 'Next he'll be wanting avocado pears!'

More whistles followed. Ned brought Abel close in an embrace and clutched his chin in his fist. 'You know what awaits you in the West? Cholesterol overload!'

'Go, Freddy!' shouted someone close to Alice.

'Freddy, my friend,' Ned continued. 'Your body is not accustomed to anything but thin soup and cabbage. What will happen to it when you feed it a juicy T-bone steak?' He stared round the room. 'Cooked medium rare with a side order of fries and a pile of onion rings?'

'Torment!' cried a voice.

'Or a cheeseburger with bacon and pickle?' said Ned.

'Stop it! Stop it!' groaned another.

'Shrimp salad sandwich on toasted rye, with melted Swiss?'

'Broiled lobster!'

'Grilled kippers!'

'Enchiladas!'

'Or take barbecued ribs!' continued Ned relentlessly.

'You bet!' shouted the audience. 'We'll take barbecued ribs!'

Ned slapped Abel on the back. 'Friedrich. Hear it from us. We have eaten at McDonald's. What is good for your stomach is a bowl of bortsch and a simple glass of water. So, please. No more of this nice drinks nonsense. Times are changing. Of course Soviets must learn to stand on their own two feet. But they are not supposed to use them to walk out through Passport Control.'

'They will prefer to lie flat on their backs in the snow.'

Ned pushed Abel away from him. 'What is it with the anti-social wisecracks, Freddy? Where do you think this is?'

With one voice the audience dutifully chorused, 'Upper Volta with rockets!'

The familiar punch line having been achieved, the audience relaxed and waited. Ned coughed into his fist and drew himself up. In his normal voice he said, 'Abel Kaufmann, a man with three years in Moscow to his discredit, whose perceptive reports of this confusing period have become required viewing in his mother's sewing circle, take your crackling microphone, the pens you've stolen from me, your terrible jokes, and get you gone to Brussels.' He embraced Abel for the last time. 'We're gonna miss you, you jerk,' he said softly.

At once people rose to their feet to reach for him. Abel held up his hand. 'You'll be glad to hear I'm fresh out of jokes. Local *defitzit*, I guess.' He pinched his nose tightly and blinked at his audience. 'In fact, I'm really going to miss this goddam place' – he looked up at the ceiling – 'did you get that, you guys? It's been the best. And not least for all the good friends I've made, the support you've all given me, through good times and bad, bad, bad! Let's keep in touch. And come and see me on the other side, OK?'

He held up his hand again before the crowd could cheer.

'While the boys upstairs are still tuned in, I'd like to pass along a message.' He stared fixedly up at the ceiling. 'Would you please send my heartfelt thanks to the militia-man in Kutz who had the courtesy to telephone the maid when I was – how shall I put it? – engaged in undiplomatic negotiations' – there were knowing snorts – 'with a certain very lovely diplomatic lady, to warn me her husband had just driven into the compound. I really appreciate it, boys.'

Yelps of approval broke out around him. Then he jumped from the table into the press of people who pushed closer to embrace him. Alice, sitting back against the sofa, was moved. She didn't know Abel well, but she would miss him all the same. The departure of a comrade from behind the wires was unsettling.

Suddenly Abel was raised aloft, borne above the crowd on the shoulders of the laughing young cameraman Alice had met at the Beriozka. Abel spread his arms wide, his awful basket swinging.

'Tovarichi!' he called out. 'Who is ready for a last dance with the brightest and the best of the world's brightest and best?'

He jumped from the cameraman's shoulders and was surrounded, people pushing up behind him and linking arms. Alice was grabbed around the waist and pulled into the circle. Then it broke into a chain and began to conga. With whoops and yells the party left the flat and made its way towards the freezing compound outside. Briefly Alice thought she heard the lonely wail of bagpipes far ahead of her. Anything was possible.

In the courtyard Abel was attempting to dance a Scottish reel with Lisa on the tiny iced-over skating rink. Here the noise of bagpipes was clear. Slowly the party moved off towards the sentrybox and into the street beyond. As they passed by the militiaman on duty, he suddenly clicked his heels together and sliced his hand up to his hat in salute. He stood there rigid, holding his pose, and smiling broadly until the whole column had gone by. The dancing snake turned in a wide loop to rumba back into the compound and up the stairs, Abel tossing unopened beer cans from his basket at the grinning sentry as he passed.

In the confusion that tumbled into Ned's apartment Alice was kicked sharply in the ankle. She fell back in pain, stumbling slightly, into the curtained alcove where the freezer stood, throwing her arms wide to steady herself. To her surprise she felt through the material the shape of what seemed to be someone's back. She stepped away and the curtain fell slack again. There was no sign that anyone was standing behind it. She must have imagined it. Overcome with curiosity, she carefully edged the curtain minutely aside.

Standing in the shadows, his trousers held up around his bare buttocks by someone straddled upon the freezer, was

Charlie Prowse, his face now turned towards Alice, pinched in the anguish of enjoyment. In shock Alice flapped the curtain and light fell on to the freezer. The woman in control of Charlie's trousers was Nadya.

Chapter Seventeen

George returned to life in Moscow with a sense of deflation. Out in the wilds of Siberia he had heard tales of long, long winters stretching relentlessly into the middle of the year, of deep, deep cold so specific and vicious that the water on the eyeballs could freeze. He had learned from stout, raw-skinned, jovial women of methods of pickling, and smoking, and drying to preserve precious foodstuffs for the interminable haul from brief autumn to briefer spring. He had spent long evenings in fur-trappers' cabins heated to the temperature of sauna baths where the stale air swilled with the sweet, oily, private smell of iced vodka. He had flung it repeatedly at his shocked tonsils, tasting it later on his lips as he staggered up the steps of his hotel near dawn. His hot mouth had tingled from contact with the frozen cheeks of young women under tickling fur hats who, giggling, reached for the pressmen as they lurched back on to their train. He had slipped on snowshoes across drifts as fathomless as the ocean, watched red-veined hunters set their snares among silver-peeled trees, and seen his own urine rise horrifyingly, predatorially, to meet him in a frozen yellow arc.

Ah, the pleasure! The sense of mischief as he plotted his next attempt to give the harassed Foreign Ministry minders the slip! How satisfying it all had been.

Here, back in the real world, as Harold insisted upon

calling it, George felt out of touch with life. He had dispensed mementoes to his family: a sable's tail for Alice (so she could say she owned a sable, ha ha), a small embroidered purse for Harriet, and a painted wooden rattle for Daisy that Alice at once removed for fear of lead poisoning. Then he had sat back to relish the anguish that welled inside him for the loss of Siberian purity and simplicity.

What did Foreign Ministry pronouncements upon OPEC price rises and 'deliberate American provocations' off the Libyan coast have to do with those stalwart citizens out in the tundra eking out an existence at minus 45 degrees centigrade and only a few hours of daylight? Harold delicately pointed to the stalwart citizens of Moscow. What of them?

What indeed, thought George, alert to his new perceptions. What lack of sensitivity allowed the foreign community to throw extravagant parties with gourmet delicacies on printed menus and limbo dancing to follow, while beyond the steamed up windows the cabbage lorries lumbered by in the dark? Or glamorous masquerades with revellers dressed in exotic costume – or worse, in flippant mock of senior Soviet figures? George remembered with shame a fancy dress party he had enjoyed at the American Embassy. Three news cameramen in evening dress, red carnations and medals pinned to their tuxedos, their faces painted a deathly white and bodies framed by coffin-shaped boxes had, to hysterical approval – George's included – impersonated the three most recently dead leaders, Comrades Brezhnev, Andropov and Chernenko. Had they not prickled with remorse as the Soviet staff passed tight-lipped around the ballroom bearing trays of drinks, even if they were KGB employees? Did no-one feel any fellowship for the arthritic women with bulbous legs who would be beginning their day not so many hours after the revellers rolled home, doggedly setting out with limp string bags down dimly lit streets in search of supplies? George took modest comfort from the fact that another senior ambassador, attempting shortly before the arrival of a flood of guests to dismantle what he thought was a bug from the imposing fireplace in his residence, had wrenched away the wiring for the front-door bell and got stuck in the chimney. But it hardly redressed the balance.

When he voiced his outrage to Charlie Prowse, Charlie had shaken his head and said, 'What can you expect, comrade? If we're all going to be confined to quarters like boarding school children, you're bound to get midnight feasts in the dorm the moment the form monitor's back is turned. It's almost one's duty to show a little defiance, don't you think?'

George considered it, sympathized, and became even more dismayed. How could there ever be any genuine rapprochement between nations when individuals behaved like either oppressive petty bureaucrats or mildly delinquent schoolboys?

Then his romantic vision of the stalwart Soviet citizen took a sharp knock when he was called upon by several members of the press to join them in a formal complaint over the repeated harassment of Svetlana Kirilina by the KGB.

Agents had twice visited her at her flower shop to pull her in for questioning, so unnerving the shop manageress that the woman had asked Svetlana if she would please not return to her job. And the questions were spurious: why did she hate the motherland? She did not hate the motherland. Then why was she applying to leave? She was, as they were well aware, married to a citizen of the United States. Not unnaturally she wished to join him. What conspiracy against the motherland was she fomenting with the foreign correspondents in whose apartments she spent so much time? And so on.

What, wondered George, did it take to produce in people the lack of humanity and tenderness that seemed essential requirements in anyone desiring employment with Soviet officialdom? Once more Charlie volunteered the answer.

'Stalin,' he said simply.

Neither Nadya's nor Alice's behaviour smoothed George's rehabilitation. Nadya slid about the office with a secretive, supercilious smile plucking at her cheeks, while Alice had become transformed into a determinedly cheerful, breezily bossy district nurse figure, clapping her hands together to make bright announcements and pronouncements. Normal conversation seemed beyond her these days.

This was Alice's method for coping with life's daily demands while at the same time allowing her mind free range over the subject of Myra Drewsbarr. The woman was now hardly ever far from her thoughts, causing a pain so excruciating that the empty knocking inside went far beyond anything she had ever experienced from physical causes.

She attempted to unravel some cool lines of analyis from the tangle of her emotions. There were, finally, two crystal clear convictions that predominated above the continual heavy jolting of her heart and her general sense of loss: one, that this meant the end of any kind of trust in George, if not the end of their marriage; and second, that the entire suggestion that George might be having an affair was totally preposterous. When, for heaven's sake, did the man find time to run a second relationship? But then, she argued, in practical terms perhaps not so much time was necessary for the fundamentals that were the essence of an affair. Actual love-making never, after all, seemed to take more than a few minutes, except in films.

Assuming, though, that George did have another woman, what should Alice do about it? Her options ultimately came down to two: challenge George with her knowledge, or sit on it. Like the youngest son in a fairytale, journeying to seek his fortune and faced with regular forks in the road, Alice found that each step she considered led to two further choices. If she confronted George and he agreed to give up Myra Drewsbarr – what kind of a name was that anyway? – she would be forced, if she wanted to keep the family together, to accept the situation and try to establish some kind of foundation upon which to build a different future. Not easy to do within the confines and pressures of bugged apartments, bugged restaurants, and days in which every minute belonged to some other master. And if George insisted on keeping his houri going, Alice would simply have to up sticks and children and go back to England. Did she want that? How would she cope with divorceedom in a North London suburb and an ex-husband in foreign parts? Was that fair on the children? It felt a far bleaker prospect than living with the status quo.

The element in all this that Alice found hardest to deal with was that George seemed to her such an unlikely candidate for philandering. He was a steady, not to say conventional, man with an almost bureaucratic approach to life. Still, Moscow did funny things to people. Behaviour that would have made them blench back home became quite acceptable out here.

Alice's tormented analysis finally concluded thus: if George had a mistress, she was more a symptom of the peculiar nature of the Masons' living circumstances than a reflection upon their marriage. As long as she was not so important to George that he felt obliged to mention her, then Alice would not mention her either. Myra Drewsbarr (how *could* George fall for a woman called Myra Drewsbarr?) would occupy as little place in Alice's thoughts as Alice could control. Should it transpire – hope glimmered briefly – that she was no more than some random colleague George had elected not to introduce to Alice, nothing but wasted hours of emotional despair, exhaustion and frenzied tachycardia would be lost. Except that whatever, whoever, she was, George would certainly be made to pay. For having a life and leaving Alice out of it. For causing her this humiliation and this pain. At least she wouldn't be bothering with Suzie Sapmann's ridiculous book any more. She could give it back.

George, preoccupied with his own agony, was not inclined to step outside the comfort of his introspection to discover what was amiss with Alice. Yet it occurred to him with sudden horror in the office one morning that perhaps she had discovered she was waning under some incurable disease and this was her courage-in-the-face-of-adversity manner of dealing with the tragedy. It would be just like Alice to go down selflessly, a heroine to the end. Her way of taking her revenge on those who weren't noticing. But in the evening, having rushed through work to get home and delicately investigate this possibility, he was snapped at so unexpectedly for such a triviality – he would have picked his socks up eventually – that they had a row instead.

His drive between home and office became his refuge. Harriet would sit quietly in the back of the car, strapped into her child's seat and humming tunelessly. At times she murmured bizarre dialogues with herself which George, in lighter mood, would have enjoyed. But George was engaged tight-lipped in battle with the traffic. The daily confrontation helped to release the tension that was building in him.

The melt had begun, the snowbanks turned now a gloomy brown. They subsided further each day, loosening lumps that sagged into hollow caverns of slush and dripped into thick puddles of liquid mud that slicked the roads, concealing the potholes under a new camouflage. Every day Sasha, having received the car into his care and made his surruptitious note of the mileage that the *nachalnik* unfettered had achieved during his absence, would fill the windscreen bottle with fresh sudded water. Each truck that trundled ahead on the Koltso, jolting in and out of the silted crevasses, shovelled a continual stream of thick brown gravy at the windscreens of the machines that followed. Across the city drizzled a relentless ground-level spraying of diluted dirt. Muscovites in queues at bus stops reeled disgustedly backwards, shaking fists and shopping bags at cars which had cut too close into the moated curbs. Pedestrians, mud splats high up the backs of their legs, delicately skipped and hopped between glutinous gaps in the pavements. Only the elderly, the unvigilant or the deliberately uncaring plunged ankle deep in their plastic boots and shoes into the tacky sludge.

It smelled. This silt was stale. It carried with it the pulpy carcasses of rats and cats and dogs. And worse. Here and there a human body was rumoured to have languished, vodka-sodden, concealed by winter until the melt. Cigarette butts, previously discarded into snowbanks, blossomed on the pavement floor, *papirossi* tubes unfurling in the wet. The once pure fresh city looked foul, befouled, raw. Noble Siberian hunters, strangers to portable stereos but at one with nature, would surely never despoil the snows of their terrain with such casual lack of grace. At least, so thought George in his new and relished gloom.

The demands that awaited him from his employers and their array of editors were excessive. Unreasonable, in his opinion. The foreign desks required an overview of his trip, the features pages, individual subject pieces, and the *Sentinel* leader writers, briefing updates. Several telexes announced the women's page editor of the *Post* in urgentest need ex Myra Drewsbarr of separate thousand-word interviews with six fascinating Siberian females from different walks of life to run each day of a fanfared Week in the Lives of the Wonder Women of the Tundra. George thought the wonder would be in conjuring six different subjects from his imagination to fit the bill. Walks of life in the tundra, he had noted, had been considerably restricted by the nature of the environment and the sterling type of womanhood that had volunteered to tackle it. But: don't get it right, get it written, he reminded himself. The journalist's adage did not lift his mood of despair.

On his third day back in Moscow, a fearsome storm gathered in the ragged sky about the Kutz compound. As George watched from the office window, small gusts of wind began to lift pieces of rubbish from the great containers of waste and toss them carelessly across the car park. Then the sky suddenly turned purple and the wind swelled to an awesome force that bent the thin branches of the barren trees to tap upon the car roofs. George could see the enormous removal vans parked below him tremble and all at once the current of air began to rock the militia-man's sentrybox gently but firmly back and forth.

As he stared at it in fascination, the box took up a remorseless momentum of its own, left, right, left, right, thump, thump, swaying faster and faster, lower and lower to either side in a widening arc, till finally with a satisfying crash the box toppled on its side, the militiaman still in it.

George flung the window open wide and shouted exultantly up to the heavens, 'Do it again, God!' Then he left the office and went home to the flat.

He announced to Alice that he was retiring at once to bed. Furthermore, he would be taking the telephone by the bedside out of its jack, and if anyone required to speak to him, Alice was to inform them he was unavailable.

'What, everyone?'

'Everyone.'

'But what if the paper calls?'

'Tell them I'm sick.'

'Are you, George? You don't look it.'

'I feel it.'

'Would you like me to drive you to the embassy doctor?' Alice enquired doubtfully.

'No,' said George. 'I am simply going to bed. All I ask is to be left in peace.'

'Should I bring you some broth, or something?'

'No, Alice. Thank you. Just leave me alone. Please.'

Now Alice began to take George seriously. And to worry. George was not a man who courted solitude. Nor did he ever ignore his responsibilities. To the paper, at any rate. Something clearly was wrong with him. She bustled about the flat, plumping cushions, adjusting knick-knacks, straightening magazines, establishing order to counter-balance her mounting feeling of anxiety. She lost her temper unnecessarily with Harriet, then confused the child further by at once sweeping her into a penitent embrace. Galina had already left for the day. There was no-one but Alice to take Harriet's part.

'I tell you what, Hattie. Let's go out and see if we can buy Daddy a get well present. He's not feeling too bright. Perhaps we might cheer him up, do you think?'

Harriet nodded unconvinced and stuck her fingers into her mouth.

'Don't do that, sweetheart. You'll give yourself rabbit teeth.'

She bundled her into her snowsuit, swaddled Daisy, protesting, into her several layers and carry pouch, and tiptoed along the corridor to the bedroom. There was no sign of George, beyond a canyoned mound in the duvet. He had disappeared completely, protectively, suffocatingly, beneath it.

Alice led Harriet out of the compound into Serpuhovsky Val. It was quite dark now, the evening pierced along the boulevard by small violet beads of light high upon the lamp-stands. Then a tram rumbled up from Tulskaya, casting squares of amber glow across the muddy road.

'We should have put out wellies on, Hattie, shouldn't we? It's got quite slushy.'

They crossed the central garden, skirting the softening islands of snow that still clung to the pathways, and reached the far side of the boulevard. Alice stood indecisively for a moment at the edge of the pavement, gazing up and down the buildings.

'I wasn't really thinking, was I? Buying a quick present is not the simple enterprise it sounds.' Harriet nodded solemnly. 'What do you think Daddy would prefer? A bag of beetroot? Or a dried fish?' She squeezed Harriet's hand and smiled encouragingly down at her.

'Eeeww,' said Harriet obediently.

Alice led her up the boulevard to the sports shop. It was the only likely hope. 'We'll try in here.'

They mounted the short flight of steps into a dimly lit room that smelled of garden twine and tar. Displayed under glass at the two counters was a small selection of lurid plastic fish floats flanked by a sturdy parade of penknives. Each was labelled with a code number and a price. Alice rose on tiptoe to peer between the huddle of men that lined the counter. Most of them were flapping their hands like bookies in a fruitless attempt to engage the attention of the salesgirl staring sightlessly through them from her fortress behind it. Alice sighed. Really, there was nothing that was likely to restore George to good humour and health. With a penknife he might slit his throat.

But as Alice turned away, her attention was suddenly caught by an object that lifted her spirits. On a shelf above the salesgirl's head, displayed in both collapsed and erect positions, was a small metal barbecue. Only five roubles. With plastic carrybag. What a find! Who would have expected to see a portable barbecue in the Soviet Union!

'What do you think, Hattie?' She pointed.

'What is it?'

'It's a genuine, fold-away, portable, socialist barbecue!'

'Oh.'

'It's terrific, Hattie! A real prize! I've not seen one before.' Alice paused. 'Perhaps we ought to buy two.'

'Why?'

'Well,' she said doubtfully. 'Someone else we know might like one.' The Soviet approach to shopping.

'Why couldn't they buy their own?'

'They might have got sold out.'

Harriet looked unconvinced.

'You're right. We only need one.' Alice shifted Daisy off to one side and pulled her wallet out of her pocket. They stood patiently at the cash register while the cashier worked her abacus, then queued silently at the counter where the salesgirl wrapped the barbecue carrybag in thick unyielding grey paper and yard upon yard of nylon twine. With the deliberation of an automaton, she wound the string round and back, round and over, round and under, armouring the package and crafting an impeccable, symmetric, indestructible handle. All this she achieved without any acknowledgement of Alice. Then, still without engaging her eyes, the girl pushed the parcel towards Alice, tendering the handle.

'*Spaciba*,' said Alice.

The girl nodded. Alice pulled the parcel off the counter. It slumped heavily against her knee.

'Oof!' She listed to one side. 'Good grief, that's a weight and a half.'

She staggered back across Serpuhovsky Val, unevenly balanced between inert barbecue and trotting child. In the bedroom, the light was on. George lay slumped back into the pillows, staring at the ceiling. Make a good Soviet sales clerk, reflected Alice, as the parade trod softly into the room.

'George? How are you feeling?'

George remained mute, his eyes fixed somewhere beyond Moscow. Alice sat down beside him on the edge of the bed cradling Daisy while Harriet burrowed in under the duvet. She peered anxiously into his face.

'Daddy? Mummy and me and Daisy, we got you a get well present.'

George turned his head and focused confused upon her. What was the child muttering?

'Shall I help you open it?'

'Open what?'

'Your present, Daddy!'

'I have a present? Why have I got a present?'

''Cause you're ill, of course. It's a get well present. Me and mummy and Daisy got it. Shall I help you open it?'

Tentatively George inched the duvet down his neck and popped his arms out over the mallowy barricade. To Alice's astonishment he was wearing his thermal underwear. He dragged the package towards him. Daisy, lying on her back, rolled sideways to watch, grinning toothlessly. George plucked weakly at the stiff nylon twine.

'Hang on. Scissors,' said Alice. Taking them from her, George attacked the string with feeble thrusts.

'Here. Let me do it.'

Briskly, Alice snipped at the nylon. It wouldn't give. She hauled the package closer and began sawing at the twine with an opened blade. The room was silent as they all watched her. Outside there was a spatter of wings and gentle cooing as the pigeons shifted about in the corner of the balcony. Alice worked away, the nylon squeaking, the rings of the scissors biting into the flesh on her thumb. All at once the tension gave. The string sprang apart and curled defeated in its separate strands upon the parcel. She pushed it once more towards George. His hand fluttered ineffectually over the stiff folds of paper. Then, with a jerk, he wrenched at a corner and tore the paper free. The barbecue, in its thickly saddlestitched brown plastic carrier, lay revealed in all its socialist glory.

George studied it doubtfully. 'What is it?'

Alice grinned with delight. He had asked the very question best to pave the way for her triumphant revelation.

Then the telephone rang, with the long, insistent peal that signalled an overseas call. George, unthinking, reached his hand automatically towards it and lifted the receiver to his ear.

'I thought you were going to take the plug out of the wall,' hissed Alice. She could hear someone talking, a sound like summer flies buzzing in the earpiece. Yet George began to shout deafeningly into the instrument.

'Hello? Hello? Anyone there? Speak up! I can't hear you.'

Alice frowned. The voice coming through was almost clear enough for her to take dictation. Then George shoved the receiver under the duvet.

'It's the office,' he muttered. 'I don't want to talk to them.'

'Then why didn't you take the jack out?'

'Forgot.' He pulled the telephone out of the bedclothes and held it as far as he could away from his mouth. 'Who's there?' he bawled. 'Speak to me, speak to me, whoever you are.'

Alice heard a sudden burst of birds outside the window as the pigeons rose in fright at the noise. George cupped his hand over the mouthpiece.

'Here, tear me off some of that wrapping paper, Alice,' he husked.

She passed him a piece. He snatched it from her and held it close to the receiver, crumpling it slightly. Then he brought the instrument back up to his face and with the other hand began frantically to crush the paper crisply against the mouthpiece while shouting through it.

'We seem to have a shocking line!' he bellowed. 'Can you call back?'

Then he slammed down the phone.

Leaning out of bed towards the floor, he reached over and yanked the line out of the wall. With a weak groan he subsided back into his pillows. 'Peace,' he murmured, and turned out the bedside light.

Alice was thoroughly perturbed. She picked up Daisy and the barbecue and ushered Harriet off the bed.

'Rest, George. See if you can't sleep some more.'

The little troupe tiptoed theatrically from the room. As they headed towards the kitchen, Alice could hear the telephone ringing anew at the far end of the flat. This time the peal was local. She ran to the sitting-room and scooped up the receiver.

It was Harold. He sounded sober. 'I've had the *Sentinel* on. They can't seem to get through to your number.'

'It's George, Harold. Something's awfully wrong with him. I think he's having a breakdown. He's gone to bed and pulled the phone out at the jack.'

There was a pause at the other end of the line while Harold hummed. Then he said, 'Has he retired with a crate of whisky and a luscious blonde?'

Alice's heart soared into her throat as swiftly as a towerblock elevator. Did the whole of Moscow know about George's affair?

She was crisp. 'It is hardly likely, Harold, that I would allow another woman in my bed with my husband in my presence.'

'No, my dear. Indeed not,' Harold soothed. 'A remark in poor taste on my part. I shall clarify. George is clearly a victim of the Moscow Blues.'

'What kind of sickness is that?'

'One probably unrecognized by the British and American medical associations, I grant you. But it exists, none the less, as many of our compatriots will tell you. I have witnessed numerous incidences over the years. The symptoms are easy to spot. In less severe cases the victim retires to bed with a blonde and a crate of whisky – thus my frivolous enquiry. In its more severe manifestation, the blonde is omitted.'

Alice almost giggled with relieve. 'So what is the cure, Harold?'

'My dear, the man is under stress—'

'Aren't we all?'

'—and should simply be left alone. There is no cause for alarm. He needs a break. He will recover. Indeed, if I have correctly assessed the tenacity of your husband, his collapse will be brief.'

'What about the *Sentinel*? They certainly won't appreciate your diagnosis.'

'I will see to it that Nadya dispatches an appropriately couched telex informing them of a more acceptable indisposition.'

'Harold, I can't thank you enough. You're an angel.'

'My dear, please! You will tarnish my reputation. If you have further doubts or requirements, do not hesitate to call Nadya or myself.'

He cut the line before she could say any more.

Chapter Eighteen

George continued to languish in bed. Alice was almost beside herself with irritation. This tiny flat she regarded as her exclusive territory during formal office hours, even if she did have to include Galina in the rollcall. What right did George have to succumb to any disease that would confine him so long to quarters? Let alone an affliction as vague as the Moscow Blues.

And at the present time it seemed to her that her quarters positively pullulated with alien forces. While George occupied one end of the flat, Galina had taken over the other with a flow of aged cohorts who came daily in faded dungarees and woolly hats to nod sagely over the still-incapacitated washing machine and then make no effective correction to it. The wretched device still hunched half crippled in the corner of the one-time bathroom, spewing gallons of sudsy water on to the tiles at the point in its cycle when it was supposed to spin. On Mondays and most of Tuesdays, the flat's open doors, bookcases, chairs and tables were draped funereally with the family's sodden linen.

A pre-wash ritual had evolved of late. Galina would squint hopefully at the sky, stick her hand out of the kitchen door into the air of the balcony, then withdraw it with a sigh, clicking her tongue disparagingly at the weather. It was still too early to hang the laundry on the line. Alice, crouched defensively over her letter-writing at the dining-room table, decided that as soon as George elected to present himself once more at the office she would instruct him to order a new washing machine. It was all too much. Besides, they were running low on vodka.

The positive side of George's confinement was demonstrated in the amount of concern for his condition – and Alice's – expressed by their fellow inmates (as Alice had taken to calling the foreign community). Fatma had sent a dish of warm baklava round in the embassy limousine. (Alice scoffed them secretly in the lavatory whenever she could palm one out of the fridge without exciting the attention of Galina, who she was sure was doing the same.) Nadya telephoned daily for a bedside update and to reassure Alice that the *Sentinel* appeared totally relaxed over the collapse of their correspondent. Privately, Alice found this rather surprising. But the convenience of it helped her keep her disquiet to herself. Lisa Prowse turned up unexpectedly one afternoon to commiserate over the unreliability of husbands. Alice, uncomfortably aware of how accurate was this judgement in respect of Lisa's own, was uncertain whether Lisa also knew and was using her for a display of sophisticated nonchalance, or whether she was not perhaps dropping hints about George. Eventually Lisa left her, with a grim smile, a sisterly hug, and a copy of Erica Jong's *Fear of Flying*.

Babs popped relentlessly in and out of the flat, dispensing boxes of Night Nurse and Lemsip and Vick's Vapour Rub she had coaxed out of a chum who acted as receptionist for the British Embassy doctor. Alice suspected that George's collapse had restored in Babs the element of missionary zeal she had lost with her job.

Hazel was beginning to wear Babs down. With each day came a new drift of notes, supplications and memoranda to God, deposited in the holy in-tray of the Simpsons' belongings. Most of these Babs had managed to conceal from Jonathan. One morning, however, he had discovered a message crumpled into the toe of one of his glossy brogues. He had, Babs exclaimed indignantly, been unnecessarily angry with her. Alice had not listened with absolute sympathy herself. Harriet, little short of heathen in her grasp of religious fundamentals, had returned in tears from playgroup one lunchtime to announce that Horace Hamster had been spirited from his cage during free-time by God and the Ugly Ghost. It transpired under questioning that Harriet had been discussing the playgroup pet's demise on her way home with Hazel and Hazel had taken it upon herself to introduce the child to the heavenly cast list. While Alice lamented the lack of opportunity in Moscow for regular exposure to Christian instruction and ceremony, in her opinion Hazel had overstepped the mark. The girl should be got rid of.

Babs prevaricated. Of course it was trying. But to sack her would mean a trip to London, advertisements, interviews to find another nanny – in short, Lisa Prowse's objections. And what would Babs do with the children? Besides, Jonty was expecting several delegations in over the next few months. He needed her there. It simply wasn't convenient.

Yet one night, eager to escape the stuffy confines of the flat for an instant, Alice descended into the compound courtyard to stroll damply around the parked cars and breathe some fresher air. To her astonishment she found Babs slumped silently in the dark behind the wheel of the Simpson Volvo. She tapped on the side window, startling Babs upright.

'Babs? Is everything all right?'

Babs raised her hands and let them fall back on to her thighs. She slowly wound down the window. 'I suppose.' She gestured vaguely at the passenger door. 'Want to join me? Seat's not taken.'

Alice climbed in alongside. Babs had wrapped an eiderdown over her track suit and tucked her legs into the bundle. She stared mute through the windscreen. Alice studied her in silence for a while. The glass around them began to mist over and Babs dabbed at the windows with a corner of the eiderdown. Alice reached and touched her tentatively on the shoulder.

'Come on. Spill it out. What's up?'

Babs slowly turned to face her. Alice had the impression she wasn't seeing her at all.

'I had a row with Jonty. We never row. It was awful.' She thumped the steering wheel with the flat of both hands, then gripped it tightly. 'I stormed out. Then remembered, of course, I had nowhere to go. Quite funny, really.' She turned her head towards Alice.

'Babs, Babs. Why on earth didn't you come to us? You should know we would hardly turn you away.'

'Ah, well. I wasn't actually seeking refuge. More a place to sob a bit. Scream a primal scream or two. You can't have a proper row here. Can't write fast enough.'

'Write?'

'Jonty says we must never give the Sovs any rope with which to hang us. No indication of marital discord, that kind of thing. So we sat there at the dining-room table with our magic slates scribbling away frantically. I mean, it's a hoot, really, isn't it, rowing on paper?'

Alice thought it sounded totally barmy.

From out of the night the crunch of footsteps approached the car. The two women tensed and fell silent. Then a flashlight beam suddenly flooded first one face then the other, catching them staring with the wide eyes of roadside animals before it was extinguished and the militiaman trudged on.

Babs grunted. 'Well, that's our reputations gone for a burton. He'll probably report we were locked in each other's arms. I might as well have shrieked at Jonty and got it off my chest.'

'What was your row about? Or shouldn't I ask?'

'Oh, I don't mind telling you. Though you're not likely to offer much sympathy.'

'You don't know. You haven't tried me.'

'I do know. We discussed Hazel.'

'Ah.'

'Precisely. Ah. Jonty thinks I should sack her at once. He found her in bed with the Prowses' nanny.'

'Oh, my.'

'They did have their clothes on. Apparently they were studying the Bible. They said. And they felt cold.'

Alice thought about the belching heat pumping remorselessly through the compound pipes.

'Jointy was furious. So was I. It was Hazel's day off.'

'What's that got to do with it?'

Babs gestured vaguely. 'I think she should be given the benefit of the doubt and anyway her free time is her own. I mean, what are all these young girls supposed to do with themselves? The choice is either the raunchy guards at the American Embassy or cunning Soviets trying to worm a marriage certificate out of here.'

She sighed and leaned her head against the side window. 'I'm not being honest, am I?' She trailed a finger through the steam and drew a childish flower on the glass. 'I was angry with Jonty for barging into her room. You know, 'what the eye doesn't see', and all that. He rather forced a confrontation. He says he knocked and there wasn't any answer so he opened the door just to double check she was out.' She paused, considering. 'But I don't believe him. I think after he found that note in his shoe he wanted to poke about her things.'

Alice was silent for a while. 'So what are you going to do?'

Babs ballooned a breath into her cheeks and expelled it loudly through her nose. 'She's only got another three months to go with us. If it were any longer, then yes, OK: I'd probably flog back to London to find another girl. But it's not long to wait. And the weather's about to change. Soon enough she'll be out and about in the fresh air and down at the beach. All this indoor living is bound to get anyone down. Winter's got on top of all of us, hasn't it? I mean, look at George. And it's far worse for the nannies. There they are, young girls, with nothing to do and nowhere to go. They've got even fewer outlets for their frustrations and energies than we have. It's bound to drive them bananas.'

'So you're going to turn a blind eye.'

'Whatever she wants to do, as long as it doesn't harm the children—'

'And frighten the horses.'

'—and I honestly don't believe it does, then I'm prepared to ignore it.'

'Will Jonty let you?'

Babs noisily sucked in air and grasped the steering wheel with her arms rigid. 'I'll have to do my best to make sure he does, won't I? I shall go back upstairs, prostrate myself in front of him, and apologize abjectly. If I am sweet enough for long enough, he'll blur over. I won't officially get my way because I shall try and make sure we keep right off the whole thing. Anyway, he's much too busy. He thinks the subject's closed now; settled as he wants it. And that's really all he needs, even if he does go on seeing Hazel in place. It's how it always works.'

'Babs, that sounds a humiliating way to operate.'

'Not if it works. Different marriages have different game plans.'

Alice reddened in the dark.

Babs reached for the doorhandle. 'Shall we go?'

By the middle of the week a green fuzz had appeared on the flat brown islands of Serpuhovsky Val, as soft and vague as the first hair on a baby's head. The sun shone down upon the asphalt, lifting the smell of warmed dust into the air. Alice strode into the bedroom one morning and flung open the door to the balcony. The reek of flatulence and feet, of old food trapped between stale back teeth, of sweat-dried bedding, stirred with the fresh breeze and floated off into the blue. George flexed beneath the duvet and poked out his head.

'What're you doing?' he grunted.

'Spring is coming, George,' said Alice briskly. 'It's time you stopped hibernating.'

'Go away.'

But two hours later, as she sat with Harriet at the dining-room table eating bread and soup while Daisy in Galina's lap mumbled over mashed carrots, George bounded into the room. To Alice's surprise he was wearing one of his worsted suits, although they were not expected anywhere for dinner that evening.

'Ho! My little family! What picture of domestic bliss is this!'

'Daddy! It's Daddy!'

'I'm glad you still recognize him,' murmured Alice.

'Look! He's not sick any more!'

'And on tip-top form to boot,' George announced. He deposited kisses upon Harriet's cheek and Alice's head. 'Hello, haggis,' he said to Daisy. 'Never felt better in my life. Though it must be said, my sweet Alice, Florence Nightingale you are not.'

He rubbed his hands together and peered into their bowls. He spoke in Russian. 'Is this some of Galya's excellent borscht I see before me?'

Galina squirmed with pleasure. 'Ah, the *nachalnik* is in

223

health again! Let me bring you a dish. *Nachalnik* must build his strength up.'

'Yeah,' observed Alice. 'Lying in bed half the month must have sapped it badly.'

George held Galina down. 'I shall help myself, Galya, thank you. Then I to the office to see what chaos reigns.'

'Actually, George, the *Sentinel* seemed remarkably composed at your absence. They did ring once or twice to find out how you were, but no one appeared particularly worried. I was quite surprised.'

George looked put out. 'Perhaps there was no news.'

But when he arrived at Kutz, he learned that his British colleagues had covered for him. Every day Winston or Charlie or Harold had filed on his behalf enough colour for the *Sentinel* to lead into basic wire service copy. He was touched. What a bunch of real troopers. What a set of solid mates!

Nadya had stacked his telexes into two orderly piles, one communications from the *Sentinel* and the *Post,* the other general matters.

'I have put the most important from both in the centre.'

She stared meaningfully with what struck him as a certain amount of amused malice. He picked off the top one.

PRO MASON EX FOREIGN DESK, SENTINEL

EDITOR KEEN U CONFIRM SOONEST JUNE DATES MOSCOW VISIT CONVENIENT STOP.

George sighed. He had been urging a visit from his foreign editor for some time. It seemed the only way to convince the paper that his operating budget fell hopelessly short of adequate and to demonstrate the restricted conditions in which he worked and lived. Predictably, it would now be almost summer before it happened, when there would be better food supplies in the shops and a more relaxed atmosphere about the city. Worse, his visitor would not be the foreign editor, with whom he could have freely raised his (and Alice's) gripes, but the editor of the *Sentinel* himself, who had never been a foreign correspondent and never acknowledged that his journalists might be plagued by problems.

'So how have you been managing without me, Nadya? All dull and desultory? Life lacking a certain vibrancy, a certain sparkle, hmmm?'

'Actually, George, I enjoyed myself quite well, thank you. It is very refreshing to be dealt with as an individual of some intelligence.'

'Really? And which misguided persons have been trying to upset the finely tuned balance of our relationship?'

'Your British colleagues, George. Who have, I think you should agree, saved your ass.'

George's eyebrows shot up in surprise. 'I see,' he said. He studied her, his hands arched as for prayer and set against pursed lips. 'It sounds to me from your idiomatic interpretation of the Queen's English, my dear Nadya, as though you have been overexposed to my esteemed fellow hack, Mr Prowse.'

Deftly Nadya flicked the pile of telexes on to the floor and disappeared from beneath the desk. Her voice floated up to him. 'Charlie has been most helpful. This should make you grateful to him. No?'

'But I am indeed. And what should it make Harold, may I enquire?'

She popped fiercely above the desk again. 'Harold also has been helpful.' She smiled slightly. 'He has been taking over Myra Drewsbarr. Actually, he has been feeling rather proud of himself for a change, I think.'

'That can't be bad, then. Where is he now?'

'I suppose he is upstairs in the apartment trying to write to Cynthia.'

'Cynthia?'

Nadya made herself even busier with the telexes, smoothing out their folds, stroking them flat. 'His first wife.' She gave a brittle smile. 'Each time his self-esteem is raised, he writes to ask her if she will take him back. This reveals much about his feelings for me. No?'

George was embarrassed. Above all things he loathed intimate revelations. They discomfited him beyond measure. 'I'm sure you're mistaken, Nadya.' In some dismay he saw that his dismissal was too curt. With trepidation he added, 'What gave you that idea?'

She shrugged. 'Harold is a man of predictable behaviour. Every year it is the same. Winter is ending. He is becoming light of spirit. Very Soviet, yes? So. He fills his waste basket with his efforts to appeal to his wife. Ha!' She caught herself. 'That is funny, no? I am his wife. Anyway. He does not like anything he writes. He does not know how to approach her. So. He becomes depressed. He gives up. He reaches for the vodka bottle. And back we are to normal one more time.' She paused. 'I know all this to be true. I look through his rubbish.'

That figured. George fiddled with a pencil. 'Ah, Nadya. What can I say?'

'I think, George, if it is anything of your usual preference, nothing is best. Yes?'

'There are times, Nadya, when you sound like Alice.'

'There are times, George, when you are quite astute.' She pushed the sheaf of telexes she had been cradling at him. 'You have not finished your reading.'

He took them from her, holding her eyes in what he hoped was a look that spoke volumes, for certainly, at this moment, he was at a loss for words.

The telex from the *Sentinel* surely he had already read:

Then he looked more closely at the heading:

PRO MASON EX POST

'Shit.'

Something akin to satisfaction crossed Nadya's face.

'The dates, Nadya. What are they?'

She touched a finger delicately to her tongue and leafed through the telexes, pulling out one close to the bottom of the pile. George peered at it.

'Bob Mathisson, ninth to twelfth of May. Well, thank the Lord for that, at least. Couldn't have coped with the two at once. Hardly worth my life, let alone my job. Can't you picture it?' Nadya looked blank. George elaborated. 'Banging in and out of doors, rushing into cupboards.'

'The editors do this?'

'No, no. I do. As in restoration comedy. You know, trying not to be discovered in an incriminating position by the other side. Lots of hiding behind curtains.'

'Ah.' A flicker of understanding crossed her face.

George tapped the telexes with his pencil. 'There's a message I'd like you to send to Justesen's.'

Nadya's expression changed to one of satisfaction. Plus a touch of smugness? George was not sure. 'The washing machine?'

'Precisely. The washing machine. How long do you reckon it will take to deliver from Denmark? I have to say, each new week of the flat draped in sodden sheets is driving me closer to dementia.'

'I am not a sales representative, George. Why don't you look in the catalogue? You will find all the information there. Anyway, you must choose which model you want.'

She pulled from the bookshelves a tome as thick as *Who's Who* and twice its surface size. George flicked through pages of camping equipment, teak furniture, monogrammed shirts, handkerchiefs and thermal underwear, past glossy photographs of barbecue, garden tools, shower curtains and hairdryers, hesitating at pictures of rubbery-skinned models sheathed in virulent nylon negligees, two-piece suits, cocktail dresses and bathing costumes. He tired eventually at the bulk sales of gelatine, cornflour, tinned goods, dried goods, luxury goods, the taco chips, the salted nuts, the candied fruit – pacifiers that expatriates cannot live without.

'My God! Is there nothing you can't buy?'

'It is a wonderful book, yes?'

'I think it is thoroughly corrupting. I hope you have not read it.'

'You, George, are free to fly out to buy all of those things any time you choose.'

George flushed. He thumbed slowly back to the intensive household appliance section and stared at the array of washing machines.

'God, I don't know, for heaven's sake. Do we want an 800 rpm cycle or a 1000 rpm one? Should we have four different programmes? Or six? Or eight or ten, even? I've absolutely no idea.'

Nadya said nothing. His focus glazed and he felt his concentration seeping away. He slammed the catalogue decisively shut. 'Order the cheapest.'

Nadya nodded and leaned forward to haul the mighty volume slowly towards her. She stood there at the desk, her hand toying with the corner of the cover until George looked up.

'You have a question, Nadya?'

She sucked in her lower lip, tracing the words Peter Justesen, Denmark, slowly with her forefinger. At last she spoke.

'Your old machine. George. May I have it?'

George began to shrug offhandedly and nod when some chord in the back of his mind pulled him short.

'Now hang on a minute. What would you want a broken washing machine for?'

'Oh, that's no problem,' she said easily. 'I can get it mended.'

George slammed the flat of both hands smartly on the desktop and soared out of his chair. He leaned to within inches of Nadya's startled face, his arms trembling in his fury.

'You said it couldn't be done, Nadya. You said no-one in Moscow would know how to mend it.'

She paled. 'That was months ago, George,' she said weakly. 'Everything is changing so fast these days. I am just now hearing this. Of people who will do special jobs. Before, nobody was interested. Now there is a new attitude. Gorbachev, he is making people think maybe it is good to make efforts.'

'Bollocks. You've always known where to get things done. What do you need a washing machine for, anyway? Hasn't Harold got you one?'

Nadya brought her hands together and slotted her fingers into a tight lock.

'To live in the Soviet Union, George, in just the simplest kind of comfort, you must have *blat*. Influence, yes? All the time, every day, with every opportunity, you work to build your *blat*. If I need something, I must be able to offer something in exchange. Money buys nothing. It is simple for you, George, you and the other foreigners. All you have to do is to telex Denmark or Sweden or London and everything is put on a plane or a ship or a truck. How many Soviet families do you know who have washing machines? Even among the kind of intelligentsia you are meeting?'

George's lips tightened. How did she know?

229

'I am not completely stupid, George. I do not believe that Harold will be with me for ever. If he does not go back to his wife, he will probably kill himself with vodka. And before he does, he will lose his job and there will be only my salary for the hard currency rent – if they don't kick us out of here – and the food and the drink. I need to build my *blat*, George.'

But George was snared in the fangs of his anger. 'You duped me, Nadya. You Soviets treat us foreigners as if we're some kind of endless vein you can tap for luxury goods. If you don't like the present system, you should have voted for the other party.'

'Don't be absurd.'

'I do not like being ripped off. Even when the sob story wrenches at the heart strings. I especially don't like it, Nadya' – he slapped the desk once more – 'when the perpetrator is a signed-up member of the system that supports this way of life. Along with the dirty duty of reporting on the activities and connections of friends, neighbours, and work associates.'

George stared pointedly at Nadya. She, for her part, merely looked blandly back at him. Furious beyond belief, confused by the depth of the betrayal he felt, he declared with a final thump, 'If that bloody machine is going to anybody, it is going to Galina.'

Chapter Nineteen

The approaching weekend was Easter. While this was clearly not a festival worthy of the notice of any ambitious Soviet citizen, it was still celebrated by the Russian Orthodox Church, which the Soviet Foreign Ministry minders who watched over the press corps were aware could always generate sympathetic copy. Well before the end of the week, therefore, George and his colleagues were fully versed, through a casual word here and a hint there, in the times and places of the most colourful Easter services.

Alice, disturbed of late by Harriet's complete ignorance of Christianity, was anxious that the Masons should also celebrate. She planned a traditional weekend that would ignore as far as possible the fact that they were in Moscow.

On Holy Saturday George woke to Harriet crawling in beside him and a tray being laid across his stomach. Alice stood by the bedside with an ominous grin of particular satisfaction on her face.

'Ho, George. You won't believe what we have here!'

George unpeeled an eye and squinted down at the tray. It was no good; the angle was too tight. He wasn't focusing.

'Move the tray a sec, Alice. I have to sit up.'

He heaved himself vertical by his fists and looked down at the plate before him. He stared at it silently for a minute. Sitting up had not corrected the view. He was still seeing what he had seen before through one eye, flat on his back. To wit: a tiny cube of toast no larger than a postage stamp, flanked by two minute fried eggs the size of coins. Whatever cooking method Alice had employed, she had obviously established a culinary breakthrough. These eggs had shrunk in the wash.

'Don't tell me,' he volunteered at last. 'I've got it. The Teddy Bears' Picnic.'

Harriet buried her face, squealing with delight into the pillow.

Alice laughed. 'Almost. Try again.'

'The rejects from an outdoor state chicken farm north of the Arctic Circle?'

'Quails' eggs.' Alice made the announcement with some justifiable pride. 'Would you believe it?'

'No,' acknowledged George. 'And I wouldn't believe what you've done to them, either.'

'Aren't they fun? I did think about boiled with minuscule soldiers of toast, but that would have been silly, wouldn't it?'

'Absolutely.'

'Go on, then. Eat them up. I'll do you some more, if you like.'

'No, no. Please. This is ample.' George hooked an egg on the tine of his fork and held it aloft. It hung there translucent, like a pearl button. 'Where did you find them?'

'In the shop that sells lumps of frozen turkey and chicken near Kutuzovsky Market. The woman said they were a freak delivery.'

'I'll bet. Someone will be sent to Siberia for this.'

'Not at all. I rang and told Fatma. She sent round her driver to buy the lot. Two dozen boxes, would you believe. I wonder what she'll do with them? I only bought one box. I thought they'd be a witty way to start our Easter festivities.'

George felt a familiar tiredness settle about his forehead. 'What particular Easter festivities have you got in mind, Alice, my sweet?'

She clapped her hands together brightly. 'Well. First of all I thought we should include the Simpsons.'

'In what, exactly?'

'The Sunday activities. After breakfast we're having an Easter egg hunt for the children around our flat—'

George threw up his hands in irritation and despair. 'Alice. We are in Moscow. Where in heaven's name do you expect to buy chocolate eggs?'

'Did I say chocolate? If you had waited till I finished, George, you would have learned that Hattie and I have been collecting painted wooden eggs at Chiriomushkinski Market. Haven't we, Hattie? The farm women sell them. And stacking eggs, like the dolls.'

'I see,' said George, subdued. 'So, all right. We've done the eggs. What then?'

'We all pile into the cars and drive into the country for an Easter picnic. First of the year.'

'What's wrong with eating here?'

'Has anyone ever told you, George, you have no soul?'

'You have. Often.'

'Well, it's true.'

'I have never felt that eating in a field disguises the fact that English picnics are uniformly disgusting. Soggy tomato sandwiches, hard-boiled eggs with grey-rimmed yolks, cold grease-silted sausages, and bits of chicken flopping about in jellied socks of loose skin.'

'Which is why we're going Greek.'

'What?'

Alice smirked slightly. 'Humus, Georgian lavash bread, hot moussaka, tomato, cucumber and onion salad with bits of a cheese from Bulgaria that's almost like feta.'

'Hot moussaka, did I hear? Ha! And how long do you

233

think it's likely to keep hot after tooling around for hours down country lanes? You're out of your tree, Alice.'

As he steered the car down the gravelled road to the edge of the Bay of Joys, Babs in the passenger seat, Harriet and Rebecca bickering behind, he reflected that he certainly would not be participating in this idiotic expedition had he not gone to midnight mass the night before. It wasn't that the ceremony had uplifted him to the point where he had resolved to be more indulgent towards Alice, though he had been deeply moved. It was simply the guilt factor. Alice had been unable to find a babysitter at short notice and had had to stay behind. He owed her this picnic. She had missed a quite special occasion.

By eleven o'clock at night, the grounds of the tiny red, green and white wedding cake church of St Nicholas of the Weavers had been crowded, each silent figure clutching an unlit candle. Some held Easter kulich bread to be blessed. Old women in flowered scarves and crocheted shawls, men and young children in their best suits, stood shoulder to shoulder without speaking. Then the doors of the church were flung wide and George could see above the heads of the crowd into a gilded interior ablaze with flickering candlelight. Quietly people pushed their way inside, to press their lips to the icons and burn a taper. George relaxed into the current and was eventually carried forward into the church.

Inside, the air was stiff with the pungent smell of incense. He could see nothing but the heads of the congregation pressing towards the iconostasis that divided the church. From behind the ornate screen came the murmuring of priestly voices and the regular hypnotic incantation of religious chanting.

At midnight the congregants tensed. Men drew themselves upright while the women rose on tiptoe, lifting their

234

faces as far as they could. Then from behind the screen emerged the priests dressed in white, bearing aloft the crucifix. Preceding them were young altar boys swinging golden censers, and a choir whose chants the congregation took up as if followed the procession out of the church. From candle to candle the flame was passed and cupped, moving in a wave of light across the mass of people. The subdued mood of before had lifted, and a tremendous spirit of exultation filled the crowd as the joyful declaration from the priests went up and was echoed by the congregants.

'*Khristos voskrese*! Christ is risen!' they cried as they circled the church, a slow torrent of worshippers following flickering candles in the darkness. '*Voistine voskrese*! He is risen indeed!'

But Easter morning was less than glorious. The weather, bright the day before, was overcast and dreary, scraps of grey cloud scudding across a stony sky.

'Are you sure we should be doing this, Alice?' George had asked after the raucous tumult of the Easter egg hunt had subsided. George and Jonathan were standing at the sitting-room window clutching glasses of aggressive Bloody Mary and staring gloomily outside. 'Why can't we eat at home?'

Babs came in from the kitchen and dumped a cool-box in George's arms. She was wearing a polo neck, a thick Guernsey sweater, a scarf round her neck and a shawl over her shoulders, as though the expedition were North Pole bound.

'Because,' she said.

Why did women always think that that patronizing, inane reply settled matters, wondered George.

In fact it had. For here they were, struggling along the forest path with picnic rugs and plastic bags and warm, tin-foil-wrapped dishes that gave off the fusty smell of school kitchens. The pines rose tall and tight to either side of them, preventing any long distance view. Ahead ran the children, jumping the runnels of earth, darting in and out of the forest, squealing madly. Hazel was with them, making as much noise as they were.

Alice had been dismayed to see her and had greeted her somewhat curtly. Babs, uncomfortably embarrassed, had drawn Alice aside in the kitchen and explained that Hazel had come back from the church service at the American Embassy depressed and homesick and with no-one to spend what she had called 'this triumphal day' with. Unusually, her friends were all involved in separate activities. Babs had taken pity. She had persuaded Jonathan that Hazel could take the children off for a walk and leave the adults to get sloshed in peace. Alice, she reminded her, had no need to feel awkward, since there was no way that Hazel could know that Alice had identified the author of her note. Certainly Alice had found the girl perfectly polite, though no more than that. Her earlier warmth had entirely evaporated.

Closer to the lake the breeze suddenly became acutely frigid. Alice put her arms protectively around Daisy, slumped in her pouch.

'Good Christ!' exclaimed Jonathan, drawing the lapels of his twill coat together.

'Jonty!' cautioned Babs, glancing anxiously towards Hazel.

As they emerged on to the spit of land that looked across the wide bay, the reason for the chill became apparent. A few inches below the surface of sepia water, the lake was still frozen solid in a pale platform of ghostly ice a full foot thick. The party stood silently on the small hillock above it and stared in wonder at a figure in bathing trunks which had emerged from somewhere to the side of them and was walking, it seemed, across the water.

'Jesus!' exclaimed George, impressed.

'I think not,' Jonathan commented drily.

They all laughed. Hazel wheeled sharply away from the group. She called tersely to the children and shepherded them off into the woods. Babs sighed. 'Oh dear.'

'Silly cow,' said Jonathan.

Alice began unpacking the bags. 'Let's have something to drink.'

The clouds had drawn together across the sky and formed a solid ash-coloured cloth. Babs shivered.

'Got anything hot?'

'Coffee. For after,' she added sternly. Plans had been made.

Babs looked put out.

'Come off it, Alice,' objected George. 'Can't you see the woman's chilled to the marrow? Pour her a cup.' Really, he would have to have words with Alice. This regimental behaviour was quite out of hand.

Alice's lips tightened. 'How about a helping of hot moussaka, Babs? That'll put you right. In fact, why don't we all eat,' she said briskly. She prodded her fish slice at the sky. 'While we still can.'

They looked up. The clouds above their heads were now the colour of rotting plums and the breeze had become a bitter wind. Jonathan stamped his feet and hunched his shoulders, his hands thrust deep into his pockets. 'Nice weather for Easter,' he remarked.

'It was wonderful yesterday,' said Alice crossly. 'Here. Take this, Jonty.' She handed him a plate of vaguely steaming moussaka. 'Soon feel better.'

'Soviet revenge upon religious festivals,' said George. 'Lenin did a deal with God.'

'Ssh. Please!' Babs looked behind her nervously. Hazel was slowly trooping back towards them with the children hand in hand.

'What did God get out of it?' Jonathan enquired.

'Poland.'

Soon they were all positioned about the hillock with their food, Rebecca, Harriet and Emily crouched over their plates on the ground, quietly shunting forkfuls of mince into the soil, the adults standing around stamping their feet. They began to feel more content.

Then slowly, softly, as the warmth rolled through their bodies, flakes of snow drifted quietly down from the skies. Nobody said a word. Studiously they carried on eating. The flow of flakes increased. Hazel stared immobile, uncomprehending, at these extraordinary people frenziedly devouring food in a gathering snow storm. Now the snow fell swiftly and thickly, laying on the shoulders of the children at their feet.

Suddenly Jonathan let his plate fall to his side. The remains of his meal flopped to the ground. 'Excuse me and all that, but what the fuck are we doing here?'

Wordlessly Alice began to pack up again, stacking plates, crimping foil. Meekly Babs followed suit.

'Christ, Alice!' Jonathan protested. 'It must be several degrees below freezing, not to speak of this wet stuff tumbling out of the heavens. Have a heart! It's not our fault it's snowing on your Easter picnic!'

'What's the betting tomorrow will be gorgeous?' said George.

Alice cuffed him.

Of course he was right. The following day was sunny again. And each successive day it became warmer.

'Is winter finally over?' Alice asked Glaina.

Galina shrugged indifferently. 'I've known it to snow on May Day.' She saw Alice's face fall. 'But not this year. I think we've seen the end of it.'

The counters at the free markets began to fill with the first of the spring produce. To the tang of brine from the vats of pickled cabbage and apples and tomatoes was added the heady hopsack smell of fresh coriander, the nasal zest of spring onions and the fresh mown scent of lettuce thinnings. ('Five pounds sterling!' Alice announced to George, flourishing a tiny bunch.) Carrots the size of fingers ('You won't believe this: fifty pence apiece!') lay in ferny bundles, orange hands along the marble slabs. The first of the season's veal appeared, and lamb, the pathetic skinned heads of the animals displayed beside their hacked up bodies.

It was all for a steep, steep price, but Alice didn't care. She and Babs drove almost daily from the Centralni Rinok to Cherimoshkinski Rinok to Riszskaya Rinok and any other market whose produce was said to be fresh or varied or irresistible. What did it matter, with a winter as long as the one that had finally passed, that the prices were exorbitant, insulting almost? They all needed fresh fruit and vegetables.

And it could only get better. April was almost over. By the middle of May, they would be spending regular time at the river beach on the banks of the Moskva in Moscow's Western suburb. Then in June, she and Galina would begin to shop in bulk to preserve in the freezer (Alice) and in glass jars (Galina) the spoils of summer for the next long winter.

Alice's spirits rose high and took wing. The windows of the flat were flung open in the morning to release the central heating that Galina assured her would continue to be pumped into the building until after May Day. Galina moved the wet laundry to the balcony clothes line, rejoicing in her acquisition of the old washing machine. Alice's rating had soared. For the present, at least, there was nothing Galina would not do for her. No, she didn't mind if the spin cycle didn't work. She would carry on wringing by hand and maybe one day she would find someone who would know how to fix it.

Meanwhile, the old washing machine was set outside the

front door to await its removal to Galina's flat, a process which had caused a certain amount of dissension at the office. George, preoccupied with another matter and asking Sasha with a vague wave of the hand to pop over to Serpuhovsky Val to drive the machine round to Galina's, was startled to hear a perfunctory 'No.'

He looked up and asked Sasha to explain.

'I am a chauffeur.' He pronounced it in the Soviet fashion: 'Shaffure'. 'I will run the *nachalnik*'s office errands. I will drive him where he wants to go. I will even deliver his daughter home from school. But I am not a removal man. I will not shift machinery into or out of Galina's flat.'

By this George understood that Sasha too must have had his hopes set on acquiring the old machine. Indeed, Alice had once remarked upon his silent interest in the attempts by Volodya and Ivan to put it right.

'Never mind,' said Galina gaily. 'I'll get one of the other drivers to do it. I'll offer him a couple of bottles.'

However, the machine languished in the corridor. Alice made no remark, unwilling to get involved. It was early days yet. She only uttered the odd expletive as she caught her hip on its corner, turning quickly out of the flat and forgetful that it squatted there. And the machine was a useful fixture when one returned heavily burdened with shopping, as Alice now was, and in need of a place to dump bags while searching for keys.

She had had a particularly satisfactory Monday morning shop. She had found new potatoes, with the pearly sheen of thin skins and cheaper by the kilo than older ones twice the size. A butcher at the Centralni Rinok had been persuaded to rescue from the mound of massacred meat upon the counter a piece of veal from which he could shave scallopini. Then on the stalls outside she had come upon chanterelle mushrooms, yellow trumpets tumbled into small piles. Some fresh parsley, some almost paperless heads of the new season's garlic, and she was ready to conjure for George a feast to knock his socks off before she helped him along with his trousers.

Spring is here, she told herself, and so is Myra Drewsbarr. The sap is rising and we can't have George breaking into leaf in the wrong forest. So to speak.

She could hear the telephone ringing in the sitting-room as she swung her shopping on to the washing machine and fumbled through torn tissues for her keys. Certain the peals were about the end, she kicked the front door open and caught Galina full in the chest as she slopped along in her slippers to answer the call.

Alice snatched up the telephone, and brightened as she heard George's voice. Then, as Galina watched, her face went the colour of cement. She tightened her grip on the receiver and began to shake.

'Oh, my God,' she said. Over and over. 'Oh, my God.'

She listened again.

'It can't be true,' she whispered. 'Come home, George. Oh, George. Please come home!'

Mumbling filtered down the line.

'Yes, of course. I understand. I wasn't thinking. Come back whenever you can, then. And let me know the instant you hear any more. I'll have to decide what to do about the children.'

Gently she placed the telephone back on the hook as if fearful it would break. She turned towards Galina. The woman was still massaging her breast, transfixed by the tone of Alice's voice. She must really have dealt her a blow with that door.

'I'm so sorry, Galya. I hurt you. I was rushing to catch the phone. I shouldn't have thrown the door wide like that. I wasn't thinking. I'm sorry. I'm so sorry.' Suddenly Alice clamped her hand to her mouth and stared in anguish at

Galina over the top of it. 'Oh, Galya. Oh, God. There's been a dreadful accident. A nuclear reactor's blown up. Days ago. They've just admitted to it. At a place called Chernobyl.'

Chapter Twenty

That evening Alice crossed the hall to the Simpsons' flat to watch the nine o'clock news. This was no time for lip-reading. They were playing Trivial Pursuit with Angela and Geoffrey Rimstead from the British bank.

'Life must go on, Alice,' said Jonathan. 'What do you expect us to do? Start whitewashing the windows and squatting under the dining-room table?'

Alice had no idea, except that she found the thought of sitting down and carrying on as normal quite intolerable.

'I wondered if you would be watching *Vremya*.'

Geoffrey guffawed jovially. 'My dear girl! You don't imagine they'll tell us anything, do you?'

'Well, they must say something, surely? It's a catastrophe that affects the whole of Europe. Besides, what about glasnost?'

'Openness, schmopenness,' joshed Geoffrey. He clearly found Alice naïvely droll. 'I don't think a nuclear accident is something Mr G is going to be broadcasting from the onion domes, do you?'

'Actually,' said Babs quietly. 'I'd like to see too if they're going to make any kind of statement. I mean, you tell me there's nothing to worry about, Jonty. I'd like to know what the Soviets say.'

They sat in a row on the sagging sofa, faces turned towards the television. Geoffrey drained peanuts from his fist into his mouth. Angela twisted a crisp curl of hair round and round her finger. Babs sat leaning forward, her hands clenched tightly between the legs of her bulky track suit. Jonathan moved about behind them, handing out drinks. Colour blazed from the screen, suffusing them with a gruesome scarlet and turquoise glow. We look radioactive already, thought Alice, staring at them all.

Leading the news was a long feature film on combine harvesters. Then followed an in-depth story on the production of a new heavy truck, studded with figures and projections, and interviews with designers and workers, foremen and plant managers.

Angela yawned.

'Another whisky, Alice?' said Jonathan.

'I don't see how Gorbachev can expect us to take his reforms seriously if they won't give us a proper news broadcast,' said Babs testily. She was ripping little shreds of skin off the side of her thumb with her teeth.

The newscaster stared out at them, and lifted his papers. 'An accident has taken place at the Chernobyl power station, and one of the reactors was damaged. Measures are being taken to eliminate the consequences of the accident. Those affected by it are being given assistance. A government commission has been set up.'

They sat there in silence.

'That was it?' said Angela.

'Oh, my God,' said Babs. 'If they've said as much as that, it must be bad.'

Alice could not speak. Her brain seemed to have stopped working.

'Jonty, isn't there someone you can phone at the embassy, find out what's going on?'

'I shouldn't think at this stage they'll know any more than what you've just heard.'

'Now there's no need to panic, girls,' said Geoffrey. 'If

we were in any danger, you can be sure they would get us out of here pronto.'

'What if no-one knows what the danger is?' said Babs.

No-one answered.

'It doesn't seem to me it would be in anyone's interest to get us out,' said Alice.

Babs looked at her. 'What do you mean?'

'Well, on the one hand it could be a political embarrassment if Western countries started advising their people to evacuate. We're all supposed to be putting our trust in Gorbachev. Giving him room. A mass exodus of foreigners isn't going to do much for demonstrating support, is it? Then there's our own nuclear policy they've got to consider.'

'There is?'

'Don't you read the papers, Babs?' Alice found it hard to keep her voice steady. 'They're trying to get public approval for plans to open another reactor at Sizewell. My mother lives near there. She says they're concerned about safety. And nuclear waste. The locals have been up in arms against it. It's hardly going to help the nuclear power lobby if the Brits are rushed out of Moscow because of a radiation leak in the Ukraine.'

'Alice, I really think you're over-dramatizing the situation,' said Jonathan. 'You're taking it all much too seriously, and you're upsetting Babs. There's no kind of hard evidence yet for stirring up this sort of alarm.'

'I'm not stirring up alarm, Jonty. I'm just trying to get some idea of what is going on. What measures we should take. You're treating it as if it's some minor accident in a fireworks factory. It's ridiculous not to be taking this seriously. I've got children to think about. So have you, for that matter.'

'All right, all right. But calm down, will you? It doesn't do any good getting worked up. Look, I suggest you go home and wait to find out what George knows. I'm sure he's better informed than any of us. And tomorrow you can talk to the embassy. Ring the Minister's office, why don't you? There'll be some sort of position established by then.'

Alice snorted. 'The Minister! Any position he takes will probably be supine.'

'That's quite enough, Alice. It's a complete waste of time even talking about it when none of us knows what the picture is. Now do as I say, all right? Go home. Have a hot bath. Have another whisky. And wait and see what George says. I'm not having you scaring Babs unnecessarily.'

Babs touched him on the arm. 'Jonty, it's all right. She's not scaring anyone. Alice is worried. Just like me. I'm sure we all are. And really I wish someone with proper authority could advise us what to do.'

'Well, I must say,' said Angela comfortably, 'a pair of old bods like Geoffrey and me aren't in much danger, are we, dear?' She nudged her husband in the ribs. 'Long past having to worry about what could happen to the kids.' She giggled. 'We've had a good run, and if I'm going to be doomed to spending the last years of my life with four arms and two heads, then Geoff'll just have to buy me a whole new wardrobe!'

Babs and Alice stared at her amazed. Babs rose and put her hand to Alice's elbow. 'The children are on their own. You should be getting back. Is there anything I can get you before you go?'

Alice rose obediently. 'I'm OK. Thanks for letting me watch your telly. I'm sorry if I've ruined your Trivial Pursuit.'

'No worries,' said Geoffrey. 'Angie's been keeping them nice and warm, haven't you, dear?' He patted her knee.

'Better let you get back to them, then,' said Alice. 'Don't want them going off. 'Night, Angela. Babs. Goodnight, Jonty.'

'Talk to you tomorrow, Alice.'

'Talk to George. He'll be more use. And less ratty, probably.'

She let herself into the flat and stood at the window of the unlit sitting-room staring out into the dark. What did radiation look like? Nothing. Was it at this very moment seeping through cracks in the doors and window frames? Insinuating its poisoning, deforming, killing rays into the clean, vibrant, living cells of men, women and children across the Soviet Union?

Children. She moved swiftly across the room and down the hallway to the rooms where Daisy and Harriet slept. They both lay puffed and peaceful, curled up on their sides. Alice stared down at them. Would they be tainted? Were they already? How could one tell?

She forced herself reluctantly back to the sitting-room and sat in the dark, her hands folded quietly in her lap, back erect. Like waiting for an interview, she thought obliquely. As, indeed, she was.

George returned shortly after midnight. At the sound of his key in the lock she sprang up and rushed into the hall.

'What's the news?'

George looked grey, his skin tight with tiredness and his eyes red. He rubbed at them with his fists before he spoke.

'God, I don't know, Alice. No-one seems to have much concrete information as yet.' He turned the sitting-room light on. 'Let me sit down. Get my breath back. Jesus, what a day. Bring me a whisky, would you? I'm wrecked.'

'Do you want anything to eat?'

George shook his head, then leaned it back against the wall, his eyes shut. Alice went quickly to the kitchen for a glass and some ice. She watched George as she poured the whisky. He seemed to have gone to sleep.

'George?'

He reached his hand out for the glass without opening his

eyes and took a long pull at the liquid. She waited.

'Apparently what happened was that a nuclear power station in Sweden began recording what they call "abnormal levels of radiation" around nine this morning. Forsmark. It's about seven hundred miles north of Chernobyl. They straight away evacuated the workers, about six hundred or so, and checked them out for radiation. Their clothing was contaminated. So was the grass. And the air. Initially, they thought the leak might have been theirs. Then they started getting similar reactions from other parts of Sweden. And Finland. Tests were showing that the radioactive wind drift was coming from the Soviet Union.'

'Oh, my God.' Alice sank down beside him. 'What did the Soviets say?'

'Nothing. None of us got anything from any of them all fucking day. But there was a cocktail party at the Swedish Embassy this evening and the Ambo finally told the Sovs that whether or not they came clean, Sweden was going to file an official radiation alert with the International Atomic Energy Agency in Vienna.' He drank the rest of his whisky.

'Were you there?'

'Sweetheart, I haven't been off the office phones all day long. No. Svenson was. He filled me in. According to him, some of the Sovs at the do were going round telling the press the leak was coming from Sweden. That was the Foreign Ministry line, too, would you believe? They were saying the Swedes were stirring up trouble to deflect attention from their own nuclear problems.' He snorted and reached for Alice's hand. 'Bastards.'

They sat without speaking for a while, George with his eyes still closed, Alice watching him. Eventually she spoke.

'What should we do, George? With the children.'

He rolled his head towards her and opened his eyes. 'I can't tell you, Alice. I don't know what to advise. Fly them out if you'd feel happier. But if the wind drift did blow towards Sweden, then it probably missed Moscow altogether.' He squeezed her hand. 'I must get some sleep. It'll be a long day tomorrow. Why don't you ring around the other mums, find out what they're doing, then decide?'

The other mums were as confused as she was. The only subject they were clear about was food.

'We should buy all the fresh stuff we can,' said Babs. 'Before new supplies come into town.'

'You're not suggesting they'll sell contaminated vegetables, are you?'

'They've got to make a living, Alice. Besides, how many ordinary Soviets do you think understand the implications of what has happened? Or even know it has happened? You say we have no concrete information. What about them? They haven't been told a thing.'

Babs was right. George telephoned a hostel for foreign exchange students in Minsk, about two hundred and fifty miles to the north of Chenobyl, and talked to a girl from Kent who had heard nothing of the calamity until she had switched on the BBC World Service.

'I rushed to the university to ask people about it, but all I got was absolute incomprehension,' he recorded for his copy.

Only the British Embassy had been in touch, to counsel the students to stay indoors, to take showers, and rinse their hair every few hours to get rid of radioactive dust.

'Where the hell are they going to get hold of that much shampoo?' George asked Nadya.

At least the embassy was advocating some kind of action. 'In the absence of any real information,' said a spokesman somewhat apologetically, 'there is not a great deal of advice we can give.'

Then Charlie Prowse came up with a bunch of Western technicians in Kiev who confirmed that five hundred square miles round the nuclear plant had been closed off.

By the evening of the day following the Soviet television announcement there was still nothing in the Soviet press. But the Swedes were able to report the chilling information that the Soviets had asked their advice on fighting nuclear fires. Finally, the day after that, Soviet authorities gave their official version of what had happened.

'The radiation leak has been stopped,' the TASS statement said. The remaining reactors at the plant had been closed down, four nearby towns had been evacuated and while two people had died in the initial explosion, a team of scientists and technicians had brought the situation under control.

The announcement brought Charlie Prowse round to George's office in a lather of excitement and rage.

'What do you make of it, then? The sods.' He towered over George's desk, refusing to sit down. George noticed distractedly that there seemed to be a pattern of rather suggestively intertwined dragons writhing across Charlie's dark blue shirt. He wondered vaguely where the dickens Charlie shopped.

'It's the best we can hope for, I suppose.'

'Stuff that for a lark.' Charlie leaned across the desk and fixed George with a stare. He seemed to be weighing him up. 'Look. I've got a helluva lead. Shit, I'd really like to go with it alone.' He paused. 'But I'm not sure enough of it.' He sat down and stroked his moustache thoughtfully with a stiffened finger.

'Well, go on, then. Are you going to tell me or not?'

Charlie was silent.

'Christ, Charlie, you're about as bad as the Soviet authorities.'

'Shit!' The expletive sounded vicious. Charlie swung round and placed his arms across George's desk. 'Right.

Here it is. I have a woman in Kiev, a hospital worker. She says two thousand people have died.'

'Fuckaduck. You're joking.'

'That's what she says.'

'Christ almighty.' George absorbed the information, Charlie watching him closely. Then he said, 'It can't be true.'

'Why not?'

George pondered for a moment. He picked up a pencil and began slowly scratching it through his hair. 'Let's see now. If they had a bigger explosion initially than they've told us about – but then, what would that many people be doing in or near the plant? No. Hang on, where's the TASS statement?' George called out to the kitchen. 'Nadya? Where's the TASS release?'

Nadya wandered into the office, a glass of tea in one hand, chewing a slice of buttered bread. 'Harold took it. *Privyet*, Charlie.'

'Christ, where did he take it?'

'To the US Embassy briefing.'

'Oh, good grief. Listen, pop upstairs, would you, and see if you can't bum a copy off the *Chicago Tribune*. Or take a note of it, or something.'

Charlie said, 'What's so important about it?'

George thrust his pencil down the back of his shirt. 'I think we should double check exactly what they are saying about the deaths. There was a reference to medical aid still being given to victims. I'm just wondering if your two thousand figure could be read into that.'

'I still don't see why you don't think they would have died anyway. We're talking Big Disaster here.'

''Course we are, Charlie. But the real disaster of radiation is that it doesn't kill people at once. It does it slowly. Over the years. Just when you thought you had escaped, kerplunk.' He slapped the desk.

'Very graphic, George. Mind you, I'm not sure how much it matters.'

'I don't get you.'

'Well, you know my illustrious organ. Accuracy tend to play second fiddle to a strong front page header.'

'Charlie, you can't run this one. I mean, it's way outside the bounds of common responsibility.'

'Not a phrase that appears on their credo. How about as an "unconfirmed report"?'

'It's not on, Charlie.'

Charlie sighed and pushed himself out of the chair. 'I knew I shouldn't have come to you for advice. You're far too conscientious. The *Sentinel* should be proud. But don't think you have me persuaded. I feel in my waters this is one story too strong to pass up. My editor has a profound reverence for the print-now-confirm-later school of journalism and believe me, he's on my back for a mega scoop.'

'You might please him but you'll bring a ton of shit down on you from the Soviets if you haven't got some pretty strong evidence to back you.'

''Twas ever thus.'

George sighed and went back to work. He filed two stories on the evacuation of British students from Minsk and Kiev, with a side-bar for the *Post* on hospitals in Kiev overflowing with patients. He did not refer to two thousand dead.

His blood was up. He filed another immensely informative piece on the effects on dairy produce of radiation for the *Sentinel*, and one in terse staccato sentence to the *Post* about the Poles and the Swedes pouring away a sea of milk. He felt his senses as finely tuned as a hound's on the hunt for a fox. The telephone interrupted him intermittently. Sometimes it was Harold bringing him up to date between briefings at different embassies, sometimes other journalists with questions or leads. Mostly it was radio stations. He had recently taken to appearing in the office only in his better suits. It did wonders for his self-esteem, besides sharpening his intellect and his comportment to match his tailored cut. Rising to stand braced with a sense of purpose, legs planted firmly apart, hand on hip, George broadcast to Britain, to Ireland, and on one heady occasion, to France. In French.

His final telex back from London was a brief note from the *Post* to the effect that in view of present circumstances, Bob Mathisson would be postponing his Moscow trip until early June.

Something in this message bothered George but he was too pressed to take time to identify what it might be. Harold returned from trawling the embassies for facts. He had little to offer but a bottle of vodka which he assured George was the perfect antidote to the effects of radiation. The Soviets were saying so. Gravely George swallowed a slug and relinquished the telex machine to Harold.

Then Gosteleradio shut down its TV satellite for what was described, to Harold's immense satisfaction, as maintenance work.

'Ah, glasnost, glasnost, where are you now? At last they have come to realize, like us journalists of the old guard, that access to accurate information can ruin a story. Speculation is so much more satisfactory and never did anyone any harm.'

The American, the Japanese and the European networks were at once denied their critical – in both senses – televisual link and George's telephone rang with greater urgency. Now he stood to broadcast even more widely – to the television masses. Harold remarked that posed like that, all he needed was a cliff at his feet and the wind rushing through his hair. At nine the first pictures appeared on Soviet television of the battered reactor, a faint plume of smoke filtering into the heavens, with the announcement that a hundred and ninety-seven people had been admitted to hospital and forty-nine of these already released. It was not Charlie's two thousand. But in all other respects, a satisfactory day for a foreign correspondent.

The following morning George joined the press corps behind its cordoned off section of Red Square to celebrate May Day.

'The show must go on,' Winston remarked.

'Poor bastards,' said Ned. 'They have no idea the fuckup their leaders have gotten them into.'

Balloons and flags fluttered coquettishly in the wind as phalanx upon phalanx of Soviet workers marched towards the far end of the square where the assorted domes of St Basil's Cathedral rose like a series of crazily corcheted teacosies above the milling crowds. The journalists were tense and tight-lipped. The ambassadors of Europe had been summoned the previous evening to the Soviet Foreign Ministry to be assured that there was no danger of radiation to their countries. With these thousands of heads bobbing under placards in the parade beneath them. it was hard to believe that the statement was anything but reasonable. But the journalists, of course, still had pages and prime-time to fill while the story remained the current focus of world attention. Students were arriving from Kiev and Minsk. They should be good for several emotional paragraphs on how the disaster had affected actual people available for interview. And in English to boot. Having sized up the May Day parade, the press corps was ready to move on to the next item, the clinic in the north of Moscow at which the students would be checked over. But how to get to them? May Day was a public holiday, a day off that included all Russian staff, crisis or no crisis. Who would drive?

'I can take three. Four at a pinch,' said George. 'But I'm really going to have to write the parade up as we go.'

'Me, too, old chap,' said Winston. 'Besides, things with wheels and I are not overly compatible.'

'Ask Svenson to come with us,' said Charlie. 'He's radio. He was doing his stuff as it happened. He can drive. And if he needs, he can probably shout some more into his microphone as we go.'

The clinic was a confusion of embassy officials, white-coated doctors, camera crews and press corps all shouting at one another while the local manager of the British airline into Moscow passed quietly among the bewildered students dispensing fresh track suits and stuffing their contaminated clothing into garbage bags. George, Svenson, Charlie and Winston moved about, taking notes and quotes.

Then it emerged that some of the students had already been released and were at the airport waiting to board the British Airways plane. The journalists broke for their cars and a phalanx of foreign vehicles travelling in the Zil lane at eighty miles an hour with their headlights on tore up Leningradsky Chaussee towards Sheremetyevo Airport. God, but if this wasn't what journalim was all about!

George couldn't bear the momentum to drop. At each assignment he issued invitations to everyone around him to participate later in a May Day celebration at his flat. He continued to offer them throughout the day to anyone who came through the office, until some time mid-afternoon when it occurred to him that perhaps he ought to alert Alice to the imminent arrival of a cast of thousands.

Her response to the news, George reflected, could have been usefully compared to the explosion at Chernobyl. Still, he thought comfortably, she would have been 'stabilized', to use the current jargon, long before he returned with the advance guard and several crates of beer to open the proceedings.

He and Harold took turns at the telex machine. He filed a thoughtful op-ed piece to the *Sentinel* on the challenges to Mr Gorbachev that this disaster represented. He filed colour pieces to the *Sentinel* and the *Post* on the Red Square parade and finally he filled an up-date to each on the state of the students.

To the *Sentinel:*

AS MOSCOW CELEBRATED MAY DAY WITH PARADES IN RED SQUARE YDAY BRITISH STUDENTS FROM KIEV AND MINSK WERE BEING SCANNED WITH GEIGER COUNTERS AND TOLD THEY WERE QUOTE EFFECTIVELY HEALTHY UNQUOTE

And so on
To the *Post:*

A HUNDRED TIRED AND WORRIED BRITISH STUDENTS LEFT A MOSCOW CLINIC LAST NIGHT WITH A CLEAN BILL OF HEALTH FROM THE SOVIET AUTHORITIES STOP BUT THE STUDENTS WERE NOT REASSURED STOP PARA QUOTE THE GEIGER COUNTER THEY PASSED OVER ME FLICKERED BETWEEN 10 AND 20 UNQUOTE SAID ANNIE THORNTON 21 OF BLISHAM POLYTECHNIC, QUOTE BUT I DON'T KNOW WHAT THAT MEANS AND THEY WOULDN'T TELL ME STOP CLOSE QUOTE

Etcetera.

Thoroughly satisfied with the day's work he left for home.

By ten o'clock the flat was tight with bodies. George had concocted a May Day radiation cocktail, an awesome vermilion mix of vodka, grenadine and soda which he gleefully touted as 'lethal'. Alice had made an enormous tub of chilli, an enterprise which had spread to several Serpuhovsky Val ovens to minimize the threat of wattage overload on any one of them. The lifts still reeked of spiced mince.

'I get it, Alice,' said Winston, prodding his. 'Red hot. Very clever.' Alice was appalled. She stared at the mixture in horror.

People lay about the floor, sated, empty bowls streaked a rich terracotta beside them. Alice and Babs stepped around them, collecting debris. Babs was packed into a scarlet track suit with a curious sheen to it.

'The May Day special. You like? My latest catalogue acquisition,' she said. 'I thought the Spandex made my bottom a bit smaller.' She gazed hopefully at Alice.

Charlie was hero of the hour. He had gone ahead and filed his '2000 Dead in Horror Holocaust' story. The instant his paper had hit the streets the wires had begun to buzz with demands to all bureaux for confirmation and follow-up. Journalists crowded about him either grimly furious or openly admiring of what most saw as an act of blatant irresponsibility and cold professionalism. As if his dubious bid for fame were not enough, he had somehow contrived to colour his moustache a vivid red in honour of the day.

Even Winston had made an effort to acknowledge the occasion. He was wearing a bright red tie, a manifestation of lightheartedness that his colleagues found mildly surprising. Kurt, the curious military man from the German Embassy, turned up encased in aluminium foil, explaining that if it did not protect him externally, then at least he was ready for cooking.

In the sitting-room a young Russian refusnik poet Harold had brought along delivered an impromptu and dreadful Ode to the Valiant Fire Fighters of Chernobyl. Svetlana arrived with the information that her neighbours were pointedly blaming the Jews for the whole catastrophe. There were tense jokes about new career possibilities such as road reflectors, luminous speaking clocks, and bedside lamps. Someone produced a guitar and extemporized four verses, uneven in quality but enthusiastically received, of something called Moscow May Day Radiation Blues. Alice stood with a stack of bowls in her hands. Was this bravery or lunacy? At what point did you decide to get up and get out?

As the Masons and the Simpsons gathered at their front doors the next day to usher their children off to school, the little Japanese from the end of the corridor emerged from his flat. Instead of bowing and turning smartly towards the lift, he approached them, brandishing his shiny briefcase. He stopped in front of the group, swung the case towards him and snapped it open. From it he withdrew a small object the size of a tape recorder and flourished it at Jonathan. Jonathan took it, Babs peering curiously over his shoulder. Jonathan looked at the thing, puzzled, then studied it more closely.

'Geiger counter?' he asked, passing it across to George.

The Japanese gentleman brought his heels together and bowed. 'Geiger counter,' he agreed.

'Oh, dear God,' said Alice. The tiny machine suddenly brought home to her more forcefully than any detailed information the implications of the disaster. The Japanese retrieved the instrument with a happy smile and retreated to the lift. Wordlessly, Babs disappeared into her flat. Without a sound, the men ushered the silent children down the corridor and Alice was left alone wondering what she was supposed to do next.

Mid-morning Babs knocked on the door to tell Alice that some official embassy action was at last being taken. Samples of foodstuffs and grass were being sent back to London for analysis and the British Embassy was advising its Moscow residents not to touch local milk or dairy products, to peel all fruit and vegetables and not to buy meat offal.

'Meat offal, for heaven's sake? That's the least of my worries.'

'The embassy's under pressure to fly in food for the children,' Babs said. 'The Japanese are already doing it.'

'Thank God. When's it going to begin?'

'They haven't actually decided if it's necessary yet.'

Alice clutched at her forehead in despair. 'What kind of disaster does it take to get the embassy to look after us?'

'A geiger counter is coming from London. I think they're going to let us use it to check the food we buy.'

'I should bloody well hope so. What else would they want it for?'

'Look, I shouldn't have told you this, you know. You'd better phone the embassy to hear it officially.'

'Babs, I find this outrageous. Why shouldn't you have told me? What damage could I do with the information? Aren't we all in this together?' Babs was silent. 'All right, who do you want me to call? The Minister?'

'Actually, the Minister is – well, indisposed.'

'Oh, for God's sake. What a time to choose!'

George's own sense of outrage was also receiving a fine tuning, though his concern was on behalf of the Soviets. Nadya, who had been dismissive of the disaster and sceptical of the Westerner's response, calling it an anti-Soviet destabilization tactic, suddenly expressed alarm on behalf of a pregnant relation. The woman had been advised by her doctor to eat plenty of cheese and yoghurt and to drink quantities of milk. Hadn't George said dairy produce was contaminated?

George telephoned round some Soviet doctors. Then he left the office for a covert meeting in a boulevard park with a Moscow gynaecologist. The man's explanation was the same as the others'.

'If I tell them to stop taking dairy products because it will damage the foetus I will be in trouble for spreading alarm.'

Typed George to the *Sentinel*:

SOVIET MEDIAL SOURCES CLAIMED YDAY THAT THEY WERE HAVING TO RELY ON WESTERN INFORMATION ON HOW TO COMBAT THE EFFECTS OF RADIATION STOP SINCE SOVIET AUTHORITIES WERE INTENT ON MINIMIZING THE SIGNIFICANCE OF THE DISASTER COMMA A TOP MOSCOW SPECIALIST TOLD THE SENTINEL COMMA DOCTORS WERE UNABLE TO ASVISE PATIENTS WHAT PRECAUTIONS TO TAKE STOP

To the *Post*:

AS TOP US BONE MARROW EXPERTS FLEW INTO MOSCOW LAST NIGHT TO HELP IN THE BATTLE TO SAVE RADIATED VICTIMS OF THE CHERNOBYL NUCLEAR DISASTER COMMA SOVIET DOCTORS WERE BITTERLY ATTACKING THE CONTINUED SILENCE OF THEIR GOVERNMENT ON THE DANGERS THE POPULACE IS FACING STOP

Still, some appropriate advice was filtering through, albeit carefully disguised. A Soviet contact called to tell him that his son had come back from school with the information that all fruit and vegetables should be peeled because foodstuffs in the city warehouses had been accidentally infected with rat poison.

Then trains coming into Kievsky Voksal began debouching children by the score, arriving unescorted from the Ukraine, dispatched to friends and relations in Moscow by frightened parents. The press corps were prevented from approaching the evacuees by a cordon of militiamen.

Finally, when it seemed there could be no further shocks,

the telephone rang once more on George's desk. It was Lisa Prowse. Her voice was clipped.

'George. I'd like you to come to Charlie's office if you could. As soon as possible. I've called a press conference. I think you should be there. Charlie's been arrested.'

Chapter Twenty-One

George walked briskly across the compound towards the Prowses' apartment block. The day was surprisingly hot for early May, the sun beating down on the stale dust of the rough pavement. On the thin trees dotted vaguely about the car park small nibs of green had begun to sprout. George noticed that beyond the rows of Volvos, Saabs and Mercedes fronting the side of the wide quadrant a small black Volga was parked. Poking from the top of one of its darkened windows was the lens of a video camera. George turned into the doorway of Korpus 5 and climbed the stairs to the fourth floor.

He could hear the murmuring of voices long before he arrived. The landing was an obstacle course of trailing leads and filming equipment. He pushed his way into the flat, nodding to grave-faced correspondents. People were crowded into the corridor leading to the dining-room, where a space had been left at the head of the table behind a hedge of microphones. Camera lights were set up around the walls, and journalists stood about grimly subdued, their notebooks open. They had been badly shocked. The worst punishment that any of these correspondents had ever considered was expulsion. Imprisonment had seemed utterly out of the question.

Lisa Prowse emerged from the kitchen, followed by Winston Fitch, his pale hair falling across his forehead.

She looked dishevelled and exhausted, drained of colour. The big black shirt she wore tucked into a pair of purple pantaloons was crumpled like a paper bag. As she passed through the phalanx that opened before her, people reached across to squeeze her shoulder reassuringly, pat her back in sympathy. But no-one spoke. What was there to say?

She pulled out the chair at the head of the table and sat. She studied her hands clenched in front of her for a moment, then looked up, turning her head to absorb all these faces of friends and colleagues of her husband.

'Thank you all for coming. I think perhaps if I tell you what happened, insofar as I know it. Then you ask me any questions.'

The camera crews adjusted their lenses, the radio correspondents their tape recorders, and the rest their notepads. She stared down at her hands again and drew a deep breath.

'Charlie got a phone call. Late this morning. He'd come back for a quick sandwich on his way over to the American Embassy. He answered the phone, not me. But he said it was a contact from Kiev who had some papers for him. He didn't say this out loud. He wrote it on our magic slate. He just put "woman from Kiev. May have info, confirm 'Dead' story." I said "Where?" and he wrote "Gorki Park riverside folly." Then he gave me a kiss and told me he'd be back at the office in an hour and he would call me from there. And that's the last I saw of him.' She gave a short intake of breath and squeezed her knuckles more tightly. Winston rubbed her shoulder. There was a rustling of notepads. 'That's all I can tell you.'

'How did you find out he had been arrested?'

'I waited to hear from him and when an hour and a quarter had gone by and he hadn't rung, I telephoned his office. Irina said he was out somewhere, she didn't know where. The moment I hung up, my phone rang. When I picked it up a voice announced that I was to be advised that my husband had been arrested in Gorki Park and was being held in custody. When I asked what the charges were, the line went dead.'

'What did you do next?'

'I telephoned the British Embassy and spoke to the Consul. As soon as I'd finished, the phone rang again. And another voice, a different one, informed me that Charlie was being held on suspicion of accepting sensitive material.'

'Shit,' someone muttered. 'That's spying.'

'Sure,' whispered another, 'but suspicion is not the same as proof. He hasn't been charged yet.'

'I talked to the Consul again and he is now in the process of lodging an official complaint. I understand there is not much more they can do at this stage. The embassy is trying to find out when I can go and see Charlie.'

'Where is he being held?'

'Lefortovo Prison.'

'Boy oh boy. The Moscow Hilton.'

'Do you know anything about the woman who made the rendezvous?'

Lisa shook her head. 'Charlie just went straight out to meet her. He seemed to think she was bringing him some concrete evidence on the two thousand deaths story. He had been working on tracking down hard numbers so he could keep the story running. But I don't know for sure.' She spread her hands helplessly.

'Do you think he was set up?'

'Of course he was set up! Charlie is not a spy.'

'Why do you think he was set up?'

'Because they didn't like his story, of course! It's been an appalling embarrassment to them at a time when they're being shown up as not having told the truth at any point about Chernobyl. Either to their own people or to the rest of the world. Besides, Charlie's always been a thorn in their sides.'

'So you do think that particular story is to blame?'

'Yes, I do think that particular story is to blame.'

'What are your plans?'

'I don't have any plans. Just to try and see Charlie as soon as possible. To do whatever I can to get him freed as fast as possible.'

'Will you take the children out of the country?'

'I can't leave now! Not without Charlie. They might never let me back in again.'

Winston gently squeezed her shoulder again. He explained that he was going to help Lisa put together a small suitcase of things for Charlie – his shaving tackle, toothbrush, fresh underwear, some books – then drive her to meet the British Consul at Lefortovo. Lisa said she did not know if she would be permitted to see Charlie, but where else could she go? She wanted to be as close to Charlie as she could. The children were with neighbours, confused but calm, pacified with an extremely vague explanation of what had happened. If anyone wanted to telephone the flat to check if she had returned, they were more than welcome. She would be happy at all times to respond to calls.

'I really feel very strongly,' Lisa said, knocking her fists against the table for emphasis, 'that the more noise you can make on this one, the more you can help Charlie. I will be grateful for anything you can get your papers and producers to do to cover it. The Soviets have got to be made to see that they can't get away with this.'

The journalists filed out in respectful silence.

'There but for the grace of the KGB,' murmured Ned.

George strode back across the compound to his office. The Volga was still in place, camera angled at the entrance to Korpus 5. Nadya was punching away at the telex machine. Harold was sitting at his desk, swinging gently back and forth on the back legs of his chair.

George bent and peered closely into his face. 'Harold? Are you with us?'

Nadya snorted. Harold flourished his hand in the air. 'Are you not witness, dear boy? Where else should I be?'

'I meant in spirit as well as in body. You've been drinking.'

'My dear fellow! I have been but partaking of my medication! As befits the dutiful Soviet citizen!' He reached down beneath his desk and re-emerged brandishing a half empty bottle of vodka. 'Have you not heard? Large quantities of this restorative liquid taken with spoonfuls of iodine have been identified as the best possible antidote to radiation poisoning. I have, of course, omitted the iodine. I find it an unpalatable addition.'

'Who told you this?'

'I gleaned it straight from the horse's mouth. Indeed, several herd of horses. I have been standing vigil at Kievsky Voksal to witness the arrival of the innocent children of Kiev. Too touching. They come alone, the simple creatures, by the several hundred, on every train. When I asked of them, in my most fatherly fashion, if they were not a tiny bit concerned for the health of the loved ones left behind, they were able to assure me of the efficacy of this most admirable remedy. I confess I found my excursion into the world of investigative journalism thoroughly rewarding.'

'Harold, you'll have to sober up. We have another story on our hands.'

'That the Soviets are closing down their other twenty-four reactors of the Cernobyl type? It is not true.'

'Harold, what are you talking about?'

'There's a telex from London. Two papers are running the story – a Yank and one of ours. London wants to know if there's any substance. There is not. Since the two correspondents concerned were seen lunching together yesterday, it is widely believed they made it up.'

266

'Who saw them lunching together?'

'I did.'

'Ah.'

George moved thoughtfully round to his desk. 'Still, that's not the story I'm talking about. Charlie Prowse has been arrested.'

The demented chattering sound of a single key eating rapidly into the ticker tape issued from the direction of the telex machine. George and Harold turned their heads. Nadya was sitting white-faced, her hands fallen flat across the keyboard. George looked at Harold.

Harold stared blandly back. 'Has he, by George?' he said. 'Couldn't have happened to a—'

'Shut up, Harold. Sober up. This is about the only event in the world that could upstage Chernobyl and they'll be screaming for copy any minute now. Besides, a little solidarity might be more in order. You'd better think about knuckling down to it.'

'*Absolutna*, dear boy. I assure you I shall rise to the occasion with my usual verve.' He flexed his fingers together and peered at George over the top of his gold-rimmed spectacles.

'So tell me, veteran Moscow observer. What should we make of this? How will it play?'

'Well now. What has Master Prowse been charged with?'

'He doesn't actually appear to have been charged yet. But they've apparently got him on suspicion of handling sensitive documents.'

'Not promising. And where do they have him?'

'In Lefortovo. At least he's not in Lubyanka.'

'Why, have you heard the service is better in Lefortovo? I assure you, it is said to be far more efficiently run.'

'Perhaps, Harold, you should think about doing a colour piece on the Hell-Hole Cells of Moscow. You're about the only one of us who could provide a personal view.'

'Tsk, tsk, George. We fight on the same flank. We must adhere in the face of adversity. Cheek by jowl.'

On the other side of the river Alice was beginning to wonder how many alternative flanks were currently taking up their positions. For her, the only battle she was aware of was Chernobyl, and the various flanks the growing factions that were coming together, colliding, then splitting, like incompatible microbes on a lab slide, into fiercely opposing groups.

The Soviet authorities were lined up on two separate fronts, facing an increasingly alarmed populace on one side and the rest of the world on the other. The foreign community had already devolved into several alternative cliques: those who were considered too complacent, and those too excitable; those who were judged helpful and those who were thought obstructive; those who had decided to leave, and those who scoffed at their panic and were staying.

Among these last was a subsection of those like Alice who would have preferred to go but were beginning to wonder whether the countries for which they would be bound might not have suffered worse contamination than Moscow. After several days of fruitless endeavour, she had finally managed to get a call through to her mother, who talked with weathermen impassivity of wet fronts bringing radiation-laden rain from the Soviet Union.

Then there was a growing bitterness between each of the nations and their embassy officials. The Japanese were flying in fresh supplies to Japanese residents. American civilians were receiving regular information on food safety and precautionary advice. European embassies volunteered a constant flow of information, advice and access to embassy supplies to their citizens. The French Embassy had warned its countrymen not to buy veal. The Italians had advised against pork. They and the Germans already had geiger counters in situ and samples of foodstuffs were being regularly flown by each of them for analysis back to their homelands. None of their nationals thought any of this was enough. Yet here was Alice, weighed down with three plastic bags full of produce, unable to check on the British Embassy geiger counter whether or not it was edible.

'See, miss,' said the security officer, looking small behind the imposing front desk, 'we haven't got one. I don't know where you would have picked up the idea we did have a geiger counter, I'm sure. I dare say they may send us one in time. But we haven't got one right at this moment.'

Alice looked down. One of the plastic bags was leaking a thin stream of brown across the aqua embassy carpet. 'What do you suggest I do?'

'I don't know, miss. It wouldn't be right for me to say.' He leaned forward confidentially. 'You could boil it all before you cook it, couldn't you?'

'Boiling is cooking. It would probably seal any contamination in for good.'

Alice gazed towards the wide mahogany staircase, at the tapestries hanging above the linenfold. She glanced around the wood-panelled hall. All was silent. The building might have been empty.

'Thank you,' she said to the security man. For what? Despair submerged her like a fog. She dragged her bags back out to the car.

She drove back to Serpuhovsky Val and hauled her shopping upstairs and on to the washing machine. It was still there, unloved by all but Galina, its right to respect usurped by the new model nonchalantly agitating clothes in the bathroom. Today the sight of the machine enraged her. She kicked it, then kicked the front door. She marched into the kitchen and dumped the bags on the floor. Galina was at the freezer, wiping potatoes with a damp cloth.

'Galina, what on earth are you doing?' Alice asked irritably.

'Sterilizing the vegetables.'

'With what, for heaven's sake?'

'Iodine,' said Galina comfortably.

'Explain to me, Galya, what iodine can possibly do for the common tuber.'

She shrugged. 'It purifies. There was a queue so long this morning at the *Apteka*,' she chuckled, 'iodine will be *defitzit* by the end of the week, mark my words!'

'That will certainly seal its reputation, if nothing else can.'

Galina plunked a potato into the bowl of rusty looking liquid. 'You take things too seriously, madam. So long as you make a few sensible adjustments, there is no reason why you can't eat as normal.'

'Iodine with everything?'

Galina nodded complacently. 'Of course. And you must boil the milk and boil the water and cook all the food for a long, long time.'

'There's a man at the British Embassy, Galya, who you should get to meet.'

The advice, which was being widely broadcast by the Soviets, was looked upon with considerable scepticism by the foreigners – even those foreigners from countries deemed by Western nationals to be on a par, in the information stakes, with the Soviet Union. It was advice, Alice learned, that was even less acceptable to the nanny faction. As she emerged from the flat towards teatime to collect Harriet from her afternoon with Ben, she found Hazel in the corridor struggling with a large placard on a stick.

'Can I give you a hand with that?'

Hazel blushed and Alice glanced down at the board.

'Perestroika for the Moscow nannies,' it read. 'Don't make Chernobyl victims out of us!'

'Good grief. What is that all about!'

Hazel said primly, 'It's all right for you, Mrs Mason. You're free to decide what you want to do about this calamity. We can't. We've got to go along with whatever you all choose. And nobody's bothered to ask our opinion. We're people too, you know.' Hazel's thin face glowed with indignation.

'So what is your opinion? If you have any better ideas than anyone else, I'm sure we'd all be glad to hear them.'

'Then why doesn't anyone ask us? We're exploited, us nannies. We're no more than extra staff, to go with the maid and the driver.'

'I don't think that's fair, Hazel,' said Alice reasonably. 'After all, nannies are included in the family. However, the fact is, if there has to be a final absolute distinction, staff is exactly what you are. Where are you taking this thing, anyway?'

'We're protesting in the Sad Sam compound.'

'Does Mrs Simpson know?'

Hazel looked defiantly at her. 'I don't see this is any of her business. It's my free time. I can do what I want with it.'

'Yes, of course. But it might be a little less provocative if you simply told her how you felt. Haven't any of you talked to your employers?'

'They don't talk to us. Anyhow, what kind of discussion do you think I could have with someone who pinches my things?'

Alice was shocked. 'Hazel, that is a very serious accusation. I find it hard to imagine you can have any foundation for making it. But I hope you believe you do have, because it would be extremely unwise to repeat it otherwise.'

Hazel drew her gaunt frame erect and spoke indignantly. 'I certainly do have foundation. They've taken one of my books. I know they have because I haven't lent it out and I've asked around all my friends and none of them took it. They wouldn't have without asking.'

Alice went cold and felt her face begin to suffuse with colour. She gestured vaguely. 'It's probably mislaid somewhere. Behind the bed or under a cupboard, or something. Or perhaps the children?' She couldn't bring herself to finish the sentence.

Hazel shook her head. 'I've talked to them and I looked through their things. No. Mr or Mrs Simpson has taken it.'

'Well if I were you I would put that idea right out of your head. I feel absolutely sure it will turn up', said Alice with finality, wondering how she could possibly infiltrate the copy of *Utterly Female* back onto Hazel's shelf without focusing even greater suspicion upon the Simpsons. 'I'm going down in the lift. Do you want any help with that thing?'

'I can manage, Mrs Mason, thank you,' Hazel said primly. She hauled the cumbersome piece through the sliding doors, leaning it against her angular shoulders. The slogan bore down on them both. 'I know you think we're just causing trouble. But we do have some feeling. We were going to protest in Kutz. We would have had much more impact there.'

'Why don't you? You might as well, if you're going to do it at all.'

Hazel looked affronted. 'We wouldn't have wanted to draw attention to ourselves when there's poor Mrs Prowse sitting upstairs with all her problems. We felt it wasn't right.'

'What particular problems are these that you're so sensitive to?'

'Didn't you know? Oh, Mrs Mason. Mr Simpson telephoned from the embassy at lunchtime. The KGB has arrested Mr Prowse.'

Alice felt the lift lurch slightly and the dim light blacked out for a brief instant. She put her arms out to steady herself.

'Mrs Mason? Are you all right?'

'Yes. Yes, thank you. I'm fine. It just gave me a bit of a shock, that's all. I didn't know. My god, poor Lisa.'

'Yes, well you see, that's why we're demonstrating in Sad Sam,' said Hazel. 'Like I said, it didn't seem right.'

'Yes, of course. I don't suppose it would.' Alice felt quite faint. What was the girl gabbling about? 'Can I – do you want a lift somewhere?' Where was Hazel going?

'It's OK, Mrs Mason. I'll get a cab.'

Alice drove by some sort of remote control that guided her round the traffic-charged Koltso. She could only think how despite the taps on the phone, the bugs in the walls, the tracers on the cars, the reports, the steamed-open letters, the militiamen, and the foreigners' deliberately provocative response to all these official challenges, she had never really perceived the KGB as anything more than a shadowy instrument of intimidation, malevolent but contained. Never, never would she have believed that they would take action against a foreigner.

How safe, then, had any of them ever been? If Charlie, with his glibness, his jokes and asides to the ceiling, feeding a popular newspaper with simplified politics, could fall victim, how secure were the rest of them? It was all too much to take in one short period, she thought. First the bodies are slowly poisoned by contaminated air, by contaminated food, then they are thrown into jail.

When she returned to the flat, dragging a tired and protesting Harriet behind her, Galina reported that the *gospadin* required her to telephone him. Alice did so willingly.

'George, I've just heard about Charlie. Is he all right? What happened?'

'Lisa's at the prison with the Consul at the moment. We

don't know if they'll be allowed to see Charlie tonight, but they'll probably be given some formal meeting arrangement if not. As you can imagine, this is going to be keeping me in the office late again, Alice. Sorry, and all that. It's a real bastard of a time.'

'Why did they pick Charlie, George? I mean, his paper isn't taken that seriously, surely.'

'Everything is taken seriously here if it suits. I really don't want to talk about this on the telephone, all right? Look, I rang because I've decided we should order in some fresh food from Helsinki until we know what's happening with the local stuff. So draw up a list, will you, and I'll telex it across tomorrow.'

'Food? Real food? Gosh, George.' Alice was almost alarmed at the prospect. 'Can we afford it?'

'The *Sentinel* can damned well help out. If they want coverage from the war zone, they can subsidize the troops.'

'But what should I order? I mean, I hardly know where to begin!'

'How about avocado pears for a start?'

Alice laughed rather shakily. 'Avocado pears! Of course! God you're so right!'

'And cornflakes.'

'And cornflakes!'

'What about Marmite? Marmalade. And bacon? Come on, Alice. We've spent practically every night for the last few months lying in bed imagining what we would buy when we next got out. Just write it all down!'

'What can I say, George? Every cloud has a silver lining, it seems.'

'Even irradiated ones.'

Despite his rejoinder, Alice felt her spirits rise.

Next morning they plummeted once more. Passing through the office for coupons on her way to the Diplomatic

Gastronom (Babs had observed that if there was any safe food to be had in Moscow, it was bound to be available at the secret Kremlin stores and the D), she found George and Harold assessing a call Harold had just received. A young Soviet student staying in Moscow with friends had telephoned at their insistence. She told him that when she had rung her family in a village near Kiev to say she was coming home, they had pleaded with her not to.

'They said they were sick,' the girl had sobbed down the line, 'with streaming eyes and headaches and skin cracking round their mouths.'

'Oh, God, can it be true?' cried Alice in anguish.

George spread his hands. 'That is the point. It may well be. In fact, it probably is. But without a proper source we can check out, we really don't feel we can run it – especially in view of what's happened to Charlie.'

Controls had tightened on the reporting front. The television satellite link was still closed down and now the Russian language broadcasts of the BBC World Service were being jammed.

Harold took off his gold-rimmed spectacles and rubbed them thoughtfully with a small square of chamois leather he retrieved from a pocket.

'You know, dear boy, I think I could have the way round this vexing problem.' He returned the spectacles delicately to the tip of his nose. 'We could give the story to Myra.'

Alice's heart crashed into something close to her ribcage and a small bubble pressed hard in her throat.

George slapped his desk. 'Harold, you genius! The perfect person!'

Alice looked at George in dismay. His enthusiasm for this mysterious trollop, this Delilah, this Jezebel, this slut, was clearly unabated. Stung, she snatched up the coupons and stormed out of the office. George and Harold exchanged a glance of surprise.

'You don't suppose, dear boy,' Harold began. Then the telephone on George's desk rang with the single peal of the international call. George plucked up the receiver and listened at length. Then he dropped the receiver back on its hook and turned to Harold.

'We may have movement on the Charlie story. The Prime Minister has been asked questions in the House. The Soviet Ambo was summoned to Downing Street an your ago and a formal protest made at the imprisonment without charges of a British citizen.'

Chapter Twenty-Two

For the next two weeks Charlie's confinement shoved Chernobyl to the bottom of the front pages of the world's press. Here was a tangible attack against a known being, instead of the insidious hidden threat in the air and the soil. Here, in Lisa Prowse, was a single visible woman in distress, instead of the faceless thousands in the Ukraine whose individual names no-one knew and whose individual pain could only be guessed at. The Moscow wives took as many precautions as before in food purchase and preparation, but the shift of focus instilled a certain nonchalance in their anti-radiation vigilance. After all, the calamity that had befallen Charlie could so easily have struck their own husbands.

Alice found a frozen Hugarian fowl in her local supermarket and decided to cook Peking Duck. She set about readying it under the inquisitive eye of Galina, who described at length what her previous German employers would have done with it. Alice plunged the defrosted bird briefly into boiling water, then looked about for a suitably airy spot in which to dry out its skin. She wandered fruitlessly through the flat, the duck dripping honey and soy as she went, and eventually decided that it would have to be suspended from the washing line on the balcony. To Galina's intense interest, Alice plunged a meat hook through the neck of the fowl and hung it outside the kitchen window. Alice's grasps of Russian was not adequate to explain in depth the principle of the Peking Duck ritual.

Twice during the night, tiptoeing naked through the flat in response to Daisy's summons, Alice diverted briefly on to the balcony to coat the duck with her soy and honey solution. The second time was just after dawn, and Alice could feel the rising sun's rays upon her bare back as she stroked the bird with her dripping pastry brush. Between now and Daisy's breakfast feed, she reflected it would probably grow a good deal hotter, and, the duck fat would begin to melt, undoing all her careful ministrations. Alice clutched her naked buttocks in thought a moment, then went inside and fetched an umbrella. Back on the balcony, she leaned nonchalantly bare against the railing and surveyed her equipment. The umbrella she opened and to its point attached a string. Then she hauled herself up on a chair to fix the string to a nail in the wall, cunningly suspending the umbrella above the duck to shade it. Pleased with her handiwork she clambered down, wiping her hands on her flanks with satisfaction. Suddenly her eye was caught by a movement across the compound.

Slowly Alice turned about. Directly opposite, vacantly shaking an eiderdown over the balcony of her apartment, a woman was staring mesmerized at the tableau before her. The previous few minutes replayed at speed through Alice's mind. Nude; dead duck, brolly. What explanation could possibly satisfy any Soviet? The scene merely confirmed what all of them knew to be true: Westerners were an exotic and shifty lot.

Alice suddenly roused herself, clapped her hands over her breasts and backed into the kitchen, her eyes locked with the woman's. George was at the stove in his towelling dressing-gown, watching the kettle boil. His hair was tousled and his face greasy from the warmth of the bed.

'George! You're up!'

He shrugged. 'I can't seem to sleep much lately. Too strung up, I suppose.'

'You're not planning to get the Moscow Blues again, are you, George?' Alice asked suspiciously.

'I didn't plan to get the Moscow Blues. Anyhow, this is different. I don't feel tired. Just edgy. Can't sit still at all. Plus I've got a horrible analysis to do on Chernobyl's effect on the economy. I woke when you went for Daisy and couldn't get back to sleep so I thought I might as well get up and try to make a start on it before the office.' He pulled his sleeve down over his hand and grasped the handle of the kettle. 'Tea for you?' Alice shook her head. 'What were you doing out on the balcony?'

'Painting the duck.'

'Why did I ask?'

He carried his mug over to the freezer, where he had spread out sheaves of telex clippings. Then he turned and pulled Alice to him. He wrapped his arms tightly around her and said, 'Painting the duck. You know, Alice, I am a lucky man. I can't think there are too many people whose wives make them feel very affectionate towards them.' He kissed her on the nose.

'How about erotic?' Alice asked hopefully.

George tucked her head into his shoulder and stared wistfully over it out of the window. 'It used to be such an essential part of our relationship, didn't it? But I'm finding it hard to spoon up the extra energy it takes to do anything but flop whenever I get home. It's not the perfect set-up at present, is it? But it has to change. This kind of pace can't go on for ever. Think how Mrs Gorbachev must feel.'

Any hope that the focus upon the dramas of the Soviet Union would soon diminish dissolved that day.

It was suddenly wonderful weather, hot but not heavy, the city freshly green with shining new leaves and the roads cleared of the last of the old winter dust. Instead, balls of white woolly stuff rolled along the gutters. The *pookh* had begun to fly – fluff from the cottonwood poplars that Stalin had planted all over Moscow. When George turned on the venting system in the car, it shot out at him like popcorn in a funfair machine. He was still picking little bits of it off his jacket as he walked into the office.

On the way, he had called in to see Lisa Prowse. The maid had opened the door, her finger to her lips. George had followed her on tiptoe down the hall and peeped into the kitchen at Lisa asleep at the table, her head on her folded arms. He had retreated softly without waking her.

He arrived in the office to find Nadya bent over Harold's desk reading out loud from *Pravida*, Harold sipping steadily from a glass of clear fluid. Harold had begun to drink openly in the office, starting earlier and earlier each day. Nadya no longer bothered to restrain him.

Harold looked up as George came in and waved him to approach. 'Listen in, dear boy. The confessions of Gorby's personal science adviser. Most instructive.'

George pulled up his chair.

'Now you must bear in mind that Professor Velikov is speaking of Russian efforts at control during a period in which the IAEA experts were swarming all over the site and we were being told foreign nationals in the area were quite safe. It adds colour.' He patted Nadya's shoulder. 'Proceed, my dear.'

Nadya raised the newspaper once more. '"The reactor is damaged",' she translated. '"Its heart is the white-hot core. It is as though in suspension. The reactor is covered on top with a layer of sand, lead, boron and clay, and this is an additional load on the structure. Down below, in a special reservoir, there might be water. How would the white-hot core of the reactor behave? Would we manage to keep it intact or would it go down into the earth? No-one in the world has ever been in such a complex position. It was essential to estimate the situation very accurately, and not to make a single error.""'

Nadya stopped and closed the paper. They were silent for a moment. Then George said, 'He's talking about possible China syndrome, isn't he?'

Harold released a short expulsion of breath. 'My own conclusion precisely.' Slumping back into his chair, he pushed his spectacles up on to his forehead and pinched the bridge of his nose between thumb and forefinger. His other hand hung limply over the arm of the chair, clutching his empty glass. 'A veritable dog's dinner, wouldn't you say?'

George could think of nothing to say, so he said, 'You're drinking too much.'

Harold flapped his hand dully in George's direction without opening his eyes. 'Please, dear boy. Don't be tedious. Take note of the excellent example of my wife. Keep your counsel. Life is too short.' He raised himself and bent towards his typewriter. 'Or not short enough, perhaps.'

Nadya looked at George. 'How is Lisa?'

Harold threw back his head in exasperation. 'Oh, spare us the solicitous enquiries, Nadya, do. They are most unbecoming.'

She reddened and rose. 'I will make tea.'

'That would be a far more politic strategem,' said Harold. 'God, how tiresome it all is.'

'What all?' asked George.

'The works, dear boy, the ageing process, incipient hair loss, life, the universe, glasnost, perestroika. At least under Brezhnev one would have been told absolutely nothing and thus been free to go about one's business as normal.'

'I don't exactly agree we've been told a helluva lot under Gorbachev.'

'Ah, but we know just enough to reach for our lifebelts.'

'Are you particularly fearful, Harold?'

'If this were a play,' Harold intoned, 'we would currently be acting out the final scene.'

'Good lord, I don't think things are quite that critical. Or do you have some more revealing information?'

'No. Indeed I have no information on anything. I speak not of personal safety. I refer to the waning of a certain historical period. I have only my own "overview" to offer.'

'Which is?'

'Simply that Chernobyl marks the watershed. As, in its smaller way, does the arrest of Master Prowse. Neither should have occurred. But since they have taken place, we watch, with the handling of both events, the death of the old order, the struggling to its feet of the new. So.' He raised his glass. 'Eat, drink and be merry, for tomorrow us old fogeys will be out of synch and die.'

'It's a wonderfully colourful scenario, Harold, but it really doesn't make a whole lot of sense. It seems to me both Chernobyl and Charlie's arrest show us just how little fundamental change has taken place under the new regime. In each case, the immediate response was secrecy and defensiveness.'

Harold peered at George over his spectacles. 'George, it is not necessary always to take me so literally. Incidentally, I was with the Minister last night—'

'A drinking companion of yours, is he?'

'You are disrespectful, George. I shall let that pass. He tells me the embassy has finally succeeded in persuading the Foreign Office to provide a geiger counter.'

'A month and a half after the event. Almost in time for Christmas.'

'This news is of personal concern. I trust it will not mean the end of the *Sentinel*'s Helsinki food run? Nadya and I are much enjoying our avocados.'

'Who am I to deprive a poor expat of his simple

pleasures, Harold? We can leave that kind of policy to the embassy. When does this machine arrive?'

'I am not a postroom boy, George. I have no idea.'

'Did the Minister say what spurred them on?'

'Apparently the FO in London checked on a consignment of veal bought at the Centralni Rinok last week. It was found to contain caesium at levels one hundred and thirty seven-times higher than that considered by the EEC acceptable for human consumption.'

'Holy shit.'

'Or not so holy, in this instance. Personally speaking, since I have not yet found the optimum moment for looking caesium up in the encyclopaedia, I am presently not overly concerned.'

'I don't think you'll find it's a substitute for monosodium glutamate, Harold. Did your drinking pal give any indication of when the embassy is like to brief us?'

'I wish you would not refer to the Minister with such irreverance. I harbour a good deal of professional admiration for the man.'

'He's a soak.'

'Not full time.' Harold stretched his arm beyond his double cuff and looked at his watch. 'If you make haste, you should catch a briefing in the embassy Dive Bar. It starts at ten.'

'Christ, Harold. Why didn't you tell me sooner?'

'The message is on your desk, dear boy.'

Sasha transported George at eye-shutting speed across Moscow and shrieked through the embassy gates with a grin to stamp on the brakes directly the other side of the sentries. George flung his hands out to brace himself.

'I wish you wouldn't do that, Sasha.'

The car slid at a more matronly pace round the side of the tennis court and deposited George outside the stable entrance to the basement cellar that was the Dive Bar. George descended and looked about him with interest. This was territory not normally within the bounds of non-embassy personnel.

There were surprisingly few people gathered in the Dive Bar, considering the degree of alarm spreading through the community. They were seated around the cream-painted walls, staring towards the well-stocked pub bar at the end of the room. To one side hung a dartboard. Like a northern working men's club hall, George reflected. He saw Winston Fitch, a couple of people from the wire services, but no substantial media presence. Geoffrey and Angela raised their hands to him.

'Got a nice one for you, George,' grinned Geoffrey as George passed by. He patted the empty seat beside him. George shook his head but bent to listen. 'Down at the market, OK? Ivan Ivanovich, with a queue a mile long at his counter, is shouting "Apples from Chernobyl! Apples from Chernobyl!" So the bloke at the counter next to his says, "I admire the honesty, Ivan, but how come your queue's so long?" And Ivan says, "Shut up, comrade, and listen to the end of it."'

George joined in and chorused with Geoffrey, '"Fruit for the mother-in-law! A kilo for the boss!" Christ, Geoff, it's a pretty foul joke.'

'You heard it already!' said Geoffrey, disappointed.

'Svetlana told me.'

Alice was sitting in a corner, reading a letter. George was put out.

'You're better briefed than I am,' he remarked as he sat down beside her.

Alice looked up from her letter in surprise. 'Hello, George. Is this newsworthy?'

'Everything is news,' he said solemnly. 'How did you get to hear about it, then?'

'The embassy phoned. They said there was a visiting scientist here who didn't mind advising us about food. Funny place, isn't it? Very British.'

George stared at Alice's knee. 'There's a big ladder in your tights.'

Alice plucked at her skirt. 'I know. I'm running out of good pairs. It's that damned washing machine. I catch them on it as I come out of the flat. If Galina doesn't get rid of it soon I'm going to sue her for physical damage.'

Babs crossed the floor and sagged down next to Alice. 'Well, this is all very jolly,' she said brightly.

'It is?' said Alice.

George looked about him. 'Quite a little pleasure dome you've got yourselves here, Babs. Taxpayers' money, is it?'

Babs flushed. 'Must you always mock, George?'

'Got to keep you in your place, Babs. Otherwise you diplomats might get the impression you were somehow better than us civvies.'

The Minister stepped hesitantly off the bottom stair down into the room. He reached out briefly and lightly touched the wall. Behind him came a ruddy-faced elderly man, short and stout, whose yellow-stained white hair and shredded eyebrows shone almost luminously against the redness of his gleaming skin. The two men ambled forward and leaned against the front of the bar, the Minister drawing the flaps of his tweed jacket round himself as though warming his posterior at a burning fire. He cupped one hand over the immense beak of his nose and stared thoughtfully at the carpet for a moment, stroking his receding hair with his other. His audience waited in silence. Lifting his weight from one foot to the other, his scarlet-flushed companion watched him uncomfortably. As people began to shift uneasily in their seats, the Minister said suddenly, 'This is our scientist. Visiting academic. Nothing to do with embassy. Wants to remain off the record. Kindly volunteered to help with advice. No names. All right?'

Then he grasped his nose again, flapped the scientist forward and dropped his chin on to his chest to listen. With a bewildered look, the scientist took a step away from the sanctuary of the bar and began to speak.

He was not reassuring. No-one really knew, he said, the long-term effects of eating even slightly contaminated food over an appreciable period. It wasn't the kind of thing testers volunteered for, ha ha. There had never been a situation before where experts and civilians were kept so much in the dark. And what one did know about, one fundamentally disagreed with.

'Such as?' Geoffrey demanded.

'Could you clarify, please,' said a wire service reporter.

Milk, said the scientist. The Soviet policy of processing their contaminated milk into cheese and butter, and dried milk powder into ice cream.

'It is difficult to see any justification for processing contaminated milk in this way,' he said. He pulled at one of his eyebrows. 'If you process twenty-five litres of milk into a block of cheese, the cheese will still contain all the original contamination from the milk. Most countries would simply throw away the milk, even for some days after the half-life of the iodine isotopes was over.'

'What about fruit?' snapped Alice. 'And vegetables?'

George looked at her in surprise.

The scientist shrugged. 'Depends where they have been harvested. All I can say is that everything is at risk. If you find that tomatoes at one shop have been contaminated, then go somewhere else.'

'Good grief, man,' expostulated Geoffrey. 'This is a state-controlled country. One shop stocks the same as all the others.'

'Then you will just have to check everything out on the geiger counter.'

The Minister stared fascinated at the ceiling.

'What geiger counter?' fumed a young woman with a small child on her knee. Another beside her clapped briefly.

'When are we going to get one?' called out a third.

The scientist deferred to the Minister but the Minister was still engrossed in the plasterwork above his head.

Winston Fitch rose to his feet. 'Minister, may I ask why it is that the German Embassy considers the danger of irradiated foodstuffs so acute that for the past month they have had a geiger counter available for the use of their nationals while the British Embassy still does not?'

'Ha!' exclaimed the Minister, shooting his arm to point triumphantly at Winston. 'Foreign office agreed now geiger counter be supplied.'

George joined Winston on his feet. 'But, with respect, Minister,' (he wished Harold could have heard him) 'you have not addressed the question of why it has taken the embassy so long.'

The Minister rocked back and forth in his brogues. He crossed his arms over his chest and leaned with interest towards the carpet. Suddenly he loked up and said, his eyes fixed on a point above everyone's head, 'Absolutely recognize whole community's feeling, failure from London to comprehend our particular predicament. Too much readiness, most people's liking, tell us not to worry.' Then he was silent again.

Alice stuck up her hand. The Minister, who was on the point once more of clutching at his proboscis, flung out his arm and pointed at her instead. 'Alice.'

'Is the embassy going to allow non-diplomats to shop at the Commissariat?'

Babs flushed.

'Under consideration,' said the Minister.

'Means no,' muttered George.

'When will the geiger counter arrive?' Angela demanded.

'Three four days. Will shortly issue timetable for use.'

'Timetable?' Alice protested.

'Timetable,' the Minister repeated. He looked at the scientist and rubbed his hands. 'All clear now? Good, good.'

He coughed and held his clenched fist at his mouth, considering. Then he looked up above their heads once more.

'British press in attendance. Small matter should announce. London uncovered number of Soviet spies.' His audience became suddenly alert. 'To be precise, four. Embassy attaché. Businessman and' – the Minister looked towards George and Winston, who were exchanging startled glances – 'two journalists. Strong complaint formally lodged Soviet Ambassador. Expulsion called for. Immediate. Effective end of fortnight. Official announcement on wire services now. Wanted to advise you personally.' He plunged his hands into his pockets and swung his head around at each of their faces. 'Thank you all for coming. Thanks to – er – our scientific adviser. Grateful, all of us, I'm sure.'

Then the Minister turned about, placed his hand upon the scientist's back and propelled him ahead of him up the steps of the Dive Bar.

'Relatively sober, I thought,' said Winston.

'What do you make of that?' said George, in wonderment.

'The spies? God knows. PM making some sort of point, I'd guess, though I can't imagine what it is. One thing you can be sure of, there'll be repercussions here. Always are.'

'How do you mean?' Alice had stood up between Winston and George. Babs appeared at her side and Geoffrey and Angela approached, hand in hand.

'That's a turn-up for the books, then. Spies in London?' said Geoffrey. 'What d'you reckon the Reds'll do?'

Winston flipped his hair out of his eye. 'What they always do, of course. Tit for tat. We expel theirs. They expel ours.'

'We haven't got any,' said Babs indignantly.

'If we don't,' said George, 'I shall be the first to complain. I pay good taxpayer's money to make sure we know at least some of their secrets.'

'Anyway, it's not relevant whether we have or not,' said Winston. 'What are we sloughing off?' He ticked them off on his fingers: 'Couple of journos, a businessman and an attaché, did he say? Well, you can bet your bottom rouble that before the week is through the Sovs will suddenly have discovered there are spies in the British community. And precisely one attaché, one businessman and two journalists will be shipped out west.' He grinned and opened his eyes wide. 'You never know, with any luck that could be the four of us!'

Chapter Twenty-Three

The Soviets did not wait a week to respond. They allowed the British community enough time to speculate, to hope, to dread, that each might be the chosen martyr (for no-one bothered to believe there might be any grounds for the allegations of espionage). Then they presented their own formal complaint to the British Ambassador.

Alice was sitting cross-legged on the floor playing with Harriet, Daisy propped against her thighs. She had taken both children down to the river beach at Serebryanny Bor after playgroup. The grassy hummocks had been dotted with babushkas sitting on opened newspapers weaving dandelion crowns for their charges. Alongside stretched Moscow's young elite, in the kind of loin coverage more closely associated with unique jungle tribespeople. Except that the strategic pieces were in assorted shades of dayglo nylon. And though the boys were demonstrating macho feats with penknives and sharpened sticks, their female accessories attended instead to crisp foreign clothing catalogues spread before them on the ground.

It had been hot and Alice had sat in the shade of a large bush beside Daisy's carrycot, considering the outfit she might wear to the approaching Sad Sam Summer Soiree. As the Broomball Ball marked the end of winter, so the annual compound thrash was a celebrated festivity that signalled the beginning of the foreign community's long summer break from Moscow. Planning one's dress for such an event involved an immense amount of thought and indecision. It had been a pleasantly distracting afternoon.

Both children had been fractious in the car on the way home. Now she was winding them down for the evening. Harriet was in nurse's uniform, testing Alice's blood pressure with a lurid plastic contraption and tapping Daisy's bare knees with a little yellow hammer. Alice was studiously devoting her full attention away from the contents of her wardrobe towards their entertainment, as part of a continuing effort at diversion from the deep dismay at herself that she had so far managed splendidly to ignore.

She had taken a stew round to Lisa Prowse – though heaven knows the Prowses' maid was hardly prevented from cooking by the imprisonment of her employer – and had been forced, in effect by the stew, to confront the difference between herself and Lisa Prowse. Alice had found herself wanting.

During the period of George's Moscow Blues, Lisa had come without summons to bolster Alice. Now, to Alice's shame, Lisa herself had had to provoke a similar initiative by Alice. She had telephoned to ask if Alice had any sleeping pills in her medical supplies. Lisa had finished hers and did not wish to go to the embassy doctor for more, since he would thus discover that she had been taking them two at a time instead of his prescribed one.

Although Alice had called upon Lisa once or twice, she had always contrived to be in the company of another of the compound wives. Lisa made Alice feel uncomfortable.

Lisa was a modern woman: clever, with a career of her own in a highly specialized field, self-confident, and independent, with a strong sense of the place of women in a world not subservient to men. Alice had looked gloomily down at the steaming casserole she had between oven-gloved hands. While Lisa had sought to soothe Alice with a mildly pornographic account of a woman's attempt to wing it alone, Alice had volunteered a comforting stew.

The doorbell chimed. Alice lifted Daisy off her lap, rose and went to the door. Babs faced her in silence, slouched inside her track suit with the deflated sag of a cold baked potato.

Alice looked at her brightly. 'Babs!'

She stared back without speaking.

Blood rushed to Alice's face, then she felt suddenly cold. 'Oh no!' she cried, and reached out her arms. Babs stumbled forward into them.

'Oh, God, Babs! I'm so sorry!' Alice patted and stroked the back of the gently sobbing figure. 'God, how bloody unfair! Of all people. Why does it have to be you two?'

Babs snivelled and wiped her nose on the sleeve of her sweatshirt. 'It's funny, really. I've not exactly enjoyed myself here. But still it's home. We've settled in. We've got a routine. We've got friends. Special ones. You know how kind everybody is here, Alice. We all look after each other, don't we? We make a team. It's like being in hospital. All organized and regulated but sort of safe. I don't want to leave. Not before time, anyway, I'm not ready for it.'

She sniffed. Alice fished in her pocket for a crumpled tissue. 'Here.'

Babs took it and blew her nose loudly. 'Besides, where are we supposed to go? Our house is let. We couldn't get it back in under three months. We'll have to stay with my mother-in-law. Oh, God!' She began sobbing again.

Harriet regarded the two women with fear. 'Why is Becka's mummy crying, Mummy?'

'She's had some bad news, Hattie. Come on, let's put the kettle on.' There she was again: stew, tea.

Alice led Babs into the kitchen. Galina was at the chest freezer making little *piroshki*'s. She glanced up at Babs and

Alice was startled to see a look of instant comprehension flood her face. Was there anything this woman did not know? Doubtless the maids too had been speculating among themselves over which one would be losing an employer. Galina retreated discreetly with her bowls to the dining-room table.

Babs slumped against the freezer and trumpeted again into the soggy scrap of tissue paper.

'How did you hear?'

'The Ambo called in the victims. Jonty telephoned me just now.'

'Who else is being chucked out? My God! It's not us, is it? It can't be, or we would have been told.'

Babs snorted. 'Can't you guess? And you the wife of a journalist? It's the story of the year – plot and double plot. You're slipping, Alice.'

Alice was astonished by her venom.

'It's Charlie Prowse, of course. Isn't that what this whole thing is about? Getting shot of him without losing face. It's one great big put-up job. Diplomatic dancing. The rest of us are just window-dressing.'

Alice stared at Babs, her dawning understanding of the subtlety of the deal lighting up her face in grudging appreciation. 'My God, they're clever. It tidies up the problem very neatly, doesn't it just?' She thought for a moment. 'Then who's the businessman?'

Babs shrugged. 'A pawn. It doesn't really matter, does it? It's such a farce, you could take your pick. But it happens to be Geoffrey Rimstead.'

'Geoff?' Alice was astonished. 'Why him? He's as straight as the day is long.'

'His bank has been pushing the Sovs to pay up instalments on loans and the Sovs have been trying to delay. That's what Angela says, anyway. Ya boo sucks diplomacy, she calls it.' Babs grinned ruefully. 'Ange, as you might expect, has really risen to the occasion. She's going to order a whole ton of food from Helsinki and empty out her freezer and all her stores and party every night until it's all finished or they leave – whichever comes first! She says if we've got to go at all, we have to go out in style. I wish it was an option for us. We've got to sell everything we can. You don't want a couple of sides of beef, do you? Or some Pimms? We've got crates of the stuff. We can't take it with us.'

Alice suddenly felt weighted down with depression. 'Stop it. Babs. I'm just beginning to realize you won't be living across from us any more. It's dreadful! I can't imagine the fifteenth floor without you all. It'll just be us and the Yemenis and the Japs!'

'And the cockroaches.'

'What will we do?' Alice stared mournfully at Babs who, by contrast, seemed to have cheered up. 'When do you have to go?'

'They've given us a fortnight. Exactly what we gave theirs. In fact we leave the morning after the Sad Sam thrash. Not a bad way to go, really. Look on the bright side, Alice. It's going to be party, party, party for the next two weeks. Hazel will finally be out of your hair – mine, too, of course. She can go straight back up to Huddersfield or Wetherby or wherever it is. I don't suppose there's many born-again whatsits up there. And your friend Charlie goes free!'

'I hadn't thought of that.'

'You also haven't asked who the second journalist is.'

'No, nor have I. So who is it? Wait, let me guess. Winston?'

'No, no, no.' Babs sounded impatient and looked smug. 'You haven't got the hang of this at all, have you? They're much more canny than that. Winston would be a wasted opportunity. He hasn't bothered the Sovs. He's only his own worst enemy.' She paused, enjoying herself. 'You'll love it. It's pure genius. You can't guess?'

Alice shook her head.

'It's Harold.'

Alice expelled a long breath of genuine admiration. 'You're right. It is pure genius. How very, very clever.'

In the office in Kutz, except for the chink of bottle against glass as Harold poured himself a shaking draught of vodka, this act of pure genius had stimulated only silence. George contemplated Harold across the desk, his hands locked under his chin. Nadya was sitting white-faced in the telex chair, her face tight, on the verge of tears.

Harold raised his glass. 'Comrades! Let us drink! To freedom, folly, and the future!' He took several deep swallows and very carefully positioned the glass in the centre of the pile of newspapers laid out in front of him. His skin was ashen and every now and then his body jerked violently inside his baggy striped shirt.

'Pour me a tot, Harold.' George rose and handed Harold his tea mug. 'It's bad luck to toast alone.'

'Dear boy, my days of bad luck are over! I am to be dispatched to the land of my fathers with the blessing of this great land of mothers.' He sighed theatrically. 'It is time I was reunited with the soil of my home. One cannot deny one's *amor patriae* for ever.'

George stared down into his drink and said nothing.

At the telex Nadya stirred. 'What of me, Harold?' she said dully. 'What will become of me?'

Harold flung his arms into the air. 'You will become a *cause célèbre*, my dear! I shall remonstrate! Demonstrate! I shall march in the streets! My wife shall not be denied a visa to follow her victimized spouse! It shall become an Incident. An Issue. A scandal of international proportion, never fear.' He took up his glass again and leaned towards

Nadya across his desk. 'In the meantime, my dear, you are free to bid for the pickings of the supply cupboards of my unfortunate fellow-expellees. Make hay while the sun shines. Tomorrow lightning may strike.' He drained the rest of his glass.

Nadya rose heavily. 'Why you do always attribute to me such mercenary appetites?'

'Come, come. You do me wrong. I have the highest regard for the Soviet instinct for self-preservation, my dear Nadya. I am not so mean-spirited as not to recognize that without it my life in this admirable country would not have been half so comfortable. I merely point out to you that with these departures there are opportunities to increase your *blat* which I trust you will not deny yourself out of respect for my delicate sensibilities. Now, more than ever, is the time to look to the feathering of your little nest, my pigeon. Who knows how long your so-called "security clearance" may be stuck in the works before you are at liberty to follow me to the shopping centres of the West?'

Nadya smiled emptily. 'You like me so much, Harold. We shall enjoy such a happy life together in the United Kingdom of Great Britain, no?' She put her hand softly to the top of his head as she passed. 'I will make tea.' Joylessly she left the room.

Harold sighed. 'Tea. Always tea. The universal solace. The very air we breathe must surely be compounded of sweated tea molecules.'

George ran his finger thoughtfully round the rim of his mug. 'Will they let her go, do you think?'

Harold shrugged. 'Who can predict? Do you imagine it will make a difference to my life? I have no expectation of her seeking me out if they do.'

'What will you do, Harold? Will you go back to Cynthia?'

Harold clicked his tongue with irritation. 'The essential to grasp about fantasies is that one should never be granted the opportunity to play them out. Dear boy, I don't know. I imagine the reality of the particular little scenario is not unlike that you once painted so colourlessly over lunch.' He poured more vodka into his glass and gestured at George with the bottle. George proffered his tea mug. Harold filled and they clinked rims together.

'One can only admire the Soviets for their sense of tidiness. How neatly they have resolved the awkwardness of Master Prowse's internment and my own affection for unfashionable public displays of inebriety. Two birds with one stone. Very satisfactory.'

'Nadya looses her right to live here once you go, doesn't she?'

Harold examined his glass thoughtfully, twisting it in his hands. 'Umm. I wonder who will shelter her then, poor thing?' He looked blearily up at George and squinted. 'I have absolutely no doubt that Nadya will be accommodated somewhere close to the heart of the foreign community. There have been moments when I have paused to wonder at the connection between Master Prowse's association with Nadya and his arrest.' He paused. 'At any rate, I do not believe the burden of concern for her wellbeing need rest upon your shoulders, George.'

George was silent.

'No, as soon as dear Nadya has adjusted to the initial shock, she will join, if not head, the queue of callers – predominantly Soviet staff – who will fall like vultures upon the cast-off goods and produce of the expellees. Sentiment must stand aside for opportunity.'

'You're pretty rough on Nadya, Harold.'

'Actually, dear boy, I am right behind her. You forget I have lived here long enough to appreciate just how propitious is this crisis for the compound Soviets. They can expect to pick up on valuable articles of essential merchandize. I merely find it disappointing that after all this time this great superpower offers the hoi polloi no simpler means of acquiring domestic appliances, furnishings, clothing and the like than to wait for the departure of foreigners to other climates and voltage systems.'

Though she wasn't there to hear it, Alice would have testified to the accuracy of Harold's observation. Galina had excused herself to follow Babs back to her flat for a private conversation. Alice hoped that Galina was not negotiating for the frozen fillets of Smithfield beef that Alice had her own eye on.

She raised this aspect of the expulsions with George when they had finally exhausted all the others over a supper of noodles, cabbage and carrots.

'It's the end, isn't it, for the staff of the people who are being chucked out? Of course it's a bonus shopping chance for the ones whose employers are staying. But for the others, we're their lifelines to Western consumer goods. Some of the staff of the expellees might well have been put in a real fix by this.' She prodded the mass of colour-studded pasta in her bowl with her fork. 'I mean, suddenly they're losing their access to all those Western trophies. All that stuff we give them for birthdays, Women's Day, Christmas, when we come back from abroad, all those things they swop up for dental treatments or better schools for their children or food or books and stuff. I hadn't really thought about it until I saw Galina scurrying across to Babs'. But these expulsions will have a devastating effect on the Russians too, won't they? Until they get reassigned. It isn't just the foreigners whose lives are suddenly turned upside down, is it?'

George was watching her speculatively, his mouth full. He chewed for a while. 'Why don't you write it? For the *Sentinel*? I bet it's an angle they'd be interested in.'

Alice looked startled. 'I can't write, George. You're the journalist. You do it.'

''Course you can. You just put down exactly what you just said. I can't do it. I've far too much on my plate as it is.'

They stared at each other across the table, their forks in mid-air until Alice finally spoke. 'Maybe,' she said. She stabbed into her food. 'And maybe not.'

'Atta girl.'

'You'd have to check it. If I did.'

'Happy to. Six hundred words or so. Not too much. By tomorrow night, or it'll be cold.'

Alice said, 'I might. Perhaps.'

She spent most of the night thinking it through, writing the piece in her head. Before she began the following morning, she drove to the Centralni Rinok to clear her brain and to demonstrate to herself that her real mission that day was in fact to get some shopping in. This would establish a fall-back position, in case her attempt at journalism fell flat.

She looked longingly at the lettuce and the spinach, sodden, according to the French Embassy, with radiation, and bought instead the less risky potatoes, carrots and beetroot. The family had eaten these all winter long and now it seemed that they would be doomed to continue during the brief growing season of the summer vegetables. Still, the long holidays were looming. Term, as it were, would be over soon and she and George and Daisy and Harriet could fly out like the rest of the foreign community to a beach somewhere in the West and laze and bathe and eat and eat and eat without fear. She bought some stewing beef, a white lard-streaked lump that looked as though it had been detached from the cow by a lumberjack. The British community had yesterday been formally advised that the geiger counter had finally been installed at the embassy. It would be an interesting exercise to test how high meat was ticking.

She drove to the embassy and found herself once more

with dripping plastic bags facing the same security officer at the front desk.

'I've come to test my food.'

The security officer sucked in his cheeks regretfully and clicked his tongue. 'Oh dear oh dear,' he said in a put-upon tone of voice. 'Well, you can't do that now, can you, miss?'

'I can't? Why not? The geiger counter's arrived, hasn't it?'

'Yes, miss. The geiger counter's here. But so is the Duke of Gloucester.'

Alice toyed with 'So what?' but felt aggression at this stage might be premature. 'I'm not sure I understand.'

'I can't be looking after the geiger counter and the Duke of Gloucester at the same time, now can I?'

Alice leaned forward and peered down over the desk. 'Where have you got the Duke of Gloucester?' she said, looking pointedly about.

'He's in with His Excellency', said the security officer stiffly.

Alice lifted her shoulders. 'So?'

The security officer bent forward confidentially and cupped his hand to his mouth. 'They're looking at the plans for the new embassy,' he whispered. 'The Duke's the architect for the FO.' Then he settled back in his chair as if that explained matters and Alice would now take up her bags and leave.

'What new embassy?'

'The Russkies want us out of here.' He stared around the great hall. 'Too good for them, if you ask me.'

'Why should all this prevent me from using the geiger counter?'

'Because the geiger counter's in there' – he pointed across the hall to an anteroom – 'and the Duke's in there.' He shoved his thumb back over his shoulder in the direction of the Ambassador's study. 'It is my duty to keep the desk manned at all times when there's' – he leaned forward and whispered again – 'Royalty about. Else it's not safe.'

Alice glanced through the glass of the inner embassy door beyond the open front portals to the armed Soviet sentries at each of the two gates. 'Aren't they guarding the place?'

The security officer sank his chin scornfully into his shirt and plucked at his home-knitted waistcoat. They, he was managing to imply, were what he was protecting the Duke of Gloucester from.

'You'll have to come back, miss. Give it another hour, I'd say. Then it'll be his worship's lunchtime.'

Wordlessly Alice turned and carried her bags back to the car. Would it have helped if she'd made a scene? If she'd weighed the importance of architectural plans against the safety of her children? No. What was the point? Royalty with an audible capital R counted for far more in Britain than small children squalling, snotty-nosed results of furtive, feverish activity. Besides, to cause embarrassment among the British was always unproductive. People only pretended they were deaf and behaved as though it wasn't happening.

Alice went home with her blood singing furiously in her ears, her mind crystal clear with anger, and wrote what George, that night, called – to his own surprise as much as hers – 'a bloody good piece of work'.

Chapter Twenty-Four

When Alice returned from collecting Harriet at the playgroup the following morning, she bumped into one of the compound maids. She recognized her from among those who lined the benches of the yard each of these now regularly hot afternoons, watching over their young foreign charges as they played on the rotting swings. She was coming out of the Simpsons' front door, clutching to herself a vacuum cleaner and an arm full of children's clothing.

She looked furtively over her shoulder, though there was nothing behind her but closed doors. She touched Alice's sleeve and bent confidentially towards her. 'Madam,' she whispered. 'You are a good woman. Galya tells me of your kindnesses to her.'

'Yes?' said Alice suspiciously.

'She is my friend. I cannot tell her this. It would upset her. You can tell her.' She nodded at Alice encouragingly.

'Tell her what?'

The woman lowered her voice even further. 'Sasha, your good husband's shaffure. He has instructed the drivers of Serpuhovsky Val that they must not help Galya with the transportation of her washing machine.' She patted the cause of this provocation in confirmation.

Alice stared at the woman. 'How do you know this?'

'I heard it from my *nachalnik*'s shaffure. He thirsted for the bottle of vodka that Galya promised him. But he didn't want the trouble. He was considering' – the woman spread her hands – 'how could he get the vodka without doing the work?' She laughed in appreciation.

'And what would Sasha do to him if he did do the work?'

'He would report him, of course!' She winked and slashed twice at her upper arm with the side of her hand. 'For using the car for personal business.' Alice took her gesture to mean two stripes and reflected with surprise upon the superior nature of Sasha's KGB status.

She felt her teeth clench involuntarily and breathed out slowly. 'Thank you for telling me. I will certainly pass the information on. We had been wondering why the machine has stayed here so long.'

The woman shrugged. 'That Sasha, he is not a bad man, madam. He is a good Russian. But he wants the machine for himself.' She laughed. 'We all do.'

'It does seem, even broken, a popular piece of equipment,' Alice gruffly acknowledged.

'Well,' sighed the woman, 'what can you do? A broken foreign machine probably works better than a new Soviet one.' She nudged Alice in the ribs as she turned to go and laughed again. 'If you can find one at all in the shops.'

Alice smiled with her. At last the matter of the immobile machine was explained and she felt uncommonly relieved. Alice had wondered if it hadn't taken root. Now all she need do was accept that it was still her concern and prevail upon some friend with a large car and good muscles to help cart it across Moscow. In truth, she knew she ought to have done this a long time ago. But she had lazily opted, in donating it to Galina, to abdicate further responsibility for it. Rather a Soviet approach, Alice reflected.

She entered the flat humming. The worst of the news – that the Simpsons would no longer be their neighbours – weighed down upon her whenever she was reminded of it. Silly old cushioning Babs, a human kind of fond spaniel, waggy of tail and pleading of eye, was a good-hearted person, just the sort of uncomplicated neighbour one most needed in a place where little was ever as clear as first it seemed. Alice would miss her badly, and could already feel a strong tinge of resentment that she would have to control towards the successors to the Simpsons, whoever they might be. With the departure of the expellees, the class, so to speak, was being broken up. Freshmen would jolt the equilibrium of the community. They wouldn't know the codes. They would have to be taught the rules. There were, of course, newcomers arriving every month, for the most part perfectly charming, affording George and Alice gratifying opportunities for displays of the blasé wryness of the old hand. The previous week, indeed, they had attended the dinner party of the new representative of the European bulldozer firm downstairs and had exchanged ironic glances as their hostess had enthused upon the astonishing versatility of the humble beetroot. These, however, were newcomers, not usurpers. It was an important distinction.

But in all other matters, everything seemed to be working out well. The summer was turning out to be wonderful. The geiger counter was at last in operation, so that there was now the possibility of broadening the shopping list to include local fruits of the field. There was the weekly delivery by train from Helsinki to Leningradsky Voksal of a varied shipment of produce from Stockman's department store, with a fixed order to include a handsome supply of avocado pears. There was now an understanding among the compound mothers that they would gather each afternoon at a very particular spot down at Serebryanny Bor (to which of course only the chosen would be given directions), bearing their bathing costumes, their young and their picnics. Here the self-appointed crème de la crème held summer court and turned a succulent golden brown, while their offspring dug castles in the sand and splashed in the icy winter waters of the Moskva. Only the soaring tower blocks to the east forced a reminder that they were not part of an impressionist painting by Seurat.

And, most stimulating of all, there was George's sudden, speculative, admiration for Alice. Over breakfast that morning he had paid more heed to her than to his shortwave radio. 'You should seriously consider doing regular pieces,' he had said through his toast. Alice had protested bashfully, while considering inwardly that it was certainly an interesting thought. It would give her a job. Wasn't that what so many of the women in the compounds were missing? George had telephoned later to announce with pride on her behalf that he had telexed the piece across, the *Sentinel* was delighted, and would be publishing it in the following day's paper.

George was hugely pleased by the reception of Alice's article. He always knew that Alice had it in her, if only she didn't let herself get bogged down by babies and housework and stuff. Motherhood was terrific and essential and tremendously fulfilling (George was not a *Sentinel* man for nothing). But here revealed was a talent that could bring her a different kind of satisfaction, and status – she need no longer think of herself as Mrs Sentinel – plus a well-paid alternative to frustration in a capital city that offered few opportunities for stimulating distraction. What could be better? Galina was on hand to look after the children, wasn't she? And a proper job wouldn't bar Alice from doing her maternal thing if she still wanted to, would it? He remembered Alice before Harriet was born. She had revelled in her work, had blossomed under the responsiblities thrust upon her. That was what she needed: the opportunity to blossom. Not, of course, that as a mother she wasn't in full bloom, but—

George tailed off. His attention was distracted by two telexes laid out carefully side by side under his folded arms.

He had been staring, unseeing, right at them while reflecting upon Alice. Now he took them, one in each hand, and felt the blood drain from his face.

One was familiar, dated way back in April, and read:

EDITOR KEEN U CONFIRM SOONEST JUNE DATES MOSCOW VISIT CONVENIENT STOP

EX FOREIGN DESK, SENTINEL

The other, with today's date, read:

ALL FIXED 25 JUNE STOP LOOK FORWARD TO MEETING U + THE LOVELY MYRA STOP

CHEERS, BOB MATHISSON

'Nadya!' George bellowed. There was silence. He began to flay through the mass of correspondence and papers on his desk, tossing stuff on to the floor. Where was the telex with his editor's dates? Where was his diary? Where was Nadya? George shouted for her again.

He threw back his chair and swung into the kitchen. It was empty. Flinging the front door of the office open wide, he stormed up the stairs, two at a time, to Harold's apartment. He thumped on the door with his clenched fist.

Eventually Nadya came, opening the door a crack and peering through at George.

'So. George.'

'So, Nadya. What's up? Why aren't you in the office?'

'Harold has locked himself inside the lavatory. Before he was just throwing up. But now I can't hear him at all. I don't know what to do.'

George stepped into their hallway. It smelt musty and flat. 'I can't remember, is it locked with a key?'

Nadya shook her head. 'With a small bolt.'

'Shit.'

He strode through the apartment, past a bedroom stale with rumpled sheets and strewn clothing, to the lavatory. He felt the door, stroking it with the flat of his hand. It was made of balsawood, terracotta-coloured and thin. He leaned against it.

'Harold? Are you there?' He looked over his shoulder at Nadya. She shrugged helplessly. 'Harold? Can you hear me? You'd better answer or I'll have to break the door down.'

'George, no!'

'What else can I do, Nadya?'

'Why don't we try to slip a knife through?'

'To do what?' We'd need a metal saw to cut through a bolt. I don't suppose you've got one?'

Nadya shook her head. George put his mouth to the crack of the door again. 'Harold?' He turned back to Nadya. 'Look, he's obviously out of it. But he might have fallen and hit his head. We can't just leave him. Harold?' He bashed again. 'Right I'm coming for you.'

He braced his foot against the door, grasped the handle, and, leaning briefly back, flung himself forward with full force against the thin wood.

'Christ!' yelled George. He reeled backwards, clutching his shoulder. 'Jesus wept! What do they do with those doors, bake them?'

The door remained intact. George inspected it more closely, tenderly squeezing the flesh of his shoulder. 'Whereabouts would you say the bolt was?'

Nadya stepped forward and pointed.

'Right. Now keep well out of the way, Nadya. I'm going to take a run at it.'

George walked backwards as far as the hallway would allow and then pelted forward at full tilt. As he gained upon the door, he suddenly bent his knees, sprang into the air, and with all his force punched the door with both feet. There was a tremendous cracking sound, followed by a groan as the door fell inwards. Harold was squatting down cradling the lavatory bowl in his arms, his head against the rim, his eyes closed and the splintered door resting heavily against his shoulder. George pulled off the door, hooked his hands under Harold's shoulders and dragged him out of the lavatory to the bedroom.

Nadya followed and swung Harold's legs on to the tousled bed. She wiped her hands together. 'Harold takes very seriously his leaving celebration. Only he is doing it on his own.'

George looked down upon the crooked figure on the bed. 'Poor bastard,' he said fondly. 'I shall miss him, you know.'

Nadya smiled an empty smile. 'I too.'

'They are going to make him a special presentation at the Sad Sam party. Did you know? As dean of the journalists. We've been taking a collection.' George began to feel embarrassed. 'For long service. Everyone's really rooting for him.' He reached down and squeezed Harold's ankle, the smooth cotton sock hot in his palm. 'You have no idea how much you mean to us, you silly sod.' He looked up abashed, at Nadya. 'What do you suppose he'd like? As a suitable gift?'

Nadya shook her head. 'To be allowed to stay, of course.'

Her reply made George feel cross. 'Before this he talked so wistfully of England,' he grumbled. 'I thought he might begin to look forward to going home again.'

'Home?' Nadya scoffed. She gestured around her at the flat. 'This is Harold's only home. Maybe you should buy him a Palekh box, one that is painted with strong colours and a picture of troikas and dragons and castles. Do you know, the dentist who comes to the American Embassy – Harold took me to him once – he finds Moscow so drab and discouraging that he keeps a Palekh box in his coat pocket so that when he is walking the streets he can take small glances at it and refresh his spirit. Maybe such a box could do the same for Harold when he is what you call "home".'

Nadya and George regarded each other in sadness.

Nadya broke the pause and said, 'You came here for something, George. What did you want?'

George plunged his hands into his trouser pockets and sighed. 'I was just trying to sort out the dates for my editors' visits. I couldn't seem to find where I'd put them down.'

Nadya looked at George surprised. 'George! I am astonished that the dates are not engraved on your brain for ever! They are both coming at the same time, of course. You will have your restoration comedy after all.'

If George was honest, his knowledge of restoration comedy was far from scholarly. All he knew for sure was that they created great laughter among the audience while causing immense discomfort and embarrassment to the characters. The thought did not soothe him. This was a time when, were George a player of chess, he might have planned some nifty moves upon the board that would save his game and his face. George sensed he was undoubtedly on the verge of losing the latter through his over-enthusiasm for the former.

What could be the worst consequences of his editor's discovering that one of his more respected correspondents was acting as a stringer for another paper? The deceit itself was not quite so bad as George's choice of string. A *Sentinel* man working for the *Post*? The suggestion was insupportable. The two newspapers were incompatible in every possible respect! What if it became public knowledge? Where would George's credibility be then!

Of course it would only get out if Bob Mathisson were to push for a revelation. If his own editor somehow found out, God forbid, through guesswork or intuition, he could be absolutely guaranteed to keep mum. No question. The potential embarrassment would make of him a silent accessary. But if Bob Mathisson were to reveal the deception, it would be curtains for George. The thing would be to keep the two apart.

Even this would not be so easy. Nadya informed George that although his editor was arriving from Bonn while Bob Mathisson was coming on the London flight, both were staying at the Rossiya Hotel on the far side of Red Square. Still, it was unlikely they would be on the same floor. They would probably not even be placed in the same annexe. The vast featureless edifice with its six thousand rooms was the largest hotel in Europe. Guests were rumoured to have been found wandering in delirium along its anonymous corridors hours after they had set out in search of their rooms. With any luck, George would manage to keep his two editors quite separate.

It was a teaser that provoked George to such a degree that he almost volunteered it as a test to the guests that evening at the Simpsons' 'Farewell Freezer Fest'. Any group who so regularly threw itself into enthusiastic rounds of charades, murder games and Monopoly could surely help him resolve this problem.

Instead he got drunk. Jonathan had decided the best way to share quarter and half full bottles of Pimms, vermouth, gin, scotch and a colourful array of peculiar duty free liqueurs among forty-odd people was to fling it all together into a deep pan and sprinkle it with lemonade and soda water. It really tasted quiet pleasant, though went rather better with the fillet of beef than with the fish fingers. However, it seemed more to stimulate thirst than to quench it, so that George, along with most of the guests, found himself knocking the stuff back like pop.

The packers were coming the following morning and things lay in large mounds along the corridor. As he became more and more tipsy, it seemed to George that these obstacles in the path between food and drink had grown taller and wider and more difficult to negotiate. At one point, he was startled to witness Alice glance surreptitiously about her before slipping a book from her bag into one of the heaps. He also observed with interest that despite the removal from the sitting-room of all the Simpsons' belongings, the room looked quite as it always had.

George negotiated in the kitchen with Jonathan for the remainder of his wine and his D coupons. Then they sat together, arm in arm on the kitchen counter, swinging their legs and singing 'Auld lang syne', George with his head on Jonathan's shoulder. The freezer door hung open, dripping slowly on to the floor, an Aladdin's Cave whose treasures had now been plundered. Alice, her temples pounding ominously, helped George back across the corridor to their flat and several glasses of Alkaseltzer.

George slept late. But not nearly as late as his digestive tract and purification system would have appreciated. The telephone woke him. He unsuctioned his eyelids on sunshine streaming through the thin curtains and hauled his wrist towards him. His watch said nine o'clock and the bed beside him was empty. He would have to answer the phone himself. He lifted the receiver.

'Hello!' sang out a cheery voice. 'George Mason, please! British Embassy here!'

George's lips appeared to be glued together. He thrust forward the piece of chewed steak that had once been his tongue and trailed it round them. He cleared his throat.

'Speaking.' But only just.

'I have the Minister for you!' yodelled the switchboard operator. 'Putting you through now! Hold on please!'

George held on with all his might. He dragged his naked body up the bed. It seemed to go on for ever, or else his legs had grown in the night. He swung them round and off the bed. This hasty act set up a momentum all of its own. His weighty head followed his feet downwards till it reached his knees, and George found himself peering closely at his genitalia.

'George?' came a voice like a mouse's squeak from somewhere close by. George had let the receiver fall on to the sheets. He snatched it to his mouth.

'Yes?' He breathed heavily into it.

'Minister here. Good, good. Look, want you to come into the embassy. Any chance this morning?'

George puffed into his fist. The energy to cough seemed to have left him. 'Ermm, of course, Minister. When?'

'How soon can? Nine forty-five? Good, good. See then.'

George stood under a cold shower, mesmerized by its unbroken chilling force upon his head. He shaved and brushed his teeth with his eyes closed, unwilling to confront what others could not avoid staring at. Alice had left a cold pot of coffee on the hob. George spooned sugar into the pot and drank straight from its lip. In the car he turned the air conditioning on to maximum and set the vents to funnel at his face. By the time he reached the embassy he felt more compos mentis and risked a glance at himself in the driving mirror. He didn't look it.

The security officer asked him to wait in the anteroom. In the corner stood a curious instrument with a numbered dial, much like a weighing machine but with an empty plastic bucket on its head.

Upon this, George pondered, we depend for our health and well-being?

The Minister's secretary, a sterling member of the female broomball team, George remembered, led George down a dark panelled corridor to an open door. George stepped through into the Minister's office. He rose from behind his desk, holding out his hand. The room smelt faintly of methylated spirits.

'Minister.'

'George. Have seat.' The Minister retreated behind his desk and brought his hands to his pursed lips, touching as for prayer. Then without looking up, he removed one hand and pushed a newspaper clipping towards George. 'Foreign Office, embassy, deeply regret story. Most unseemly. Most untimely.'

George leaned forward to look. To his surprise, it was Alice's article on the expulsions.

'I don't think I understand.'

The Minister reached for the piece and pinched it off the desk. He read from it. '"Stocks of special treats imported from Helsinki for impressive dinner parties will have to go, along with the cross country skis, the bulk buys of Smarties that are the centrepiece of every child's birthday tea, and the impressive sides of beef that only the diplomats are allowed to buy from the Foreign Office."' He looked expectantly at George.

'I'm sorry, Minister. I don't see what your objection is.'

'Beef, George. Sides of beef.'

'Beef?'

'Sides of beef give quite wrong impression of life here. Tax-payers object. And this.' He lifted the clipping close again. '"There will be farewell party after farewell party in foreign compound flats and perhaps the British embassy dacha,"' he read. 'And this: "The British will toast their compatriots in the last of the gin and Pimms"' George gently rubbed his temples – '"and make spoof speeches in rolling accents laced with a measure of bravado and defiance on behalf of Mr Gorbachev, Lenin and appropriate Politburo officials."' He laid the cutting sadly on his desk and sighed. 'Quite wrong impression, George. Most regrettable. Simply not done.'

'What isn't done, Minister?'

The Minister looked solemnly at George. 'One does not write about the embassy.'

George was astonished. This was the first complete sentence, to George's knowledge, the Minister had ever uttered.

'Forgive me, Minister, but the press writes about anything that is of public interest or concern.

'Taxpayers no proper understanding life in Soviet Union. Could absolutely misconstrue tenor of hardship, reference sides of beef, Pimms parties, Smarties.'

'Minister.' George was patient. 'Number one, this is the *Sentinel* readership you're referring to. Not the gutter press. Our readers are all pretty well educated, thinking people. They're not going to read this piece, home in on the beef and start firing off angry letters to the Prime Minister. If they notice it at all, they're probably thankful that at least the people who have to work so bloody hard here on behalf of their country are getting properly fed. Unless they're vegetarian, of course. Which, with our readers, is a strong possibility. But that would produce a different kind of protest. Number two, everything in that story is true. I myself was at one such party last night, thrown I might add, by a member of this embassy, in which quantities of Pimms and other stuff were drunk and FO sausages, legs of lamb and fillets of beef were accompanied by Commissariat baked beans, tinned peas, fish fingers and Angel Delight.'

George felt quite sick.

'Foreign Office expects an apology, George.'

'For what! There are absolutely no inaccuracies. Why should Alice apologize!'

'Would like a written letter for the files.'

'You're talking about press freedoms here, Minister. What you're saying is that we can write what we like about the Soviets, so long as we don't mention our own.'

'Stick together, George. Representing our nation abroad, each and every one of us.' The Minister put his head down and clutched his nose thoughtfully. 'No letter, George, have to take action.'

'What kind of action?'

'Not sure courtesy of frozen embassy milk be extended any longer.' The Minister trailed off, toying now with a fountain pen. 'Access embassy doctor? Also understand your daughter British Embassy Playgroup.' He shrugged regretfully.

'My God, that's not Queensberry Rules, is it? The milk you can keep. But in this godforsaken hole are you denying us the use of the doctor?' George rose off his chair. 'And are you going to take your rancour out on a four-year-old? If you want an enraged taxpayer, you're looking at one right now. No, Minister, no play game. Sorry and all that.'

He stormed towards the door as the Minister stood up behind his desk. He turned as he grasped the handle and said, 'If you want to ban Harriet from the playgroup, I'll tell you what. I shall call a press conference. And I shall invite not only the members of the world's press but also Soviet journalists. And I shall put little Harriet on top of my desk and I shall say. 'At last the British Embassy has taken on somebody its own size!'

With that, George yanked the door open, passed through it and out of the embassy. His hangover had quite gone.

Chapter Twenty-Five

Alice was appalled that she should have upset the embassy. The embassy, like traffic wardens, priests and head-mistresses, was a symbol of authority she had always felt one should toady to. Or at the least avoid provoking. The whole affair was mortifying. And at the same time, very odd. She read and reread her piece until she knew it by heart and found it merely – bar, she did concede, the mischievous reference to beef imported exclusively for the diplomats – a curiosity that was mildly amusing. She was, therefore, adamntly in agreement with George that she would not write any letter of apology to anyone. Still, how would this affect their, albeit tenuous, relations with the embassy? Or embassy people at large in the com-pounds? Would they find out? Would Babs and Jonty come to hear of it? And how would they react?

Of course in a ghetto as enclosed as that of Moscow's foreign community, news travels faster than fire. Within days everyone knew. And reactions were twofold: Alice was a traitor to her nation, or the whole thing was a hoot. Supporters of the former view parted at the farewell parties like the Red Sea before Moses to let George and Alice through without verbal or physical contact. These indi-viduals also heaped a measure of their disapproval upon the heads of Babs and Jonathan who staunchly and publically stood by their friends.

316

The sympathetic faction passed the tale along with increasingly fanciful twists and, to their alarm and glee, the Masons suddenly found themselves taken up as a Cause. Repeatedly the Serpuhovsky Val doorbell would chime and a uniformed 'shaffure' from one embassy or business or another would appear, tendering a large box or bag of exotic tinned and dried foodstuffs. Cartons of milk were left in anonymous tribute to the children upon the washing machine by the front door. Supporters pressed colouring books and pencils upon Harriet.

One morning when the doorbell chimed, Alice opened it to find Sasha loaded down with a crate of apple juice Alice had sent him to forage for. Behind him stood Kamal and an Egyptian busboy in starched white jacket, bearing a large platter covered with silver foil.

Alice let Sasha push past and her eyes flickered quickly from Kamal to the dish. She and George would have to clarify their status. This was becoming uncomfortable.

'Kamal! What a nice surprise! Won't you come in?'

Kamal shook his head. The jacket of his suit was draped nonchalantly over his shoulders and the top button of his blue silk shirt was open. He held up the flat of his smooth gold hand. 'No, no, thank you. I am expected at luncheon across town. I have brought this small offering from Fatma. She is worried that you might not be eating well, so she has prepared for you some Imam Biyaldi. This means 'The Priest Fainted', which we sincerely hope you will not do. It is stuffed aubergine and I must state, without bias, that she makes it most excellently. Where can we put it?'

Alice looked about her, confused. 'Goodness! This is incredibly kind of you. Fatma really shouldn't have. Why don't you put it on the washing machine? I can take it in.'

'You do your washing in the corridor?'

'No, no,' said Alice, flustered. 'No, this machine belongs

to our maid, but we haven't yet found anyone with a large enough car to transport it to her apartment.'

'Is that so?' Kamal stared at the machine. 'Is your maid's apartment so far away?'

'It's just off Gorki Street.'

Kamal turned to the busboy who was still holding the platter and murmured something to him. Then he turned back to Alice.

'Please, Alice. Show my boy where he can carry this food. I am going to return now to my driver and ask him to help load the machine into the limousine. He can deliver it – if, of course, you can spare me your maid to direct him – while I am having lunch.'

At once Alice became rattled. 'Oh, but you can't, Kamal. I couldn't think of allowing it, it's far too much trouble! Really, there's no problem. George and I can absolutely arrange it.' But of course it was the perfect solution.

Kamal layed a hand on Alice's arm. 'Alice. Hush. You will offend me. It is already done. This will be my pleasure. Please, ask your maid if she will be ready for us. You will forgive me for stealing her from you?'

'Heavens! Absolutely! And the dish. I'll put the aubergines on something else and you can have your dish back.' It seemed of supreme importance to Alice that she should give something to Kamal in return, if only his own plate.

He bowed lightly. 'Thank you, Alice. I shall wait downstairs in the car.'

Alice, grinning widely, with a bubble of glee rolling in her throat, bore the platter triumphantly into the kitchen. She placed it carefully on the freezer and turned to Galina at the kitchen sink. Sasha was kneeling at the juice crate, unloading bottles. With a delight almost impossible to suppress at the fortuitous composition of her audience, Alice put her hands ecstatically to Galina's cheeks.

'You're not going to belive this, Galya. You must get

your coat at once. I've got a lift for your washing machine. You and it are going to your apartment now, this minute, in the limousine of the Egyptian Ambassador!'

Down among the juices, Sasha let a bottle slip from his hands and shatter.

George, meanwhile, was engaged in solving his own vexing problem: he was attempting to ensure that the registration desk of the Rossiya Hotel would room his two editors as far from each other as the hotel's massive structure allowed. He had telephoned repeatedly in vain for assistance. Each time he had been connected to a different Natasha, Ivana, Natalya, Irina on the front desk, none of whom could make head or tail of his concerns and wishes and cared even less. Surely just to have the good fortune of being allocated a room in the Rossiya at all was enough! Some people were never satisfied. Eventually George, pockets bulging with loot from the slush fund, instructed Sasha to deposit him at the hotel while Sasha went off to chase up some vital juice delivery, so that George could tackle the issue face to face.

His first difficulty was that there was not one front desk but three: at the south, west and north entrances to the mighty edifice. At each there was a press of people several rows deep, waving arms, waving papers, waving fists, while about the general foyer milled different flocks of tourists craning their necks anxiously like turkeys for some kind of saviour who could guide them on what they should do next.

George, in the south wing, pushed through to the front and thumped his elbow into position on the desk. 'Comrade?' he called to a pretty young girl with long dark hair and biteable lips. 'May I speak with you, comrade?' As she glanced up from her registration book, he smiled encouragingly at her and unfurled his fingers. Inside his palm lay a lipstick in a gleaming case.

'*Minutichku*,' she murmured to the guest she was signing

319

in, and rolled laconically towards George. He spread his palm flat and replayed his encouraging smile. She in turn smiled lazily at him, snatched the lipstick out of his hand, and rolled laconically back to the guest, turning herself away from George.

Shit, he said to himself, and headed out to the north wing. Here the receptionist was more helpful. Indeed, all three were. Once the other two had somehow sensed a negotiation had taken place to the benefit of their sturdy colleague, they abandoned their impatient clients and focused their attentions exclusively upon George, who had to fish into his pockets for further tributes. The ladies were anxious to help. *Absolutna.* If only the *gospadin* could make it a little more clear quite what he desired. Yes, indeed, the two foreign gentlemen in question were assuredly booked into the hotel. The *gospadin* himself was saying so. Could not the accommodating comrades see if they could confirm this for certain? Surely if the *gospadin* knew so firmly that the two gentlemen had reservations, what was the need to confirm this fact? Please, *gospadin*, clarify. George bit on his tongue until the saliva rushed from his cheeks. Very slowly he repeated himself. Would it be possible to arrange for the following two highly important, greatly distinguished (George emphasized this firmly). British newspaper editors who he had been led to believe were booking into the Rossiya, to be given rooms, regardless of which desk they should register with, as far from each other as possible? George fully appreciated the demands this placed upon their time, diligence and energy and would recognize their trouble in no small way. He waggled his eyebrows.

The ladies clapped their hands together in delight. The *gospadin* was so amusing! Surely he understood, as the cultured foreign gentleman that he himself undoubtedly was, that the matter of room allocation was a complex and subtle procedure. There were floors for prestigious foreign guests and floors for less prestigious foreign guests. There were floors for foreign guests of no consequence at all. There were annexes for prestigious Soviet guests and annexes for less prestigious Soviet guests. (Soviet guests of no consequence would not be housed by the Rossiya.) There were delicate distinctions between guests who merited the view of Red Square and those who could enjoy the view of the power station on the island in the river. Further, there were those who would merely stare across Kitaisky Prospekt at old Chinatown or towards Ploshad Nogina. This was not simply a matter of exchanging room keys. Each guest was placed according to a detailed assessment of his appropriate position in a complex game plan that simply could not be altered. George didn't bother to trek around to the western desk.

What else could he do? It was all in the lap of whatever gods still included the Soviet Union in their beat. Besides, he had Harold's present to take home and wrap before the Sad Sam Summer Soiree that evening.

It was, as Nadya had suggested, a hand-painted lacquer box from the village of Palekh. George had mobilized all the 'blat' he could to acquire it. The best of these exquisite boxes, miniature masterpieces, seldom saw the light of the souvenir shops and hard currency stores; but with the right strings pulled, they could be found. George had had to traipse out to Lefortovo to quiz Charlie on the whereabouts of one vital link in the chain of anonymous Soviets that lay between the Japanese tape deck that the press corps had clubbed together to buy and the box for which it would be exchanged.

Now that Charlie was simply languishing in prison until the moment when he could be transported directly to his flight out of the Soviet Union, George felt it was a bit of a traipse. Before, when Charlie's future had been in jeopardy, the journey to do supporter's detail had had something of the sacrificial pilgrimage about it.

George accompanied Lisa on her daily encounter with her husband in Lefortovo's bizarre visitors' room. The prison smelt sourly of cheap disinfectant and floor polish, but the room into which they were led was decorated like the set of a bourgeois French period comedy. Charlie was slouched on a brocade-covered sofa beneath an exceptionally bad pastoral oil painting. George and Lisa manoeuvred past the net curtained windows to the neat armchairs on either side of the rococo coffee table and sat.

Charlie was in remarkably good form. He looked as though he had spent his entire life incarcerated, not just the past few weeks. He had been subsisting off soup and buckwheat kasha, pushed four times a day through a window in the door of his eight by ten cell, and it showed. He also smelled. But his spirits, now that it was only a matter of counting the hours, were reasonably high.

'Really pissed off I can't make the Sad Sam bash. Best fucking do of the year. Would have been a great way to go. You'll drink my quota for me, George, won't you? Wouldn't want it going to some wimp.'

'I'll bring some British Airways bangers to the airport.'

'There won't be any left, you mark my words,' said Charlie mournfully. 'Load of bloody gannets when it comes to real food, you lot.'

'Us lot,' corrected George.

'Ah, but I won't be there, will I?'

Before George had left, he had contrived in oblique and laboured fashion, full of obscure references and hints, to bring the conversation round to his purpose. Charlie, eventually, had understood what George was after. His own method for relaying the name of the place the Palekh painter liked to use for his black market transactions was far more convincing than George's efforts at casual subterfuge.

'Listen,' he said, almost as an afterthought. 'A tip for you. You have to try the Georgian breadshop on Olympichiski

Prospekt. Gruzinsky Kleb, it's called. Does fantastic flat bread – great for humus, if Alice makes it. And kachapuri. A sort of cheese smothered thing. Isn't that just what you always wanted to know?'

With a wink, George rose and left Charlie with Lisa. 'See you at the airport, Charlie. Not long to go now.'

Charlie checked his watch. 'Twenty-seven hours, forty-three minutes, and nineteen seconds. Goodbye, George.'

George hurried along the red carpeted corridor, past bulletin board line ups of this month's most effectively beastly KGB men down the stairs, out through the brown metal door, and back into the relative freeom of Energya Ulitsa.

The Palekh box was indeed worthy of all the subterfuge and trips hither and yon across the suburbs of Moscow. George wondered briefly whether he couldn't just buy Harold another one from the Beriozka and keep this box for himself. Alice fell upon it with awe.

'You know, I've never really caught on to Palekh. All those rows the diplomats have lined up on their coffee tables. But this is quite lovely.' She traced the figures with her finger.

'You're looking quite lovely yourself, Alice.'

'Why, George! Mind you, I emphasized the "lovely". You emphasized the "quite".' George spread his arms wide. 'No, George. If you don't mind, I'll take a rain check on hugs. Galina spent all afternoon ironing this.'

George inspected it. 'This' was a voluminous calf-length dress of finest apricot lawn, gathered layer upon layer at a low-necked yoke. The colour made Alice's gentle tan hum with life.

'Nighty, is it?'

'Honestly, George. You really are the answer to a poor

girl's prayer! No, it is not a nighty. It is what I was proposing to wear to the party.'

'Jeans. It's more a jeans party. That's a bit, what, flighty?'

'How do you mean, flighty? I thought it was rather Midsummer Night's Dream.'

'The whole point of the Sad Sam Summer Soiree, Alice,' said George patiently, 'is that it's a knees-up in the face of adversity. A kind of rollicking, beer-swilling, jazz-orchestrated, up-yours-Commies, barbecue.'

'It sounds perfectly ghastly. I thought it was quite a different kind of do. I'm not sure I want to go.'

But of course she did. For the expellees it would be their last night in the Soviet Union. She should say goodbye. Besides, no-one turned down an invitation to the Sad Sam Summer Soiree. It was the compound equivalent of Commem Balls, signalling the end of the working year when Moscow began to empty of as many foreigners and Soviets who could escape the stifling city summer. It also was the foreigners' most public, most exuberant, most harmlessly delinquent expression of defiance towards the careful apartheid system that made privileged pariahs of them.

Such rebellion was considered contagious. Before the last year's celebrations, the inhabitants of the Soviet apartments overlooking the Sad Sam compound had been evacuated to prevent their leaning out of the windows and shouting encouragement at the revellers below as they had in the past. This year, too, their windows where dark.

Alice and George walked arm in arm into the compound yard and the clamorous tooting of a jazz band in rollicking rip. A piano had been hauled out on to the concrete walkway that ran around two sides of the compound and a pianist with a full beard, a loud lumberjack shirt, sleeves rolled him, and a tiny bowler hat perched on his thick black hair was thumping at the keyboard, head down, elbows up, like a washerwoman tackling sheets.

Next to the piano, bobbing about like a plastic duck in a turbulent bath, was a trumpet player with a long black t-shirt that declared in citrus yellow that he loved New York. The man at the drums was wearing a green pool-hall eyeshade and waistcoat over a low cut undervest that exposed a mossy lawn of dark hair, while the trombonist was dressed in denim dungarees and a thin red satin baseball jacket. They gave the sartorial impression of having rummaged together in a trunk marked 'Universal Jazz Cellar Gear'.

Above their heads and along every wall flapped red, white and blue bunting. Ropes of candle-lit Japanese lanterns crisscrossed the courtyard, casting a soft peach light on to the heads of the people pitching and rolling beneath them to the music. Below the walkway nearer to the compound entrance were two barbecues cut from oil drums, gusting smoke. Alongside them stood several tables with so many different dishes of food that in places they balanced in double tiers.

George squeezed Alice round the waist. 'Glad we came?'

'It's quite extraordinary. In Moscow! Where did they get the jazz band from?'

'Repin and the Refusniks, would you believe? They're Jews who can't get exit visas.'

'Don't they get into trouble?'

George shrugged. 'What have they got to lose? In any case, it's said they're allowed to play for foreigners so long as they include the trumpet player, who's a UPDK man.' George tapped the side of his nose and winked. 'Come. Let's mingle.'

Suddenly and simultaneously the spirit of the evening took hold of them. The smell of wood smoke, the clamour, the bouncing music, the sight of all the glorious treats prepared by the multi-national compound women for the gratification of their fellow inmates – the sushi, sateg samosas, tzadziki; the pilaffs, pasties and pastas – the swirling skirts and bending bodies, and above all the fact that they knew everybody, knew their lives, knew their woes and their triumphs, caught them and seduced them. They belonged more closely with these people than they ever had with anyone, anywhere else.

As the evening grew swiftly darker, the compound yard filled. George and Alice were soon snatched apart by hands that pulled them here and there to talk, to drink, to laugh, to dance. Josh Klaczynski, the American Embassy attaché, swung towards Alice. He snatched up her left wrist and scrutinized her fingers. 'No divorce yet?' he bawled at her hopefully.

Alice smiled and he rolled on. Alice and Nadya embraced as old friends. The German Military attaché, this time dressed as Superman, flickered in recognition and silently dabbed her cheek with his gloved forefinger as he flitted by.

Lisa linked her arm fondly through Alice's and Alice squeezed it to her side.

'Poor old Charlie, eh?' shouted Lisa into her ear. 'He's been racking his brains about how he could steal out for the night.'

'Well then: almost out of the Soviet Union.'

'And not sorry either.'

'Where do you meet tomorrow?'

'They'll bring him straight out to the plane in the paddy wagon. I must say, I'm almost grateful to the Sovs. Packing and queueing and getting through customs is a whole lot smoother without Charlie. Just two kids instead of three.'

Winston at on the edge of the walkway, shaking beercans and squirting the foam above the heads of the dancers. Harold was there, weaving his way through the crowd, a glass in one hand, bottle of wine in the other. He seemed happy, expectant even, bobbing here to listen, there to murmur a word, never staying long with anyone. Despite the informality of the night, he was dressed as elegantly as ever, allowing himself only to open the buttons of his double-breasted suit as he grew warm with the Scottish dances he occasionally executed on his journeys across the yard and back.

Kamal and Fatma watched from the walkway, talking with Ned to the British Minister who had pressed himself against the wall. Alice glided swiftly away towards the food.

'Tip for you, Alice,' came a voice at her side. She turned. It was Geoff, his face shining and red. He had his arm round Babs' shoulders.

'Why, Babs! George and I were looking for you! We thought we could share a lift.'

'Actually we came with Geoff and Angela. We spent the day together.'

Alice felt a rush of jealousy. Adversity was binding.

'Great picnic, Alice,' Geoff enthused. 'Down at the Secret Lake. Mind you, bloody chewed up by mozzies.'

'Secret lake?'

'Yes,' said Babs, smiling lightly. 'Shame we aren't staying longer, really. We could have shown you where it was.'

'Not to worry!' said Geoff. 'Still got one tip for you. Listen to this. Babs and I, we just tossed the last of Ange's Memorial Marinated Helsinki Lamb Chops on to the barbecue.' They laughed together. 'If you rush now, you'll still get one.' They spun away from her with a wave, propelled by their satisfaction at this beneficient announcement.

Alice continued towards the trestles. Across the tables hands stretched out, dipping like humming birds at dishes here and there. The smell of grilling chicken and roasting sausages hung richly in the warm night air. Alice leaned forward for a kebab and felt her elbow being fiercely grasped and shaken very slightly. She peered over her shoulder, and her kebab stick fell from her hand.

It was the Minister. She turned to face him, her heart crashing about in her throat. As people around her became aware of just who was her companion, they began to edge away and to watch, leaving Alice backed against the table, facing the Minister in an empty semicircle. The Minister looked about him, surprised. He grasped his nose firmly and studied the ground, swaying very gently back and forth in his brogues. Alice waited. Eventually, as the small group of people about them began to rustle edgily, he spoke.

His words came slightly muffled. 'I want to know,' he enunciated slowly and with great care. 'I want to know on what side of the Union Jack it is you stand.'

Alice was utterly baffled. She was sure she had correctly heard the question. It had been stated so ponderously that she had the strong impression that it might even be a pro forma enquiry with officially designated status. But what could be the correct answer? She considered carefully. Much depended upon her reply. Here clearly was a tentative proffering of the flag of truce.

'On our side,' she ventured.

'Good, good,' said the Minister, pleased. 'Think we ought clear up whole unfortunate matter, don't you? Telephone office in the morning.' He patted her on the upper arm and she caught a strong whiff of parma violets before he bent carefully back into the crowd.

At once Alice was surrounded by people pressing her for an exact rendition of everything that had been said, suggested, implied, inferred. Alice was not much help. The whole encounter had been so unexpected and so peculiar. Why had the Minister not confronted her before this moment? It was she, after all, who had written the offending piece, not George.

'I think it's outrageous,' expostulated Lisa. 'Mind you, it was pretty low of George to go along with it. Personally speaking, I've always wondered why he didn't tell the Minister that very first time that since he wasn't the author of the piece he was hardly the person to talk to about it. Raging sexists, both of them.'

In this instance, Alice had been rather grateful for the fact. Confrontations were not her strong point.

Up scuttled George. 'What did he say? What did he say?'

Alice shrugged helplessly, still bewildered. 'I don't really know. He wants me to ring him tomorrow.'

'Fantastic!' said George. He wrapped his arms about her and lifted her off the ground. 'He's going to retract!'

'Some hope,' grunted Winston. 'Ministers never retract. It's not good policy.'

'All right. He's going to fumble for a meeting point. About time too.'

'Don't you think we should wait and see what he actually does instead of deciding what he's going to do?' said Alice. 'Maybe he's going to ask me to write that letter he wants right there in his office. What would I do then?'

'Tell him to stuff it,' said Lisa.

Angela plucked at George's sleeve. 'George? Your Nadya's looking for you. She says if you don't make your presentation to Harold soon, he'll be too blotto to accept it.'

'Cripes, I forgot all about it. Come on. You lot go and group around him. Make sure he doesn't fall over. Christ! Have I still got the box?' He patted his pocket and felt the small lump.

George strode along the walkway up to where the musicians had temporarily given way to the kindergarten teacher from the Anglo-American School. She was exorcising from her writhing body a raucous rock classic backed by the hi-tech musical hardware of the American Television Network cameramen, who swooped their arms like rodeo riders across their guitars with agonized frowns and fiercely pursed lips. The young woman's normally placid hair had risen about her head in a Medusa halo of thick dark clumps and she reeled, slumped and twisted about the microphone to an audience of open-mouthed parents. George waited until she had yelled her way to the end of the rock anthem and stepped forward for the microphone. He cleared his throat into it and the sound of distant thunder filled the courtyard. Down below him, hands were passing a confused Harold forward like a parcel, standing him at George's feet.

'I hate to cut into your appreciation of this – er – revelatory new aspect of Ms Lafferty's talents, but I wanted to say a few quick words about a member of our company whom we are shortly to lose.' Thunder rumbled from George's throat again. 'We are, of course, about to lose more than one member. But I'm sure the others – even the stalwart Charlie Prowse who regrettably has been detained tonight – and for several other nights' – laughter rippled gently – 'I am sure the others will agree that the loss of Harold Armitage will leave a gap in Moscow that no-one could fill.'

Below him Harold stared up astonished, then began to shuffle his feet.

'Harold, as no-one needs to be told, is Moscow's longest standing foreign resident. More than anyone else, Harold opened up the riches of the Soviet Union to British readers, interpreting for us the complexities of this vast country's politics and culture in a light and readable style. His dispatches were always well-balanced, never hysterical, always measured, never biased, always fond, never offensive, even when he was being highly critical. And over the long years of Western fear of Soviet socialism, Harold gave us the personal side of the political picture, introducing us to the Soviet man in the street and his particular concerns.

More than anything, in a period of Western prejudice, Harold humanized the Soviet Union. The British press now serving in Moscow and those who served before us owe a singular debt to Harold: he taught us that if we looked hard before we leapt into print, we would find not a cold nation of implacable monsters bearing no relation to ourselves, but a fascinating people who would amply repay our curiosity, study and concern.'

Harold had his head in one hand, the other stretched protectively across his body to grasp his elbow. He was trembling very slightly. George fished in his pocket.

'With great respect for Harold's achievements, in gratitude for his example, and with the hope that his new life will be as' – George thought hurriedly – 'intriguing as his old, his fellow hacks would like to present him with this small tribute, a painted box from Palekh.' George peered at it. 'It is a little small, but rather exquisite, I think you'll agree. Harold.'

Harold drew his hand slowly from his eyes. He seemed to be sweeping them carefully with this thumb and forefinger. He stepped hesitantly towards the walkway and George reached down his hand. Harold proffered his and George hauled him up beside him. Harold took the box and examined it closely.

'As almost always, George, you are correct in your judgement. It is an exquisite piece of Palekh. I infer from this that your *blat* is more potent than I suspected. My thanks. To you, who have afforded me much amusement and pleasure as office mate, and to my esteemed colleagues. I am touched. My deepest gratitude to everyone who has contributed in currency and in spirit to this most generous of gifts. What can I say? I should say something, shouldn't I?'

George patted him on the sleeve and retreated to the shadows. Harold pinched his nose thoughtfully. Eventually he looked up with a ghost of a smile.

'We observe today not a victory party but a celebration of freedom, for Charlie Prowse, and for me, symbolizing an end as well as a beginning, signifying renewal as well as change.

'The Soviet Union is very different now from when I was first sent all those years ago to cover it, for this great nation too now holds in its hands the power to abolish all forms of human life.

'We, the members of the press, dare not forget today that we are the recording heirs of the October Revolution. Let the word go forth from this time and place, to friend and foe alike, that the torch has been passed to a new generation of journalists, both in this century, tempered by limited expense accounts, disciplined by hard and bitter foreign news editors, proud of our ancient heritage, and unwilling to witness or permit the abuse of those human rights to which the Soviet Union has bever been committed, but to which it appears it may conceivably, under this new leadership, become committed today.'

'Gawd,' murmured Lisa. 'He's being a bit heavy-handed, isn't he?'

'Ssh!' said Winston. 'Listen.' He held up his hand. 'He's taking off Kennedy's inaugural address. Don't you recognize it?'

Harold studied his toes again, then looked up once more.

'Let every Soviet Ministry official know the foreign correspondents of Moscow shall pay any price, bear any burden, meet any hardship, support any friend, oppose any foe, to ensure the survival and the success of liberty.

'And so, my fellow hacks, ask not what Harold Armitage has done for you, ask what you could have done for Harold Armitage.'

'That's a bit off,' Lisa muttered out of the corner of her mouth.

But the crowd roared supportively.

'Deeply embarrassing,' stated Lisa. 'What did that last bit mean?'

All at once, as Harold stood there swaying slightly and staring amiable at his audience, a dark shape whizzed through the night sky and smashed at his feet. Harold stared down with interest and the crowd pressed forward to see what missile it was that had exploded on to the walkway.

'Jam,' observed Harold. 'A jar of jam. Someone didn't like my speech.' He considered the gooey mess thoughtfully.

People turned. There was nothing to see behind them but the darkened façade of the neighbouring Soviet apartment block.

'That's where it came from!' came a cry from the crowd and heads turned up towards the unlit building. On the sixth floor a window was open and a curtain fluttered in the dark.

Alice shivered. 'They could have hurt somebody. Killed them, even. It's a long way for something heavy like that to drop.'

'Or be thrown,' reflected Winston.

'Come on, Alice.' Lisa linked her arm through Alice's and pulled her towards the barbecues. 'Let's grab some sausages and get right out of the way.'

The walkway had cleared. Harold and George had both disappeared into the crowd and the jazz band was back in place at its instruments. The frisson of unease was carefully suppressed and the dancing began once more.

Alice and Lisa pushed through to the barbecues. British Airways' Moscow manager in butcher's apron was tossing bacon about and coaxing fat sausages with his long fork to roll over.

He waved his tongs at them. 'Come and eat! Flown in today!' he announced jovially. 'Fresh off the shelves of Sainsbury's, Hounslow.'

Lisa cuffed him on the shoulder. 'The only man in Moscow with our true interests at heart. Feeds us and flies us out. Hero.'

He passed them each a banger on a paper plate. The strolled companionably away to the edge of the party and leaned against the compound wall, tearing tentatively at the hot sausage with their teeth. The dancers were still reeling and lurching, the band still frenziedly bending and swaying at their instruments like reeds in an uncertain wind. Alice and Lisa watched, at peace.

Suddenly their attention was caught by a movement above their heads. A dark fluttering, it seemed, tumbling from the sky.

'Oh, my God,' groaned Lisa. 'Not another disapproving brickbat!'

But it was moving too fast, too heavily, a chaos of shadow touched here and there with pale. It fell wide, spread like a parachute all flapping material. A cry went up among the dancers. Then a shout, passed urgently from mouth to mouth. Heads raised. They stared upwards, swiftly appraising, and anxiously shrank back, clearing space. The thing, big now, hit with a thud that came quite clearly to Alice and Lisa at the wall. They pushed forward brusquely through the press of resistant backs, propelled by a feeling of dread.

Tossed down upon the concrete like a large discarded rag doll lay Harold, his arms stretched submissively to either side.

His left hand was tightly clenched. George, white-faced on the edge of the circle, dropped to his knees by the lifeless body. Gently he uncurled Harold's fingers. Gleaming with a vibrant life of its own in the palm of Harold's hand lay the Palekh box.

Chapter Twenty-Six

The plane that was to carry Harold's coffin back to England brought out Bob Mathisson. George greeted him with the harassed resentment of someone who has spent hours of intimacy with a book or television serial and who is asked by an interloper to explain the story so far.

Bob Mathisson had no right to the knowledge. He had expended neither time, nor energy nor emotion to acquire it. He therefore had no briefing privileges. With all the official activity surrounding the British Airways flight that, having disgorged its virgin travellers from Heathrow, was to accept on board five adult expellees, four expelled children, one untried spy and one coffin, it was hardly surprising that Bob Mathisson's appetite for gossip and news was stimulated. But George had no desire to fill the outsider in.

It had been a day of exaggerated emotions. Alice, having telephoned the Minister, had been summoned at once to join him at morning coffee. Life went on. She approached the meeting with a certain frisson of anticipation. The realization that she had, after all, had it in her power to cause such a great deal of alarm and despondency was not entirely unattractive.

'Bit early in the day for the geiger counter, aren't we, Mrs Mason?' joshed the security officer. Over their weekly visits, he had become a modest accomplice of the compound wives, lamenting with them the necessary rejection of ticking foodstuffs.

The Minister had clearly been mourning the loss of his drinking companion all night but seemed to have passed through some threshold where gravity and grief had instilled a certain composure. She had found the confrontation as nebulous as her conversation with him the night before, but had understood that the hatchet was to be buried, without apology due on either side, and with full restoration – the Minister spoke magnanimously – of their embassy privileges.

Alice had felt the resentment at the loftiness in his tone infuse her cheeks with red. But she had remained silent. The Moscow compounds were too claustrophobic for prolonged antipathy. Besides, she was too cowardly to protest. Thank heavens Lisa Prowse had not lent an ear to the proceedings. Alice conveniently set aside this aspect of her dialogue with the Minister and drove on to George's office in triumph.

It was not, of course, she remembered at once, a suitable backdrop for displays of jubilation. George was hunched over the telephone. Sasha was slumped into Harold's chair, grieving openly without a sound. Alice gently touched his shoulder and he raised his heavy head, exposing, to her shock, the full measure of his pain.

Eventually George dropped the receiver back on to its base and scrubbed his face slowly with both hands.

'I must say the Consul has really pulled his finger out. The Sovs are letting Harold's coffin go on tonight's flight without any court formalities.

'Who is it going to?'

George looked up at her bleakly. 'His first wife. Cynthia.' He spread his hands impotently. 'I couldn't think of anyone else who might take him. It's ironic, isn't it? He used to fantasize that one day he'd go back to her.'

Alice came round the desk and laid her arm across him. 'George. It's not your fault.'

'"Ask not what Harold Armitage has done for you,"' he quoted '"ask what you could have done for Harold Armitage." You don't think so? No, I suppose not. Still, I should have tried harder. Understood better.'

'Phooey! That was just maudlin melodramatics!'

'Yet he threw himself from the topmost balcony.'

They were silent for a moment. Then Alice ran a hand down George's back. 'Where's Nadya?'

'Upstairs in the flat. She's packing. She's going back to Murmansk.'

'For ever?' Alice exclaimed in surprise.

George shrugged. 'I don't know. Who can say? Who knows what plan they've got for her.'

'Should I go to her? How is she?'

'I'd let her be for the moment. She could do with some motherly comfort, if that's what she's going home for. She's devastated.' George turned and looked bleakly at Alice. 'You know, I think she really loved him. After all.'

He buried his face against Alice's stomach and she brought her arms around him and held him close. They stayed together for some long time, Sasha's phlegm-filled snuffling the only sound in the dusty office.

George had cautiously explained to Bob Mathisson as he saw him to his room in the Rossiya [how near was it to his editor's? Shit, who cared?) that he would be unable to extend Mason hospitality that night. It had been one helluva day, as Bob might have guessed, and there were still some loose ends to be tied. But would Bob join him and Alice the following evening?

Not to worry! enthused Bob Mathisson. He wasn't expecting to feed off the Masons that night anyway. No, no, Bobby boy was an old hand at foreign assignments. Knew how to feel his way about all kinds of alien territory. Didn't serve in Bangkok, heh hey, for nothing. All those stints in Belfast? Beirut? Bucharest? No, no, Bob Mathisson could always find his feet. Besides, he'd done a little sleuthing already, hadn't he? He winked and tapped his nose. He'd discovered his young fella-me-lad was expecting other company. Am I right? Am I right? And Bob had set himself up for a wee nightcap with – no less (bet George couldn't guess) – George's very own official boss, the editor of the *Sentinel*!

George drove wearily home, the floodlit Kremlin behind him reflecting in his driving mirror. The night was balmy and all his windows were rolled down. But for once the car was silent, The Beach Boys encased in their plastic envelope. He parked the car in the last space left in the compound and stood for a moment in the still night, his head cocked, listening to the sounds of the city muffled by the summer heat. Then he sighed deeply and headed for the barren lobby entrance. There was nothing for it but to tell all and fall upon Alice's mercy.

She was leaning over the balcony of the sitting-room, a drink in her hand. She turned as he came in.

'I watched you drive in. You looked so forlorn standing there.' She turned back to let her eyes rove across the industrial suburbs of the city. 'Isn't it peculiar how heat renders everything tranquil?'

'Exhausted, more like.' George stepped forward to join her and they stared out over the buildings into the far distance of nothing at all. 'Alice?' said George eventually. 'Won't you come inside and sit down? I've something to tell you.'

Alice's flesh began to ring with the sensation that each of the tiny hairs upon it had erected themselves in one movement. She wondered if there were a limit to the stress and distress that normal individuals could handle. And how could you tell when you had reached it? Did the hearing give out?

Block out what was not acceptable? Did whatever nerves that intertwined behind the chest cease to respond to shock and never more jump and squeeze and pitch about from stomach to throat? What was she about to go through now?

'Sit, Alice.' George pressed her gently down into the sofa. He settled beside her on the edge, his elbows planted on his knees, contemplating the rug. 'Actually, I need your help. I don't know how to put it, but I've got myself into a most awful mess.'

Alice's heart seemed to have slowed down considerably and become immensely heavy. She could hear it lumbering forward for each measured thump. She sat there, back erect, her chilled hands clenched together, and waited.

George spoke. 'I've been filing for another paper.'

'George!' Alice was startled. This was surely not the ghastly revelation to which he was building. But a surprise none the less.

'Some months ago,' George continued. 'I took on another string. It was supposed to be Harold's. Only Harold didn't want it. He wasn't up to it. So I took it.'

Alice waited, but George did not continue. She spread her hands, bewildered. 'And so?'

'I didn't tell the *Sentinel*. I didn't ask them if I could. I knew they probably would have vetoed it. So I went ahead without their agreement.'

He stopped again. Alice watched him for more. Eventually she said, 'I still don't see what the problem is.'

'My editor flew into Moscow tonight.'

'Don't I know it. We have a dinner party arranged for him on Thursday, remember? I must say,' she added, 'I shall look forward to meeting him after all these years.'

'My other one flew in too.'

Alice stared at him. 'Ah.' She fiddled with her fingers in her lap. 'What do you plan to do? It can't be too difficult to keep them apart.'

339

'They're staying at the same hotel.'

'Ah.'

'And drinking together tonight.'

'Oh.' Alice thought for a bit. 'Is your other editor likely to be discreet?'

'I think he probably is.' George paused. 'I hope to God he is. No, he won't tell, though he will have a lot of fun with innuendo and double entendre if he can get away with it. No, no. It's part of the working deal that he doesn't say anything. And he doesn't want to lose my services. No, the problem is that now they've linked up with each other, they'll probably want to stay together.'

'Well, that's fine, then!' Alice clapped her hands. 'Parcel them off with a map of Moscow and a few choice pointers and let them get on with it.'

George sighed. 'Alice, you know that isn't how editors like to be treated. They want to be cosseted and cushioned and mollycoddled by their very own correspondents. Both of them.'

'Yes.' Alice stretched the word thoughtfully. 'I do see now.'

'If I could have kept them apart, I could have handled the tourism aspect no problem. One in the mornings, the other in the afternoons. Now my editor is bound to suggest we all join up together and make a team.'

'Which editor?'

'The *Sentinel*. He loathes Bob Mathisson but it wouldn't be good Fleet Street politics to ignore him. Especially in Moscow.'

'Won't the other one try and save you?'

'Bob Mathisson? Not a chance. He'll play it for all it's worth. It's the most animated drama he'll have been part of for months.' George slumped back on the sofa and stared into space. Then he screwed his eyes up a little and said thoughtfully, 'Of course, if I could get someone to do Myra—'

'Myra?' squeaked Alice.

George rolled his head heavily towards her. 'Myra Drewsbarr. You wouldn't like to impersonate her, would you, Alice?'

'Impersonate Myra Drewsbarr! Jesus, George. I'm buggered if I would!'

George frowned. Such profanity was most unlike Alice. 'I don't see why you should take that attitude. It would certainly get me out of this mess.'

'If Myra Drewsbarr has anything to do with getting you into this mess then you can stay in it, as far as I'm concerned.'

'Of course she got me into this mess! Nadya was right, too. It's a bloody silly name. I wish I'd given myself a masculine pseudonym.'

Alice stared at him. 'I beg your pardon?' George remained sunk in thought. Alice sprang off the sofa and stood, her feet planted accusingly apart, before him. 'Do you mean to tell me Myra Drewsbarr is you?'

'Of course it is,' said George mildly. 'Who did you think it was?'

Alice stode angrily towards the balcony, then reeled abruptly about as she reached the door. 'Bloody hell, George. I have spent months. I mean painful, ghastly months, convinced that Myra Drewsbarr was your lover.'

George's mouth sagged gormlessly. 'What?'

'That's right. Can you imagine it? On top of everything else that Moscow has to throw at you, I honestly believed my husband was having it off with another woman. That's who I thought Myra Drewsbarr was.'

George shook his head, perplexed. 'But why didn't you ask me?'

Abruptly Alice felt deflated. 'Pride. And the belief that if we didn't confront it, then it would go away. I could carry on pretending everything was all right so long as you didn't think she was important enough to you to mention.'

George rose and reached out for Alice. She shivered slightly and clasped her arms around herself. 'No, George. Not just yet. And as far as Myra Drewsbarr is concerned, no, I shan't impersonate her. You got yourself into this mess. You caused me weeks of unnecessary heartache. Now you can suffer just a little bit. If you don't mind.'

And, head held high, she marched out of the sitting-room to bed.

She lay for a long time motionless in the darkness of the bedroom, George tossing uneasily bedside her in his sleep. The door on to the balcony was open but the curtains hung still in the summer night. How long ago the snow seemed in all this languid heat. Those exhilarating times tobogganing with Babs, the broomball games, cross-country skiing through the woods of white-skinned birches; they all seemed such simple and innocent activities now. Harold was dead. His coffin would recently have landed at Heathrow, with the Prowses and the Rimsteads and the Simpsons. Babs and Jonty and the children would have been swept into the comforting arms of their family; the married daughters would have come to support Geoff and Angela, and Charlie would have been in his element elaborating for the waiting press the precise nature of his first taste of freedom. Lisa had revealed that Charlie would be using the flight to knock off the opening instalment of 'My Life in Red Hell' for his anxious paper.

Alice felt bereft. She should have been there with them. Her history was tied up with theirs. Now they had gone, she would have to develop a new one for herself, with a different cast of characters. Life in Moscow would never be quite the same. The innocence had gone, the pretences stripped away, the games exposed. What she needed at this juncture was a radical change in direction, a new persona. It was time for a fresh start.

It was a long time before she slept.

Alice woke in the morning with her spirits high. She was careful not to reveal this to George. He was already on the telephone talking to the editors. Now that school had broken up for the summer, Alice left Harriet to sleep on. Daisy sat on the kitchen floor, pulping a piece of milk-soaked bread with her gums.

'What's your plan?'

'Do you care?' he said crossly.

'George, of course I care! Anyway, I'm curious as to how you'll juggle it all.'

George was pleased enough with his scheming to want to show off a little. 'I've told my editor I'll meet him at the office at ten fifteen. Nadya will be there. She is staying on until she finalizes her plans. I reckon she needs to be busy. So she can chat him up while I pop over to the Rossiya at ten, tell Bob Mathisson I've got an unexpected but essential press briefing. Then I'll drop him off at the Novodyevichy Monastery to wander round by himself for an hour or so. Meanwhile I dash back to the office, have a quick chat with the ed, and tell him I've had an unexpected call to go into the Foreign Ministry. Then I'll rush over to the Novo-dyevichy and—'

'Sounds to me you've got the whole thing very neatly worked out.'

No thanks to you, thought George. 'Nightmare. Absolute nightmare. I don't know how I'm going to keep it up for four days.'

Alice patted him. 'You'll manage, George. You'll manage.'

He grunted. It would have been so easy if Alice had offered to co-operate. But he could sense an aloofness in her that prevented him from hinting again that she should. Hinting? Begging, more like. George felt as close as he had ever come to panic. He drove along the river bank towards the Rossiya with a premonition of doom and disaster and an excruciating pain across his shoulders. He was far too early yet for his appointment, but better to meander the back streets of the old merchants' quarter round Bolshoya Ordinka than to spend the time cooped up in the flat with Alice.

Alice, meanwhile, moved through the flat humming. Galina arrived and took the children down into the compound, Harriet to churn up the sandpit, Daisy to roll about upon a rug in the sun. Alice checked her watch and made a quick telephone call. Then she strode briskly into her bedroom and pulled a chair over to her wardrobe. She climbed upon it and shuffled briefly through a pile of clothing before extracting, with a look of supreme satisfaction, the scarlet Soviet basque.

She wriggled into it and clipped black stockings to the suspender catches. Slipping her feet into her gleaming patent leather party stilettos, she reached into the cupboard and withdrew a smart black suit. She pulled the skirt over her head, zipped it, then slid her arms into the jacket. In the bathroom she carefully applied a glistening coat of scarlet lipstick to her mouth, gave her eyelashes an extra twizzle of mascara, and brushed her hair into a soft brown cloud. She made a small moue at herself in the mirror, then strode back down the corridor to the long bedroom looking-glass. The effect was good: aggressive suit, power shoes, provocative bodice, television hair. In sum: totty with brain. And balls. With a surge of confidence she drew herself up and left the flat.

George at the Rossiya was finding it difficult to move Bob Mathisson with the speed that he wished. The man was apparently enjoying himself slouching in the lobby, his large posterior pressed into a low Soviet chair, watching the comings and goings of the tourists and the maids who crossed back and forth, slopping mops about the marble floor.

'Good looking bints, the Russkies,' he said cheerfully. 'Bet they keep a body warm in bed in winter!'

George stared pointedly at his watch. 'Look, I really think we should be getting a move on, Bob. You won't have much time at the monastery and I'll be late for my press briefing.'

'Can't have that, can we? Why don't you leave me here a bit? To tell the truth, George, I'm not in any hurry to see a monastery. I'm happy sitting here' – he swung his short arms in a wide embrace – 'absorbing. Press conferences don't take that long, in my experience. Why don't you nip back for me afterwards?'

That wouldn't do at all. George stood up anxiously. 'No, really, Bob. I've got it all planned. Honestly, I do recommend the Novodyevichy. A really lovely place, fine example of old Russian—'

Bob reached up and plucked at George's sleeve to draw him down beside him again. 'Listen, George. Me and culture. You know how it is. With some people, they can have orgasms over a painted ceiling. To be honest with you, my expectations of a good cultural experience in Russia is a sit down by a bottle of iced vodka and a bowl of caviare, with a row of pretty girls in national dress dancing whatever it is they dance around my table. Why don't you save your cultural plans for your editor? Much more up his street.' He squinted over George's shoulder. 'Speaking of the devil. Good morning to you, comrade.' Bob Mathisson began to rise. George, distracted, glanced up. Oh, my God, there was his editor, extending his hand.

'Ah, George! You've connected up with Bob. How do, Bob.'

'But I thought we were meeting at the office!'

'Well, we were, until I got your telephone message.'

'Telephone message?'

'Yes. Changing our rendezvous. Nice sounding voice. I thought it must be your secretary.'

'Nadya?'

'Whatever. Anyway, she told me you wanted me here.' The editor sat down opposite Bob.

George's neck began to hurt. He should have bought larger shirts when he was in London. What the devil was Nadya playing at? Had grief affected her brain? Surely she of all people was aware how devastating was the confrontation she had contrived. Or was this precisely her reason? Did she wish to avenge herself upon George for Harold's suicide? Well, why not? Poor bloody woman. Bloody, bloody, bloody woman!

George's editor and Bob Mathisson were bent towards each other in consultation.

'Look here, George. I don't know how you feel about this. But Bob and I think we should pool resources. I appreciate you have work to do. Always a newspaper to fill, isn't that right, Bob? So I wondered if we shouldn't split chaperon duties. What would you say if I suggested you handled the a.m. schedule and—' George's editor turned to Bob Mathisson. 'What's your stringer's name, Bob?'

Bob Mathisson glanced towards George and lifted his shoulders very slightly. 'Myra Drewsbarr.'

'And Myra Drewsbarr did the p.m. shift. I dare say there'll be occasions when we'll have to go our own ways. I don't know what Myra has organized for you, Bob, but I know George has lined me up to press the hand of a number of leading Soviet officials and intellectuals.' George's editor smirked slightly.

'Right. Me too.'

'But when we're simply seeing the sights, I don't see why we can't do it together. Any objections?'

George wanted to spring to his feet and jump frantically

up and down, petulantly screaming 'Yes, yes, yes, I have!' in furious frustration. Instead, avoiding Bob Mathisson's gaze, he nonchalantly flicked his wrist and said, 'Aah, can't think of any.'

His editor rubbed his hands together. 'All right, then. So, Bob. When are you meeting up with – Myra Drewsbarr, is it?'

Bob Mathisson smiled vaguely. It was time to help George out. Best tactic. George would have to pay for it later, though. In hard copy. 'Well,' he drawled, 'you know how it is, these Iron Curtain countries. Lots of pressure. Schedules always going up the spout. She's going to contact me as soon as she's' – he cleared his throat – 'got her act together.' He looked fixedly at George. 'Perhaps this morning, first day and all that, is not the ideal time to muck in together.'

George wanted to kiss him. Instead his eye was caught by a striking figure that had flitted behind one of the ochre marble columns supporting the high foyer ceiling. Looked a bit like Alice. Not bloody likely, though. Still, remarkably similar. But something in that brief glimpse of the clothing wasn't quite her. Besides, Alice had made her position perfectly clear. She wasn't coming within a million miles of assistance. He leaned forwards on his knees and focused briefly upon the floor. Bob Mathisson was waiting for him to pick up the towel he had thrown into the ring. How best to develop this tenuous advantage? He pulled a deep breath in through his nostrils, drew back his shoulders ready for the fray, and raised his head decisively.

Behind his editors stood Alice.

He made to speak, startled. Alice put a black-gloved finger to her lips. With slow emphasis, pointing first to him then to herself, she stood alongside the column in the most suggestive, most becoming, most un-Alice-like outfit he had ever seen her in, and mouthed, 'You. Owe. Me.' Then she stepped forward into the semicircle.

Surprised, the two men rose to their feet as Alice drew off her glove with slow deliberation. Bob Mathisson rubbed his hands together, running his eyes over Alice's gently bulging scarlet bustier, elegant legs encased in thin black stockings, the just so slightly short skirt and the padded shoulders of her jacket. She smiled gently, and proffered her hand.

'I don't know who I should introduce myself to first,' she said coyly. She turned to George's editor. 'How do you do. I'm Alice. George's wife.'

His editor took her hand, looking mildly taken aback. George caught his expression and groaned inwardly. Not only was George a soon-to-be-unmasked traitor to the *Sentinel* but he was married to what looked not far short of a tart.

Alice languidly stretched her hand towards Bob Mathisson. 'I also go under another name.' Her eyes flickered briefly towards George. He held his breath. Then, her hand still firmly encased in Bob Mathisson's, she said, 'You're familiar with it, I think. Myra Drewsbarr.'

George's heart soared. Alice had come through! Good old Alice! Then he stopped himself mid-exclamation and studied her. Today that cosily reassuring description did not quite fit.

Bob Mathisson glanced quickly at George, then brought Alice's hand to his lips. 'Well, well, well. Myra Drewsbarr. Very pleased to meet you. It's been good to have you on board.'

Alice pointedly held George's eye. 'I hope we can work well together in the future too, Bob. I'm certainly looking forward to it,' she said serenely. And smiled.

THE END